Like Nowhere Else

Denyse Woods was born in Boston in 1958 and is
the daughter of an Irish diplomat. She studied
Arabic and English at University College, Dublin,
and subsequently worked as a translator in Iraq.
She has travelled extensively in the Middle East,
and also lived in the USA, Belgium, Australia, Italy
and the UK before settling in Co. Cork with her
English husband in 1987. She has two teenage
daughters.

Like Nowhere Else

DENYSE WOODS

PENGUIN
IRELAND

F14 3,769

€15.00

PENGUIN IRELAND

Published by the Penguin Group
Penguin Ireland, 25 St Stephen's Green, Dublin 2, Ireland
(a division of Penguin Books Ltd)
Penguin Books Ltd, 80 Strand, London WC2R ORL, England
Penguin Group (USA) Inc., 375 Hudson Street, New York, New York 10014, USA
Penguin Group (Australia), 250 Camberwell Road,
Camberwell, Victoria 3124, Australia (a division of Pearson Australia Group Pty Ltd)
Penguin Group (Canada), 10 Alcorn Avenue, Toronto, Ontario, Canada M4V 3B2
(a division of Pearson Penguin Canada Inc.)
Penguin Books India Pvt Ltd, 11 Community Centre,
Panchsheel Park, New Delhi – 110 017, India
Penguin Group (NZ), cnr Airborne and Rosedale Roads, Albany,
Auckland 1310, New Zealand (a division of Pearson New Zealand Ltd)
Penguin Books (South Africa) (Pty) Ltd, 24 Sturdee Avenue,
Rosebank 2196, South Africa

Penguin Books Ltd, Registered Offices: 80 Strand, London WC2R ORL, England

www.penguin.com

First published 2005

1

Copyright © Denyse Woods, 2005

The moral right of the author has been asserted

Set in 13.5/16 pt Monotype Garamond
Typeset by Rowland Phototypesetting Ltd, Bury St Edmunds, Suffolk
Printed in Great Britain by Clays Ltd, St Ives plc

A CIP catalogue record for this book is available from the British Library

ISBN 1–844–88042–7

In loving memory of my exceptional parents,
Finola and Gerard

She is the capital
Of the soul
Her gates are seven
— And the gardens of Paradise
Their gates are also seven —
Each gate realizes a wish
For a stranger
And whichever gate you enter by
Peace upon you

from *The Book of Sana'a*, Abd al-Aziz al-Maqalih

PART I

I

Sana'a must be seen,
even if the journey is long

(Old Arabian proverb)

The journey *was* long. Seventeen hours in Cairo airport – in any airport – would try the most patient of souls, and I am not one such soul. After a long flight from London, I was ill-disposed to spending an even longer spell in a bucket seat, so it was a good thing that I had no idea, when I arrived, exactly what lay in store.

I knew I would have to endure a change of pace on this trip and found it sooner than I expected at several different departure gates that night. Cairo International is not the most comfortable airport in the world, but it runs high on aspiration. When the flight to Sana'a was called three hours after I arrived, on schedule, I made my way, with other passengers, from the transit lounge to the departure gate. All as expected. But the flight never left. In fact, it had not even arrived. There was no information, no explanation, only shrugging shoulders. *It is the will of God.*

The delay was like stepping through the footbath

3

before getting into the swimming-pool – a procedure meant to cleanse me of irrelevant Western expectations of time-keeping and bring me within the local speed limit. Here, in transit, I would be calmed, but it was going to be cold turkey.

There were no more than fifty passengers bound for Sana'a, and only six other Westerners, all men. Three were travelling together, one was trying to sleep, and another was hidden behind a newspaper. I paced. I counted the orange bucket seats, the minutes between jets taking off, and the scrawny cats putting their heads round the partition, like people looking into a bar to see who is there. Another Westerner was equally restless. We kept passing each other as we paced, throwing our eyes up and shaking our heads: the language of those who cannot wait.

My mind kept bouncing off the glass partition like a ball in a pinball machine, but this was not only impatience. It was also apprehension. Many people had told me not to travel to Yemen; this was hardly a propitious start.

'Yemen isn't safe,' they had said.

A text message from a caring friend: 'Do NOT go to Yemen.'

The Department of Foreign Affairs, the Foreign and Commonwealth Office in London, all Western governments in fact, had warned their nationals against non-essential visits, and this visit was certainly not essential – but it was necessary, for me. I wouldn't wait any longer. I had a score to settle.

*

4

A huddle of passengers gathered in one corner of the room. I watched to see if they had gleaned anything about our flight, but they dispersed despondently, and, as they did so, revealed the man who had earlier been hidden behind his newspaper.

Christian Linklater.

Astounded, I stared at him from the other side of the enclosure. He picked up a bottle of water, threw back his head to drink. I looked away, my pulse banging against my wrists. Linklater, in the flesh. *Jesus.*

I knew him well – too well, for my liking – but he did not know me. We had never met.

He raised his chin to scratch his neck, then frowned at the ceiling, and in those slight gestures I began to understand.

Now I had something to do. A project to pass the time. Responsibilities, even. I would have to memorize every scant detail, every mannerism. Did he fidget? Sulk? Did he have any unpleasant habits when he was trapped in an airport, like biting his nails or scratching his scalp? He ran his fingers down his neck, unconsciously checking the growth. It was definitely him. The half-inch scar running from the right side of his upper lip confirmed it.

Not long after midnight, when we were moved to a different gate, on the ground floor, we perked up in the belief that something was about to happen. It wasn't. This waiting room was half the size of our former enclosure and offered no sweeping view of runways, only grubby windowpanes reflecting our restlessness.

My brain clicked over in irritation. I take delays as a personal affront. When a bus doesn't come or a waiter is slow, I seethe. Then I complain. In writing, usually. One of my fortes is the letter of complaint. I also write letters of approbation, when they have been earned, but friends say I am like a cranky old biddy, not a woman of thirty-two who should have better things to do with her life. I argue that the latter is as entitled to good service as the former.

We were evolving, hour by hour, as delayed airline passengers often do, into some kind of family. More frequent eye-contact led to little smiles and shrugs of resignation. No longer individuals, we had become a group. An abandoned group at that – climbers stuck on a mountain ledge, unable to go either up or down until someone came to fetch us. The Yemenis, returning home from their jobs in Egypt, were laden with ghetto-blasters, foodstuffs and huge boxed parcels for their families. I stretched across several seats, a sharp plastic rim digging into my hip, and tried to rest.

'Sit up straight and close your eyes. It's the only way.'

I sat up. Linklater was standing behind me. 'Excuse me?'

'If you really want to sleep, sit up,' he said.

Ah, the voice. That mellifluous voice. I had heard it before, and its unexpected familiarity here, in an airport in the middle of the night when I was betwixt and between and out of sorts, was curiously soothing. 'I can't sleep upright. I'd fall over.'

'You can't stay awake all night either.'

'We're not going to be here all night, are we?'

6

He glanced around. 'Looks like it.' He sat down a couple of seats to my right in the row backed up against mine, so that we were facing in opposite directions. He looked over his shoulder at me. 'If I could make a suggestion?'

'Be my guest.'

'You've been fidgeting about, expending energy when you have a long wait ahead, whereas if you were to follow the example of our Arab friends here, you'd be much calmer and resigned to your powerlessness to alter your situation.'

'Like you?' I said.

'I can't quite match the Eastern art of passive acceptance, but I do travel without expectations.' He raised his eyebrows, widening his eyes.

Ever the anthropologist, I thought. With his legs stretched out and his hands deep in the pockets of his khaki trousers, he looked like a man on a park bench having a chat with the old wino behind him. He had a creased, lived-in face. I calculated that he must have been about forty-one by then.

I got up and walked around our box, stepping over snoozing passengers on the floor. This was difficult. I had not expected Linklater to take the initiative, to put me on the spot with his renowned affability, and my ambivalence about him made no sense at all. He could not be held accountable for what had happened in Durham.

'Helps, does it?' he asked. 'Pacing?'

'Not really. I mean, why won't they tell us what's going on?'

'Because this is Egypt, and Yemen will be Yemen,

7

and neither can match the zippy efficiency you seem to require, so huffing and puffing will only make you breathless. It certainly won't get us off the ground.'

'What do you suggest?'

'You could read.'

'Can't concentrate.'

Linklater frowned. 'How long are you planning to stay in Yemen?'

'Three weeks. Why?'

'I have certain concerns about your mental well-being.'

He was being overly familiar, which was disconcerting. I had to remind myself that he did not know me as I knew him. I sat down behind him and crossed my arms. 'Don't mock the afflicted.'

'Oh, you don't look the least bit afflicted to me.'

Christ. 'Well, I am.' I went on quickly: 'I was born without the patience gene – you know, the virtuous one – and life is tough on the impatient. We're always out of kilter with everyone else.'

'But you probably get more done.'

'Quite the opposite. We're far less efficient than most people, as you've just pointed out: I am not using my time here well. I could be reading *War and Peace*, *Ulysses*, *The Complete Oxford English Dictionary*. All of the above.'

'Have you tried yoga?'

'Yes, but I was asked to leave the class.'

'Why?'

'Drumming my fingers on the floor must have done it.'

He laughed.

'It isn't funny,' I said. 'It's exhausting. I've been in a hurry all my life. I was even born in a hurry – both prematurely *and* swiftly.'

'Maybe there was somewhere else you needed to be,' he said, smiling.

'Yeah . . . Maybe there still is.'

He glanced at my knees, which were jigging about. 'You should be going to New York, not Yemen.'

I nodded. 'New York about suits my speed.'

'But you're going in the opposite direction because . . . ?'

'Holiday.'

'Really? Not a very popular holiday destination at the moment.'

'The problem with popular destinations is that they're popular.'

'Yes,' he said, 'but many people would say Yemen is dangerous.'

'People used to say that about Ireland too, when most of us were living perfectly safe lives. Yemen is the same, I imagine. All we ever hear is the bad stuff. The Irish know how that feels.'

'So it doesn't worry you that a number of foreigners have been lifted there?'

'Not really.'

'That's refreshing.'

'It's realistic. I mean, let's face it, you're more likely to be beaten up on a Friday night in any European city than kidnapped in –' I stopped abruptly, horrified at what I had said.

9

Linklater didn't flinch. He just said, 'You're clearly determined to get there.'

'Absolutely.'

'Why?'

I sighed. 'Such a small word for such a big question.'

He smiled. 'And so much time to answer it.'

Oh, yes, I could see it now. Lively green eyes, good hands. 'Well,' I said, 'shall I take you all the way back to my childhood or just to the recent past?'

'Oh, let's have the whole catalogue.'

He asked. So I told him.

It is a hazy recollection now, that glossy page opened before me, in *Paris Match* or *Life* magazine, offering a panoramic view of a mud city rising out of a desert. Its outer buildings stood side by side, tall and narrow, no gaps between them, like an uneven rampart with windows in it. I was only ten when, lying on the floor in a shaft of light that warmed the carpet, I looked at this place and wondered, Where *is* that? The article might have mentioned Yemen, or the Hadramawt, but such details made no impression. The only thing that registered was that such a place existed, that people had made something so extraordinary, so beautiful, out of mud. There were no shiny white columns, gracious porticos or glass atria, just windows and walls, but it was a living town, simple and brown, in what looked like the middle of nowhere. I resolved there and then to go one day to this remarkable place. Years later I read about Sana'a and, seeing pictures of its own tower houses, mistakenly concluded that this must have been the town that had featured in the magazine. In fact, it was Shibam that had entranced me: the 'Manhattan of the desert'.

Perhaps because of this, I developed in my teens a fascination for travel literature, for writers who had known the desert. At fourteen, I discovered Thesiger's *Arabian Sands*, which transported me several times across the Empty Quarter. Thirsty for more, I went burrowing in bookshops until I found Richard Burton, Freya Stark, Doreen Ingrams. I even unearthed Charles Montagu Doughty. He, too, had donned the robes, taken the camel and written the book, but his arcane use of language left him in the shade of more accessible writers. Getting through his *Travels in Arabia Deserta* was a labour and a badge.

But my childhood resolution to get to Yemen was refuelled by one man: Carsten Niebuhr. An eighteenth-century German surveyor, Niebuhr joined a Danish expedition to Yemen in 1761. Five of them set out, but only Niebuhr returned alive. In fact, by the time he got back to Denmark, even the king who had commissioned the expedition had died. As a tribute to his dead colleagues, Niebuhr wrote a book detailing their discoveries. It is an antique now, but it was lent to me when I was sixteen and I never returned it. I kept it instead as a keepsake, a reminder, of that moment on the sunlit carpet when Yemen had first called to me.

More recently, it had called again, and that was why I found myself, in March 2002, waiting out an Egyptian night, on my way to Arabia Felix. The elbow of the Arabian peninsula.

'But why now,' Linklater asked, 'when the world is all at odds, and East and West are glaring at one another like bulldogs across a fence?'

'Another book.' I pulled a paperback about Yemen out of my bag.

'Ah,' he nodded, 'Mackintosh-Smith. Prescribed reading.'

I dangled it between my fingers like a textbook, remembering the moment I had seen it in a shop and had struggled to resist the urge to pick it up. 'I'd got over the Yemen thing until this came along. So it's this man's fault I'm stuck in a bloody airport. What about you?'

'I'm going out to do fieldwork. I lecture in anthropology.'

'There must be rich pickings for anthropologists in Yemen,' I said.

'Absolutely. And archaeologists. In fact, I'll be piggy-backing on an archaeological dig for the next few weeks.'

'Whereabouts?'

'Marib.'

'Queen of Shebaville.'

'Well,' he smiled, 'you make it sound like a theme park, but many would call that region the cradle of civilization.'

'I've heard that said about Mesopotamia.'

'*And* the original Garden of Eden.'

'I've heard *that* said about Damascus.'

He smirked. 'It's because of cynics like you that we have to dig. Yemen is bursting at the seams with pre-Christian, pre-Islamic and Sabaean sites. It's like

Mesopotamia at the beginning of the last century, or Egypt at the beginning of the nineteenth.'

'What will you be doing? Looking for Sheba?'

'No. Generally speaking, it's the archaeologists who are trying to establish who she was, *if* she was.'

'And was she?'

'If she did exist, she's proving elusive,' he said. 'There's scant reference to her in the Holy Books, so the legend has grown out of all proportion to the evidence.'

'All I know is that she ruled Arabia and went to Jerusalem to seduce Solomon.'

'Or he seduced her. The thing is . . .' He stopped to gauge the level of my interest.

'Go on.'

'Well, her visit to Solomon would have taken place in the tenth century BC, but the first Sabaean inscriptions at Marib date from the eighth, so the jackpot would be to find some reference to a queen dated a little closer to Solomon's rule. Find a name. That would make history out of folklore.'

'And Sheba would rival Cleopatra.'

'Certainly. But I'm more interested in the Sabaeans who definitely did exist, and then definitely died.'

'How do you mean?'

He widened his eyes again. 'I *love* the dead.'

'I thought anthropologists studied the living?'

'Not exclusively. I'll be doing some work with the living, but I have a great sideline in cemeteries. There isn't much a good necropolis won't tell you about the way a society lived.'

'Sounds a bit morbid.'

'Well . . . it would be,' he said, and we laughed.

Affable. Definitely affable. Warm and engaging, too. 'Is this your first trip to Yemen?' I asked him.

He shook his head. 'Several years ago I hiked around looking at turret tombs – ancient burial mounds in the desert – so when a friend of mine needed an anthropologist for her excavation of a cemetery near Marib she asked me along. The timing is perfect. It gives me the opportunity to pursue some of my own . . .'

'What?'

'Trouble is, once I get started I tend to forget the difference between a lecture and a conversation.'

'Either will do. The night is long.'

So he told me about his work, and it was immediately clear that his lively enthusiasm, coupled with that voice, would certainly have made him a riveting lecturer. 'At the moment,' he said, 'I'm looking at how . . . tribalism, for want of a better word, works in a modern political context. The community versus the state, if you like. Yemen has a strong tribal tradition, which is now operating within a democracy of sorts, and while the tribes rightly want services provided by the government, they retain a degree of autonomy and are sometimes reluctant to put the state ahead of the community, so the line between the two is fuzzy, and that's my point of interest.'

'But where do the Sabaeans come into it?'

'Ah, well, they come into the bigger, Khaldunian, picture. Ibn Khaldun was a fourteenth-century Moroccan philosopher who had a theory that all civilizations rise and fall in cycles, going from nomads, to villages, to cities, always driven by the needs of the community, and become increasingly developed until they turn into empires, which inevitably collapse under their own sense of well-being, then return to the nomadic life. Are you sure I'm not . . . ?'

He was a bit, but I said, 'You're not boring me, no.'

'Well, the Sabaeans followed that curve. It all relates to a concept known as *'asabiyya*, or group solidarity, which is still strongly tied up with many Islamic communities today.'

'And brings us back to tribe versus citizen.'

'Exactly. Here endeth the lesson.'

'So is Western civilization on the downward slope?'

'Many would say so. Ibn Khaldun's model is ultimately pessimistic.'

'Cheer me up, why don't you?' I quipped, then blushed. Now *I* was being too familiar. I cleared my throat. 'Will you spend long in Marib?'

'Six weeks, I hope, and I'll have to spend some time chasing paper in Sana'a.'

'It must be hard, being away from your family.'

'Yeah, but I love the work. I love being . . . *out.*'

'Your wife must be very accommodating.'

He caught my eye. 'She would have to be, yes . . . if I had one.'

My first slip. 'I'm sorry, I . . .'

He elaborated no further.

Curious. How very curious, all the same. '*If* I had one . . .' What could it mean? Had the perfect couple been unable to live up to their own propaganda? After twenty-something years, had they come asunder? And what about those girls – their kids, three of them, triplets, actually – to whom they were so devoted? For the second time since I had set eyes on him, my head raced.

Linklater stood up and stretched. 'What part of Ireland do you hail from?'

'Dublin.'

He reached over with outstretched hand. 'Christian Linklater.'

'Vivien Quish.'

We meet at last.

The hours passed slowly. Linklater crossed his arms, dropped his head and slept. I managed only to doze. It was difficult, under the harsh fluorescent lighting in the middle of the night, not to be weighed down with apprehension. Quite apart from the global unease, with extremists on the rampage and Israeli incursions into the West Bank fermenting anger in the Arab world, I had my own reasons for being shy of Yemen. And yet I had to go, in the lull, before things got worse.

At five, people began to stir. Linklater looked refreshed; I felt like death. Still determined to pick up every snippet and store it away in my newly opened file, the Linklater Chronicle, I watched him discreetly. He was attractive, no question, in a crinkly, used sort of way. If anything, he had improved with age. He was less chubby around the jowls than he had been; the youthful good looks had matured to his advantage. The green eyes, which had been rather bright and eager in his thirties, had become more hooded. His sandy-blond hair was greying. His was a rested face, even after hours of inertia. I noted all this in the name of research, but I watched for too long. Linklater looked up, straight at me.

In an otherwise empty restaurant, which offered panoramic and tantalizing views of planes taking off, we were given a square omelette, sliced tomatoes and stale rolls. Linklater, sitting at an adjoining table, persisted with his legendary friendliness. I found it mildly irritating. It would have been more satisfying to find an unmitigated bastard beneath the charming reputation. Instead, I liked him, which was ironic.

'You're frowning,' he said, 'and I don't think it's the food.'

'Hmm? Oh, no, I was thinking about the guy who's supposed to be meeting me in Sana'a. I wonder how long *he*'s spent at the airport.'

'A friend of yours?'

I shook my head. 'That's what makes it worse. He's a friend of a friend of a friend, but he's very kindly agreed to put me up for a few weeks, and the trouble is, I don't have an address for him, just a phone number, so if he's given up on this phantom flight . . .' The prospect of not being met seemed, all things considered, like an insurmountable challenge.

'Don't worry. If he doesn't show, we can share a taxi into town and you can call him from my hotel.'

'Thanks. I'd appreciate that.' Outside, the sun beamed down on the busy runways. 'The Pyramids,' I sighed, 'so near and yet so far.'

'You've been to Egypt?'

'No. No, I haven't been anywhere much. But you've been in all sorts of untoward corners of the globe.'

He grimaced.

'I do have a television, you know.'

'Ah.'

The meal finished, we were led back downstairs by a woman in a uniform who told us nothing about anything. And so, on with the day, the sun adding to our discomfort by beating through the high windows at our gate. I walked, I sighed, I cursed the sluggish efforts of my watch. There was little else to do.

We were almost beyond caring when, in the early afternoon, the plane that had been flown in to replace ours, which had suffered a malfunction, touched down and taxied in. Two hours later I raced across the burning Tarmac, ran up the steps into the aircraft and settled into my window seat. There could be no turning back now.

Not long after take-off, Linklater's voice purred in my ear: 'May I?' he asked, gesturing towards the empty seat beside me.

I didn't react, but he sat down anyway. His interest, which I gauged as fluctuating between flirtatious and genuinely attracted, was unsettling. The flirtatious I could handle; the alternative didn't bear thinking about.

He handed me my tray.

'What is it?' I quipped. 'Lunch or dinner?'

'It could be breakfast for all I know,' he said. 'I've lost track.'

'Me too.'

He ate with appetite, chewed with determination. He also talked a lot. Stubble had appeared across the fresh, clear face of the previous day. His eyes had sunk. I wanted to press him about his marital status and was about to do so when I looked out and saw below us the Red Sea and the dry coastline of the Arabian peninsula. From my little hole of a window, I could see the coast of Africa and the edge of Arabia in one glance. Blue and brown, as in a satellite shot. Down there, Thesiger had explored with the Bedu. Down there, Burton had trespassed into Mecca disguised as a Muslim. That featureless place was smeared with the trails of Western men and women drawn to its savage emptiness. To the space, the blank. Above the trail of Niebuhr's long voyage, I flew, two hundred years later.

2

We arrived in Sana'a after dark and in a downpour. The only sound, when I stepped out of the aircraft, was the rush of rain, exhilarating after Cairo's grubby airlessness and two days without a shower.

I hurried across to the terminal. In contrast to Cairo, where we had wandered around like a nomadic tribe, the atmosphere in the arrivals hall was immediately welcoming. And yet I was edgy. Standing by the carousel, biting my lip, I looked about expecting to see faces I knew. My host, Theo Klaassen, could hardly be blamed for giving up, and I was still worried that he would not be there to collect me. I knew little about him, except that he was a Dutch cartographer working on an agricultural census for the EU. The power failed just as I grabbed my suitcase. My nerves jangled. People called out. Torches came on and beams of light, like swords sparring, threw a dim glow around the hall. Linklater was gathering his own belongings nearby.

'Hi,' I said. 'I mean, 'bye. I'm off, I hope.'

He hesitated, then gave me a warm handshake. 'It was lovely travelling with you. Good luck.'

My passport was checked by torchlight, along with the letter of invitation without which I could not get into the country, and I was waved through Customs. I took a deep breath and made my way out to the crowds pressing around the arrivals gate. I had no idea what Theo looked like, but my eye immediately caught a European face. His head popped up and he smiled. Relieved, I went towards him, but he looked right over my head, calling, 'Charles!' so I had to freewheel past him with a redundant grin on my face and nearly ran over another man bearing a sign with my name on it. It was surprising I had not seen him. He towered at least a foot above everyone else.

'Theo?'

'Vivien! Welcome.'

'I am *so* glad to see you.'

'Me too,' he said ruefully. He took my case. Outside the building, the rain continued to pour down. 'We must run for it.'

I followed him through the car park until we reached his jeep. 'I'm really sorry,' I said, when we sat in. 'I was stranded in Cairo for seventeen hours. Have you been here all day?'

'Don't worry. It happens. They keep saying, "It's coming, it's coming," but it never does.'

'How awful.'

'Much worse for you. And seventeen hours – that's a record, even for Cairo.' He pulled out of the car park. The streets were unlit. 'The storm has caused a blow-out,' he said. He had near-perfect English and spoke it in the clipped, efficient manner of Netherlanders.

I tried to see beyond the wipers and the beam of headlights, but the rain was too heavy.

'We get a lot of rain at this time of year,' said Theo, 'especially in the evenings. But the days are pleasant.'

'Have you been living here for long?'

'Six months, on and off.'

'Do you like it?'

'Very much,' he said warmly.

When we came into the city along a broad, uneven road, it was impossible to define anything other than a few scruffy buildings. Sana'a was hiding, making me wait, but I was elated to have arrived at last and to find myself in someone's care. We turned into a back-street and pulled up beside a high wall.

Theo led me through two wooden gates into a court-yard, then straight into the house proper on the left, where he lit a candle. We were in a whitewashed hall. I followed him up a stone stairway. There were rooms on every level: a bathroom at the turn of the stairs, and further up, on the first floor, two bedrooms and a *mafraj* – a room traditionally used for entertaining.

'This is your room,' said Theo, stepping into a small bedroom. He handed me another candle and lit it. In the halo of light I saw a stack of thin mattresses on the floor, made up with yellow cotton sheets.

'Very basic,' he said.

'It's fine.'

'There's hot water, if you'd like to shower in the dark?'

'I'd shower in sulphur if I had to.'

In the bathroom, a bare stone room without tiles, Theo lit a few more candles. 'When you're ready, follow the steps up until you reach the kitchen.'

He left me there, in flickering light. I was afraid of the dark, afraid of what lurked beyond the inadequate glow. I half expected to see myself – my younger self – emerge, wide-eyed and stricken from the umbra, so I jumped swiftly behind the shower curtain to avoid me.

When I had dressed, I made my way upstairs until I came to the kitchen, a small, cluttered room at the top of the house.

'Tea?' Theo asked, standing by a gas cooker.

'Please.' There was just enough space to step round the rectangular table and take a seat by the small window. Open shelves on two walls were stacked with pans and jars and packets of food.

'No milk, I'm afraid.' He poured mint tea from a large copper kettle.

'Nice house,' I said, 'what I can see of it.'

'Yes, it's great. This area, al-Qa, used to be the Jewish quarter.'

He started telling me about al-Qa, and I struggled. It didn't really matter that I had not been wholly honest with Linklater, but Theo was different. He would be my host and companion for three weeks. To pretend for that long would be dishonest, and yet owning up never came easily.

'So,' he said, 'how is it your boss knows my boss? I didn't get the connection.'

'Shoukria knew him in London, years back, when they were both working there – that's why you've got stuck with me.'

'Not at all. It's nice to have the company.'

'Do you live here alone?'

'*Ja*, but people come and go. People involved in the project.'

'I'm afraid I don't know much about it, except that it's an agricultural census.'

He nodded. 'It's very important for Yemen, actually, because there is a lot of information that internal bodies and international organizations are waiting for. Agriculture is the most important economic sector here.'

'But surely cartography is about making maps, not counting people?'

'You can't count people without accurate maps. We have to update the co-ordinates of many villages and take those of others that do not have them at all before the census proper can begin. I do some training also.'

'Sounds fascinating.'

'Oh, it's an amazing place to work – the morphology of this country is so varied, with high mountains, deserts, coastal plains . . .'

'And lots of bureaucracy, I suppose?'

'*Ja*, bureaucracy – but what about Europe?' He slid a Spanish omelette on to my plate. 'I'm sorry I didn't have time to cook something special to welcome you.'

'That would have been a bit difficult from the airport.'

He lifted his leg over the back of the chair and sat down.

'So are there many foreigners working here now or did everyone run scared after September eleventh?'

'Dependants left, but they are filtering back. There are many big projects going on here, sponsored by the EU and the World Bank.'

The shadows jumping on the wall, like figures in a

nightclub, made the small room seem crowded. I wanted them to go away. I wanted lights.

'The problem now is the trouble on the West Bank, and also this risk that the Americans are going to storm Yemen and "cleanse" it of al-Qaeda.'

'Is that likely?'

'The Yemeni government is co-operating. So far, that has been effective.'

We continued chatting through dinner, over tea, and for several hours afterwards. Theo asked about my boss, Shoukria, and our work in the gallery. I wasn't tired. The elation of reaching the end of the journey had quashed any weariness, and there was relief too, about Theo. I had come blind. He might have been unfriendly, uncouth and resentful of the favour bestowed upon me at his expense. Instead, he was courteous and easy-going. But speaking to him was disconcerting: he had several mannerisms in common with my former boyfriend, Bill. By candlelight, he didn't look much like him, which was just as well.

The lights came on. We blinked at one another. Theo was really very tall, but slight; light brown eyes behind gold-rimmed specs; a long face, fair hair, thinning slightly, and dark hair protruding from the open neck of his shirt. William Hurt came to mind. We smiled, acknowledging this proper visual introduction, and he had a quirky, lopsided smile that was immediately endearing.

He stood up. 'You should take things easy until you get used to the altitude. You'll feel a bit, you know, sluggish.'

*

25

A bit sluggish. That was one way of describing it. I felt the altitude in my legs, in my stomach. Every time I went downstairs to the bathroom, I had to face coming all the way back up those six steps again. I got up long after Theo had left for work, and found my way around the kitchen: bread in a green plastic bag, tea in a dented tin. This will do nicely, I thought.

So I sat at the little table by the window in a room at the top of a house in Sana'a, and everything was all right. I didn't look out or go to the balcony. Enough to sit, drinking *shai*, Yemeni tea, and eating *khubz*, the great flat disc of bread, knowing that I had arrived and that everything was all right.

Exhausted, I went back to bed. There was much to do, explore, confront, beyond the small windows, but sleep was more enticing. After all, I was on holiday. I didn't have to buzz about and be the busy tourist. Or so I told myself. In truth, I was afraid to go out, too frightened of what Sana'a might throw down before me.

It was more a question of what Sana'a would throw *at* me. Occasional but persistent 'ping' sounds drew me to the window. Little boys were aiming their catapults at the small windows on the side of the house. Their targets were the crows, but in the absence of birds they had turned their attention to our house. I sat on the edge of my bed with my head in my hands, cursing. The windows snapped and cracked. A cloud had come across the pleasant morning. I could not let this unsettle me, could not begin this way, so I phoned Theo and told him about the target practice. He came home straight away.

'*Rotjongens*. Catapults are very popular here. There is no one out there now.'

'Sorry for disturbing you. I was afraid they'd break your windows.'

'That's okay. How are you feeling?'

'Hung-over.'

'How about a late lunch in a place nearby?'

'If you carry me there . . .'

We stepped into the courtyard. An old woman called a greeting to us. She was sitting outside one of the two other houses that shared our enclosure – hers was squat and shabbier than the one Theo lived in, while the other, nestled in the corner, was taller than either. There were also storage huts and a goat pen made of chicken wire; several goats were wandering around. It was an untidy place, with tyres, planks, empty paint cans and general rubble strewn about, but it felt intimate and safe.

The little boys were nowhere to be seen when we walked through the back-streets to the restaurant. My mouth was dry, my eyes furtive. My long headscarf, crossed under my chin and thrown over my shoulders, was like a protective shell. I could pull it over my face and peer out. In spite of the heat, I didn't mind being covered from ankle to wrist – the only appropriate way to dress in Yemen; I quite enjoyed the privacy of concealment.

The restaurant had two wide entrances. On the pavement, men were crouched around large silver platters of food. We had to step round them to get inside, where rows of tables along each wall were mostly occupied, also by men. Outside, both men and women gathered around a large window that opened on to the kitchen – the takeaway section – calling out their orders.

We took a table. The men were dressed in *zannahs*, long white shirts, and jackets, with their curved daggers, the *jambiyahs*, tucked into their belts. To set eyes on the *jambiyah*, this most singular of national symbols, was to arrive in Yemen all over again.

'The hilts are made of rhinoceros horn,' Theo explained. 'People think rhinos are being killed for the aphrodisiac in their horns, but many are brought to Yemen.'

A niggling concern that he might prove a bit of a bore, a fact bore, crossed my mind, but I liked him. He was about my age, a bit younger maybe, and we got on with remarkable ease in view of the fact that we had only just met.

When a large Asian man came to take our order, I looked around again: the kitchen at the far end; two double doorways; sky blue shutters; another Asian man in the kitchen, twice the size again of the slight Yemenis around him.

'I've ordered a standard Yemeni –'

'Chicken and chips.'

'Sorry? You want chicken and chips?'

'No. That's what . . . they used to serve here.' I nodded towards the owner. 'He's Vietnamese, isn't he?'

'Yes.'

'Funny . . . I thought it was in the other direction. Over by al-Qa Square.'

Theo frowned. 'What was?'

'This place. A big Vietnamese woman used to run it. These must be her sons.'

'But how do —'

'I've been here before, Theo.'

'Here in Yemen? When?'

'Twelve years ago. Just after unification.'

'I was told this was your first trip.'

'The last one didn't count.'

'Why not?'

I thought about it, wondering how best to present this hard pea that still lay beneath my mattress. Theo didn't press me but, as he sat with his arms crossed along the edge of the table, occasionally waving flies away, I knew that telling him would be a challenge. He lived nowhere and everywhere, going wherever his company sent him for short to medium stints in mostly challenging territory. He was unlikely to understand.

'Have you ever thought you'd be really good at something,' I asked, 'but when you tried it, you found you didn't have what it took? I mean, not at all?'

'Ice-skating.'

An image of this gangly man on skates flashed through my mind. I snorted.

'The messages from my brain took too long to reach my feet,' he said, deadpan. 'What about you?'

'. . . I thought I'd be a great traveller. In fact, I bet my career on it. Only I wasn't. I didn't get past the first post.'

'And that was Yemen — the first post?'

I nodded. 'I wanted to cross the Sahara with a

caravan, or the Empty Quarter alone . . . I fancied being the Freya Stark or Doreen Ingrams of the late twentieth century – you know, see the world the tough way and then write the book. So I came out as a volunteer with an aid agency. It's the way it's done, isn't it, when you can't afford to travel? You sell your services. It was perfect: two years in Niebuhr's Arabia Felix, during which I could acclimatize, learn the language, and sniff out whatever venture would make good fodder for a book.'

'You were here for *two years*?' he said.

'No. I didn't last that long.'

'You got sick?'

'I chickened out. Couldn't handle it.'

Theo shrugged. 'It happens.'

'Does it? The resident field director didn't see it that way. They'd trained me. Paid for my flight and accommodation. They'd invested a lot with a view to getting two years' work out of me.'

'How long *did* they get?'

'Nothing. Zilch. Zippo. I left almost as soon as I arrived.'

Our meal came, piled high on one of the great silver platters. My cheeks were raging.

Theo considered the food, as if planning his next move on a chessboard. I had expected disdain, but he simply reiterated, 'It happens,' and pressed his fingers into the rice.

'It's kind of you to say so, in view of your lifestyle, but it is embarrassing nonetheless, which is why I tend to keep it to myself.'

'Why have you come back? Do you still want to write a book?'

'God, no. Not much use being a travel writer if you're no good at travelling.'

The patient cats skulking around our ankles were rewarded with scraps from the tables. The restaurant was noisy, but in spite of the flies and cats and sticky fingers, it was a civilized place to be, as it had probably been the last time I was there. Back then, it wasn't so frenetic and there were no customers hunkered down on the pavement outside. Back then, I was a bit of a case.

'By the way,' said Theo, 'I got a call this morning from a Dr Linklater.'

I looked up.

'You travelled with him, *ja*?'

'How on earth did he get your number? All I told him was that you were working on a census for the EU.'

'So he called the Central Statistics Organization where I work,' said Theo. 'He's invited us to dinner tonight.'

'Oh.'

'I wasn't sure . . . I felt I should accept.'

I had been trying not to think about Linklater, but he had been sliding into my thoughts all morning, like light under a closed door.

'Do you mind?' Theo asked.

'Er, no, that's fine. If you're okay with it?'

'I'll take a free meal from anyone – but who is he?'

'He's an anthropologist – lectures in one of the big

London universities – and he used to make documentaries.'

'Good ones?'

'Yeah, not bad. He'd go to far-flung places and live as the villagers did for a month, with a camera crew in tow. He made an excellent series in Bhutan, I seem to remember, living up in the hills in really dire poverty.'

'Sounds interesting.'

'It was intriguing in a soap-opera sort of way, I suppose. You know, the marriages and mothers-in-law, petty arguments and all-out feuds – not much different from the goings-on in any affluent suburb. He approached things from a very human point of view, not professional or academic. I liked that.' Was this *me* speaking? 'Anyway, he had quite a high profile for a while, but then he disappeared.'

'I look forward to meeting him.'

I slugged back some water. It was probably good that Linklater had maintained contact – more fodder for my chronicle; less good, however, that I was quite so pleased about it.

Theo was smiling.

'What?'

He shook his head.

'I'm not interested in him, if that's what you're suggesting.'

'Of course not. And he's asked us to dinner because he's not interested in you either.'

'Probably because he's a long way from *his family*.'

'Still,' he shrugged, 'if you'd like me to catch some

unpleasant disease that prevents me from joining –'
'Don't even consider it.'

After lunch, Theo took me to his office and introduced
me to his colleague, Fadhl Khadami. He was a hand-
some man, and although he was of average build, he
seemed small and portly next to Theo's gangly frame
as they looked up and down at one another like two
adjacent buildings in Sana'a's old quarter.
    'It is very wonderful you have come to Yemen,' Fadhl
said. 'We have hardly any tourists now, and tourism
is so important, not just for dollars, but for the jobs
it creates. Some years ago we had over one hundred
thousand visitors per year, but now hardly any.'
    'Because of September eleventh?'
    'Yes, that made our problems much worse. So if
there is anything I can do for you, Vivien, please let me
know.'
    'Actually, there is something. Theo tells me you know
the writer Tim Mackintosh-Smith.'
    'I met him once. You know him?'
    'No, but I've got his book and I'd like him to
sign it.'
    'No problem. I'll find out where he lives.'
    'Thanks.'
    'Would you like to walk over to the old town now?'
he asked. 'I can show you how to get there.'
    What a prospect. Walking alone to the old town?
No chance. There was somebody waiting for me there,
at Bab al-Yemen, and I wasn't yet ready to see her.
I pleaded exhaustion.

'Of course,' said Fadhl. 'You have had a very long journey.'

'Yes.' Yes. Much wiser to go back to the house and have another nap, and pretend not to be in Yemen at all.

I was short of breath when we arrived at Linklater's hotel that evening, but this had nothing to do with altitude. He was sitting in the lobby, looking smarter than he ever had on television, in a freshly pressed shirt and a light jacket, and as he stood up to greet us, a shiver passed through me, like a breeze rustling the leaves before a gale blows in. Trouble ahead. He shook hands with Theo when I introduced them, then lightly touched my elbow, the formality of a handshake already behind us, apparently. This was no television personality, no phantom from the past. 'Linklater' was right in front of me, for real, and it was very peculiar. He had become someone I knew; someone, even, whom I was glad to know.

On our way to a fish restaurant Theo recommended, I sat in the back of the jeep, looking out. The afternoon heat had given way to the wet again and the sky kept smarting with flashes of lightning. Thunder rumbled. People – men mostly – hurried about the streets. They shopped, talked, and drank tea in bare, dimly lit cafés, their cheeks swollen with *qat*. The bulge had alarmed me the first time I'd seen it – not because I didn't know Yemenis chewed the leaves of this mildly stimulant plant and stored the mulch in one cheek to savour the juices, but because I had not expected it to be any

34

bigger than a golf ball, perhaps. Instead, the men looked like they had tennis balls in their mouths. The traffic surged and stopped, rushed and crawled. There was no rhythm in the fuss of cars that filled the streets.

'You must have to travel around a fair bit,' Linklater was saying to Theo. 'Are there security implications?'

'I have to have armed personnel sometimes, but I hate this. I feel more at risk when I'm protected, and it really isn't necessary.'

'What about kidnap?' I asked.

'Kidnapping is not so bad here. They call it Four-star Kidnapping: the hostages are treated like guests. Once, the authorities went to free an Italian from the village where he was being kept and he didn't want to leave.'

'What about ninety-eight?' Linklater said. 'That was no family picnic. Four people died.'

'Yes, it was terrible. But in that case the army got involved and the hostages were killed in the crossfire. People here were very shocked by that. They say those kidnappers were a group operating from abroad – native kidnappers would never bring harm to their hostages, they are almost always released – because, historically, kidnapping is a bargaining tool. Anyway, there haven't been many incidents recently. The government has had success in preventing hostage-taking. It carries the death penalty now.'

We parked in a narrow side-street and made our way into the restaurant, stepping into a vast, tiled area, more like a fish market than a place to eat. We selected our fish from a pile on a table. Emperor fish, Theo said: big, fat guys. The man who picked them out for us wiped their insides with a sponge and directed us towards the seated area beyond the kitchen. We stopped by the kitchen door where, in spite of a great kerfuffle of activity – half a dozen cooks under pressure and flames leaping high from pans – we were waved in. Nobody was too frazzled for a smile and a welcome. Along the back wall, three men were making bread – the first was twisting cords of soggy dough into spirals, which he curled into huge circles and slid along to the next man, who moulded and kneaded and tossed them like pizzas. They whirled in the air and landed on his fist like pale, armless squid. The third chef flung these plates of dough into his oven, a large chimney-like furnace that rose from the floor. The scene gripped me. It offered everything I had once come looking for – an escape from the West and its insidious, creeping cultures. I peered into the oven, shielding my face from the heat. At the bottom, flames toasted some shrivelled-looking emperors, while the breads were stuck to the side. I had read about this somewhere – Ingrams, probably – and to see it now, seventy years after she did, was as effective as being sucked back through time. Behind me, other fish were being fried in a screech of heat and oil. Linklater stood close by my shoulder.

Theo led us into the dining room. I made a point of sitting beside him, but this meant that Linklater was opposite me and he caught my eye at every opportunity. I longed to explain that I was merely observing him, that he was little more than a specimen to me. One could even say that I had become an occasional anthropologist on his account.

'So,' he asked, 'what did you see on your first day?'

'Boys with catapults. Men with *jambiyahs*. Cats with scraps. Mountains.'

'Busy day.'

'I slept a lot too. I feel like I'm walking on thin air.'

'You are.'

'I think it is more the delay in Cairo that exhausts you,' said Theo.

'Oh, it wasn't so bad, was it?' Linklater said to me. 'We kept one another pretty well entertained.' There was no question but that he was flirting, and even less doubt that I was enjoying it, which struck me as nothing short of unbelievable.

'Indeed,' I said to Theo. 'I learned a great deal about *abassiya*.'

''*Asabiyya*,' Linklater corrected me.

'A Khaldunian concept,' I parroted, 'whereby intense notions of solidarity are more likely to be found in tribal contexts, where there is greater loyalty to their own than to the state.'

Linklater raised his eyebrows. 'Impressive. You were awake, after all.'

'You will be studying this here?' Theo asked him.

'Among other things. I'm writing a paper about its role in contemporary politics.'

'Vivien said you were going on a dig.'

'I am, and that'll be my morning job, but I'll be doing my own fieldwork in the evenings. First of all, though, I have to sit around the Ministry of Information and wait for them to issue my permit to leave Sana'a.'

'Will I need one of those?' I asked.

'Yes,' said Theo, 'but it won't be a problem. Where do you want to go?'

'Shibam.'

'There are three Shibams,' he said.

'You know the one I mean.'

Theo smiled. 'I'll take you there – the best way: driving across the desert from Marib. It's an amazing trip. You cross the sands to Shabwah, and then go on to the Hadramawt.'

'Thanks, but if it's all the same to you, I'll fly.'

'I thought you wanted to see Shibam rise out of the desert?' said Linklater.

'I do, but in my own good time and in my own sweet way. I'm no good at roughing it. I'm better suited to sit-upon lavatories, toilet paper, and hearing the news on the hour. I'm not doing the donkey bit.'

'I didn't say anything about donkeys,' said Theo, perplexed.

'If you do go ahead,' Linklater said to him, 'you can certainly count me in.'

'Not me,' I said. 'I'll fly to Seyun and get to Shibam from there.'

Linklater shook his head. 'What *would* your pal Niebuhr say?'

'Listen, I'm here, all right? I've come when no one else has, all by myself, to stay with a complete *stranger*, when the West Bank is in chaos, al-Qaeda are on the run, and the Americans are coming.'

'God forbid,' said Linklater, drily.

'Are you planning to hide in my house for three

weeks, then go home and tell everyone how brave you are?' Theo asked.

'Absolutely.'

They laughed.

The food arrived. The fish was toasted, the bread crackled and warped. 'It's called *rashoosh*,' Theo said.

I tore a chunk off the enormous disc and noticed, with some surprise, that I was enjoying myself. The anxiety was receding. I looked around the restaurant. Driving across the desert to Shibam. Not quite the expedition I had once envisaged, but some compensation, perhaps, some part of a dream realized. On the other hand, what if the car broke down? What if we got lost? ... And what would Shibam look like, approached in that way, after winding through Wadi Hadramawt?

As we left the restaurant, our emperors scraped to the bone, Theo suggested a drive through the old city and so, without preparation, I came once again to Sana'a proper, this time in the rain. A simple turn off the main road and we were immediately weaving through the narrow passageways of the old town, houses towering over us.

The paving stones glistened. The streets, the width of one car, ducked and dived between buildings. Theo drove into a dead end to give way to cars coming in the opposite direction. Another car shunted in behind us for the same reason, so we pushed further into the blind alley. Brown walls rose up around me, glowing in the headlights. Nowhere to go. My breathing grew shallow.

The two men talked about the World Bank, investment, the old city.

'Forty thousand people live here,' said Theo. 'This is no museum.'

I felt like a cat in an alleyway, the beams of lights in my eyes.

'And if they want to add on,' Linklater asked, 'can they do so?' He was leaning on the back of my seat; I could feel his breath on my neck, and it was making my blood stomp through my veins.

'Of course. They go up. Whenever Sana'anis need more space they add another floor, but they must stick to regulations. This is a World Heritage Site, so they can't mess with it.'

When the log-jam freed up, we backed out and resumed our tour, which allowed me to breathe easily again. Men hurried along, cheeks swollen with *qat*, their eyes bright in the night, splashing through the water with the hem of their shirts, the *zannahs*, pulled up and hung around their daggers, revealing large roomy shorts underneath. The *suq* was busy with people, moving from stall to stall, jumping over puddles and into them. A woman stood under an awning, a stack of breads balanced on her head. There, in the night and the wet, the love affair that had been thwarted struggled to resume, but bitter memories continued to spoil it. There was such professional mortification and personal failure linked with this place that a great chasm lay before me. It remained to be seen whether or not I could bridge it within three weeks.

I like Spain. For years I went there for my holidays,

with a friend or two. I'd go from the plane to the bus to the hotel, with its pool here and its beach just there, and for two weeks would read heavy paperbacks of no weight, speak to people who also brought teabags from home, and listen to children playing in my own language. All this, of course, within the confines of our 'complex' – a curious word for such a simple place. If pressed, I'd take a bus to some village and dally among the trinkets and postcards that lined the pavements, and when I got home I'd rave about the places I'd seen, carrying my passion for Spain like a banner. But it was more a veil than a passion, for it concealed disappointment. I returned eagerly to Spain every year so that nobody would notice I never went anywhere else.

I had scarcely been a tourist, let alone a traveller. Instead, I spent most days in the gallery, minding other people's visions, my own having being crushed by my inability to carry them through.

Bumping along those back-streets, I could see Sana'a only through the eyes of failure. I looked up at the multi-coloured fanlights, glowing in the dark, and wondered what went on behind them. We pulled out on to a broad unmarked carriageway with high walls.

'This is the *sailah*,' said Theo. 'A riverbed. In the wet season, it floods.'

We were driving through a foot of water. 'Like now?'

'Oh, much more than now.'

At the hotel, Theo said, 'Christian, I'm taking Vivien out to Wadi Dahr tomorrow afternoon. Would you like to join us?'

I glared at him.

Linklater noted my reaction. 'Lovely,' he said. 'Thanks.'

We stopped at Theo's office on the way home so that I could send the requisite emails. I reassured my mother, via my brother, that I had arrived safely; Theo was great, the house amazing, and I was holding my own. Then I sat and stared, a blank email page before me. I wanted to be clever, sharp. It occurred to me to say nothing, but mischief got the better of me.

'Arrived safely in Sana'a,' I wrote, 'in the company of one Dr Christian Linklater.'

I thought it was funny, but an odd feeling filled my belly when I clicked on 'Send'.

3

In the stifling heat of my tight little room, with the sun beating through the yellow curtains, I woke the next morning to find that Christian Linklater was all over my mind, like prickly heat. Although the horse had already bolted, I told myself not to cave in. That would be too ridiculous, too unaccountable, and too bloody complicated. I had let myself down in Yemen before; surely, this time, I could not do so again.

Driven out of the stuffy room, I went upstairs for breakfast. A door led from the small landing – between the kitchen and Theo's bedroom opposite – straight on to one level of the whitewashed roof, so I took my bread and tea outside. Low walls partitioned the different levels of the roof. The sun was hot. Already that shading of freckles would be appearing across the bridge of my nose, and the spiky tips of my short hair would be turning blonder (and would soon end up so light that I'd look as if I'd been electrocuted). The rooftops around me, most lower than ours, were busy. A goat was tethered on one, women put out washing on others, and someone was cooking across the street. In the distance, Jabal Nuqum, the great mountain that stands by the city like a proud grandfather, was purple against the clear blue sky. Sometimes it was green and imposing, as if it were on the very doorstep, but in the crippling summer heat, it shimmered in the distance, further away than ever.

In the crippling summer heat . . .

I had not returned to lay my ghosts at Sana'a's door, for the ghosts were a permanent fixture. Decisions, whether considered or rash, stay for ever, leaving their imprint on a life. Fate is baloney. Decisions, not destiny or defining events, create the gains and losses, the pros and cons, the trajectories we follow. I would never come to terms with the decision I had made twelve years earlier. It had been ill-judged, immature, and there could be no undoing its consequences, so I had returned, not to restore myself to Yemen, but to restore al-Yaman to me. During my teenage years, it had been the vessel into which I had poured my aspirations; it was the place I would take myself, make myself. Like an undeniable vocation, it was the direction I had looked towards. Since then, it had been the direction from which I turned away.

I sat on a whitewashed ledge, the sun burning my shoulders, and forced myself back. The house in which I'd stayed had had a roof like this, a view like this. Every part of my psyche resisted. Memories had to be hauled through the intervening years like a screaming child.

I had no clear idea, while I was still at school, how I would become a travel writer or get to Shibam or find that camel to take me into the desert, but I never doubted that I would succeed in all three, which was slightly odd because I was neither adventurous nor particularly brave. My best friend told me frequently that I was far too timid to take on the world, and I *was* timid, but not incompetent. I painted well, held my own at hockey and, according to teachers, my academic results were only undermined by my tendency to rush. One teacher wrote in a report, 'She could go far, if she would only slow down.' But I already knew I'd go far. It was merely a question of choosing the route.

My conscience played a large part in the direction I eventually took. In 1985, when I was sixteen, the Live Aid concert was broadcast and Bob Geldof rattled my comfortable cage. Watching footage of the Ethiopian famine made me realize that I had been born lucky – I had landed on the right side of the economic divide, in a democracy, even in the right climate, for God's sake – so when Geldof smashed his fist on to a table and said, 'Give us the money *now!*' I did. But it wasn't enough. The gesture didn't satisfy my conscience in the least. The notion of volunteering for an aid agency working in the third world came to me soon afterwards. With one shot, I could do my bit and get to travel. I would go East, learn the language, save the world, and lay down the foundations for my great adventure. It would take careful planning, but in this instance, as in no other, I would demonstrate remarkable patience. One day I would find myself perched on a camel's hump, swathed in robes in a sandstorm, with my own posse of noble Bedu leading the way . . .

I shied away from taking Arabic at college because of a general ineptitude in languages and a reluctance to embark on such an unknown subject from scratch. Instead I followed the safer option of continuing with

45

subjects I was good at – English and history – and achieved the kind of results for which I had hoped. On completion of my degree, I singled out agencies active in Yemen and offered my services. A London-based charity took me on as a junior administrator. Their offer of a stint in a village called Abs, helping to run a clinic, oiled the wheels of my dreams. Within weeks of finishing college, I had achieved two goals: I was on my way to Arabia Felix, as the Romans (and many since them) called Yemen, and salving my bad conscience to boot.

The sun grew very hot on the roof and my skin was stinging. I went into the dim kitchen, poured another glass of mint tea, and sat down. There was only a grubby wall to look at, but I was seeing another wall entirely – the one I'd hit the moment we'd landed in Sana'a.

By the time we touched down, the thrill of the adventure had already been crushed by my lover, Bill, who didn't appreciate being abandoned and had filled my head with notions that we were meant to be together. It wasn't entirely his fault. I learned quickly that my Yemen was completely unrelated to the real thing. The intensity of the heat was the first shock when I stepped on to the Tarmac. It was July. With three other volunteers, I ran towards the transfer bus as if I were hurrying away from a conflagration. Inside the terminal, I was harassed at Customs because I had not had the foresight to pull out the photographs of semi-clad women from my magazine. The surly official flicked through the pages, glancing at me with distaste. Then he ransacked my luggage and turned out my handbag. One of his colleagues muttered, '*Bas, bas!*' Enough, enough.

Nobody had come to collect us. Little boys climbed all over our trolleys and could not be shaken off, and as we stood forlornly outside the airport, soldiers asked to see our papers. None understood our pidgin Arabic and their few words of English amounted to a lot less than a sentence. I had never before been without language. Instead of being captivated, I was thrown off kilter.

When our lift eventually turned up, we were taken to the volunteers' house in Sana'a, where three of us were to share a room until we were taken to Abs. We were made to feel welcome and yet treated like first-formers, so I duly began to miss home as violently as if I had indeed gone away to boarding-school. I pined for Bill, and felt as if I had been wrenched from my home and taken to some far distant outpost, never again to return to the familiar. My excitement at being at last in Sana'a had crash-landed.

Over dinner, the established volunteers seemed intent on disabusing us of any notions of the romance of the East, emphasizing the very basic amenities in Abs, the drought, the poverty, the dirt. And there was bowel talk, too, of course. Tales of dysentery and relieving oneself at the side of the road made me break out in a sweat. One girl described how she had recently blocked herself up with toilet paper in case she didn't hold out until she got to the clinic where she worked. This suggestion was meant to be helpful, in the event that some time we might need to apply such a preventive measure. It became clear that in the event of diarrhoea, I would not be able to stay by a loo all day: it was an occupational hazard and one was expected to work regardless. For the first time, I wondered what kind of a Doreen Ingrams I would make.

Ingrams had travelled all over the Hadramawt valley in the 1930s, sometimes with her children tucked into boxes balanced on either side of a donkey. In her writings, she made little of the difficulties and discomfort, which belied how extreme conditions could be. That she and I were in different leagues was fast becoming obvious. It was clearly not enough to want to take the donkey and see the land: one had also to be blessed with a peculiar disdain for comfort and modesty.

That night, wedged between two English girls on the floor of our room, I had the first of several panic-attacks. My thoughts were jammed into that shrouded corner of the mind where light refuses to go. Two of Niebuhr's colleagues had died in Yemen, I reflected grimly, as I lay stiff and jet-lagged, listening for disease-laden mosquitoes.

'But disease began now to fall severely upon us,' Niebuhr had written in Mokha. 'Mr Von Haven . . . became much worse . . . He then sunk into a deep lethargy, and expired in the night.' Another colleague, the botanist Peter Forskaal, died soon afterwards. 'We were deeply affected at his loss,' Niebuhr wrote.

I, also, was deeply affected at his loss, in the dead of night two hundred and thirty years later, and I was unable to rationalize that those men had probably died of malaria, from which I was protected. Freya Stark, too, had had many low times while travelling in the Hadramawt, and as I tried to catch my breath on that thin mattress in that bare room, I could see her as clearly as she had portrayed herself, lying fevered on a mattress in a bare room in an isolated village surrounded by 'motionless cliffs'. 'A sense of prison overshadowed me between those perpendicular buttresses; they seemed as unescapable as the delirium of the night.' The delirium of the night . . . It was unfortunate that I dwelt on the darker passages and chose to forget that when Stark came close to dying of a heart complaint in Shibam, it was not her sins she regretted, 'but rather the many things undone'. Had I remembered this one quotation, instead of all the others, I might have acted differently.

The following day, the field director, Marcus, took us out to the bank, to get permits and to visit the office. In Dublin it had been easy to see Yemen as I wished, all towering brick buildings and sloping green terraces, but now I had to see it as it was, and as we made our way through the streets I noticed only mayhem. I had never been beyond Europe and could barely assimilate the breadth of disparity. The rigid heat and whirling dust; the bedlam of cars and Toyota pickups honking and screeching; the old man begging at traffic-lights, carrying a large crippled boy on his back . . .

What had I expected? Camels wandering car-free streets? Or Lawrence of Arabia, perhaps, riding into town with his faithful retainers, his pristine robes flowing behind him? For all my reading, I had been prepared only for pretty pictures – glorious architecture, *qat*-filled cheeks, *jambiyahs* stuffed into belts. I actually knew very little. Rather than being an asset, my extensive reading, selectively remembered, disabled me.

Externally I maintained a sulky, aloof demeanour, but inwardly I had flipped. I lost my appetite, couldn't sleep, relax or enjoy. By the evening of the second day, Marcus knew he had trouble. He took me aside and gave me a pep talk, explaining that the culture shock would ease after a bit. Patting my back, he said, 'You'll be fine.' Instead I worried my homesickness until it took over. I rang Bill and blubbered down the phone. Rather than rally me, he begged me to come home. 'We're both miserable,' he said. 'I told you this was a mistake.'

On the third day we were driven out to a village where the agency held clinics much like the ones we would be running. Seeing some of this beautiful country would help, Marcus assured me, but my nerves rattled when we were nearly knocked off the road by a lorry coming round a bend, and they never recovered. The mountainsides were dry, bare. Towers perching on the rims of hills seemed to be spying on me. In the village, grubby children rushed around the jeep, pushing into us, and teenage girls with babies on their hips stood about, watching. Their faces were dark, their eyes intense. The heat sucked me in. I wondered what Bill was doing just then and imagined him standing in our local supermarket in the icy glow of the frozen-veg cabinets. Marcus showed us into an unadorned building with one table in the middle of the room, a few chairs, and several shelves leaning at an angle on which were stacked health pamphlets. He passed round the leaflets, written in Arabic, and explained that we would be working in a similar environment, though more remote and a great deal hotter than on the 'lovely cool plateau of Sana'a' – his little joke.

My breathing grew even more strained. I couldn't hear properly, such was the thumping of veins in my eardrums, so I went to the door to catch my breath and was confronted by my new existence. The way heat kills, stifles any sense of life, meant that the street was a dead place. I didn't wonder about the teenage mothers who stood at a distance wondering about me. I didn't care about them. I wanted only to be away from it all, from the snotty children with beautiful eyes, from the thumping sun and the bleak mountains that had me cornered.

As we headed back to Sana'a, nothing could pull me from the encroaching panic. I had no sense that I would wake up the next day feeling better – though everyone told me repeatedly that I would – and there seemed no escape from the desperate mood that gripped me. I was held in a wrench. If the destitute existence of those whom I had come to help left me cold, I would never care enough to endure the tough conditions.

We went to the Vietnamese-run restaurant that night, where I found solace in chicken and chips and Coke. A feeble attempt to relate to my colleagues failed: there was no connection. I was the oddity already, the one who wasn't measuring up. These people were genuine, game, while I amounted to a lot of hot air. My state of mind was as alien as my surroundings. It seemed to exist in a box separate from the rest of me. I could see my hands, down there, grasping a moist glass, a fork, and I could hear voices, but my thoughts were somewhere else entirely, racing along like a stallion on the loose. My only objective was escape. At whatever cost to my integrity, leaving was the only thing worth thinking about. Another sleepless night followed.

The following day my reading habits took another negative turn. We were left to our own devices, so the volunteers decided to go to the old town. I followed, nervous and newly agoraphobic. I didn't want to go out into the streets but could not stay alone, and there was some hope that the old city I had waited so long to see would cure me.

We walked the length of Az-Zubayri Street heading towards Bab al-Yemen, the gateway to the old town. The women, sailing along the streets like moving shuttlecocks in long black skirts and capes, unsettled me. Many covered even their eyes. Faceless beings slid past me. Were they looking at me? Could they see me looking at them? Were they not suffocating beneath all that black? Breathing had become an obsession. I hadn't taken a satisfying breath since I arrived: it was always too short, too shallow, too hot. For the women, it must have been intolerable, I thought, and I railed with self-righteous indignation: how could I work in a country where girls gave birth at twelve, often had a dozen children and were old by thirty? Why should I go into a dustbowl to help young mothers when nothing would ever change? What was the point and who did we think we were, in the final analysis, coming over to save them all? My fellow volunteers, as I hurried along behind them, suddenly looked to me like misguided imperialists.

We went through the archway at Bab al-Yemen, and the old city of Sana'a, like an old man rising from a bow, reared up before me. It brought us to a halt. The others gasped. I continued to gasp. 'Amazing,' they said. 'Like a diorama, except real.' 'Sandcastles.'

We stood gaping. There was a bustle of people all about us. Out of nowhere, a peasant woman, draped in a great colourful cape, accosted me and shook a bar of vile green soap in my face, squealing at me, mouthless, in unintelligible gabble, for only her eyes were exposed. I recoiled – from her, from the soap, from Sana'a. When I looked at those extraordinary buildings, nothing stirred; no sense of recognition rumbled in my gut. The woman shouted at me. My companions moved on towards a narrow street into which the great mass of people were pressing, but I couldn't get past her. She was determined to sell me that soap. Her face was ever closer to my own and the smell of the green soap sharp in my nostrils. She was laughing, enjoying our battle of wits. I bolted. I pushed through the crowds at the gate and went back the way we had come, stumbling on cracked pavements, stepping in front of cars as I ran from myself. I hurried along Az-Zubayri Street, thinking about home, friends, family, and wove through the men who came at me, some calling out in anger when I barged past, until the crowd became too oppressive and I took a right, and then another, to reach quieter streets. Within minutes, I was lost. I went back to Az-Zubayri street to start again. Under my all-encompassing clothes, sweat poured off me. I couldn't stand it. I pulled at the scarf round my neck, opened my shirt and rolled up my sleeves. A man nearby shouted at me and shook his head vigorously. I couldn't get air into my lungs and he was telling me not to undress? In semi-collapse, I sat on the pavement. A crowd gathered – a *crowd*, compressing the air, pushing into me, a circle of dusty sandals and dirty hems surrounding me like a fence – and a din of curious voices hammered in my ears. 'I need space – *space!*' I cried. Arabic was thrown in my direction and I felt as if I was swimming through a lexicon, trying to outpace these garbled sounds, drowning, drowning in words, dry, hot words, burning words. It was a language without shape, without sentences, just strings of syllables, flying at me like darts at a board. Where was the meaning? Where was I?

A bottle of mineral water found its way into my hand. I drank and drank and poured it over my face. A broad man leaned forward, shouting over his shoulder at the gathered press of people, who backed away by one step. He urged me to drink more, and when I had recovered a little, offered in broken English to get me a taxi.

'I don't know my address.'

There was little he could do about that, but he and some others stayed with me, discussing my predicament no doubt and considering solutions as I sat there on the pavement. In the end, I took a taxi to the Taj Sheba hotel and phoned Marcus.

While other writers might have put me to shame, Jonathan Raban at least would have understood. He also suffered culture shock on his first day in Sana'a in the 1970s: 'Suddenly in Sana'a I was in the middle of a real maze. Its walls were oppressively high, its corridors narrow, its noise frightening.' As I sat in the cool lobby of the hotel, it gave me comfort to remember that such a seasoned traveller as he had written, 'I was down to the whimpering stage by the time I asked a man if he knew where the British Embassy was.' At the embassy, an official gave him the means to calm down and, therefore, to stay. Without that diplomat, Raban wrote, 'I would have fled the Yemen on the next plane out.'

Sadly, I had no soothing diplomat so it was the next plane out for me. When I told Marcus I had to go home, he acquiesced limply.

Several horrible days followed, during which I was counselled, bullied, befriended and excluded, but they let me go. Marcus realized I would be useless. The three days I had to wait for the flight were interminable. I stayed in the house, too ashamed for Yemen to see me or for me to see it in all its glorious disarray.

The relief when I landed in Ireland was overwhelming; the shocking sense of failure hit days later, quickly followed by mortification. Only with dire embarrassment could I look back at the frenzied, desperate person I had been in Sana'a. Whoever she had been, I did not recognize her in the comfort zone of my Dublin life, and I had no desire, ever, to become reacquainted with her. For years afterwards, whenever I was reminded of it, my brain shrank and my skin flushed. If people asked, I never spoke about my inability to cope, I talked only about Bill and our need to be together, but even that version would ricochet against me.

Theo called from the stairwell. I stepped out of the past to greet him on the landing.

The Rock Palace at Wadi Dahr is picture-postcard Yemen. No tourist brochure is without a photograph of the former imam's summer residence, so five of us set off that afternoon to see another sight that must be seen. Fadhl joined us, and Nooria, one of our neighbours, came along too, forcing me to be polite and sociable when I was becoming increasingly preoccupied by Christian Linklater's every gesture. Even with my back to him, I knew exactly where he was, how close, how still, which way he was looking . . . My radar was on, my body alert. For all my efforts, I had been unable to stem an attraction to him, though I remained determined to plug it.

Nooria, who lived alone in a flat in the house adjoining ours, was from Aden and ran an educational centre for young women. Like many women in Sana'a, she dressed in the *balto*, a long black coat, and wore a black headscarf. She was extremely familiar with Theo, teasing him in a cheeky, almost flirtatious manner, and although her bright, independent spirit was impressive, her liveliness irked me.

I had remained calm so far, thanks largely to Theo and his jeep. Theo had swiftly become the stake that held me up, and he seemed as comfortable with this as I was. If there had been any particular moment when we ceased to be host and guest and became friends instead, it would have been when I told him the truth about Yemen and me, but the transition had been more seamless than that. We had simply flowed into the same stream – by design, perhaps, but we continued together by choice. In his company, I was assured, almost confident, although I still worried that my composure might suddenly be thrown. On our way out of Sana'a, I clung to the handhold in the back seat, looking through grubby windows. Near Bab al-Yemen, decorators stood about with buckets and rollers over their shoulders, hoping for work, and along the roadside fruits rose in great pyramids of segregated colour – watermelons, oranges, tomatoes, limes – one beside another, gracing the broad street like a patient crowd watching a carnival go by. 'Fruits are, however, very plenteous at Sana,' Niebuhr had written.

It was not so hard, perhaps, to look Yemen in the eye, and it was impossible not to be drawn to the purple mountains that surround Sana'a like cupped hands.

Outside the city, Theo turned off the main road and drove along a bumpy track that led to a clifftop overlooking the valley. 'Don't fall over,' he said, when we walked gingerly to the edge of the flat red rock. It was a bright, hot afternoon. The air was clear, the view extraordinary.

In a great gorge beneath us lay the wadi, a lush valley winding its way round the curves of the bare rocky hills. Below the escarpment were houses among the orchards and a village at the foot of a rounded cliff face. To our left, rising out of the valley floor, Dar al-Hajar, the Rock Palace, stood out, a towering edifice built on a pinnacle of rock. A tall boy perched on a tall man's shoulders, to command a better view, perhaps, of the graceful lands around him.

'Right,' I said, 'let's go down.'

'Don't you want to . . . you know, breathe it in a bit?' Theo asked.

I took a deep breath. 'Okay. Let's go.'

Linklater put his hands on my shoulders. 'She needs some training,' he said to the others. 'Now,' to me, '*look*. Appreciate. And don't move.'

Arcadia lay before me, but Linklater's hands were on my shoulders, warm and steady, and his voice made my insides twist. One of the country's most stupendous views stretched out around us and all I could think about was the cultural anthropologist. He was standing between me and this place. I walked away, sat on a rock and, with some distance between us, found it easier to muse about the brochures I had once wondered at, with Imam Yahya's palace always to the forefront. It took a considerable feat of concentration to accept that I was actually looking down on it, for the panorama before me was as silent and as still as any photograph.

But Linklater followed. He hunkered down beside me, his camera dangling off his wrist. 'Glorious, isn't it?' He had long, slender fingers.

'I wonder how they built it.'

'Vivien . . .'

'Hmm?'

'Any chance we could have dinner tonight?'

'Again? Oh, I don't know. I'll have to ask Theo.'

'Actually, I wasn't planning to invite Theo.'

Nooria was standing perilously close to the edge. Theo admonished her. Her teasing, wild laughter rang out. I willed Theo to turn round, to see me perched there, stiff and trapped.

'Vivien?'

I looked away, across Wadi Dahr. *No.* I had loads to tell already. He was attractive, interesting, everything as expected – and married. Or did he play away from home? The look on his face, as he balanced on the balls of his feet, no longer spoke harmless flirtation but genuine interest. In failing to discourage it, I had allowed myself to arrive at this awkward moment. 'You mentioned a family,' I said. 'Aren't you married?'

'Divorced.'

'Let's go,' Theo called.

Divorced? Jesus. How did that happen? When?

Two youths were suddenly upon us, one with a falcon on his shoulder, the equivalent of the monkey on the Costa Brava: have your photo taken with the monkey and pay for the privilege. Before I knew it, the falcon was on *my* shoulder, stepping back and forth like a man on the deck of a transatlantic liner. I gesticulated at its owner: Thank you, but I don't want a photo with your flesh-eating bird. Linklater remonstrated with them in Arabic. As if out of pique, the bird scratched my neck with its claw as they took it away.

'Ouch.'

'He got you? Let me see.'

I put my hand over the scratch. 'It's fine.' I walked towards the others. It wasn't fine, but I didn't want him anywhere near the back of my neck. 'Got any disinfectant?' I asked Theo, showing him the scratch.

'Sorry, no, but you've had your tetanus shot, *ja*?'

'Yes, but it needs cleaning. Have you no antiseptic at the house?'

'*I* have,' came the voice behind me. 'In my kit, back at the hotel.'

'Never mind.'

Down in the valley we drove past a round water-tower with a square room built on top, then left the tarmacadam for dirt tracks that had been moulded into humps and dips and even great crevices. The jeep heaved and sighed, leaning this way and that, splashing into enormous puddles – ponds, almost. The dull browns and greys of the landscape were speckled with blue plastic bags, and there were a lot of people everywhere. Among them, no doubt, some of those who had been thrown out of Saudi Arabia in 1990 during the Gulf War, and sent back to a country that many of them scarcely knew, only to become an extra load on already burdened families. The men squatted under trees or walked the roads, sometimes holding hands. Children ambled about with satchels on their backs. Some went to school in the morning, Fadhl explained, others in the afternoon. Many got no education at all. The boys were dressed like little men, in *zannahs* and jackets, but the girls were enchanting in their multicoloured layers, baggy pants under elaborate dresses.

They crouched in doorways or stood around in huddles.

When Theo went into a shop to buy water, a little girl came to my window. She was wearing a white satin dress that looked as if it had been a First Communion dress in a previous life and had somehow arrived in Wadi Dahr from my part of the world. It was held together by safety-pins, but the child managed to look more entrancing than a Grainne might have done on her First Communion day at home, with her corkscrew ringlets, short lacy socks and shiny patent shoes. Big brown eyes stared into mine, and I stared back. While Linklater, Nooria and Fadhl discussed the environmental curse of plastic bags, the little girl and I had a long encounter. I would not allow guilt to cut it off. I needed to look into her eyes until she turned away.

'We've just got rid of them in Ireland,' I heard myself say.

'Yes?' said Fadhl.

'We have to pay for plastic bags now, so people remember to bring longer-lasting carrier-bags to the shops. The tax goes towards the environment. In theory.'

'But this is excellent! And the bags are gone?'

'Just about. You have to hit people in the pocket.'

Theo got back in. The little girl stepped away, releasing me.

Outside the palace, we parked beneath a huge tree, pockmarked with age.

'Those are *qat* trees,' Theo said to me, pointing at an orchard. 'They soak up huge amounts of water. It's a big problem. Sana'a's water-table is almost non-existent.'

'In spite of all these downpours?'

'Most of the year is very dry.'

'Do women chew much *qat*?' I asked Nooria.

'I don't,' she retorted.

Theo smiled. 'She's from the South,' he said, by way of explanation. 'In the Hadramawt, people say only sheep chew.'

Nooria seemed utterly uninterested in me. Theo had wanted us to meet, but she had barely spoken to me and I wondered why she had come. A woman draped in the *sitarah*, the large blue and red cape favoured by rural women, stopped to speak to Nooria and me. She kissed our hands with her veiled mouth, the response to which was to kiss the back of her hand. The welcome made, she moved on, waving and smiling.

The palace was glorious from every perspective. A five-storey building atop a ten-storey rock, its several levels twisting around themselves like stone topiary, it had looked from the cliff like an inland lighthouse. Two men were sitting in the administration office sorting piles of *qat*, and an eager guide ushered us through the great wooden door into the palace. We climbed twisting white steps, bent over to get through low doors and gaped down wells that dropped into darkness. We stood in ancient caves that were an integral part of the rock – prehistoric burial places – but the anthropologist who loved the dead was scarcely interested. He was more intent on keeping to my heels. Even when I took the women's staircase, up a back way, he followed. The guide showed us the bedrooms of Imam Yahya's first and second wives on one floor and those of his third and fourth on another.

My thighs were shaking.

'Get used to it,' said Linklater. 'Anyone who comes to Yemen will have an intimate relationship with stiff thighs and crick.'

'Crick?'

'From looking up.'

When Fadhl took Linklater and Nooria in another direction, Theo and I continued climbing. 'Linklater has asked me to dinner tonight,' I told him.

'If you are having dinner with him,' he said testily, 'don't you think you should call him Christian?'

'I've always called him Linklater.'

'I thought you'd only just met?'

'We have. It's the TV thing, probably. Would you mind my going?'

We stopped to rest against the walls on a bend in the staircase.

'You don't need my permission,' said Theo.

'No, but I wish you'd stop me.'

He had one foot on a higher step and his long arms dangled by his sides. 'Why?'

The wall cooled my back. 'Gut feeling.'

'That's how I felt when I met Roos, my girlfriend.'

'You have a girlfriend?'

'So surprising?'

'No. I mean, yes. You don't look . . . attached.'

'How can I look attached when she's in Amsterdam?'

'I don't know. Body language. You might have given

me the "I-am-already-spoken-for" signals in case I tried to jump you.'

He laughed. 'I had no worries. Christian spoke for you the first time we met.'

'Oh, God, did he?'

Theo nodded.

'Right, that settles it. Let's have a quiet night at home and you can tell me all about Roos.'

'That would be nice.'

We stood looking at one another, and in that quiet moment, options were considered, boundaries decided, decisions made.

Theo resumed the climb. 'But why are you hesitating about Christian?'

'Because he was married for years and he has triplets, for God's sake. Imagine the baggage he's carrying.'

'He's not asking you to marry him, Vivien. Just to have dinner.'

At the top of the building, we stepped on to the terrace, which was surrounded by a very high wall with only four small windows in it.

'One for each wife,' Fadhl explained.

Linklater was at my shoulder again. 'About dinner?' he said quietly.

No, I thought. Let him go away to the desert. 'Yes, lovely. Thanks.' From loyalty to betrayal, with relative ease.

4

Linklater's first gesture when he arrived that evening was to hand me a tube of antiseptic cream. I was agitated. I had spent hours agonizing, scarcely able to believe I had not declined this invitation. Had I no restraint? It seemed not. Whenever he appeared, all my inner resolve crumbled and I slipped gracefully into neutral. It was too easy, so far from home, to disregard the consequences.

Since it was within walking distance, we went to the Vietnamese-run restaurant, where we found a table in the corner. It was busy and sweaty beneath the harsh strip lighting. He ordered; his fluency in Arabic was seductive. There was no Theo to distract me. I had to talk to Linklater, one on one, and it made me jittery, not least because I would have to dissemble – ask questions to which I knew the answers and feign curiosity where there was none. He also seemed unnerved, and his natural flow of conversation faltered. He put his palms flat on the table and tapped his fingers lightly as he looked around. Had there been cutlery, he would have straightened it; moved it minimally, from here to there.

'What do you do when you're lecturing?' I asked.

'Sorry?'

'Every lecturer has his own peculiar body language. What's yours?'

He thought about it. 'I usually stand back from the lectern, one foot pointing up. The I-am-cool-confident-and-deeply-knowledgeable stance.'

'And are you cool and confident?'

'Course not. Students are terrifying.'

'So which part of your work do you prefer – teaching or TV?'

'Oh, I gave up the documentaries some time ago. It had got out of hand. It became a parody of ethnographic film-making.'

'How so?'

'Viewers seemed to be more interested in me, in my personal trials and whether I'd wear a penis gourd on camera or not.'

'Did you?'

'I'm afraid so.'

'I must have missed that one.'

He smiled.

'Still, it seems a shame you gave it up. I quite enjoyed your programmes.'

'"Quite,"' he teased.

'No, I did enjoy them. I always learned something.'

'Good, because that was the whole point of the exercise, to educate – and not being able to do so, now that I'm out of the loop, *is* a little frustrating.'

'You miss it?'

'Bits of it,' he said, with a shrug. 'The fact is that television remains one of the most effective ways to inform the greater population, and I miss having that opportunity, especially at times like these. I mean, the average Westerner knows as much about the Middle

East as the average Brit knows about Northern Ireland, which doesn't help the way of the world right now.'

'What made you specialize in the Arab world?' I asked, and then thought, Christ, how would I know this? Has it come up already?

He was unfazed. 'The usual, really. When I was a student I spent three months doing fieldwork in Syria and got completely hooked, but I've banged on enough about my work. Tell me about yours. You run a gallery?'

'Yeah, I work for an Iraqi, Shoukria O'Rourke, who is married to an Irishman. She owns the gallery and I run it while she's off building up her own private collection of Arab art and sniffing out artists she'd like to launch on the world.'

'Nice way to earn a living.'

'For me, yes, but she doesn't make a living out of it. She doesn't need to. She's married to a millionaire.'

'A genuine philanthropist?'

'Down to her toenails. You can't imagine what it's like working for someone who has no interest in profit, whose entire *raison d'être* is launching other people's careers.'

'Sounds wonderful,' he said. 'How long have you worked there?'

'Seven years.'

'Goodness. How come that impatient gene of yours hasn't moved you on yet?'

'I'm impatient, not stupid.'

'*Touché.*'

My knee knocked against his. Eye-contact. Too long. I politely asked about his children.

'Ah. April, May and June.'

I looked nonplussed. Those were not their names.

'They're triplets,' he explained. 'We have three girls.'

'You make it sound like a personal achievement.'

'It certainly felt like it!'

We laughed. 'Whose side was it on? The multiple conceptions?'

'Mine, I'm afraid. My sisters are twins.'

'God. Are they identical? Your daughters, I mean.'

'To outsiders, yes. How about you? Any kids? Husbands?'

'Neither. I have a clear slate in that regard. Have you been divorced long?'

'Two years. You must have had offers?'

'Just one,' I said. 'A good one. Naturally I accepted.'

'Oh?'

'He was lovely. And I did love him – that was why we got engaged. I even bought the odd bridal magazine and looked at silly dresses, but when it came to the crunch, I had to concede there was . . . I don't know, some kind of gap inside me that shouldn't have been there. Not that one's partner in life should meet one's *every* need,' I added quickly, in case he thought I was naïve, 'but this particular blank was just too big. It was as if I wasn't fully coloured in yet, you know? Giving him up was horrible. The friendship, the security of being loved, having an anchor – it was hard to let all that go.'

'So we've both lost our roots, then.' He smiled. 'Spore floating through the air.'

'Er, no, I'm not a bit spore-like,' I admitted. 'On the

contrary, I seem to be chronically settled. Breaking off the engagement did it.'

'Ending relationships usually has the opposite effect.'

'I know, people go mad with freedom, but I consolidated, and now I'm just too comfortable. I have a great job, a great flat, good friends and a gorgeous cat.' A wave of unease washed over me. It didn't sound like much: a flat, a cat – a tiny pile of a life, and all because of one bad decision that, instead of carrying me away, forced me to return like a boomerang and banged me into a dreary existence like a driven nail.

'What about the unfinished canvas?' Linklater asked.

'I have that in hand, I hope. What about you? Did you hide or go wild when your marriage ended?'

'Oh, I . . . I have kids. I wasn't free to go wild. Besides, there was no point in revisiting my youth because I was dreadfully conservative then. I married my first serious girlfriend.'

'No midlife crisis?'

'Apart from the small detail of my marriage ending . . .'

Oops.

'No,' he said, 'midlife suits me fine.'

It certainly did.

I tapped my fingers on the table, looking left and right.

'That won't work here,' said Christian.

'I know.'

He put his hand over mine. 'Is there no way to still you?'

I tried. I did try, a little. Common sense implored me

to bring to an end the lingering eye-contact, to move my knee from where it kept brushing against his. I couldn't, and it would soon be too late to turn back. He was no longer a project. He had swiftly become an obstacle bearing down on me, like a tanker on a sailboat in the night.

The Vietnamese owner also bore down on me with another superlative meal. Christian was adept at rolling rice between his fingers, while I yearned for a fork. I asked about his background – lest at some point I let slip something he had not told me himself – so we covered the early childhood in the Somerset town of Street, 'Where Clarks shoes are made', and the later move to Bristol. His mother had been a solicitor, his father a criminal psychologist. 'My father used to tell me about the cases he was working on, but it wasn't the individual criminal who interested me, it was the community behind him, the wider social context, so I turned to anthropology. A sunnier alternative than sociology or Dad's grim line of work.'

After dinner we wandered slowly through quiet streets. Christian walked with his hands in his pockets; I held mine behind my back, fingers hooked together. Our elbows made contact. Like snakebite, the heat ran up my arm. There was a yell behind us. Fearing a catapult attack, I swung round and walked backwards for several steps. Christian steered me round a pothole. Theo's street was dark. Cats mewed. We stumbled along near the walls.

'This is it, I think. Double wooden gates. Number eight.' I threw my shoulder against the door to open it and stepped into the courtyard. There was no moon, nothing to see. Across the yard, a goat bleated. Apart from one light each on the top floors, the houses were in darkness. I felt my way to the front door. Theo had given me a key, but it wasn't much use. 'I can't find the keyhole.'

More than ever, Christian was a black shadow bearing down on me. We both felt at the door. 'Where the hell is it?'

'Let me.' He felt for the key in my hand, put his fingers over mine. His arm came round my back. When he kissed me, my conscience skulked away across the courtyard.

Even with our minds more firmly on the job, the keyhole was no easier found than before. We fingered the door, its recesses, laughing quietly. 'Maybe it's the wrong house.'

'Imagine the commotion if we got in.'

'We'll have to rouse Theo.'

'You think you can throw a stone up that high and hit his tiny window?'

'Got a catapult?'

'No!'

We kissed again. 'Here it is,' said Christian, breaking off. 'My finger's in it.' He fumbled with the key, unlocked the door and let us in.

The stairwell was also dark. 'Oh, God.'

'What now?'

'I don't know where the light switch is either,' I said.

'Now you're just taking advantage of me.'

'I am not! I've only been here two days.'

'It must be beside the —' The light came on.

We went up to the kitchen. Light slipped out from beneath Theo's door. I took Christian on to the roof while the kettle was simmering.

'I can't quite believe I'm here,' I said, glancing around the lights of the city.

'I can't believe you're here either.'

The *mafraj* was marginally bigger than my bedroom, but it gave the impression of space, because, apart from the cushions along the walls and rugs on the floor, there was no furniture. Christian lay across the cushions; I sat on the floor, one leg tucked under me. He sipped at his cup, I at mine. Pointless. Neither of us wanted coffee so he put our mugs on the low windowsill and pushed me back, where we indulged ourselves demurely like a couple of teenagers.

'I should go,' he said eventually. He lifted himself off and pulled me up with one hand. 'Don't come down. I'll find my way out.' On the landing, he hesitated before making his way into the dark stairwell.

In my room, I stood for a moment, meaning to undress but unable to move. Where did infidelity begin? In a few indulgent kisses or in the bedroom? I dreaded the rest of the night; the length of it. The sleepless hours during which the evening, so physically charged, would replay in my head, battering me with guilt and recriminations.

Something moved behind me. I swung round. Christian was standing in the doorway, shaking his head slightly. 'Hopeless,' he said.

'What is?'

'This.' He stepped in, ran his finger along my lip, over my chin and down my neck. 'I should go but . . .' he pushed aside my unbuttoned shirt '. . . I don't very much want to.'

My shirt fell to the ground, along with good intentions. We lowered ourselves to the mattresses. He unlaced his boots with one hand. The bedside light shone in his face. I turned it off. Fragments of excuses hurried round my brain, looking for justification, but settled only on one insubstantial little word: *sorry*.

The sex was sharp, quick, worth it.

'Oh dear,' said Christian, afterwards. 'I shouldn't have let this happen.'

Curious, I thought, how a man's conscience always catches up with him after the act. But my own conscience was none too clear. 'Why not?'

'I should have wooed you properly, slowly, over several candlelit dinners.'

'Which wouldn't be difficult in this town.'

'I should at least have got beyond the first date,' he said.

'Trying to stop this happening would have been like trying to stop an express train with your little finger.'

He chuckled. 'It would, wouldn't it? I would have had you in Cairo airport, given the chance, especially when you were fiddling with that unsavoury omelette.'

For a fleeting moment, I felt unbelievably, disgustingly, smug. It was like getting a qualification after cribbing in the exam. 'You'd better go,' I said. 'I don't want Theo finding you here in the morning.'

'Fair enough.' He started to dress. 'I like Theo. Lovely man.'

'He's the best.'

Christian leaned over me and, although we were replete, the kissing went on for a long time, until he dragged himself away and once again vanished into the dark hallway.

It was a long night. Disturbed by giddiness, guilt and arousal, I slept sporadically. At dawn, I woke to the cry of the muezzin, doing his thing before sun-up. Around the city others echoed him, until the prayer was like a lullaby, telling me all was well, that I could roll over and go back to sleep.

Later I woke to a knock and the rattle of plates outside the door. Theo! I reached for a T-shirt, calling, 'Just a minute,' but the door opened and Christian appeared, grinning that boyish grin and holding a tray.

'Jesus! How did you get in?'

'Theo seems to have left the door unlocked when he went to work. Unwise, in my view. You might have been ravished by some stranger.'

'I was.'

'Anyway, I took the liberty of letting myself in and made breakfast. Hungry?' He sat cross-legged on the floor, poured tea and ripped up the *khubz*. His hair was tousled, his face relaxed. 'What are your plans today?'

'I don't have plans. I've made a rule to have no plans in Yemen. Let it do with me what it will. You?'

'I have some sitting around at the ministry to do, but

this afternoon we could have a swim at the hotel if you fancied?'

'A swim? In honest to God *cold* water? Yes, please!'

The swimming-pool was round, the water warm. So warm, in fact, that we had to get out to cool down. We lay in the sun then, reading and talking until, a propos nothing, Christian said, 'Let's go up.'

In his comfortable air-conditioned room, we stretched across his hard, wide bed and made good use of it. He drifted off to sleep afterwards, but loud music prevented me doing likewise. There was a child's party going on down in the garden. I got up to look out. Children were running around and jumping in and out of the baby pool while their mothers sat round tables chatting. I watched for a long time. On the lawn a party organizer was arranging a game of musical chairs. Waiters moved about with trays of tea and cold drinks. Just beneath our window a birthday cake, with a picture of a young girl's face iced on it, stood waiting for its candles to be lit. Everything, in short, was just like at home: the pretty face on the cake, the games, the kids. Only the women were different.

Fully veiled, they exposed only their faces, some just their eyes, but from up on the third floor they looked as familiar to me as my own friends – chatting vigorously, leaning into mobile phones, running after children with towels or trying to coax them into eating various treats on paper plates. As the afternoon wore on, some head-scarves came off and in one case the *balto*, the long black coat, was discarded to reveal a pretty woman in a dress and high heels. I was mesmerized by the sameness of it all, by the games played the world over, and by the one thing that stood between me and them: the veil. I wanted to get behind it. I wanted to be part of their world, to sit with them down there and enjoy the gossip. But would they not judge me? Would they not shake their heads at this unmarried, childless woman who had just had sex with a man she scarcely knew? Did I not represent everything they distrusted about the West – our quick fix to every desire, our disregard for sanctity and convention? Would they accept a woman so different? Or was I, really, so very different? I would not leave Yemen without finding out.

Christian rolled on to his belly, the sheet tangled round him. 'What's that bloody racket?'

'Kids' party. And guess what? The wretched party bag has come to Yemen.' I lay down, put my chin on his shoulder and ran my hand down his back. I wanted to find the scar. My fingertips loitered around his right haunch, but found no bumps, no grizzled skin. So I worked my way down, kissing his spine and pushing the sheet away, until I found it. It was on the other side – on the left. I drew back. It was worse than I'd expected – an ugly chaos of white and red lines, a patchwork of skins.

'Horrible, isn't it?' he said.

'What happened?'

'I was attacked by some dope-heads in London a few years ago. They took my wallet and left their signature with a broken bottle. A new slant on cash for kidneys.'

'Sorry?'

'I lost a kidney.'

'I didn't know that.'

Christian rolled on to his side. 'How could you?'

My hand resting on his thigh, I stared at the scar and wondered why he had lied about it, but he had become aroused again and I became distracted.

When Theo got home from work that evening, we sat opposite one another at the kitchen table, as had swiftly become our habit, and talked over tea. He told me more about Nooria. 'She was married twenty years ago, when she was seventeen – an arranged marriage – but it didn't work out, so they divorced and she moved to Sana'a to study, then stayed on to work. She has no family here so she lives alone. It's a little unusual but not unheard-of, especially for a divorcée who has the support of her parents, and they are less conservative in the South, after years of Communism. They're better educated, generally, and of course women were expected to work in South Yemen, so Nooria is used to running her own life. She doesn't care very much what anyone thinks, actually.'

I loved listening to Theo, to the way he spoke English – almost with a Dutch accent, but not quite – and I loved talking to him, with the evening stretching ahead, when nothing mattered beyond the stories we told and the things we learned in his little kitchen on the top floor.

He told me that he was part-English. When Holland had been liberated by the Allies in '45, his maternal grandmother had become pregnant by an English soldier who, when the party was over, decamped with the rest of the army. The legacy of those liberation celebrations was a whole generation of half-English children born to young Dutch women. Theo's mother was among those who never succeeded in tracing her father.

'Speaking of tracing people,' he said, 'apparently Mackintosh-Smith is out of the country doing research but is due back soon. Do you still want to meet him?'

'Yeah. It'll be intimidating, but I'm determined to meet a real live travel writer.'

'Why intimidating?'

'Because when I set off in the footsteps of people like him, I tripped up and fell flat on my face.'

'You don't have to tell him that.'

'I won't. He met Thesiger, you know. He actually interpreted for Thesiger. *That*'s what I'll ask him about.'

Theo looked at his watch. 'We have a party to go to.'

'We do?'

Apart from our quick drive on my first night, I had still not been down to the old town. It astounded me that I had managed to avoid doing so for days, but I had yet to take more than three steps alone in Sana'a, surrounded as I always was by my protective coterie, and although I grew more confident that way, I would make no real progress until I faced Bab al-Yemen. But I was too busy – busy with my love-affair and busy living Theo's life. There always seemed to be somewhere to go, people to be with. I hadn't socialized so much in years, and all this activity was a slur on my existence

78

back home, on my unchallenged routine of television and book clubs, and much-dreaded openings. As we stepped into the crowded, candlelit home of Jane Ware, a forthright Englishwoman who had lived in Yemen for twenty years, I realized how much I was missing.

She gathered us to her like a benevolent aunt and hustled us into the *diwan*, a large parlour. Christian was there, leaning slightly forward to listen to the woman next to him. He watched me come in, and almost smiled, and it was as if a flash had gone off, a photograph been taken. *Evidence.* I glanced around furtively, but no one had noticed the look that had passed between us. It was silly to fret. I would not be caught, not so far from anyone I knew.

He introduced me to Edda Lombardi, the project leader, who had been instrumental in having him included in what was otherwise an Italian-Yemeni excavation.

'What exactly *is* the security situation?' I asked her.

'Never as bad as you read in the papers!' She laughed. 'In Marib, it can get a little tense sometimes, but we have never had any problems. We always use local tribesmen as bodyguards, the Ashraf mostly, and we stay with families – the men leave and we move in, under the care of their women. As we are their guests, they see it as their responsibility to protect us. We have not had one incident, not in all the years I've worked here, but now the government insists on soldiers and police guarding us.'

'Good,' I said.

Across the room, Nooria was as giddy as ever, patting

79

Theo's knee and shouting at him whenever she dis-agreed with him, which was most of the time. It bothered me. There was something about Theo I wanted to own.

'Come! Come!' Jane called, from the doorway. 'Eat! Eat!'

In the kitchen, Fadhl delighted in telling me about the census. 'This is a huge project,' he enthused, 'and a vital event for Yemen, but we have to identify the problems and train enumerators in data-processing, software, GPS – this is Theo's work – before we carry out the fieldwork.'

'GPS?'

'Global Positioning System,' said Theo. 'It tells you where you are or where you should be.'

'There will be over a thousand enumerators . . .' Fadhl went on.

Christian was pressed into a corner, surrounded by three or four people, holding his plate close to his chest. My involvement with him was unsettling, and fascinating. Was it, in fact, a betrayal? And even if it was disloyal, was it not a valid move on my part if there could be substance to it? Or was I merely weak and self-serving? Does one regain integrity beyond such an affair? These were the things I pondered when I was away from him, but now I watched him and asked myself where this could conceivably go. The answer was not reassuring.

Later, we danced in the empty *diwan*; my body moulded into his like wax drying on the side of a candle.

'Come back to the hotel,' he said quietly.

'No. I came with Theo. I'll leave with him.'

'He wouldn't mind.'

'That isn't the point. I won't abuse his hospitality.'

'But I'd love to spend the night with you,' he said, using his low voice to optimum effect.

'Well, you're welcome to squeeze on to my bed. Besides, I didn't come here to stay in a five-star hotel. I like my little room. I love the dead heat in the morning and the lumpy mattresses.'

'What about the fleas? You're covered in bites.'

'I like my fleas. We don't have them at home. And you're very welcome to share them tonight if you really want to.'

He went back to the hotel.

5

Fadhl and Theo would not relent. They were determined to get me across the desert. The next day, in a steaming hot restaurant, they resumed their attempts to persuade me.

'When your permit to leave Sana'a comes through,' said Theo, 'we'll go over to Marib and then across to Shibam.'

'But things are too unsettled to be driving off into the desert,' I said.

'You'll regret it if you don't,' said Christian.

Our *saltah*, a beef and vegetable stew, arrived in a great jardinière, bubbling like a geyser, with a lurid green sauce on top. We ate from the same pot, dipping slabs of bread into the boiling broth.

'You rip your bread in a triangular shape,' said Theo, 'fold it over, like so, and scoop out the *saltah*.'

Christian chewed in that exaggerated manner of his. 'This dish dates back to Sabaean times, you know.'

'There is no problem with security, Vivien,' said Fadhl. 'I will come too. There are many things I'd like to show you.'

'Good. You can all pick me up at Seyun airport in a nice air-conditioned Land Rover.'

'Useless,' Christian mumbled, scooping another mouthful of *saltah*.

'I have to get back to the office,' Theo said to me. 'What are you doing this afternoon?'

'She's going to the old town,' said Christian.

'No, I—'

'You still haven't got there in the light of day,' he added.

'Yes,' said Theo, who alone knew why I was avoiding it, 'you really shouldn't put it off.'

It could no longer be sidestepped. After the others had gone back to work, we went along to Bab al-Yemen, the old city gate, and I held Christian's hand tightly as we walked through. Once again the vista stood before me.

'Are you okay?'

I took his wrist with my other hand. 'Yeah,' I said. '*Déjà vu*, that's all.'

'It's quite a moment. You've waited so long. Savour it.' He shuffled me away from the men hawking goods on the sidewalks. Things had changed, but it was hard to rinse off the residue. I could still hear the voices of those who had been with me, blurting out platitudes and understatement, and I smelt again the vile green soap that had made me flee.

Christian stood close behind me and a fleeting breeze of something like love rushed past me. 'Here it is,' he said, 'waiting for you. Not much changed, probably, since Niebuhr came this way.'

We walked towards the main thoroughfare and between the gracious buildings that had lived in my mind for so long. It was quiet in the afternoon lull. A man was selling cucumbers from a wheelbarrow full of water, but most of the stalls were closed for the *qat* chew, when men gathered in one another's homes to chew together, so it was not the best time to come looking for enchantment.

'Let's go back,' I said. 'It's too hot.'

'But we've been here for days already and you haven't even –'

'Not now. We could get lost. Please.'

So we spent the afternoon like tourists in Greece – lying by the pool, reading and sipping cool drinks. In an idle moment, I pulled pink bougainvillaea from an overhanging branch and ran it across Christian's cheek. He flapped about as if caught in a cloud of hornets. 'Get that off me!'

'What? Why?'

Sitting up, he said ruefully, 'This is always the worst part of the familiarization process.'

'What is?'

'I'm . . . I loathe flowers, all right? I'm phobic about them.'

'You have a phobia about *flowers*?'

'Yes, yes, I know it's ridiculous. But there it is.'

I put the bougainvillaea to my face. 'But it's lovely.'

'Just don't come near me with it.'

I covered my mouth and sniggered.

He sighed. 'When am I going to meet a woman who is even vaguely sympathetic?'

'Why would anyone hate flowers?'

Christian crossed his arms. 'Blame my grandmother. She put Barbara Cartland to shame. Her entire life was carpeted with flora of one kind or another. *Blooms* everywhere! Her wallpaper, tablecloths, sheets – every conceivable surface had some revolting floral pattern and those were only the *dead* ones. Her house stank of . . . Oh, quit giggling.'

'Sorry.'

'Think about it: air-fresheners, loo-cleaners, dried flowers, real ones in every room of her house, like it was some kind of atrium to bad taste.' He shivered. 'She kept swallowing me up in these breath-defying hugs. I spent my childhood stinking of cheap perfume.'

'Oh dear. So Granny was a bit of a case?'

'She was a horrible old hag who loved young boys.'

Ah. I slipped off my sunglasses. 'She interfered with you?'

'Not seriously, just sloppy kisses and . . . Ugh. She lived with us for three years before she died, and I reeked of her for another three years after that.'

'But there's no such *thing* as a flower phobia.'

'No? You've just witnessed it. And you know what it's called? Anthrophobia.'

'You're joking? That sounds like –'

'Yes, I know, like a phobia about anthropologists. I've heard it all before. But you've been warned. You will never receive either perfume or flowers from this particular lover.' He turned back to his reading.

I lay down, still sniggering, and raised my face to the sun. 'Oh come, you harmful rays and toast me lightly.'

Christian looked up from his papers. 'Says here that a Celtic cross has been found with *"Bism'Allah"* engraved on it.'

'What?'

'Mmm.'

'But how could that be possible?'

'Well, some experts claim – persuasively – that there was a strong Arab influence on Irish culture, long before the Romans invaded Britain, and that it affected all aspects of Celtic life. Even language.'

'Language?'

'You don't notice any similarities between Irish and Arabic?'

'*No.*'

'Apparently it's there, particularly in the guttural sounds. Now, if you were an anthropologist, you could really get your teeth into that theory.'

'I'd rather get my teeth into an anthropologist.'

We went to his room. We couldn't keep from one another. Christian wasn't doing half the research he should have been and I wasn't doing anything at all. So this is Yemen, I thought. Bedrooms, air-conditioning, sex. Christian's fault. No, mine. I had become incapacitated, like an adolescent overcome with insatiable urges. All else standing aside. Yemen, even, forced to stand aside. And Theo would say, 'So, what did you do this afternoon?' and I would have to say, 'Nothing.' I did nothing save lie about making love.

I had not come to Yemen for this, and yet I wanted nothing else.

When we were done, I pulled on one of Christian's shirts and sat on the end of the bed. He leaned against the pillows, watching me. 'Go on, then,' I said. 'Tell me how someone so happily married blew it.'

'Who says I was happily married?'

I faltered. *A slip.* 'You must have been. Eighteen years is no slouch. What happened? Another woman? Another man?'

'A ghost.'

'What?'

He turned out his bottom lip, thinking. 'You're right. We were happy for a long time, but the triplets . . . Coming all together the way they did, there was so much work, stress, sleep deprivation. It was like living in a boot camp. If you didn't stick to the timetable, all hell broke loose, but we somehow got through those early years, and then, when the girls became more independent, the relief of having held it together in spite of the strain was beguiling. We gave ourselves a medal. Because we were successful parents, we thought we were a successful couple, but in truth we'd lost touch. The awakening was sudden, like being hit by lightning. When the girls were twelve, something collapsed.'

'You met someone else?'

'I . . . became infatuated. In its own awful way it was wonderful, but it's shocking too when you realize you no longer desire your partner. Whenever I looked at my family, all I could see was doom ahead and no way to avoid it.'

'You could have avoided it by not having an affair.'

He held my eye and said, 'I didn't have an affair. I was powerfully attracted to a colleague, and rejected out of hand. Diane suspected the worst – the need to be around this woman kept me out of the house every hour possible – but she held fire, and then another factor came into play. While the tragedy for me, for my kids, was that our marriage didn't last, the tragedy for Diane was that it lasted too long.

'During those long hours when I stayed out, an old friend gamely stepped into the breach. Eric. They had been at university together. He had fancied Diane at the outset, but she wasn't interested so eventually he married someone else, and not long afterwards we got married. His marriage lasted five years, no kids, which meant that when we went through our bad patch he was there to catch Diane. I expected it of him. He was one of her closest friends.'

'You didn't mind?'

'On the contrary, it gave me leeway to pursue my pathetic little intrigue. Diane was hurt, but muted. Eric helped her stay calm.' Christian stopped for a moment, reflecting. 'Inevitably the tables turned. I realized how foolish I'd been, but when I went home, so to speak, I found I'd become redundant. Diane had fallen in love. She made no effort to conceal it, and I accepted that. Had to. So it became likely we would separate, but neither of us rushed it. We were on a slow slide to divorce and in no hurry to get there. We kept waiting for something else to happen. It was like being on a melting ice floe – as it got smaller and smaller, we still wouldn't jump in to swim to the next one because we knew the water was fucking freezing and the kids might not survive it. And they, of course, were benefiting from our inertia, which went on for months. But then, without warning, the intervention we'd been waiting for presented itself.'

'What happened?'

'Eric died.'

'*What?*'

Christian nodded. 'He was at a conference in Birmingham and had a massive coronary. He was only thirty-nine.'

'Jesus.'

'Yeah, it was a nightmare. Suddenly I became Diane's rock. I felt for her, honestly. It seemed so unfair that one of us had had another chance and missed it, in such horrible circumstances. She was inconsolable – lay in bed for days, crying and sleeping. At night we talked. She told me he had never pressurized her to leave me because having her love after all that time had been enough, and apparently their affair had been as celibate as mine. Sleeping with him while she was still living with me would have been a betrayal of the girls, she said – not of me, mind, but of our daughters. So she mourned not only Eric, but the opportunity missed, the love affair never consummated.' He stopped again, then said, 'Beware the unconsummated affair. It has powerful aftershocks. Diane said it was like missing the very last boat. She felt stranded, as if she would never get home again.

'It's curious, but it was only then that people started to see the cracks in our marriage. Her grief was so overt, so indulged, that friends concluded she'd been having a long-standing affair with him. It was humiliating – bloody annoying, in fact – but I had to get her back into gear. The girls were doing their GCSEs that year and needed us both on the job, so separation was the furthest thing from my mind. But then another odd thing happened. Two months after Eric's death, I had to go away to make one of the documentaries, so Diane was forced to pull herself together – and she did. She sounded better on the phone while I was away, but when I got home the bomb dropped. She looked serene, no longer on the edge of torment. Sad, not desperate. The ice floe had grown a little. We'd skirted the edges of disaster. That was what I thought when I got home. I was in the bath, sipping a well-earned whisky, when she told me.'

'That she was leaving you?'

'That I was leaving her.' Anger surfaced in Christian's voice for the first time. 'She had bought a house down the road. It had come up for sale before I'd left, and while I was away Diane bought it. She had inherited money from Eric so she had it all worked out: she'd buy me out of our house and I'd transfer our mortgage to this new place. Oh, and she had spoken to the girls, too, without consulting me. They were devastated, and absolutely furious, although Rebecca did say she wasn't a bit surprised her mother was leaving me for Eric.'

'But Eric was dead.'

'He wasn't a bit dead in our house. Diane had denied him long enough. Every night we spent together was a further disloyalty to him and she owed him in death the commitment she had failed to give him in life, or so she claimed. She had to become his widow.'

I couldn't think of a thing to say.

'That was how I reacted,' said Christian. 'Astonishment. I lay in the bath getting cold. I thought she'd gone mad, but this wasn't madness: this was a mother at work. With or without Eric, our separation was going to be easier on the girls if I lived down the road, and when I eventually calmed down, I had to respect her decision to . . . honour her love, if you like.'

'Nice speech, but you're still furious.'

'Not as furious as I was then. After resisting Eric for the girls' sake, she was going to mess them about when he was dead. It was ridiculous, and over subsequent weeks we argued so much that it was miserable for the girls, who pulled together and scorned us both. Their wretched exams were looming and they didn't appreciate the sour atmosphere at home, so when the other house was vacated I gave Diane what she wanted and moved out.'

'But surely all that was just depression. Grief.'

'Maybe, but she thrived on it. She really did become Eric's widow. She put photos of him around the house – snaps of him sitting with her under *our* Christmas tree, like an American couple on a greeting card. It was ghastly, but it was her way of giving him his due.'

'And you?'

'I was miserable. I hated living alone. It was hard, being surrounded by three lovely girlie bedrooms, which were usually empty, but my sisters told me that if I'd only stop hissing and smarting, I might begin to heal and . . . eventually . . . I did both. It's better now. Switching between houses for the children is like walking from one room to another, and I've learned to enjoy my own space, which I'd never had before because we married so young.'

This was the hard sell. He described the arrangement with dead eyes; I wondered if he had really come to terms with these events.

'And all for a passing crush,' I said.

'Yes, but now I'm single and,' he touched my knee with his toes, 'very glad of it right at this minute.' He smiled, the story told. He talked a lot. I was used to doing the talking after sex, but Christian's loquaciousness was alluring. Most men reveal themselves in sentences, not paragraphs. Many would simply have said, 'My wife fell in love with a bloke who then died.' Getting an insight like this was potent.

I repeated the entire tale to Theo when I got back to the house. A lack of discretion, perhaps, but it was too juicy to keep to myself and, besides, I have never been particularly discreet. Like two old women we sat at the kitchen table, dissecting every angle and eating the chocolate biscuits I had been asked to bring out to him because he had a predilection for them. What woman, we wondered, would break up her family for a dead man?

'Shall I cook something?' I asked.

'Actually, Nooria has invited us to dinner.'

'Oh.'

'We have to go. She's very bossy.'

So at eight we made our way next door. I was apprehensive, and not entirely enthusiastic. Nooria was intimidating: she had a smart mind and a quick tongue, and I was no match for her, but when she greeted us, all smiles and excitement, I was slightly bowled over and then, suddenly, delighted to see her. It seemed to be mutual. We embraced each other warmly. It was a startling moment of recognition. In spite of the reserve that had been thwarting us, we *were* friends. It felt, in fact, as if we always had been.

'Is Christian coming?' she asked.

'Sorry. He's had to go to the British Embassy to press the flesh.'

She led us through a bare tiled room to a tiny sitting room, the size of a bathroom, with cushions on the floor and a portable television perched on a kitchen chair, which stood in the opening to the larger room. There were no windows. In this box room, I sat drinking pineapple juice and staring at what appeared to be a Yemeni soap opera on the television. Nooria was wearing an apron over a light cotton nightdress and a black *maqramah*, the local headscarf, with a red line round the edge. She looked sweeter, less challenging, without the large plastic-rimmed glasses she usually wore, and had lovely almond-shaped eyes.

We moved to the long narrow kitchen for dinner and sat at the small table. I mentioned to Nooria that I would like to meet other women.

'Who?' she snapped. 'Who you want to meet?'

'Well, artists, maybe. I'd love to compare the art scene with home.'

She was concentrating on the meal and didn't reply. During dinner, she was quiet, working away at her gas stove and making little contribution to the conversation. This might have felt like a rebuff, but I was comfortable with her in this subdued form. After the meal, she poured a black brew into my glass, then stepped into the other room with her mobile phone.

'*Qishr*,' said Theo. 'It's made from the husk of the coffee bean.'

'Oh, yeah,' I said, grimacing at the bitter taste, 'I remember this stuff.'

'Tomorrow.' Nooria came back in. 'Five o'clock. You meet my friends. Someone will pick you up outside the gate.'

It was still early when we left. 'So,' said Theo. 'Shall we go into town?'

'I tried earlier. I didn't get very far.'

'It's different at night.' He took my elbow. 'Come.'

He was right – it was easier without the burning heat of day, and easier too without Christian, who had had no idea that he was making me step right back into the scene of my disgrace. But Theo knew. Theo, it seemed, knew everything about me, and with his subtle guidance I made it all the way into the heart of the old medina. My shoulders were tense, my diaphragm tight, but I eventually became distracted. There were such faces. Old men sitting cross-legged in their box-like shops; young boys, bright-eyed among their wares; old women with sun-wrinkled brows. One woman was sitting on the ground selling fruit from a tin pan. With a *sitarah* round her head and a black scarf about her nose, she looked like the soap woman. She handed Theo a piece of fruit. He split it open, took a bite and passed it to me. 'Fig.' Further along, a man was roasting nuts and selling them in newspaper cones. Theo bought some and we ambled on, chewing, through the date *suq*, where pile upon pile of sticky dates stood side by side, and the tin *suq*, where men hammered out vessels, and further on, we passed a shop where kettles of every size hung around the entrance like copper curls around a face. All I had to do was stick to Theo's elbow and allow my eyes to feed. It was that easy. There were no demons, no one jumped out at me. Instead unobtrusive cries of 'Welcome to Yemen' followed me. In a court-yard, large sacks huddled together, fat with multi-coloured spices. Orange, yellow, ochre, red. The whiff of incense mingled with the cool night air, and Niebhur walked alongside me: 'At Sana . . . Each different com-modity is sold in a separate market. In the market for bread, none but women are to be seen; and their little shops are portable. The several classes of mechanics work, in the same manner, in particular quarters in the open street.'

There were no bricks of green soap. Perhaps now they imported Lux.

That night I slept fitfully and dreamed vividly. In my dream, Sana'a was empty. There were no people, no motorbikes. Nothing moved except me. I walked through its alleyways in the shade of high buildings, but at the end of every street the blinding sun beat down, distorting my perception. This was not the *suq*. There were no shops, just buildings, all closed up. I was neither lost nor making my way out, but trying to find my way in, pushing deeper into the maze – trying to find a particular building, perhaps, because I kept stepping back to look up at the friezes, as if the different patterns could be read like a map and would tell me which way to go. The alleyways were unpaved. I was wearing the long blue dress I had worn twelve years before, with white cotton trousers underneath. Sana'a went on and on in its labyrinthine way, revealing more shaded streets pressed between more narrow houses, until I stepped again into the glare in a gracefully appointed square and saw her sitting against a wall. It was the smell that drew me to her, though dreams have no scent. I crossed the square and crouched before her, curious and unafraid. She held out a solid bar of green soap, her eyes grinning. She knew I had been looking for her for years. I smiled, and reached out for it.

'Vivien.'

The smell lingered in the air. Real soap. Not perfumed with rosemary or sandalwood. Real, honest to God scullery soap.

'Wake up, dope.'

A hand slid along my thigh. I grabbed the soap and ran into consciousness. Christian was sitting on my mattress. 'Where did you come from?'

'Same as usual – through the door. Doesn't Theo ever lock it?'

'Says there's no need,' I mumbled, still sleepy. 'Though keeping you out should be reason enough.'

He smiled. 'Want to help me move?'

That woke me up. 'What? Why?'

'I can't afford to stay at the Taj indefinitely. I only intended to land there while I looked around for something else.'

'But what about my pool?'

'You'll have to charm the leisure-centre manager for your swims. I've found a place in the old town. Wait till you see it.'

The Felix Hotel was near the *sailah*, the riverbed that ran through the city. Beyond the gate, a pathway over-hung with bougainvillaea led past garden tables to Reception. Ducking, Christian hurried ahead. A small group of tourists were sitting in the *diwan*, the greeting room on the ground floor.

'A rare sighting of an endangered species,' Christian said, in his television voice.

The manager led us through a hole in the wall, which led into an adjacent building and up countless steps. On the top floor we went through a simple sitting room, stepped over a low partition and into the bedroom. We were at the top of one of the tallest buildings in the old town. Two sides of the room were glass.

Christian smiled. 'How's that for a view?'

I stepped towards the window.

'And there's a *mafraj* on the roof. Come on.'

The *mafraj*, densely furnished with cushions, had windows on every side. While Christian chatted to the tea man, I climbed on to a higher level of the roof.

Around me, all around me, Sana'a stood in its higgledy-piggledy glory. A rare panorama. I could look down on it at last. A brown town. Reddy-brown and white. The houses, like a troop of eager Girl Guides, seemed to be standing to attention, ready for inspection. Their uniformity had so much the appeal of rows of books neatly stacked on library shelves that I felt an inclination to run my fingers along their spines. As with books, the apparent symmetry was a sham, for there was nothing but asymmetry within this vista. For all the similar shapes and raw materials, nothing was quite the same. Some houses were the breadth of one window, narrow, squashed, holding their own. Others stretched across five windows, which themselves varied from floor to floor – some filled with multi-coloured panes, others with alabaster, as in the old days, which let in light but kept out heat, a function largely taken over by lace curtains. The elaborate gypsum friezes – the white triangles, arcs, zigzags, lines and circles – gave the houses expression, stature, like women adorned with *naqsh*, each with its own statement to make. The hoops and loops created individuality within the crowd, and it was this mix of order and disorder that made Sana'a so stunning, so satisfying and glorious to behold.

I looked out at the great mountain, Jabal Nuqum, spellbound and relieved. Sana'a had been restored to me – or, rather, revealed for the first time.

Christian brought me a glass of tea. 'Happy?'

I couldn't take my eyes from the city. 'Bad news,' I said.

'What?'

'I think I might be falling in love with you.'

'Look at me when you say that.'

'No. I don't want to see you run for cover, hopping from roof to roof to get away.'

'I'm not running.'

'Thank you for bringing me up here.'

'Thank you for coming.'

'It's a clever old town, isn't it? The way it survives. Taking in electricity, but leaving out neon; satellite dishes, but no obtrusive aerials or wires. Adapting without changing very much.'

'Clever, or stubborn.' Christian inhaled. 'So it lives up to expectation?'

'It does now.'

I peeped over the parapet. On the street below, the workmen who were paving it had stopped for a late breakfast and were crouched round a platter of food. A man in denims, a Westerner, came along the road and spoke to them as he passed. They responded with casual waves. They knew him.

'God, do you think that's him?'

'Who?'

'Mackintosh-Smith.'

Christian looked over. 'As if I'd recognize him from up here. As if I even know what he looks like.'

'I have *got* to shake that man's hand.'

'Why?'

I took my tea over to one of the tables in the shade. 'Because his book gave me the kick I needed to come back here.'

'*Back?*'

Details kept emerging all around me – a small balcony here, an oil tank on the roof over there, an unfinished extension in fresh red brick that would eventually fade to dusty pink. 'This isn't the first time I've been here.'

Christian sat down. 'You hold a lot back, don't you?'

'It isn't something I broadcast. It wasn't exactly a highlight in my life.'

'All the more reason to share it.' With a sideways throw of his head, he urged me on. Unlike many talkative types, he knew how to listen, although this was probably a professional trait. Much of his work involved listening to people speak about their lives.

I went with the romantic version of what happened. I came out of it better that way. 'I'm guilty of that most stupid of all mistakes,' I said. 'I made a decision based on love.'

'Your fiancé?'

'No. Earlier. My best friend's brother.'

'Ah, let me guess: you adored him from the age of ten, but he didn't actually notice you until you turned into a beautiful swan at nineteen.'

'Actually, I *was* nineteen when it started, and we hit the ground running. First love, with all its cataclysmic possibilities. Intense, exciting and very, very painful. It was love on full blast, top volume, and so were the fights, the lows. We knew how to torture each other. Splitting up took years.'

'An *amour fou.*'

'And with very long tendrils too. There were things I wanted to do. Bill just wanted to *be*. I decided to come to Yemen with an aid organization. It was a good move: childhood passion consummated, disintegrating relationship conveniently left behind, and a chance to put down the roots of the only career I wanted – to be a travel writer.'

'Ah.' Christian raised his chin. 'Hence the fascination with Wotsisname.'

'Trouble was, Bill was devastated. It wasn't the distance that bothered him, it was the step away. He promised we'd sort things out and move to London together. It was the first time he'd suggested anything. That was the problem: he was devoid of strategy. He had no view of the way ahead – he was too scattered. Moody. He'd be one thing one day, and completely different the next. Anyway, I took the flight and it was like being lowered into a dry well. Bit by bit, hour by hour, further and further into the dark. When I got here, Bill was so far away I felt brittle. Yemen's physical location alarmed me. Being tucked away on the end of the peninsula was like being in the bottom of a bag. No trains through Saudi, no way of getting home except on a long flight. I'd spent a lot of years on Bill. To waste all that emotion seemed foolish, so instead I wasted the opportunity of a lifetime and went home. Easily the most stupid thing I've ever done, and it didn't pay off, not in the slightest way.'

'Please don't tell me you arrived home and caught him with someone else.'

I stared out at Nuqum and saw it all. Rushing to Bill's flat to surprise him. Finding his key with shaking hands, bursting in and seeing his legs curled round another woman's hips . . .

'Is that what happened?' Christian asked, horrified.

'What? Oh, no, that didn't happen, though I can just imagine it. But no, nothing so theatrical. I arrived back. Bill was ecstatic. Friends thought it sweet: she couldn't be without him, they belong together, na na . . . And I believed in our own myth until, within a month, we found ourselves in the shit again. We never went to

London. We simply continued to break up in slow motion. My career, my life, had managed to arrive nowhere at all.'

Christian grimaced.

'That's why I will never again make a decision based on love or some ridiculous perception of it.'

'What happened to Bill?'

'He went to Boston. We couldn't be in the same place and not be in one another's lives, so we trained ourselves to hold on to each other within, but be without. Still, he's the one I'll never quite get over.'

'What did you do?'

'I didn't do a bloody thing. It was awful. I couldn't seem to move. If I had stayed here, it would have altered the course of my life. Leaving also did so. I felt completely incapacitated. For years I temped, going from company to company, never settling into anything, because I was afraid to trust myself with my own future, but Shoukria saved me. Stepping into her gallery that first time was . . . almost a spiritual experience. The paintings were like windows opening all around me, letting a breeze blow in. Then Shoukria came at me in a scarlet dress and swallowed me up. She created my career by giving me that job, training me to do something I'd never done and then leaving me to it. The gallery is my buoyancy aid. It keeps me afloat.'

'But you still had to come back here.'

'Yes, but not to prove a point. I came because I could no longer bear to have Yemen spoiled. It was something precious to me once, and I ruined it. Even recently whenever Yemen came up, in the news or whatever, I still got this twist in my stomach. You know the way you feel when you remember something deeply embarrassing, and you can't wipe it out or undo it and it just keeps revisiting you when you least want it to?'

'Yeah, I've a few of those cringe-making memories stored away. They keep me honest.'

I smiled. 'Me too, I suppose. All this time I've been haunted by a recurring image of footsteps in the sand, and another set alongside that . . . turns back. My Great U-turn.'

'We all do stuff like that. And things worked out okay, didn't they?'

'Well . . . My life back home is all right, but it isn't what I'd envisaged. The fact is that I squandered the only real vocation I ever had and that makes me pretty much second-rate – at least, that's how Freya Stark would see it.'

'You're being way too hard on yourself.'

'I don't think so. Anyway, I had to see Sana'a again. It's the only way I can look back, and forward, without cringing.' I glanced around me. Minarets, squat and tall, rose among square buildings. One imposing house shot up to the right, at least ten storeys high. Brand new. The bricks still red. 'Yemen has been whispering in my ear for years,' I said. 'I want to know if it holds something for me.'

Christian took my hand. 'I'm sure it does,' he said. He was thinking about us, but that wasn't what I meant at all.

I leaned over and rummaged in his neck with my

chin, relishing the unshaven rasp and the mild smell of sweat, and we made our way downstairs, where sliding skin and graceless intimacy banished the time I had been contemplating.

6

Several women were packed into the car that came to collect me that afternoon. One of them jumped out, embraced me and hustled me into a great jumble of black in the back seat. I hadn't the faintest idea where we were going, and they weren't too sure either. It was raining, so we had to drive on the wrong side of the road to avoid flooding, and an extraordinary tree with the most lurid purple flowers prompted one of the women to screech. Someone translated: it was the same colour as some fabric she had bought recently for a dress.

The new suburbs consisted of houses dotted about on vast tracts of muddy earth, many in a state of construction. There was no Tarmac or street names, and the ladies argued amicably as they tried to locate their friend's home. When we found it – an expansive bungalow – and made our way inside, the hostess, Husnia, greeted me like a long-lost friend. I removed my sandals and was led into a sitting room where several other women had gathered. What *had* Nooria set up?

A woman sitting on the couch looked up at me. 'What?' she said. 'You don't know me?'

Blind panic. Who was it? Where had we met?

'Aiee!' she squealed.

'Nooria? Oh, my God, I didn't recognize you!' I had

never seen her unveiled, or her long straight hair. 'I'm *so* sorry!' My mortification delighted her.

The women who had brought me took a while to join us, since they had to remove their scarves, kept in place with pins, their *baltos* and shoes. The veil takes years off a woman. Some were older than I'd expected, but all were as attractive as their gorgeous eyes suggested, and there was an elegance about them, in the way they moved and dressed, that made me feel frumpy.

Husnia explained that this was an occasional gathering of women involved in the arts. 'We are very interested to meet you. Nooria tells us you run a gallery.'

'That's right.'

'You must tell us all about it. And all about you.'

But first they had a lot to catch up on, they told me, and began chattering to one another in Arabic. They led busy lives and didn't often have the chance to meet, so I sipped the juice Husnia had handed me, while they exchanged news. When we were shown into another room for a buffet dinner, I realized just how busy these women were. They had jobs, and children and in-laws to look after, but they were also passionate about improving the lot of Yemenis and gave much of their free time to doing so. They were from among the educated élite, but that made them no less impressive. Some were working in prisons, others in health, and one was trying to introduce art into schools. I was humbled, but also delighted to find myself among them, where it was warm, chummy, female.

We moved into the *diwan*, a long room with cushions around the walls and a large expanse of carpet in the middle. Cardamom tea and *qishr* were served, and the women got down to the serious business of cross-examining me. Where was the gallery? What were my qualifications? What course had my career taken? They had no interest in my private life. It was work that turned them on. The rest – babies, mothers, husbands – weren't relevant to a gathering such as this.

But this line of discussion made it difficult to bypass the great Yemeni crater in my career. I walked around it at first, skipped those years between leaving college and starting at the gallery, but they didn't miss a trick.

'And in between?' asked a young woman, who was expecting her first baby.

I could have embellished it: I could have glorified the two-bit offices or emphasized the amazing variation in my working life. To admit that I had been unable to cope with their country was daunting, but they deserved better than my usual veil of distortions. Here, I told the truth.

The electricity went off. Husnia, who moved barefoot across the room with a gentle sway, lit candles and night-lights, and the women's faces glowed in the flickering flames, their dark eyes dancing. Some chewed a little *qat*. I took a few leaves and munched them cautiously. They were bitter, and I certainly didn't need the high. I was high already, in a house in Sana'a surrounded by women during a power cut. There was a hush in the room, broken only by my voice, followed by Nooria's translating, then mine again. There was rhythm to the flow of the English and the Arabic, and although I wasn't sure how they would react, I didn't play down the culture shock I had suffered. I gave it to them bare.

They understood. Many of them had been educated in Eastern Europe and knew about dislocation. One spoke of studying in Moscow and being so homesick she could barely move. Another described the terror of seeing missiles fly right past her university accommodation when she was a nineteen-year-old student in Baghdad during the 1990 Gulf War. Yet another said consumerism in Britain had shocked her into embracing Islam, which until then had eluded her.

'But you all stayed,' I said. 'You stuck it out. I didn't.'

'We had no choice. We were on student grants, government loans, and it was the only way to be educated.'

'Yes,' I said, 'and now you have something to show for it. I came away with nothing.'

'Well,' said Husnia simply, 'you will go home with much more this time.'

An older woman in the corner spoke for the first time. 'A wise man once said, "We must not travel the road that is not ours to take." Perhaps Yemen was not the way you were meant to go.'

'But what if it *was*? Where would it have led?'

'Yes,' said Nooria, to the woman. 'She took her boyfriend's road. That was her mistake.'

'Especially since his road wasn't going anywhere,' I grumbled.

Another lady, a poet who spoke no English, talked at me in a sharp nasal voice. Husnia translated: 'Yemen is not a . . . rock in the middle of a river.'

'You mean a stepping stone?'

'Yes. Yemen is the other side, *ya'ani* . . .' Husnia struggled, her hands gesticulating.

'The other bank?'

The poet's voice grew more high-pitched. She had beady eyes and a scarf pulled loosely over her head. 'She says, ah, your feet will not slip back into the stream when you reach the other side,' Husnia explained.

'When I reach firm ground, yes. I see.'

The conversation became chaotic again, English here, Arabic there, robust disagreements all round, especially when we discussed the commission taken by galleries, of which they vehemently disapproved. It was disappointing when the electricity came back on. We grimaced in the glare of the overhead lights, and blew out the candles.

'You know,' said Nooria, as we huddled in the back of the car on the way home, 'you should not mind about running away from Yemen. God loves each single one of us, no matter how we, the poor tiny stupid human beings, assess what happens in our lives. There is always good in everything, even in what we consider mistakes.'

I had expected a lot of things from this trip, but I had not anticipated friendships, or anything as erotic as my relationship with Christian. And that was what it was, I told myself often, an erotic splurge that could not have taken place at home. I cursed myself for capitulating, but the pleasure in doing so consistently outwitted prudence.

The following morning, he was cross when he turned

up in our *mafraj* where I was reading and listening to Saint-Saëns' *Samson and Delilah* on Theo's CD player. Christian had been at the ministry again.

'Wretched *qat*. There's no getting anything done around here,' he complained.

I yawned. 'What was it you said in the airport? "Yemen will be Yemen and there's nothing you can do . . ."'

He looked down at me. 'Late night, was it?'

'Not really. Blame the "wretched *qat*". I haven't slept a wink.'

'Well, it *is* a stimulant.'

'So were the women. Oh, Christian, I came home buzzing. They're so dynamic. They put me to shame. It makes me wonder what's happened to us at home that we're so tired and apathetic. Why does nothing matter any more?'

'Because it doesn't have to. Because it *doesn't* matter where we come from.' He slumped down on the cushions.

'What's wrong with you? The permit'll come through.'

'Oh, I've got the permit – just not the right one.'

'You can't go to Marib?'

'I can, but . . .' He fiddled with tassels on a rug, then flicked them away. 'The truth is, I had other plans for Marib, and it looks like they won't work out.'

'What plans?'

'Film. I want to get out there and *film*.'

'I thought you were going digging?'

'I am, but who the hell is going to read the findings? Other academics and Arabists and students. I want to reach beyond that, find a wider audience. I mean – tourists won't come to this country because they're afraid of being kidnapped, so you could say the whole country is being held to ransom by a few malcontents, and I'd love to get some of these guys on record and give it all a context. Show it from their perspective.'

'Which is?'

'Well, there's oil out there and the people in the villages aren't seeing much of the benefits, and now there's the al-Qaeda thing. If certain groups are protecting operatives, *why* are they? Solidarity? Or is it sheer survival – financial gain? Getting out there with a camera and coming back with some kind of footage would be dynamite.'

'Better get yourself kidnapped, then.'

'It crossed my mind,' he said ruefully. 'Get a micro-camera, hide it about my person and put myself in the way of some disaffected tribe.'

'You're not serious?'

He shook his head. 'It wouldn't be that easy, believe me. So I've been trying to do it legitimately – get all the right permits and contacts, and agree to have a government minder, but the ministry won't entertain the idea. They don't want cameras where I want to go.'

'Can you blame them?'

'They're probably afraid I'll run into American special forces.'

'Weren't some BBC documentary-makers kidnapped out that way?'

'That was years back and they were let go. It would all be in a day's work for me. I'd just be consigning to film what I'll be doing anyway – drinking *shai* and chewing *qat* and getting an inside view of things.'

'I thought you'd given up making programmes.'

'I'm not talking about the whole circus of a film crew. I want to go back to the roots of ethnographic documentary. Fly-on-the-wall stuff. And I know I could do it – I've been getting under the folds of communities all my working life.'

'Oh, so you'd be a bit like Terry Waite, would you? Went off to negotiate with some group in Lebanon and disappeared for four years. Or was it five?'

'Look, there's a lot to be said for trying to throw a chink of light in a very dark corner, and how the hell else can it be done?'

The phone rang. 'Just passing on a warning,' said Theo, when I picked up, 'from the American Embassy. There's going to be a pro-Palestinian demonstration this morning so don't go out.'

'*You*'re out.'

'*Ja*, but I'm in the office. They're meeting in al-Qa Square and if things get overheated, you don't want to be a passing Westerner.'

Another suicide bomber had blown himself up in Jerusalem, taking more innocents with him. Israeli troops had marched back into the West Bank as had become their habit: the incendiary ricochet.

'I'm sure it'll be fine,' Theo said. 'The Yemenis are generally too placid to get out of control, but with the way things are in the West Bank, it's better to be safe.'

'Okay. Thanks for letting me know.' I hung up. 'Had you plans for this morning?'

'Yeah,' said Christian. 'I need to see Edda and stop off at the Internet café. One of my students has got it into his head to follow me out here. His parents want me to stop him.'

'Well, you're not going anywhere. Nor am I, as it happens. Demonstration. All Westerners stay home, Theo says.'

'Bloody hell.'

I crawled over him. 'Oh, it's not so bad, is it?'

This was a room made for love. No furniture to restrict us, no ornaments to topple, and even the coloured windowpanes offered discretion. We shed our clothes. The rug was rough against my back. '*Mon coeur s'ouvre à ta voix*,' Delilah sang, and it made me think again of love. There where I must not go. Not with him, even though I was loitering on the outskirts. I had already said too much on the roof of his hotel, and could not risk mentioning it again without becoming hopelessly embroiled. Words are as sticky as spider web. Consequently I continued to be mute when we were intimate, and Christian too proved to be a silent lover, although he moved with tenderness and affection. We never spoke, never whispered endearments, which was a pointless restraint since our eyes and bodies spoke so eloquently.

Samson called Delilah's name in reply to her love song. I bit Christian's scarred lip, which made him wince and press harder into me.

After showering, we sat on the roof and he talked about his daughters. Tania, the first-born, was assertive, bright and quick with a quip. 'No flies on her.' Rebecca, the middle one, was passive in the extreme, almost to the point of laziness, induced, her father felt, by being sandwiched all her life between two intense personalities. Melanie was fiery. Spoilt, he admitted, after being mollycoddled by her mother because she was a needy baby. 'She was the most kissable child imaginable,' he said.

'How old are they now?'

'Seventeen. You'll like them. I can't wait for you to meet.'

'Sorry?'

'I can't wait for you to meet the trips.'

'But . . . well, that's not very likely, is it?'

'Why not?'

'Because you live in London and I live in Dublin.'

'That need not be an obstacle.'

'It very much *is* an obstacle.'

His face went hard, as if someone had covered it in plaster-of-paris.

'This is an interlude, Christian. A very pleasant one, but it is nonetheless no more than –'

'A holiday fling?'

'I thought that was understood.'

'I wasn't aware we'd discussed it.'

I felt uneasy – hurt even; the incidental interlude was beginning to cloud the clear Yemeni skies. He would not be important to me. He would *not*.

'I don't see why this can't continue at home,' he said.

'"At home" is two different countries.'

'It's a one-hour flight.'

'Maybe,' I said, 'but I can't afford to make that trip every other week.'

'We can at least give it a shot.'

'*I* can't.'

He raised his chin. 'There's someone else?'

Yes. I shook my head. 'Besides, you're only recently divorced.'

'Two years!'

'But it isn't really two years, is it? It isn't really a divorce. You live in the same street. You practically have Sunday lunch *en famille*. I can't get into a domestic mess like that.'

'Can't, or won't?'

'Both.'

Christian looked out towards the mountains. 'You're the one who mentioned love, Vivien.'

The demonstration had been low key. Thousands had protested against Israel's incursions into the West Bank, but it was all over by lunchtime. Sana'anis would never let anything get in the way of the *qat* chew, Theo said. This left me free to visit Nooria at the women's centre, a somewhat ramshackle building where young women could study English and acquire computer and other skills after they had finished school. Nooria showed me classrooms, a poorly stocked library, offices and a computer room, then gave me tea at the coffee shop on the roof. 'We'll teach them anything,' she said. 'Anything that can be useful, if we have a teacher: arts, crafts, even swimming.'

'They go swimming?'

She smiled. 'Most of them jump in wearing street clothes. The dye runs and makes the water a terrible colour, but it is a new experience for them.' She looked at me directly. 'Many of the people working here are volunteers.'

'Meaning?'

'You could work here, if you wanted. I need people who can inspire these girls.'

'But –'

'You could if you wanted, that's all. It might help you to . . .'

'Make up for the last time?'

'I think so.'

'But what would I live on?'

'You could teach English to rich girls in the evenings.'

'I don't think that would cover my outgoings and, anyway, it has already been adequately demonstrated that I don't have what it takes.'

'Oh, you do,' said Nooria. 'You do.' She stood up. 'Since you are here, you might as well give some help. I need an index for our library. You could set up some kind of system.'

'Now, that's the kind of job I'm good at.'

After spending a happy afternoon among books and some eager pupils, Nooria and I walked home together. Reconciled to Sana'a, I could now not get enough of the 'splendour and havoc of the East', as Kinglake described it. I loved to feel Sana'a beneath my feet, and Sana'a liked to have me there, because still the voices called, 'Welcome to Yemen!' Nooria showed me the *qat suq*, a narrow alleyway, where men bartered among piles of green plant, leaning over low entrances to the hovel shops. We stopped outside a windowless shed where a blindfolded camel was walking in circles, a wooden beam attached to his harness pressing sesame seeds to make oil. His young minder explained that they blindfolded him so that he would think he was in the desert, crossing an endless steppe, and had to keep on going.

The city was different in the evening light from how it appeared in the clear, fresh mornings. As the sun dipped, the buildings turned golden, the gypsum cream, and the lines became muted. I sat on Christian's bed watching the light change over one of the world's greatest cityscapes.

'This feels as right now as it felt wrong before,' I said.

'You do seem to be *très bien dans ta peau.*'

'I am, somehow. It's . . . something in the streets – the feel of the place. And the people. They're so easygoing and approachable. They're so . . . Irish.'

'*Irish?* The Yemenis are Irish now?'

'They just seem familiar, that's all.'

'You're not tempted to live here, are you?'

I gazed out and, after a moment, said, ' "The favourable reception we had met with at Sana, which was above our expectations, might have tempted us to stay longer." '

'Niebuhr again? Do you know him by heart?'

'Some bits. Anyway, of course I'm tempted to stay but, let's face it, been there, done that, made a complete balls of it.'

We had dinner downstairs, a light supper prepared by the owner of the hotel, who had been forced to let his cook go in these lean times, and it was like having our very own Sana'a palace. When Christian offered to take me home, I said, 'I'll stay, if you like.'

I could not part with his window. A red light on top of the mountains flashed silently. At the end of Ramadan, Nooria had told me, they set off fireworks up there and everyone in the city had a spectacular view.

Christian stood behind my shoulder; a swell of delight surged inside me. 'Arabia Felix,' I said. 'Truly, Arabia Felix.'

'I thought you wanted to spend the night with me, but it was Sana'a you wanted to lie with.'

Our first night together was disturbed in the early hours when a loud hollering almost threw us on to the floor.

'What the fu–?'

'Jesus!'

The muezzin had started up at the mosque next door. It was like someone shouting through our window with a megaphone.

'Not so evocative this close,' Christian muttered.

I fell back on the pillows, my heart beating so hard I felt ill, and listened to the call. Even lying down, I could look out. The outline of the mountains was just visible in the creeping dawn. Christian was already asleep again. I went to the window. The tower houses seemed to be sprouting out of the ground as they became more defined. Household lights were extinguished, the voices of early risers grew louder, and the nasal sneer of a moped rose from the street below.

From the top of the world, I watched the day begin.

After breakfast we set out for Theo's house, Christian assuring me that he knew how to get there. 'Half-hour walk, tops,' he said, but when we turned into a main thoroughfare we found ourselves in the thick of a march. Another demonstration. I reached for my neck. No scarf. Nothing to shield me, to help me blend in. Christian tried to steer me out of the way, but the forward march was so paced that we couldn't get across the road, or go back without holding up the oncoming crowd. It was mostly men, shouting slogans and waving banners. I was frightened. There was such anger seething in the Arab world. Footage of Western journalists being set upon by a mob raced through my mind, but then I realized the footage I remembered had not been of journalists in the East, but of detectives in Northern Ireland who, some years before, had paid with their lives for taking a wrong turn and ending up in the middle of an angry mob. I felt naked without a scarf and Christian looked so pale, so *English*. We tried to get out without pushing. The march was as wide and long as the dual carriageway, and clearly far bigger than the previous gathering. There were thousands of students and bitter young men, fed up and unemployed, and young boys too, and women, ululating above the guttural male roar. Palestinian flags flew alongside Yemeni flags, just as they had often flown alongside Irish tricolours at home. Shoving me into empty spaces as if we were in a game of hopscotch, Christian shepherded me to the edge of the throng, but we were then hemmed in by a barrier where roadworks were taking place.

'What are they chanting?' It sounded like, '*Al huddz, al huddz!*' The young man striding along beside me in a brown *zannah* caught my eye and shouted it at me, but not aggressively.

'Jerusalem,' said Christian. 'Al Quds is Jerusalem. They're saying, "We will reclaim Jerusalem."' And he raised his fist and clamoured with them.

We were in the thick of it now: there was no way out. We had evolved into it, like flour on the side of a bowl being incorporated into the dough, and I no longer wanted to get out. I wanted to march for the Palestinians, as I had done before. The man behind me scraped my heels, stumbled and put a hand on my shoulder to catch himself. A TV crew filming from the top of a van followed us for a moment – two Westerners who clearly weren't heeding American and British Embassy advice. There could still have been a change in the tide but we marched on with the Yemenis, shaking our fists and chanting for Al Quds.

'We've got to get out of this before we reach the square,' said Christian, 'or we'll be there all day. The Taj is nearby, so come on, concerted effort.'

We squeezed our way towards the edge and this time broke free of the mass, like toothpaste coming out of a tube. My limbs rattled. The demonstration filed past, disciplined and orderly.

Half an hour later, Fadhl came rushing towards us in the lobby of the hotel. 'You okay, Miss Vivien?'

'I'm fine. Is Theo furious?'

He wobbled his head. 'Happy you're okay.' He turned to Christian. 'And angry you were not more careful.'

'Have some tea, Fadhl,' said Christian.

'There's such strong feeling out there,' I said.

'Of course,' said Fadhl, wiping his sweaty forehead, 'and I tell you this. If our government would let us, every Yemeni would cross the desert right now and fight for Palestine.'

'Surveys carried out recently in the US,' said Christian, once again using his television intonation, 'show that many Americans believe everyone hates America because we're jealous of its standard of living. They think that's what September the eleventh was about.'

'Fadhl,' I said quietly, 'see that guy sitting with those people over there?'

He glanced over his shoulder.

'Is that Mackintosh-Smith?'

'I'm sorry,' he said, shaking his head. 'But don't worry. You'll see him.' He smiled. 'His book must be very good.'

'It is, but he also has a certain quality most of my other travel writers lack.'

'What is this?'

'He's still alive.'

The lingering stress of the morning's adventure was dealt with effectively after lunch, when I went to the *hammam* with Jane Ware and other expatriate women. I could hardly see my own toes in the thick steam, and after I had sweated away for half an hour, a huge woman sitting on a stool in a sagging wet vest positioned me between her legs and got to work. She washed my hair, then scrubbed me with some kind of loofah. Peels of dirt came off me.

'Golly,' I said, horrified. 'It must be Sana'ani dust.'

'It's life, dear,' Jane bellowed. 'Life!'

'Ugh. Who's going to keep me this clean in future?'

A voice came out of the steam. 'A good scouring brush should do it.'

'Maybe I should just stay in Sana'a,' I mused, 'and be clean.'

'It can be a hard place to leave,' said the voice.

'Indeed,' said Jane. 'For my own part, I never got the hang of it.'

'But is it an easy place to *stay*?' I asked. 'I mean, is it possible for freelance foreigners to get work?'

'Not very,' Jane said curtly. 'Yemen has the fastest growing population in the world. They don't need more people coming in and taking jobs they're perfectly capable of doing themselves.'

'But –'

'I work in AIDS awareness, on an entirely voluntary basis. I live perfectly well on my husband's pension. I wouldn't want to take cash out of Yemeni pockets.'

Crumbs, I thought. I only asked.

By then I was in the rinse cycle and copious amounts of cool water were being poured over me. I lifted my face to it, smiling – not at Jane's reply but at my own question. Nooria had planted the idea and it was already throwing out shoots. A change had come over me. The fear was gone; the dread of panic and failure had been scoured off. I was no longer the hostage who had touched down in Sana'a, this time and the last. The water pelted my face, and I laughed. I was a free agent once again. My life was mine to do with as I wished, and there was a lot I wished to do.

I returned to the house all but sterilized – and completely wiped out – and struggled upstairs. Christian and Theo were reclining in the *mafraj*, their cheeks stuffed.

'Oh, my God.' I collapsed on to cushions. 'I am almost certainly dead. My life has been scraped off me.'

'You enjoyed the *hammam*?' Theo asked.

'Yeah, but talk about turbo-wash!'

Christian was sorting through their pile of *qat*, picking out choice leaves.

'This is very anti-social of you,' I said. 'Why aren't you at a proper chew?'

Christian looked over his shoulder at Theo. 'I'm chewing properly. Are you chewing properly?' Theo nodded, wide-eyed. 'This is a proper *qat* chew.'

I pulled off a leaf. 'My party piece as a child was eating nettles, you know.'

'Nettles don't have quite the same . . . properties, I think,' said Theo.

'Like what?'

'It's supposed to be good for the libido,' said Christian.

'In fact it has the opposite effect,' said Theo. 'Apparently.'

'I'll let you know,' Christian muttered, stuffing leaves into his mouth.

'So are we going to have a discussion about the pros and cons of *qat* and the detrimental effect it's having on the Yemeni economy?' I asked.

'No,' they said together.

'Just as well,' I said, 'because I need the sleep of eternity to recover from that scrub.'

'Well, you can't have it.' Theo gathered his long limbs about him, like a folding lamp, and got up. 'We have an early start tomorrow.' He went upstairs.

'Early start?' said Christian.

'We're, em . . . going to Ta'izz for a couple of days.'

His eyebrows leaped up, and he dipped his head. 'Jesus, Viv.'

'*Christian.* I have got to see some of this country.'

'But can't you wait until I've gone?'

'No. Theo's got work and some party to go to. It might be my only chance.'

'Thanks for telling me.'

'It only came up at lunch.'

He stared into the pile of *qat.* 'Well, seems our time's up, then.'

'How come?'

'I leave for Marib on Sunday.'

'Oh.'

He nodded, more to himself than to me.

'I'm sorry.'

'Never mind. The sooner I get out of your hair, the better.'

'Don't be so bloody cranky,' I said. 'We're only losing a couple of days, which won't make much difference in the long run.'

'Ah, yes, because the run was never going to be very long, anyway. I remember now.'

This little sulk was about Dublin, I realized, not

Ta'izz, but there was nothing I could do about Dublin.

'Look, we couldn't possibly re-create back home what has happened here, Christian. This was only ever going to be a Yemeni thing.'

He looked up. 'What is this? The "We'll always have Sana'a" speech?'

I turned away.

'I haven't enjoyed a relationship like this since I was sixteen,' he said, leaning towards me. 'I'm not going to give up on it.'

'You have to.'

'Why?'

'Because it's what I want.'

'Is it?' He got to his feet and looked down on me. 'Is it really?' He turned, collided with Theo in the doorway, and left.

'What's his problem?'

'Angry.'

Theo looked back towards the staircase. 'You should go after him.'

'No point going after him if I can't make it better.'

'Why do you make it so difficult?' Theo asked, exasperated. I exasperated him a lot, I felt.

'I have to. I'd rather not, but I have to.'

'Because?'

'Because I could fall in love with him and that would be a very bad idea.'

'And you won't tell me why?'

'I'd like to, but it's someone else's story. Not mine to tell.'

*

I didn't sleep that night. The *qat* probably. Not Christian. My initial mistake was running deeper than expected. This was a mire, its tendrils grasping like squid. I blamed the sex. It had been reckless, and it was careless of me not to guard against threads, nerve-endings, becoming entwined. In rushing to feed the passion, I had failed to see it transcend beyond the bedroom and out of my grasp, like a bar of soap in the bath. That I should pay for this was inevitable; that Christian should also suffer hadn't even occurred to me.

7

Theo and I set off early for the summer capital in the mountains. He had work to do along the way and had been invited to a party by a friend, a German doctor, who lived in Ta'izz. We made a staggered exit from the town, through several checkpoints. Theo had papers from the CSO – the Central Statistics Office – which gave him leave to go just about anywhere, and although my mother's poorly typed emails implored me to stay in the city, nothing could have stopped me travelling Niebuhr's route from Ta'izz to Sana'a. Here, at last, with the precious volume beside me, I could truly follow his trail.

We were soon in the mountains, where the slopes were terraced and barely farmed. Then we dropped on to the Dhamar plain, a drab plateau, whose only points of interest were the remnants of damage from an earthquake – a long, straight fissure ran across the bland earth, like a ruler left on a desk. Leaving the main road, we headed towards the hills. Theo made a few stops to consult his GPS, a gadget not much bigger than a mobile phone, and enter the co-ordinates and 'way-points' in his laptop. 'Training is okay,' he said, 'but working in the field is best.'

We headed towards a village in the foothills. 'The survey will be conducted on a sample of eighty thousand agri-holders and thirty thousand non-agri-holders, by means of an *ad hoc* questionnaire,' he explained, 'but first we must do a pilot census to verify the questionnaire's questions and the reaction of the respondents. This village is part of the pilot scheme. One of our co-ordinators is coming out here today so I said we would meet her.'

On the outskirts, he stopped to look at a walled cistern in the ground – a newly constructed well – which had been built as part of a water project, but it was on a dry, rocky slope and empty.

'Will it ever fill up?'

'*Insh'Allah*, when the rains come.'

'And in the meantime?'

'The women have to continue to carry water from much further away.'

We drove on into the village, where we were met by his colleague, Sharifa, whom I was very glad to see because almost every male inhabitant had gathered around us and I urgently needed a bathroom. A bush – if there had been one – would hardly have sufficed with so many curious eyes following me, so Sharifa led me to the *shaykh*'s house further along the track. This time it was women and girls who pressed into us when we stepped into the cool dark rooms of the house. They kissed and welcomed us, and gleefully led me to the bathroom – a small cement room at the back of the house, with a hole in the ground hanging over thin air. I had come upon a traditional 'long drop.' It was spotlessly clean. How they managed to keep it so, when every drop of water was so hard come by, was beguiling, but I was very happy to see it – in any condition.

The women pressed food on me, along with eager questions and queries about how many children I had had. The *shaykh*'s wife had three, and had lost another three in childbirth. Her sister had nine. Apart from the local midwives, there were no maternity services. If a woman had a tricky labour, they told me, she was put into a truck and taken along the bumpy, windy roads to the nearest clinic, which wasn't very near.

Children poked and teased me. I poked them back. When a little boy came to tell me that Theo was ready to leave, it was difficult to release myself from their hospitality, but we had a long way to go. The men were particularly put out that Theo would not stay to chew with them. As I got into the jeep, a woman in a doorway, slightly ajar, inadvertently made eye-contact with me; she dipped her head and pulled her scarf across the side of her face to avoid doing so again.

At the other end of the Dhamar plain, mountains loomed beneath a storm, which sat above them like a great grey trilby. We had no option but to drive right into it. It was an electrical storm, with a foul temper. Theo took the bending roads with caution. Lightning shot into the ground ahead as if Satan was stabbing his fork at us, but kept missing. After dark, sheet lightning gave us negative impressions of the mountains, then threw us back into an all-consuming blackness. Above us on the hillsides, occasional rows of arc-shaped windows glowed, too far away to be comforting. I was thrilled. On this very road, Niebuhr had had a similar experience: 'A violent storm surprised us, and gave us an opportunity of remarking how the torrents, rushing upon such occasions from the hill, produce the gullies.' The centuries peeled away. I had never been so close to the Danish expedition.

We were very tired when we finally got into Ta'izz at eight. I read out the directions, such as they were, to the house of the German doctor. Our landmark was a rubbish bin on a corner in a particular district. We bumped over every kind of side road looking for it. Theo asked in shops and on street corners, but nobody knew the German doctor, so we tried to phone him. A Yemeni answered. We had the wrong number. We set off again, and spent another hour looking for the dustbin.

'You're the bloody cartographer,' I said. 'Why don't you get out your GPS to find the way?'

'It doesn't have the co-ordinates for rubbish bins, does it?'

'All that fancy equipment and we still get lost . . .'

'We'll go to the hospital where he works.'

This he did manage to find, after driving across the city, up and down the hills of Ta'izz, but the night porter had no idea where the doctor lived. We headed back to the suburb and trundled around for another half-hour until, exhausted, we conceded defeat and went in search of a meal. We found a restaurant and took a table on the pavement, where we ate chicken legs with our fingers.

Theo was almost too tired to eat.

'I don't understand why you didn't write down the address and get specific directions,' I said.

'Addresses are no good around here.'

'Phone numbers, on the other hand, can be handy.'

'It is all my fault?'

'Well, a rubbish bin is hardly a *landmark*.'

He bit into his chicken leg so angrily that I had to suppress a smile. Our first row.

'We have two options,' he said. 'Either we stay in a *lukanda* – a sort of hostel – or we head out of town and sleep in the car.'

'Those are our options?'

'You have another idea?'

'The Four Seasons Hotel? Any nice hotel?'

'I can't afford a place like that, and it's stupid to spend so much money. You came here for adventure, didn't you?'

'Not this kind of adventure.'

'If you stay in a hotel, you stay alone.'

'So what would a *lukanda* be like?'

'Like a dormitory. Not really suitable for a woman.'

I sighed. 'Great.'

'We should sleep in the car.'

'But that would be absolute madness. You know that as well as I do. An unmarried man and woman sleeping together in public?'

'But we'll be gone before anyone even knows we've been there. We'll hide behind some bushes.'

'Oh, that'll look even better!'

'Vivien, I'm so tired. Please.'

He drove back on to the Sana'a road and some miles out of town veered off the Tarmac on to a bare stretch of gravel. He parked by some bushes. I went in one direction to pee, Theo in the other. Then, giving him driver's privilege, I made do with the driver's seat while he stretched out in the back. I leaned over the steering-wheel, praying that deep sleep would bring this awful night to a swift end. Instead I dropped in and out of dreams, none enticing enough to keep me from waking. In one dream, Christian was sitting at a desk, writing, and I was bringing him a glass of *shai*. Then I dreamed I was in my own bedroom at home and Bill was bringing me a mug of tea. I opened one eye to take the mug and saw the sky and trees of Yemen.

At five thirty, I woke to hear Theo saying, 'Better get out of here.' But I had imagined it. He was asleep. The words echoed in my ear. I should have taken heed.

At seven thirty, it was too hot to remain in the jeep, so I got out and sat on a warm rock, enjoying the gentle morning heat. The one time that my impatience could have worked to my advantage, it languished in the sunshine, too limp to activate me. Since it was Friday, there was little traffic on the road, a hundred yards away, although I vaguely took note of a motor-bike going towards Ta'izz. Some children, decked out in their colourful clothes, herded their goats and thin bumpy cows across the road and came towards me. They giggled. I smiled. A big lizard ran across the stones at my feet. At the top of the hill behind us, a tractor came and went. Every few minutes, its engine splut-tered into the silence, drowning the buzzing of insects as it appeared on the crest of the hill, then puttered off again. I needed to pee, but the meagre bushes nearby awarded scant cover. I scrambled up the hill to a thicker one that would conceal me from the jeep and the road. I had to time it carefully. The farmer in the tractor had a full view of this bush every time he reached the brim of the field, so I had to wait for it to appear, turn, and disappear before I could safely relieve myself. When I slid back down to the jeep, Theo was awake.

We were preparing to go searching for dustbins in Ta'izz when a motorbike veered off the road towards us.

The driver was a middle-aged civilian; a young soldier rode pillion. Theo greeted them, but this was no social call: the civilian's demeanour was aggressive. They began remonstrating with Theo, who swiftly became defensive. He tried to handle the situation in his still basic Arabic, struggling to find words, and although the small, swarthy man was almost spitting in his face, he managed to maintain civility.

There was a pause. The two men stepped back to argue between themselves.

'What's happening?' I hissed.

Theo's hands were shaking. 'We were seen having sex in the jeep this morning.'

'*What?*'

He glanced at me. It was laughable, but I didn't like his body language when the men resumed the interrogation, firing questions and accusations at him. Theo took his time, answering them slowly and clearly.

Once again, they retreated to discuss the matter between themselves. 'Shit,' said Theo. 'I said I wouldn't sleep with you because you're my cousin, but cousins marry here.'

'They can't be serious?'

It went on. Exasperated, Theo went to the back of the jeep, opened the doors and showed where he had slept. They pointed at me. I sat into the driver's seat and laid my head on the steering-wheel. It seemed unlikely, even to me, that anyone could sleep in that position, but I kept telling myself that as soon as Theo had made his point, we would be on our way.

We weren't. His explanations weren't working. The civilian grew more agitated. Theo asked them repeatedly to slow down, to allow for his grasp of Arabic, but they continued to harangue him.

My mouth was as dry as sandpaper. We should have known better. We *had* known better. As an unmarried man and woman travelling together, we should have coughed up and stayed in a hotel. Like I'd told him.

The pair quite suddenly came to an agreement and waved us into the car.

'We can go?'

Theo looked grim. 'They're taking us in.'

The words barely left my throat. 'You mean – *arresting* us?'

He nodded. I was rigid. The women at Husnia's *tafrita*, or gathering, had told me about the prisons. I wished they hadn't. Kidnap would have been infinitely preferable. My nearest Irish representative was in Riyadh, although the British would deal with my case, but I had none of my own to look after me. I might be left to rot. After all, I was not entirely innocent – sleeping in public with a man who was not my husband flouted Yemeni laws of decency. And yet I didn't panic. This obliterated panic.

The two men were arguing again.

'What's going on?'

'It's their word against ours. The soldier isn't so sure.'

But the older man was adamant: they would take us to the police. The soldier, armed with his Kalashnikov, got in behind us. This was a journey into a dead end. It led into a place from which I would not emerge for years, possibly. Those who had told me not to travel had been right. I had ended up being arrested for having sex with my cousin in the back of a jeep by a main road on the holy day.

As if things weren't bad enough, the jeep then got stuck in the sand. The wheels spun. Theo sweated. I remained blank. This wouldn't help. We would be accused of delaying. Instead, the Yemenis became involved. The soldier and Theo got out, while the guy on the bike considered the wheel stuck in the dirt. He told Theo to drive while they pushed. For a moment, all tension dissipated. Men and machinery. With much calling and pushing, advice and debate among them, the jeep was heaved out of its rut. Theo waited for the soldier to climb in, then drove on to the road and, closely followed by the motorbike, turned towards Ta'izz. Terror was still unable to get hold of me. I was in abeyance. My main fear was of being separated from Theo, which I knew I would be as soon as they locked us up. He, at least, could speak the language. Would I even be allowed to phone home?

As we neared the outskirts of Ta'izz, the soldier tapped Theo's shoulder and told him to pull in. We stopped under a tree. Once again, he went over it all with Theo. Questions. Answers. Theo shook his head, his hand over his heart.

Finally the soldier said, 'You know what *"Willahi"* means?'

Theo nodded.

'You must swear by Allah that you did not take her and you will not take her.'

Theo swore by Allah that he had not taken me and never would.

The soldier smiled. Theo smiled. Then the soldier jumped out.

The man on the bike walked back to us. The soldier explained that he was not taking us in. The civilian shrugged. They came to the window and, with great smiles and handshakes, wished us a safe journey. Waving us off like old pals, they called greetings and sent us on our way.

Theo swung the jeep round in the direction of Sana'a. We were high with relief. To hell with dustbins and breakfast. We were going home.

'I don't believe,' I said, when we had caught our breath, 'that I have ever been so eagerly, publicly and wholeheartedly rejected.'

'Sorry.' Theo took his eyes off the road to laugh with me – and lost control of the jeep, which slid off the road and shaved a tree. He swerved and pulled us back on to the Tarmac where he slowed down, exhaling noisily through his lips.

'Jesus Christ!'

'Potverdomme!'

'Kill me, why don't you?'

Theo threw me a sidelong glance. 'This is the last time I take *you* on a trip.'

'This is the last time I'll come! I didn't escape prison just to die on the road, you know.'

We laughed again, then motored on, gingerly, round the bends.

The hills were magnificent, deep green and stepped, a staircase for the gods. 'Like Indonesia,' I said.

'I didn't know you'd been to Indonesia.'

'I haven't.'

In Ibb, we bought a litre of water and half a dozen bananas for breakfast.

8

Dr Linklater was not amused. 'Stupid bloody way to behave,' he snapped. 'Like a pair of ignorant tourists.'

'I thought you'd be glad I'm not in jail.'

'Yes, and I'm particularly glad that I don't have to scrape you off a tree! Stunts like that get foreigners into trouble, and then the country gets a bad name.'

He was in a deeply surly mood. It was his last day in Sana'a and he was stressed. He had arrangements to make, provisions to buy. I trailed behind him, trying to gain his favour. Later, while he had a meeting with Edda and members of the team at his hotel, I read in the garden, waiting to snatch minutes with him, but he came to tell me they would be working through lunch.

'That's okay. I'll hang around until you want me.'

He leaned over me. 'I want you all the time.'

Something sparked. The rest of the day would go like this, I thought, Christian appearing at intervals to say he had still more to do and then in a blink he would be gone and this selfish affair would be over. I went inside, casting an eye in his direction. He was in the restaurant with the group, hunched over a sandwich, looking particularly good in a particularly nice grey shirt. I wanted a final blast, to be magnificently disloyal one last time, so I went to his room, had a shower and pulled on a robe. Then I rang Reception and left a message:

Christian must come upstairs immediately. I sat on the bed, shaking a little. Sana'a looked in from outside.

His belongings were stacked against the wall. The film equipment he wouldn't use; suitcases; stacks of books – Dresch, Mundy, de Maigret; his tape-recorder, mini-tapes and pristine notepads. He didn't use a laptop in the field – too much sand, he said. I looked at his things; I would miss him, this man who should never have been in my life.

He came up within minutes. 'What's wrong?'

'Nothing.'

'They said you were looking for me.'

We stood at the foot of the bed.

'I was. I am. It's just . . . I'm not very good at this.'

'At what? Vivien, I'm in the middle of a meeting.'

'It's that shirt.'

He looked down. 'What's wrong with it?'

'God, you're not making this easy, are you?'

'Nor are you.'

'Look, I've never done this before. I'm not the forward, pushy type and it isn't much my style to march into the boardroom and take off my clothes in front of the chairman, but you look bloody great and you'll be gone soon and I just –'

Christian burst out laughing. 'Is this a seduction? Is that it? You're trying to seduce me?'

'*Trying* being the operative word!'

'You're right, you know. You aren't any bloody good at it.'

'Oh, all right, go on to your damn meeting and I hope you choke on that sandwich.'

'Edda thinks there's some kind of emergency.'

'There *is*. I'm in urgent need.'

'What's it worth?' he asked.

'Blackmail won't work.'

He began unbuttoning his shirt. 'Give me your phone number in Dublin.'

'Don't turn the tables.'

'Let me come to Dublin . . . or I'm out of here.'

'Look, *I*'m seducing *you*, all right?'

'Well, get to it, then. A man hasn't got all day.'

We fell on to the bed. 'What'll you tell them down-stairs?'

'That I got waylaid.'

That evening we had a send-off for him. I had invited my little posse, and a few others, round for dinner, and had spent the afternoon shopping with Nooria. The meat hanging off the stalls in the market hadn't been terribly appetizing, so I had decided to do stuffed auber-gines and rice. But turning out dinner for such a number in a sparse kitchen was difficult, and when Christian arrived I was fussing over the cooker. I handed him a juice. 'Better enjoy a cold drink while you still can.' He leaned against the doorway, with nothing to say for once, and watched me cook. His silence unnerved me.

'No need to do the guilt-trip on me,' I said. 'I feel bad enough already without your input.'

'Clearly.'

'Look,' I said, banging the wooden spoon against the pan, 'I'm really sorry I can't make this what it might have been, but that's all there is to it.'

He shook his head. 'You try to be mysterious. It doesn't work. You think being elusive covers up infidelity? It doesn't.'

'I'm not being unfaithful.'

'Oh, come on. You've clearly got me caught up in some kind of triangle.'

'I *haven't.*'

'Look me in the eye and say that again.'

I couldn't, of course.

'So I'm right. There's someone back home you failed to mention?'

'Christian, if I could have things my way –'

'Let me call you, at the very least, when I get home.'

'Absolutely not.'

'He might answer the phone, I suppose.'

'There is no "he".'

'Then give me your number.'

'No. Please just leave it.'

He glanced at the pan. 'Haven't you ever cooked aubergine before?'

We laid out the food in the *mafraj* and crowded round to eat, cross-legged on the floor. Afterwards, curled up like a cat in the cushions, I enjoyed a feeling of contentment that had eluded me for longer than I cared to acknowledge. Perhaps I had never known it before. These cosy gatherings, this pick-and-mix of people bridging geographical divides with the invisible threads of friendship, were comforting and all-absorbing. It felt as if I had always been there, had always taken up a space among these friends, and yet I would soon be gone and the place I had vacated wouldn't even seem empty to those who remained.

Theo drove Christian and me back to his hotel, but neither of us slept. At four I sat up and gazed at the lights for the last time.

'You know I can find you in Dublin if I set my mind to it?' Christian said.

'I'm asking you not to.'

He sighed heavily. 'I thought we were embarking on something exciting, but all I've done is to walk into a cul-de-sac.'

'I'm sorry. I thought there wouldn't be time to get involved.'

'So you *are* involved?'

I looked over my shoulder at him.

'Can't you at least tell me what this is about?' he asked.

'Not now.'

'When?'

'I dunno. Maybe, years from now, I'll write to you out of the blue and explain.'

'Oh, that'd make all the difference,' he said bitterly, but then he sighed again, this time with a certain amount of resignation. 'I suppose, either way, I'll still be missing you in a few hours, whatever your reasons for ending this now.'

'Is there anything I can do to make up for it?'

'You could make love to me, I suppose –'

I rolled playfully on top of him.

'– and pretend to mean it.'

*

The garden, when we emerged at seven o'clock that morning, was bright, and tight with tension. Christian spoke to one of the drivers while I stood in the sun, wearing his grey shirt and a long cotton skirt. Theo sauntered along the walkway, dipping his head to come under the bougainvillaea. 'So,' he said, patting Christian's shoulder, 'all set?'

'Theo! Thanks for coming.' They shook hands. 'And thanks for all your help.'

'Get in touch when you get back.'

When I'll be long gone, I thought, out of the picture and out of their lives.

'I look forward to it. And you'll do the decent thing, won't you?' Christian said, nodding in my direction. 'Keep her out of trouble and so on?'

'That's if I can stop her running into the desert after you.'

'We both know that isn't going to happen.' He picked up his bags and went outside to the Land Cruisers that had come to collect him.

Theo nudged me with his elbow. 'I thought you might want a shoulder to cry on.'

'I won't cry.'

We went out to the pavement and stood watching as bags were tied to roof-racks and busy archaeologists leaned in and out of cars, calling to one another. The city was quiet, and the early warmth of the sun was, at that moment, the way of things. Staying in Sana'a while others left seemed a natural way to be.

Christian came over to us. Theo moved off. 'So, I can't even tie you down to one dinner date?'

'You could have tied me down very easily if things had been diff –'

'Spare me the cliché. You could find a way through if you wanted to.'

'No, Christian. I couldn't.'

He kissed me hard, then got into the Land Cruiser. There was a great banging of doors, voices crying out, engines starting up. With a crunch of gears, the convoy pulled out. Christian didn't wave or look back. He sat in the front seat, his fist against his mouth.

Use and be used; discard and be discarded; hurt and be hurt.

As the lead vehicle moved along the street, Christian's Land Cruiser came to a sudden halt, causing a jarring of brakes behind it. He got out, slammed his door and came marching towards us. I hurried to him, but he ducked my outstretched arms and grabbed my elbows. 'Give me your bloody number!'

I gave it to him.

'Thank you!' He stormed back to the car, and by the time I became aware of Theo standing behind me, they were out of sight.

'Oh, God,' I said, 'I've really blown it now.'

9

We had a lovely day, Theo and I. It was good to get into the countryside and enjoy sights I never tired of – villages perched on hilltops or crouched in nooks and crannies. Theo was quite a sight too, in his desert boots and shorts, standing on a crag and fiddling with his GPS. He was so much like a child with his GameBoy, I had to keep reminding myself that this was serious work.

I didn't miss Christian too violently. Perhaps I had become anaesthetized by the afterglow. Sex leaves an aura that can last for days and I was steeped in it. As the jeep took us over lumps and bumps well off the beaten track, my mind replayed our every coupling. I thought about the first time, the last. Above all, I enjoyed a powerful sense of relief, as if I had stolen something and got away with it.

We had our picnic next to a tumbledown bridge over a dry wadi that Theo had surveyed.

'Vivien, I have a plan.'

'You have a plan.'

'You must see Shibam.'

'We've established that. We need to book flights.'

'Fadhl will sort out security,' said Theo. 'We'll drive to Marib, surprise Christian, and take him with us to Shibam on Friday.'

'That would certainly surprise him.'

'Please. Let me show you more of Yemen. It would give me such pleasure.'

'You're sweet.'

'So – we'll go?'

'We'll go. By plane.'

I spent the next two days feeling my way at Nooria's centre. Young women came in shrouded in black, but uncovered their faces when they got upstairs where there were no men. I made coffee for teachers, did some work on the index in the library, and showed a group of students round the Internet. They giggled a lot and spoke so quietly that I could barely hear them, but they quickly made it clear they were more interested in my private life than the Internet. My childless, spinster state momentarily stymied them, but they moved on to ask about my boyfriend. Not wishing to appear a complete peculiarity, I invented one.

Nooria was like a whirlwind, swirling with enthusiasm, ideas, projects and plans. She had me in her sights, and it was hard to duck her ambitious presumptions. I was her new cause: she needed me, but she knew that I needed her more. The scars of 1990 were hers to heal.

The building was in need of repair, but the dynamism of teachers and volunteers alike, the rustle of cloaked students moving between classrooms, and the sense of purpose vibrating on every floor made the centre an intimidating place, as well as exhausting, for someone used to the stillness of an art gallery. On the second day I was so worn out by lunchtime that I went home to rest, excited by the prospect of returning. Nooria had me where she wanted: she had given me a space, a place to be. But had I the courage to take it?

Theo appeared in the stairwell when I got to the house. 'I have a big surprise for you.'

'Christian!'

His jaw dropped. 'Oh . . . I'm sorry, no. Come on up to the kitchen.'

The shock was like a gust of wind; it blew me sideways in the doorway.

Gemma was sitting there, her hands cupped round a glass of tea, grinning from ear to ear.

Impossible. Impossible she would go this far.

'Well?' she shrieked, standing up to grab me. 'Surprised?'

Words. Where were the words?

'I got in this morning on Egyptair. Bit scary, actually, because I didn't have an official invitation and they wouldn't let me out of the airport. They didn't understand a word, so they finally gave me a phone and I called Theo. Your mum gave me his number. He came to save me.'

'Jesus, Gem.' I turned to Theo.

'It's okay,' he said. 'I brought out a letter of invitation from the CSO.'

Gemma nudged me. 'I thought you'd be pleased! I thought you'd, you know,' she grimaced in the quirky way I loved, '*expect* it.'

'How could I expect it? What are you doing here?'

'I must go,' said Theo, kissing my cheek as he left.

He had picked up on something, had seen the index of emotions cross my face. I sank into a chair.

'Why do you think I'm here? For God's sake.'

'Jesus. I'd never have emailed you if I'd imagined you'd –'

'Imagined I'd what? Surely this *is* why you told me?'

'No. I thought . . . It was just the coincidence. Being on the same flight . . . I thought you'd get a laugh out of it.' And I had been too distracted to dwell on why there had been no reply . . .

'A laugh? I nearly had heart failure! And spending a thousand euros I don't have to get to this place is hardly my idea of fun.'

My hand went to my mouth.

'Where is he?' she asked.

I was stumped, stymied.

'Have you seen him since the flight?'

'It's a small town,' I said quietly.

'That's what I figured – that you were bound to run into each other. So do you know where he's staying? Have you seen him much? *Please* tell me you've kept tabs on him.'

'Oh, I kept tabs on him all right.'

'Great. So where could we run into him?'

'Nowhere. You're too late. He's gone on a dig. You should have asked before you . . . did this.'

She slumped back into her seat, winded. 'Shit. Can we go there?'

'Where?'

'To the dig.'

I stared at her open-mouthed, then said, 'Oh, yeah,

sure. First you need a permit, then you need a police escort, then you need to organize security with the local tribe. No prob!'

'Jesus, what's with the sarcasm? You know better than anyone what this has been like for me.'

'But what's it been like for him?'

She shrugged. Gemma was very good at shrugging.

The kitchen wasn't big enough for both of us. I went outside. The early-afternoon rainclouds had come in. It would rain soon, and thunder. Gemma followed me. 'I'm going out later,' I told her.

'Can I come?'

She could have, but I said, 'No.'

'Where is this place Christian's gone?'

'Why didn't you email me to find out what the score was before rushing out here like a teenager on heat?'

'You would have talked me out of it.'

'Of course I would!' Anger was seeping through the shock. 'I mean, God, if you're so desperate to see him why didn't you contact him in Durham?'

She fell right into the trap. 'Durham?' she said, frowning. 'He's in London now, isn't he?'

'Christ,' I said, shaking my head. 'I should have known. You haven't lost sight of him at all, have you? You've been tracking him all this time. How *do* you do it?'

'The Net. It's easy to follow academics on the Net.'

'But why?' I threw out my arms. 'Why would anyone *want* to?'

Gemma's expression hardened. 'Don't give me grief about it.'

'Oh, right. You turn up out of the blue, landing in on Theo and me, and I'm not supposed to ask why?'

'You know why,' she said quietly. 'Unfinished business.'

'Oh, for Jesus' sake, the business *is* finished, Gemma!'

'Look, the last time I saw him —'

'I know all about the last time.'

'Seeing him again, in a different context, might help me put it behind me.'

'I thought it *was* behind you, long since.'

'Well, it isn't, all right? And this is perfect — he's here, you're here, and I'm just along for a holiday. I mean, it's too good an opportunity to pass up.'

'Too good an opportunity for *what*, exactly?'

Her head jolted sideways, as if in a nervous tic.

I stared at her. 'Oh, God. You know. Of course you do. That's why you've come.'

'Know what?'

'That he's divorced.'

She raised her chin and looked down her nose at the ground.

'Is that on the Net too?'

'Grapevine.'

There was no accounting for it: her single-mindedness and my naïveté.

'Have you any idea why it ended?' she asked quietly. 'The marriage made in heaven?'

I sat on a low parapet, wearied to the core, not by this arrival but by its history. 'Nothing is ever as it seems. Marriages any more than divorces.'

'What's that supposed to mean?'

'He calls it a divorce, but I'd be inclined to describe it as a sabbatical. He talks incessantly about his wife and they live in the same street so they can still play happy families. I wouldn't go there if I were you. It's a barbed path.'

'But why did they split up?'

'He met someone else, she met someone else, some-one died.'

'Someone died?'

'It's a long story.'

Gemma looked at me oddly. 'He told you all about it? You must be pretty chummy.'

'I was working on your behalf. Preparing for the cross-examination you'd put me through when I got home.'

'What did he say about me?'

'Nothing. I didn't mention you.'

'Why not?'

'I wasn't sure you'd want me to.'

She looked towards the mountains. 'Is it far, this place he's gone? Could Theo take us?'

'Even if he could, chasing Dr Linklater around the country is not what I have planned for the rest of my holiday. What were you thinking?'

'Look, I just couldn't stick it, all right? Knowing that you were both here, in the same place, probably hanging out with the same people . . . I know it's a bit mad but –'

'A bit mad? It's completely bloody insane! You'll set the whole thing in motion again.'

'So what if I do?' She grinned mischievously, trying to rally me. 'Might be just the job . . .'

I was shaking all over, like a rabbit caught in a trap. *Caught.* The one thing I had feared but never expected.

'Come on, Viv. Don't be such a pain. I mean, where's the harm?'

I looked at her, hard. 'The same place it was last time.'

She swept over to me, took my arm in her hands. 'Vivien, don't be like this. I have to see him. Haven't I always said there was an affinity between us, that some time, somewhere, everything would make sense?'

'But, Gemma –'

'Otherwise why all this? You coming to Yemen when everyone told you not to and ending up on the same flight . . . How can I overlook that? I'd be mad not to act on it.'

'You'd be mad to let this start again. He might have someone else, he might –'

'I don't care about that. I need to tie this up once and for all, one way or another. You can't put an end to something when it's lying in front of you on the pavement.'

'Oh, please. Don't play the pavement card.'

A different bunch of women, more friends of Nooria, came to collect me. Thunder rolled round the skies. I had no idea where I was going, but we stopped outside a modern apartment block and took a lift to the tenth floor where we were greeted by a young woman in baggy trousers and a loose top. I removed my sandals, stepped on to a plush carpet and was introduced to a whole new set of faces, who embraced me warmly. Still giddy with anger or fright, or something, I sank gratefully into an armchair. I needed to be embraced. The bright flat offered an expansive view of the outer rim of the city and had a far preferable layout to my own apartment at home, where every room led off one long, dim corridor. The women went into the bedroom to take off their *maqramahs* and *baltos*, while I sat sipping pineapple juice and trying to achieve the impossible: shove Gemma and Christian from my thoughts.

There was a burst of laughter from Nooria and the woman to whom she had been speaking politely on the couch. They had only just realized they knew each other. They met occasionally through work, but had not recognized one another unveiled.

'So it doesn't just happen to me?' I said.

'No. It happens all the time!'

The hostess, Najat, rushed to the front door, giggling into her phone. More guests had been standing in the corridor knocking, but we hadn't heard them so they had had to telephone Najat to tell her they were there. They also came in to shrieks of laughter. It was awful, awful, to be confronted by my own shortcomings. I had fancied myself a good friend, but Christian had dismantled that notion, and now Gemma could claim my scalp.

We had afternoon tea in the *diwan*, where Najat laid out a selection of honey-soaked pastries. 'I baked them myself, of course,' she said. Some things were the same the world over, I thought – they had clearly been picked up in the deli at the last moment. I felt cosy, at home.

I wanted to stay there all evening, all night, for the rest of my holiday.

These women were professionals. The trivialities laid aside over soft drinks, we discussed politics, human rights, women's rights. My own questions had been lost in the fog created by Gemma's appearance. The best thing would be to come clean with her straight away. The shock might bring her to her senses. The women were discussing divorce. 'Is it easy to get one?' I asked. 'Because I've met many divorced women, all of whom instigated the divorces themselves.'

'If a girl has her family behind her,' Najat explained, 'and her husband has mistreated her, she will get a divorce. A woman can do anything when her family supports her.'

'You in the West think Arab women have no rights,' said Arwan, a feisty little doctor who had been telling me about problems in the health sector, 'but at least we get the same salaries as men if we do the same job.'

'And we keep our own names when we get married.'

They did not deny the difficulties they had to unravel in their own country, in particular the huge population growth and the desperate need for education. One of the women, a politician, alternated between anger and passion. The problem for women politicians, she explained, was that they were excluded from the true decision-making process – the *qat* chew – but the Women's National Committee had recently set up training courses to encourage more women to go into politics.

I have to stop Gemma going to Marib, I thought,

and in this at least I was sincere in wishing to protect her more than myself.

The politician was getting agitated about young marriages. 'Western organizations say they will not give us aid until we stop allowing girls to be married young. This is hypocrisy. How can you tell us not to let our girls marry when they have the support and encouragement of not one but two families, whereas your teenagers are having babies at fourteen, fifteen, outside marriage and living alone in high buildings?'

Nooria excused herself to go and pray in the next room. 'I have been so busy today I have not had time.' Another woman joined her.

An old photograph was passed round. It was grey, faded – faded, you would almost say, by the sharp light of the Hadramawt in which it had been taken. Two little girls leaned against a wall, grimacing against the glare. 'That was my mother when she was thirteen,' said the woman who had brought it out, 'and she had my sister that same year.'

I stared in amazement, but the other women were equally fascinated.

On our way home in the taxi, Nooria asked me politely why the West did nothing to protect the Palestinians. I wanted to say, 'Oh, Nooria, you won't believe what I've done,' but I forced myself instead to tackle the question put to me with such sincere bewilderment. It wasn't easy, nor would it have been even with a focused mind, so I muttered ineffectually that there was a lot of support, in Ireland and Europe, for the

Palestinian cause. Nooria said nothing because I had said nothing.

When we got back to number eight, I watched Nooria cross the courtyard, a black shadow in the dark, walking with her head high and her conscience clear. I liked her enormously. Behind the giddiness lay a depth of sincerity and an unassuming spirituality that made me feel wanting, and empty.

I climbed the stairs, frustrated by my ineffectual life, so irrelevant to the greater world. There was so much to do and these women were doing it. No matter the obstacles, they persevered, and still found time to laugh and chat, be mothers and wives. After hearing them discuss what could be done for disabled children in impoverished families, it was irritating to have to face Gemma and her petty strung-out drama.

She and Theo were sitting at the kitchen table. She had usurped me there already.

'Theo tells me the trip is already arranged,' she said curtly, 'that you're leaving for this place Marib the day after tomorrow. Why didn't you tell me?'

'You know why.' I turned to Theo. 'Will we be able to get her a permit?'

'I'm sure Fadhl can do it, since the group is already organized.'

'Excellent,' said Gemma. 'Who else is going?'

'My colleague Fadhl,' said Theo, 'and our friend Nooria.'

'I don't know how you persuaded her to leave her girls,' I said to him, in a weak attempt to gain some ground, shut Gemma out.

'It was no problem,' he said, then added, as a tease, 'She's in love with Christian.'

'Is she? Who is?' said Gemma.

'Nobody,' I said. 'Nobody's in love with Christian, Gemma.'

'You know him?' Theo asked.

She smiled. 'Oh, yes. We go back a bit.'

We made a bed for Gemma in the spare room. 'Theo isn't your personal assistant, you know,' I said.

'Is he the reason you're in such lousy form?'

I tugged on the sheet. 'I'm in lousy form because I've had years of this and I'm sick of it. You're pushing the limits, Gemma, and I won't be party to it.'

Theo's light was still on when I went back upstairs. I knocked and put my head round the door. 'Can I come in?'

'*Ja.*'

I had never been in there before. 'I owe you an explanation.'

'Not really, but . . .' He patted his bed. He was wiping his glasses with the sheet. Nice chest, I thought vaguely. I sat beside his ankles. He had slender feet and toes shaped like stop signs.

'You know all those reservations I had about Christian?' I said. 'The reason I didn't want to get involved?'

He nodded.

'Well, right now that reason is downstairs in your spare room.'

10

We were friends, nothing more, nothing less, and had been for years. At school we had been predisposed to dislike each other – I was timid, Gemma loud – and did so until we became drawn to one another like wary animals sniffing at something unfamiliar yet compelling. We were so polarized. Everything about me was muted, concealed, and she was exactly as she appeared. While my friends were sensible, studious girls, hers were smarter and often in trouble. I smoked to blend in; Gemma didn't have to smoke because she blended in wherever she wanted to. Tall and gorgeous, she had deep auburn hair and wide green eyes, and she had a huge personality: inpulsive, gutsy, opinionated.

Our friendship also became huge. For me, a day without Gemma was like chips without salt. I thirsted for her view, her wisdom, her wider knowledge of the world. I liked nothing better than to hang around her house, where we gorged ourselves on bars and biscuits, and fought with her many brothers. Her father was a hard-working orthodontist, her mother a golf-mad, fund-raising, hyperactive woman who was never at home, which was probably why Gemma, in turn, loved my home. She enjoyed the privacy and the absence of rugby teams. She also adored my mother, who did not entirely return the sentiment – the Colbert family, in her view, was altogether too unruly – but her disapproval made them all the more entrancing to me. In those days, I didn't much appreciate my parents. They were too retiring and sensible, I thought, without realizing that I was desperately sensible too. I prissily kept away from the frequent parties that Gemma's brothers held in their garage because dope was smoked and booze consumed. I was terrified of sex and drugs, and even rock and roll.

My parents were a-musical: had they not been so, I would not have believed such people could exist, but, in separate homes at opposite ends of Dublin, they had both grown up without exposure to any music, except hymns. It was simply not part of their environment, so I grew up in a house with one radio, a record-player that was never used and a television that always was. It was never suggested that I should learn an instrument, which suited me because, unlike my friends, I had no scales to practise and no piano exam in May, but Gemma showed me that this was a drawback, not a bonus. She didn't play an instrument either, but then, she didn't have to: she had the voice of a chorister. She sang at school masses, and in her brothers' band, and sometimes she sang just to be nice to me. I began to understand about music. When my brother David left home, I turned his bedroom into my own den, invested in a good sound system, and spent hours listening to any tape or record that came my way.

I soon had plans for Gemma. I fancied she had the makings of a rock diva – the hair, the attitude, the spunk. Above all, the voice. But my attempts to nurture her potential failed. She had no interest. 'My voice is for me to do with as I please,' she argued. 'It isn't for marketing. It's for giving, like kindness or love.'

Her own attempts to nurture *my* potential were more successful. When we were sixteen, she announced that it was her intention to bring out the porpoise in me. I was headed the way of the spoilt only daughter and indulged little sister of a quiet family that never rocked, except to the sound of my own ratty impatience, and it was time to break out, she said. With her help, I eventually did. I learned to smoke dope and to jive in front of a crowd and, in their garden shed where they kept the bikes, I lost my virginity to her brother, Bill.

If Gemma could be fickle, I never acknowledged it. Too lacking in self-belief to take a stand against her bouts of disinterest and exclusion, I took the blows on the chin. In view of the fact that I wasn't very hip, I took it as a given that she might not always crave my company; by the time I came to resent it, we were headed in different directions anyway. But it was at just that point, after leaving school, that I became involved with her brother and ended up seeing more of Gemma than ever before. I was always in their home, spending time with one or other or both of them, and Gemma was delighted. She liked having another female around to help dilute the testosterone-heavy atmosphere, and although initially staggered by the relationship – persuaded as she was by our absolute incompatibility – she acquired a new respect for me. It gave me kudos, being her brother's girlfriend, and confidence too. I no longer yearned for Gemma's approval because I had Bill's, and the shift in balance was good for both of us; it even brought us closer. We enjoyed some crazy times in that unruly, often parent-free house, and quiet times too, when it was just her and me, and maybe a few girl-friends, swapping stories about student life and work.

Gemma had opted to skip university. Life was too short for study, she believed, so she worked for a few years as a dentist's receptionist until she decided, at twenty-two, that life was too short to be spent as a dentist's receptionist. Students had much more fun, she now declared, and university was the only place to be, even though most of her friends had already moved on. Her choice of subject – anthropology – poured a certain amount of salt into my gaping Yemeni wound, for such a career would offer her the kind of opportunities I had squandered. She chose it because she thought she'd be good at it, and her father insisted she enrol at the University of Durham, in Britain, because it was known to offer the best course. Besides, they could afford it.

She had first taken note of Christian Linklater when she attended his series of lectures on Middle Eastern culture during her first year. There was no *coup de foudre*. The attraction simmered inconspicuously for a while, until she noticed how giddy she became before and after his lectures. She took more heed of him then, and allowed herself to be carried away by the voice until his mannerisms made her squirm in her seat. She waited for it to pass – this mild crush on a lecturer – but a Christmas break in Dublin failed to kill it off, and the following February she was propelled even further into infatuation during a seminar featuring an eminent Canadian anthropologist. Linklater had largely organized the event, but when he failed to show, Gemma became flustered. She sat at the back of the room, watching the door, and when he finally appeared and slipped into the seat beside her, the attraction pounced and made her its own. Her heart raced. She noticed his hands, his cuffs, his smell. He was renowned for his collection of ties. That night he was wearing one with pigs on it. Subsequently I heard no more about life in Durham, beyond Linklater. He was like another course she was taking. She liked to tell me what an incisive and stimulating teacher he was, but it was still a joke between us, this infatuation, and she acknowledged that it would eventually burn itself out.

It didn't. In her second year, it continued to be excruciating and wonderful for Gemma, and increasingly frustrating for me. I became very bored with Dr Linklater, with his ground-breaking research, his happy marriage and his wonderful triplets, of whom I knew he spoke often because his every word was relayed back to me. I was concerned, too, about Gemma. Apart from odd flourishes, she had no relationships. No young man could compete with the wonderful, worldly (and wordy) Linklater. Discussions between us became heated. 'He's married,' I reminded her frequently.'He is *un*available. Sold. Out of bounds!' But this was good, she insisted, because it spared her any possibility of rejection.

When she signed up for a field trip to Jordan led by Linklater that spring, I had grave reservations, and with good reason. That Easter I lost Gemma, the one I had known thus far, and so did she.

She wrote me long, rambling letters, but not a word about Jordan or the village in which they were based. Her entire focus was on the lecturer: his sense of humour, the damp on the back of his shirt, the minutiae of his being. It was impossible to know whether or not he was aware of her feelings. Gemma thought not. There would have been awkwardness on his part if he had suspected it, but he was relaxed around her and even gravitated towards her for company, perhaps because she was a little older than the other students. Keeping her cards close to her chest, she was happy to observe and absorb, and had no serious inclinations to move in on him. She did that enough in her dreams.

When she came home, she tried to pretend this was still a silly obsession, but she was too changed to carry that off. Gone was the wild party animal, always on for a laugh. Instead came a quieter individual. Daily exposure to Linklater had inspired a deeper attachment, one that, paradoxically, Gemma wore well. She had fallen in love and she nursed her love like a pet. Like a pet, it thrived in her care.

While I moved in and out of relationships, had my highs and lows, Gemma remained constant. I came to admire this unrequited love. She lived like a nun who had taken vows, like a Bride of Christ. She could never touch him, be with him, she could only yearn, as in a blind alley. I acquired new respect for nuns, but my heart bled for Gemma's celibate existence (broken by occasional one-night stands after Linklater had stood too close to her) and the time she was wasting. I longed for some other guy to steal up on her when she was looking the other way. I longed for her to be free of the leg-iron that Linklater had become.

She compounded the condition by pandering to it. That summer, she took a job in the Department of Anthropology in Durham, filling in for secretaries on holidays. 'Now you're being plain bloody stupid,' I told her, but there was nothing I could do while the non-affair grew more intense in England, except read her scribbled letters in despair, and sometimes in amusement. One day she wrote that she had nearly broken her nose. She had been walking along a corridor when Linklater had come out of an office ahead, and suddenly there was a loud crash. Everything stopped. Gemma stopped. But Linklater was still moving. She had walked into a glass door.

He rushed to her. 'Good God, are you all right?' He picked up her papers, while she stood stunned, her eyes watering. 'It's bleeding. Quick.'

He shuffled her into the ladies', thrust a fistful of toilet paper at her and hurried her into a cubicle to sit down. Then he soaked his clean hanky under the cold tap and put it on the bridge of her nose while she tried to stem the bleeding. When it stopped, he took her to his office and gave her a glass of water. 'I did that once,' he said, 'walked into a glass door, and in front of all my students too. You'll have two black eyes. Not hoping to impress anyone at the moment, are you?'

She saw something then, in his manner, and for a moment thought he knew. A new fantasy took root: he

164

had noticed her. For three days in succession he came to the office to inquire after her. As her eyes grew blacker, his interest seemed all the more ludicrous, but it was so much sweeter for her than being cast to the outskirts of oblivion. One morning he joined her for coffee in the common room, where he allowed her to wallow in his full attention, unconsciously catapulting her further into the mire, and did most of the talking, as ever. Having worked with him on equal terms, she claimed to like him now, as well as love him, and this worried me – it is so much easier to stop loving than to stop liking. Those whom we like are good for us; those whom we love, not always. Gemma had become trapped and I had come to loathe the innocent Dr Linklater. In my view, he had to have noticed the glimmer in her eye and therefore should have distanced himself. What Gemma perceived to be flirtatiousness, I now interpreted as caddishness.

As soon as the great black circles faded from Gemma's eyes, so did Linklater's interest. Shattered, she began to slide. Her appetite dwindled until the only food she could contemplate was tomatoes, and she lost sleep. She went to a doctor. He questioned her about her emotional state, diagnosed love, and wished her well. She went on eating tomatoes.

And so into the third year. It was hardly surprising when Linklater became Gemma's supervisor for her final-year dissertation – by design, of course. She had placed herself strategically in the way of his particular expertise, which allowed for plenty of one-on-one discussions. She was elated, but Linklater was becoming a thorn in our friendship. I could no longer bear the swooning conversations and what I increasingly perceived as misinterpretations – she was surely reading too much into his every gesture, his every passing comment, when she herself had once attested to his happy marriage? We argued about it often; I could not account for her motivation and felt myself slipping away from her. My own problems were sloshing around my ankles at the time, but it was impossible to get Gemma's attention. My chances of developing an interesting career grew slighter with every passing year, as did any possibility of finding again the intensity I had known with Bill. Every relationship, like every job, seemed more limp than the last. It was like swimming against a strong current – lots of effort and little progress – but once Linklater had caught Gemma's eye, I could have waved banners when she was home and shouted through a megaphone, 'I am more miserable than I have ever been,' and still she would have sighed and said, 'You should see him in his cream jacket. Sex on legs!' But that was her way, and I should have been used to it. She had a special knack of looking past me when it suited. A few years before, the sum of her response to the news that Bill and I had finally and comprehensively separated had been 'Yeah, yeah, until the next time,' which was fair enough, perhaps, but it didn't help the pain. Sometimes I moaned about this passive disregard to other friends, many of whom professed to having a similar relationship in their own lives – a sister, friend or lover who did all the talking and none of the listening, who spoke expansively about their own experiences but showed no interest in anyone else's. The glazed expression, the nibbling of cuticles and the selective deafness were all part of a subtle undermining – with Gemma, it was a practised posture – but I was learning to get round it. Besides, I was more put out by something else: Gemma had become a bore. With only one interest, one topic of conversation – this man, to whom none of her Dublin friends could relate and in whom we had absolutely no interest – she became detached from the lives the rest of us were living. I tried to hang in there, out of loyalty or maybe even habit, but, like her other friends, I was impatient for her to move on and give us all a break.

Instead she got worse. With her finals only months away, when her thesis and exams should have preoccupied her, she was unable to work, convinced once again that she was receiving subtle signals. Linklater had sought her out unnecessarily, she would write to me, had held her eye during a lecture or spent three hours discussing her dissertation. Being around him was no longer enough. Being in his office, alone and in such close proximity, had become painful, and as those crucial months passed, she admitted that she feared she would lose control.

Unfortunately for both of them, she did.

At an end-of-year party in a student house, Gemma cornered Linklater on the staircase, determined to test him. They talked for two hours. Her work rate had fallen away so dramatically that he urged her to get stuck in before her exams. His personal interest destroyed any restraint she might have had left. In a low-cut excuse for a dress, she pushed towards him every time someone passed them on the stairs, her thighs pressing against his leg, her breasts against his arm. She knew she was getting to him. When he went to fetch drinks from the kitchen, he was detained by a rowdy crowd of students who tried to force him to share their joint. Music boomed. He had taken off his jacket. Gemma watched the back of his head through the banisters.

When he started making moves to go, she left the house ahead of him so that he came out to find her standing on the pavement, wondering about a taxi.

'I'll drop you back,' he said. 'My car's around the corner.'

It was after one o'clock. There were a few stragglers on the street. Gemma leaned against the car. Linklater threw his jacket on to the roof and shuffled around in his pockets for the keys. When he leaned forward to unlock the door, she kissed him.

He struggled to disengage, but she was, by her own admission, as firmly attached to his mouth as a clam to a rock, and when he finally pushed himself away from her, he tripped on the pavement and fell into a group of passing youths. Seizing upon this as provocation, they knocked him to the ground and laid in without mercy.

Gemma couldn't even scream. Boots. Fists. Knees. Grunts of pain mingled with grunts of intent until, their anger spent, the thugs drew away, gurgling with aggression. Linklater lay on the ground, curled up like a hedgehog without spikes. One of the youths shoved Gemma, telling her to run on home, but as they moved along, Linklater was heard to mumble, 'Fuckers.'

They resumed the attack. Gemma stumbled towards the main street to wave down a car, but the sound of a bottle smashing made her turn and she heard such a groan that she was shocked into stillness.

The gang dispersed. In the dim glow of street-lights, Gemma saw the hump on the ground that was Linklater and a broken beer bottle standing proud, lodged in his flesh like a stake in the sand.

11

The room was still; Theo too. In the street below, someone was over-revving an engine.

'I saw the scar,' Theo said, after a moment, 'at the *hammam*.'

'Yeah, it's . . . It brings it home.'

He nodded. 'What a way for it to end, her little crush.'

'But it didn't end there. I wish it had.'

Theo swung his legs off the bed. 'We need some tea.'

He came back with a tin tray, two glasses and a small copper kettle of tea. 'So,' he said.

'Well, after giving her statement to the police that morning – Christian had been rushed to hospital – Gemma packed her bags and went home. She never went back to college. Nothing could persuade her to take her exams. Even when we heard later that Linklater had recovered, it didn't help. I rushed in, of course. I mean, I was shocked. It had all been very silly and tedious, but when she came home totally shattered, her friends rowed in. We sat on the end of her bed, trying to cheer her up, and a couple of her brothers were supportive, but her parents were a dead loss. They were very hands-off types. They only ever dealt with practicalities. I'd always quite liked them – they were head-cases, especially her mother – but, my God, when that happened, they went way down in my estimation. Once they'd established that Linklater was all right, they moved right along. He was the only victim as far as they were concerned, and Gemma just had to brush herself down and get on. Her father was such a high achiever that having his daughter drop out of college was devastating, and he never got off Gemma's case about it. Within a week her mother was accusing her of wallowing. They just didn't seem to understand that she was traumatized — she'd just seen someone stabbed right in front of her eyes, for God's sake! I mean, anyone else would have made sure she had counselling or something, but they did nothing. I really felt for her. Her degree was gone, her career was over before it began, and this guy she fancied had been mangled . . .'

Theo shook his head, sipped his tea.

'Anyway, she brooded for a year, sitting at home under a pall of guilt. It was her way of hanging on to Linklater, I think. As long as she focused on those grisly events, she didn't have to let him go, quite. Under pressure from her father, she eventually got a job, but there were no parties or boyfriends, just work and television. The cheerful, daring person I'd always known was well and truly buried, and I really missed her. The only blessing was that she had finally stopped talking about Linklater. We were relieved. Even though it had come to such a horrible end, it had at least come to an end.

'And then the bugger turned up on television.'

About two and a half years after the attack, we were in my flat one evening, surfing between television channels, when Gemma suddenly shrieked, 'Go back!' I flipped back a channel and there he was: the Blessed Dr Linklater, doing his thing, surrounded by street children in Kathmandu. Gemma threw herself towards the screen, repeating, 'I don't believe it. I don't believe it!'

Nor could I. She, I, *we*, could not escape him, and he had absolutely no idea.

For a few weeks it seemed as if the whole thing was starting up again but, in fact, that was the very point at which Gemma shrugged off all the maudlin behaviour she had been indulging in. Linklater himself proved to be the cure. The programmes gave her something to look forward to and something to feel good about afterwards. She was still living at home then, so she used to come round to my flat every Monday night with an Indian takeaway and a bottle of wine, and she'd wilt in front of the television while the programmes were aired. I should probably have tried to dissuade her – prevented her, even – from watching Linklater, but I did no more than warn her about getting hooked in again. Most of our friends wouldn't have been able to stomach this slavering over someone who had ended up with a bottle in his back because she had lost the run of herself, but it didn't bother Gemma. After every programme she'd spend hours mooning over the video recordings, and as the weeks passed, her good mood stretched into Tuesdays, and then into Wednesdays and Thursdays, until she was in a good humour all week. My old pal began to reappear, zany and unpredictable, maybe, but recognizable. Our Monday nights together became sacrosanct, and it was like turning back the years – pre-Durham, pre-Yemen, pre-Bill even – and we'd have fits of giggles, often at Linklater's expense, but seeing him well and successful restored Gemma. She slithered out from under that gloomy guilt and re-established her sense of herself. When the series ended, she went back out and took on the world, leaving me like a mother on the doorstep, waving a hanky at her back.

After she started her wonderful, busy and demanding job in the entertainment industry, we didn't see that much of each other. I might have been miffed, had I not been so busy myself at the gallery, where I was thriving in the glow of Shoukria's mentoring. The distance between me and the Colberts did me no harm at all. I met Gemma for lunch once every few months and sat eating quietly while she blathered on about this junket to Thailand or that conference in Turin, and then, oh, she had to dash back to work but we'd talk about me next time . . . I had become wary, and more detached. Unease about events in Durham had never quite left me and the one-way traffic was tedious. And yet whenever Linklater reappeared on our screens, Gemma reappeared on my doorstep, all cheeky and bubbling over with warmth and wine and declarations about how no one else really understood the Linklater thing. I didn't mind. It was fun. I had come to understand that at some point I had made an unconscious trade-off: Gemma was self-absorbed, perhaps, but she was also entertaining and good for a laugh, and that was often enough for me. That was what I got out of it. I liked her, and we went back a long way, so I enjoyed falling into our autumnal Linklater routine of cushions on the floor and critical analysis. We judged his haircut, his diction, his commentary, his earnestness. I liked to knock him, to tease her, and would never have admitted to her that he was fairly easy on the eye. When each series ended, we reverted to meeting for lunch, and it went on like that for four years until one autumn Linklater failed to return.

By then I was living with the man who was pressing me to marry him. Gemma decreed that marriage and babies would be just my thing. Her long-standing perception of me as tame and domestic had never faltered – I was expected to stay resolutely on the ground, rocking no boats and making no waves. Undermined by my failure to get to grips with Yemen, I suspected she was right, so I became engaged, and then quite swiftly disengaged, and lost my flatmate in the process. Before I had even decided what to do with the engagement ring, Gemma had moved in with me. Always partial to my sunny flat, she lost no time in occupying the spare room, which was a good thing because I had a stiff mortgage to pay off.

My close friend Tess was alarmed when she heard about my new flatmate. There would be partying and noise, she predicted, and Gemma would leech off me, suck me dry with one drama after another. She was right about that – Gemma frequently wore me down with her all-consuming dramas, but as long as we didn't try to be best friends or live each other's lives, the arrangement worked. She was a good tenant. She was clean, well-off, and while she was as unpredictable and endearing as a panicked mouse, she was never there long enough to get on my nerves. There were business trips and opening nights, clubbing and holidays, and few girlie moments in between. She took men like vitamins, popping them here and there, and although she never fell in love, the Linklater thing that had consumed her for so long was well and truly forgotten.

'I swear,' I said to Theo, 'when I saw that man sitting in Cairo airport, I honestly believed I was looking at the past.'

'You know,' he said, deadpan, 'I think maybe you were wrong.'

'Astute, Theo. Very astute.'

We went to Wadi Dahr, the museum, the *suq*. Gemma had no interest. She wanted only to get to Christian. I wanted only to stop her. The wildness and unpredictability I had once envied now perturbed me. It was more consuming than I had realized, as was this endless obsession, and I was seriously disenchanted. Resentment, in the form of old, sometimes very old, grievances, churned in my head. A can of worms had been opened, but lingering loyalty kept trying to close it. She had spoilt my party, but that didn't mean I wanted to see her hurt.

My own exuberant affair with Christian had always been a boil on my conscience and now it was festering. The matter could be dealt with simply: I would tell Gemma about it and she would leave the country, humiliated, and our friendship would be over. If she hadn't followed me to Sana'a I would certainly have told her, eventually, back in Dublin, but I would have done so out of cowardice, not fairness, because one way or another I would have been found out. One always is. But circumstance had outplayed me. I no longer had the option of handling this on my terms, and coming clean when she had travelled so far seemed harsh even to Theo. Now, here, there was no gentle way to do it.

I longed to discuss it with Nooria, but it was not appropriate to spread Gemma's feelings about like a blanket for us all to sit on, so I said nothing when we met up at Bab al-Yemen that Wednesday afternoon. We had an appointment with Antelak al-Shami, an artist who had invited me to visit her atelier. The building was empty when she let us in. There was a gallery on the ground floor and studios on each of the floors above.

I stepped into her studio. Her work was bright, geometric. Sunlight poured through timber-framed windows and above them the semi-circular fanlights threw green, blue and red beams on to the paintings, like miniature spotlights. It seemed an exquisite environment for an artist to work in. In another studio, the paintings were so true to life that it seemed as if we could step right into that alleyway or zone into that desert where tumbleweed was hurtling along in the wind. On the third floor, another woman's work was quite violent. One painting depicted something that looked like a foetus with a bleeding heart; another looked like a womb exploding. A woman's frustration.

'Do you come here every day?' I asked Antelak.

'Oh, no, only when I have time. I also teach, and I have two children.'

We sat then, the three of us, with our cans of lemonade, and chatted about love, marriage, mothers. Nooria talked about her ex-husband. 'He is a good man, and we were best friends when we were children, but when we married he was more like a brother than a husband. So he went to America to study and never came back, which made it easy for me to divorce him. It was what we both wanted.'

'Would you marry again?'

She shrugged. 'I like my work too much. And not many men would accept my lifestyle. I like to be free in what I do.'

'Ah, yes,' said Antelak, 'and then there are children and mothers-in-law . . .'

'But how do you manage, Antelak?' I asked. 'Where do you find the time for everything?'

'There is never enough time,' she said languidly. 'My mother helps.' She pulled pins from her headscarf and held them in her mouth while she lifted the scarf and shook her head. Her movements were fluid, practised. She pulled the fabric beneath her chin and pinned it back into place.

God bless mothers, I thought. For it was mothers, it seemed, who were behind these high achievers, minding their children, their homes, and making their own contribution now, in spite of being uneducated themselves. I looked at the paintings again. 'My boss would love to see these. She'd love to exhibit you. I'll talk to her about it when I get home.'

After Nooria and Antelak returned to work, I caught a mini-bus back to al-Qa Square and reached the only conclusion I could. Allowing Gemma to hurry out to Marib would be too cruel and in any case was beyond me. Time had come to speak up, whatever the consequences.

'So you like it here this time?' she asked, when I got home and we had taken our tea out to the roof.

'Oh, yes.'

'Looks like Yemen has a hand in both our fates,' she said, 'not just yours. Or maybe not yours at all. Maybe you were drawn here because of me.'

'Honestly, Gem, Linklater brings out the worst in you. Next thing you'll be consulting the pebbles on the street.'

'But you've met him now, you know him. You can see what I've been dealing with, can't you?'

'Yes, but –'

'So give me one good reason why I should let it go just when it's all coming together?'

'Who says it's coming together? It could fall further apart! You might be disappointed. He might not –'

'Fancy me?' An unpleasant smirk sat on her lips, and a rustle of foreboding hurried across my chest. 'Yes, well,' she said. 'That's where you might be wrong.'

I looked down the street, hoping to see Theo drive up, but there was no stopping this.

'There's something I didn't tell you,' she went on, 'way back when. That night. The night of the stabbing. The thing is . . . when I kissed Christian, he kissed me back. He responded. Big time. We . . . Things happened, you know? That's why he pulled away so violently. It wasn't to get me off him, it was to get himself off *me*. When his conscience caught up with him, he recoiled like a spring and barged into those guys.'

The sip of tea I had taken stopped in my throat. It wouldn't go up or down.

'I couldn't tell you at the time, obviously,' said Gemma. 'If it had got out, his reputation would have been shot.'

I swallowed, finally. 'You've come all this way,' I managed, 'on the basis of a drunken kiss?'

'Oh, it was rather more than a drunken kiss,' she said. 'That's why I'm here.'

The following day, laden with that amalgam of truths and half-truths, evasions and lies, we set off for Marib with Nooria, Theo and Fadhl – and the escort, of course, which we picked up outside Sana'a and which would take us most of the way to Marib. Heavily armed policemen stood in the back of their Toyota pickup, keeping their balance, as the dust spat up at them from beneath the wheels.

'What a job,' I said.

'I hate this,' said Theo. 'All these guns. It isn't necessary. I travel around all the time and have no problems.'

'We want to reassure our tourists,' said Fadhl.

'I am reassured,' I said.

We left the Sana'a basin, passing vineyards and groves, and started climbing. Long-held dreams were trying to come true, but they were thwarted. Being around Gemma was fraught with discomfort, like walking on a blister. I could never have anticipated this onslaught of determination on her part and, because of it, the ducking and diving had to continue. It would require total concentration in every conversation we had but, with assiduous care on my part, she need never know about what had happened in Sana'a. Shocked by her revelation – and silenced by it – I remained tied like a tight spool of thread round my own deception. My hand had been forced also. I would now have to come clean with Christian as well.

As we wove through the mountains, the jeep pulled round hairpin bends and Yemen fell away to the side. My mind fell away too. Everything Christian had told me had dropped into shade. His one infatuation with a colleague – unconsummated. Really? His wife falling in love with someone else – not so surprising, perhaps, if he was the sort of husband to shag a student in a street. From what I could understand, that was what had taken place. Gemma had implied it, and I hadn't had the stomach to pin her down, to anchor her insinuation in truth, because I didn't really want to know, didn't want to be forced to contend with my own jealousies. Still, I had to wonder – would he truly have jeopardized his career and his marriage for a rushed fuck?

On the rim of a bend, I asked Fadhl for a photo stop. He beeped to alert the other vehicle and we pulled in. I got out, camera in hand, Theo beside me and Yemen all around. Everything loomed over me, graceful and patient. The solitary towers on the pinnacles, the mountains, even Theo. Where I had once been intimidated by this landscape, it seemed now to have eight arms to hold me. While I was all disarray, it was solid and still. Like a cat, sure of its charms, comforting if I would only reach out. There was arrogance in the way this country looked at me, from high windows in Sana'a, from the peaks of Jabal Nuqum and from the dwellings in these hills. No other country watches as Yemen does.

'What is it about place?' I asked Theo. 'Why do certain people feel a deep connection to a particular place? It's almost like the chemistry between lovers.'

'Maybe it dates from a previous life.'

'Yeah, and maybe I'm the Queen of Sheba.'

'I'm serious.'

'I have a Belgian friend who feels this way about Ireland. It holds her soul, she says, and there's nothing she can do about it except return whenever possible.'

'Come on,' Gemma called from the car. She hadn't even got out. We were on two entirely different journeys. I only wished we weren't making them in the same vehicle.

Theo glanced at her. 'How long did you say it's been since all that happened?'

'Seven years.'

'How do you think he'll take it – seeing her again?'

'The way she tells it, he'll be ecstatic.'

Resentment gnawed at me. When Theo had persuaded me to make this trip, I had allowed myself to become excited at the prospect of being with Christian again. I had fantasized about surprising him at his dig – appearing from nowhere and throwing my arms round him – doing the one thing, in short, he did not expect of me. It had been easy, and sweet, to imagine the delight it would give him, for there could be little harm in extending our affair by a few lovely days, especially on such an adventure. Even if our subsequent separation proved to be harder than the first, it would surely be worth it.

All of this had been taken away: the pleasant anticipation, the filmic reunion, the extraordinary journey in the company of easy friends and all of its consequences. Having lost it, I was forced to accept how very much I had wanted it.

After crossing Naqil al-Farda, we began dropping towards the edges of the desert – abrupt at first, but with such views that I made myself car-sick turning my head this way and that. The descent crossed semi-desert swathes of rocky land, with occasional pyramids of black, volcanic rocks. Every now and then we crossed a dried-out wadi.

'I would never have made a travel writer,' I said to Nooria. 'I don't have the botany for it. I have no idea what those trees are.'

'Acacia, I think.'

'But *those*,' I said, pointing at the local fauna, 'are goats!'

She laughed.

I squeezed her hand. 'I'm so glad you've come – and flattered, in view of the fact that you rarely take holidays.'

'Well . . . I have never seen Marib, or even Shibam, so if you have come all the way from Ireland, I can make an effort also.'

We came into Marib at about midday. There was

nothing much to commend the new town so we drove straight through it and, as we came out the other side, the old Marib appeared on a rise on the horizon. It was far hotter down there, but in Fadhl's Land Cruiser the air-conditioning did its work. Nooria, wedged between me and Gemma, knew herself to be the wall that stood between two people who had their backs to each other. Theo rang Christian, pretending to be in Sana'a, and asked him how he was, and where he was. He was at the site, near the Awwam temple.

My guts churned. Christian would presumably be pleased to see me, but the surprise would be a two-headed spear. Gemma looked ill with trepidation and no longer questioned my dark mood, for she had too much to contend with in the chaos of her own head. They were about to meet on equal terms for the first time, with no lecturer/student ethic barring the way, and no marriage either.

Old Marib was yet another sight that held the eye, and so were the five and a half pillars of Arsh Bilqis, shooting towards the clear blue sky, as we drove past them on our way to the Awwam temple. There, eight pillars rose magnificently out of a dip in the sand behind the huge oval site. The cemetery was about a hundred metres south-west of the remains of the temple. We pulled up beside several Land Cruisers and stepped into the heat. There was activity – kids, soldiers, tribesmen – but hardly any sound.

Gemma shaded her eyes. 'Where is he?'

A hot wind buffeted us. 'Over there somewhere.' Theo pointed towards a small group and headed towards them. A figure suddenly emerged from the ground – Christian – and came bounding towards us. Theo shook his hand enthusiastically, as if to slow him as he hurtled in my direction, but Christian hurried towards me, smiling broadly. 'What the . . . ? Where did you people spring from?'

With a firm grip on his arms, I disguised the hug as casual and waved towards Gemma, as if it were she who was the surprise, but he turned towards the others as they came round the front of the jeep. 'Nooria, lovely to see you. Fadhl!'

I expected Gemma to rush and gush, but she stood behind me, dumbstruck.

There was much back-patting and many garrulous greetings before Christian finally acknowledged Gemma with a polite nod, then turned to me. 'When did you hatch this little plan?'

He hadn't recognized her.

'Oh, blame Theo. He misses you so.'

'You persuaded her, Theo! Good work.'

'And Gemma has just come out from Dublin,' I said. She stepped forward.

'Hello.' He shook her hand with friendly disinterest, saying to Theo, 'So did you have much hassle with the permits?' He just wasn't taking her in. She was wearing a hat and sunglasses, and no longer had the long straight hair of her twenties, but surely the name . . .

'You remember Gemma, don't you?' I said. 'Gemma Colbert, from Durham.'

His hopping about jarred to a halt. He looked at her

again. Emotions rolled up his face like items on a receipt: shock, confusion and something else.

She took off her sunglasses. 'Dr Linklater.'

I felt for him, a little. He had rushed over, thrilled to see me, and instead had come face to face with a former student whom he had once fucked up against a car, apparently.

'So how are things going?' Theo asked.

Christian was stunned. 'What? Oh, fine, yes.' He looked back at Gemma, as though she might be a mirage.

'We haff come to take you away,' said Theo, exaggerating his own accent.

'Hmm?'

'We're taking you to Shibam. We leave early tomorrow. You can drive back in a couple of days.'

'Can you get away?' I asked.

'Um . . . yes, I suppose so.'

Theo slapped him on the back. 'Good! Now show me what you're doing here.' He dragged Christian along in his own gushing enthusiasm, pointing here and there, asking stupid questions.

'Like being punched in the gut,' Gemma said quietly.

'What did you expect? A welcome party?'

'Something,' she said. 'I expected something.'

Nooria heard this, leaning against the jeep fanning herself. Fadhl was talking to some men who were crouched in a circle on the ground.

'You were right,' said Gemma. 'This was a terrible thing to do.'

We stood in the blistering sun. Christian kept turning

towards us, but I couldn't tell if he was looking at me or at her. When they came back, Theo took drinks from the cold box.

Christian was still dazed, perplexed at having his past fly out at him from the sands. He stared at her. 'What brings you to Yemen?'

'Vivien. I came to join her.'

He frowned. 'You know each other?'

'Yeah,' she said, 'since school. We share a flat. Well, I live in *her* flat.'

He looked at me, uncomprehending.

'Here.' Theo handed round mini-cans of cold drinks, but Gemma took him aside and said quietly, 'I need a loo.'

'I'll take you to the hotel.' He turned to the rest of us. 'Shall we get something to eat?'

Tactfully Nooria and Fadhl jumped into the jeep. Gemma sat in the front, gripping her stomach, scarcely aware that I was staying behind.

There was no warm hug after they drove off. We stood in the dust churned up by the wheels, Christian staring after them. A tear of sweat slid down the side of his face. He was gone from me. Gone back to that pavement probably. To the smash of that bottle. Or perhaps to the side of the car and the little, little dress.

The image held me in its grip. His hand on her leg, his body pressing into her. She had told me just enough to paint an all-too-vivid picture. I scorned myself for having felt so guilty about being with him because it was everything Gemma had once wanted but never had. Never had? So I had thought . . . Guilt is a wasted state.

Christian went to speak to Edda, who was working in an opened passage in the ground, then called to a young man, who followed him over and climbed into the Land Cruiser behind me. His name was Ahmad and, as I would soon discover, he had become Christian's shadow. Fifty yards down the road, Christian slammed on the brakes. Looking out over the steering-wheel, he knocked the knuckle of his index finger against his teeth. 'Where did she come from?' he muttered 'Where the hell did she come from?'

I touched his wrist. He swung round. 'And you. Where do you come into this?'

'At the beginning.'

'You knew she'd been my student?'

I nodded.

He yanked off his sunglasses. 'And you know what happened?'

'If you mean the assault, yes.'

'But you asked me about it.'

'And you lied.'

'That was my prerogative!'

Ahmad, sitting behind us, sighed patiently.

Christian looked at me for a long time. 'Why didn't you tell me you knew one of my students? Especially *that* particular student.'

'I didn't think you'd want to be reminded.'

'Well,' he said, letting off the handbrake, 'I've been reminded now.'

The Bilqis Hotel had been built to house foreign oil workers and in the hope, no doubt, that one day tourist throngs would come to view the antiquities, but that was before the kidnap attempt down south in '98, when four tourists had died, and the more recent disaster far away, on September the eleventh, so the hotel was almost empty. It was cool and spacious; after checking in to our rooms, we gathered on the circle of sofas in a sunken seating area in the lobby where staff delighted in seeing to our every need.

'How is it?' Theo asked Christian. 'Hard work?'

'The usual,' said Christian. 'We start at six, play in the sand until two, crash for a few hours and then I get down to my real job of work: chewing the fat with the Ashraf.'

'You mean chewing the *qat*, no?' said Nooria.

'That too.'

'You call this work?' said Theo.

'It's as much work as pushing buttons on that mobile phone of yours.'

'It isn't a phone. It's a Global Positioning System.'

We had lunch on the terrace beside the pool, but Gemma missed most of the meal. Her loose bowels were entirely emotional, and I watched Christian deal with the way she kept coming and going, and coming again like a whip. He was thrown. I no longer had to worry that he might squeeze my knee or make some tender gesture that would alert Gemma. My connection to her, and my failure to reveal it, had cleaned me off the slate.

Deceit has its own agenda. It takes you where you had no plan to go.

That afternoon, Christian and Ahmad joined us when

we became tourists. We began with old Marib, a medieval town built on the site of the ancient capital of the Sabaean kingdom, a huddle of shattered buildings that looked from a distance like a set of broken lower teeth, perched on an unlikely mound, not quite a hill. It had once been the centre of a vibrant civilization, a busy commercial town at the heart of the frankincense trail.

'This was the largest ancient city in southern Arabia, and it was inhabited until the nineteen sixties,' said Fadhl. 'But it was used as a base during the civil war and was bombed. It's deserted now, except for some families and their animals.'

We wandered, as in a ghost town, clambering through the disarray. It was, indeed, a bomb site. The tumbling mud houses looked like chocolate sculptures that had been partially melted by the sun. Rubble crawled up the remaining walls. Windows were like odd quirks on old faces, the great gaps of doorways like jaws dropping in dismay. Free-standing walls tilted at an angle, ready to tumble at the slightest provocation from the elements. Goats hiccuped and children giggled. A teenage girl in a long blue dress and purple scarf made her way down a rock-strewn alleyway, carrying a small can on her head. It was only the size of a can of baked beans, but she walked very carefully, her hand raised, ready to catch it. As I watched, she lost her footing and the can almost fell, but she caught herself in time, then looked up to make sure no one had seen her slip. Our eyes met. She looked down.

Christian kept close to Nooria and Theo, as if we Irishwomen were a threat to his equilibrium. In one of the more solid houses, we climbed a disintegrating staircase to the top, where the view reminded me that we were on the border of the Empty Quarter. Thanks to Gemma, I needed to be reminded. I looked west, searching for my other self. There was no caravan trudging across the horizon, no shadows that might have been me, living my Freya Stark life. I said quietly to Theo, 'Don't let me forget. With all this going on, don't let me forget why I'm here.'

We moved on. We had given ourselves only one afternoon for several sites, each of which warranted far greater attention, but it was always a relief to crawl back into the air-conditioning and cool down before throwing ourselves again into the furnace. Our next stop was Arsh Bilqis, the Throne of the Queen of Sheba, although evidence had yet to be found to prove it had had anything to do with her. The five and a half pillars had become a national symbol, and since the site had been fully excavated, there should have been the sound of clicking in the air and the ring of appreciative voices all around, but a dispute with a *shaykh* and local tensions ensured that one of the great finds of antiquity lay mostly unseen, the sands the only monitor of its survival. 'I like this,' I said to Nooria. 'I like when the West can't get a foothold.'

'Not good for Yemen, though.'

'No, but it gives me perverse pleasure that this belongs to the desert and not to Fuji Film.'

We stood in the forecourt of the temple. 'There are actually four temples superimposed here,' said Christian, who had adopted lecture mode and led us about like a band of students. 'The remains of the other three are buried under the podium of the last one.'

'How old is it?' I asked.

'It was probably built during the tenth century BC, possibly earlier.'

We walked towards the podium on which stood the monoliths.

'It was a magnificent complex,' said Christian, 'devoted to the god Almaqah, patron of the Sabaeans. It was more than fifteen metres high.'

He showed us where there had been workshops, a well, stores, but the pillars offered the beauty, the tenacity, of a work of art, and turning our backs on them seemed disrespectful.

'They are masterpieces of engineering,' Christian went on, 'eight point two metres high, the highest monolithic pillars in this part of the world, and they're constructed with such precision that even earthquakes haven't been able to topple them.'

'But these are ugly,' said Theo, pointing at steel girders at the base of each column.

'They are there to make sure earthquakes will not make them fall,' said Fadhl.

'Practical,' said Christian, 'but unsightly.'

'Imagine if they did this in the Nile valley,' said Theo. 'The peristyle hall in Karnak would look very peculiar.'

The others wandered off, but Nooria stared up at the podium. 'I can see her,' she said, 'coming along here, surrounded by her priests and her people.'

'The Queen of Sheba?'

'Bilqis, yes.'

I tried to imagine it, but failed. 'I'm no good at ruins. I can't project myself into the past and see this the way it must have been. What moves me more is what it has become.'

'You have no imagination,' she scoffed.

As the others spread out, I walked back to the monumental staircase and up to one of the pillars. Putting my feet on the clumsy girder, I leaned back and closed my eyes. The stone was hot on my back. Heat makes for good silence. It loses words, thoughts. It monopolizes the brain so that all energy is focused on dealing with the aim of the sun. You wear the heat. You cannot take it off. Wherever you go, it moves with you like a piece of unwanted clothing. It owns you, and as the day wears on it tightens its grip.

When I opened my eyes, Christian was leaning, with one hand against another pillar, watching me. Ahmad sat on the step in front of us, a little boy at his elbow.

'Well,' said Christian slowly, 'aren't you just so full of surprises?'

'I had no idea she was coming.'

'Is that so?'

'She just turned up.'

'I'll bet.'

'Christian —'

'Flatmates, she said? *Room*ies?'

The stinging sarcasm hit its target. I had no defence to make. I had owed him this much at least: to reveal the unlikely tangle in our otherwise separate lives.

Roomies. No doubt he imagined we were bosom buddies, sharing our secrets in our cosy flat over wine and chocolate, but it was no longer so. I was still fond of Gemma, much as I would always have feelings for her brother, and we sometimes still had an old-time giggle, but it was not the friendship it had been. Durham – and the way in which she had helped herself to her married tutor – had put an end to that.

She was at the other end of the forecourt. 'It must be odd,' I said quietly, 'seeing her again.'

'It's rough. Very rough.'

'The attack?'

He kicked the girder. 'And the other stuff.'

'Other stuff?'

'What's going on, Vivien? You've both of you brought yourselves out here – for what?' He motioned towards Gemma. 'What does she want? What do *you* want, that you've come hurtling across the mountains with your jolly Dutchman?'

'I want to see Shibam, as you very well know, and Gemma wants to make her peace with you. She blames herself.'

He snorted. 'Not without reason.'

I gaped. 'You don't hold her responsible, surely?'

'Was it someone else's fault?'

'You cannot blame her for the actions of a gang of thugs!'

'Why not?'

'You . . . How can you be so –'

'Look, I admire your loyalty,' he said, 'but frankly you would've done her – and me – more favours by putting the brakes on her back then.'

'How the hell could I have done that? I wasn't even

there,' I hissed, struggling to keep my voice down, but he had hit a raw nerve. I *should* have tried harder to restrain Gemma, to pull her off his back. Had I done so, she would be an anthropologist now and he would be an anthropologist with two kidneys. '*You*'re the one who should have put the brakes on her.'

He looked away.

'She did something stupid – granted,' I said, 'but she has never stopped beating herself up over it, so give her a break. She acted on impulse –'

'She compromised me and very nearly compromised my career!'

'The way I heard it, you did a fair amount of compromising yourself.'

His shoulders tensed. Gemma was watching us. I walked down the steps and went towards her.

'He doesn't seem very happy to see her,' Theo muttered, as we made our way to the cars.

'He's angry with her. Really furious. After all these years. What does that tell you?'

'I don't know. What does it tell me?'

'That he has a guilty conscience – a *very* guilty conscience – which means it must be true, what she implied.'

'You should ask him.'

'I will.'

We drove back to the Awwam temple, once southern Arabia's most spectacular shrine. The eight pillars there, though less grand than those at Arsh Bilqis, were somehow more beautiful. The sand made the difference.

The pillars were not fully excavated and emerged from the ground like the rigging of a ship sunk in shallow waters.

'It was first excavated in 1951 by Wendell Phillips,' said Christian, 'an American archaeologist – the original Indiana Jones, they say – but the tribes got agitated so he had to scarper. He left most of his equipment behind.'

'And then the sand came back,' said Theo

'Yeah, the place was buried again. Wendell never returned, but his sister has recently been excavating here. She's determined to prove the existence of Sheba.'

'God,' Gemma muttered to me, 'he really is in teacher mode.' I sniggered, and suddenly we were back at school again, giggling at the back of class. We whispered to each other behind our hands, resurrecting private jokes, while Christian droned on. The giddiness was refreshing, *cooling*. The rigidity in my back loosened, but that was the Gemma Effect. She had an unerring ability to pull me this way and that, between ire and affection, and she had always been able to make me laugh. The intimacy of laughter, my mother believes, is the breastplate of every friendship.

The huge oval precinct was like a football pitch carpeted with sand. We walked across it. Christian stomped on the ground with his boot. 'Under all this, geophysicists have detected half a dozen man-made structures, but millions of tonnes of sand will have to be shifted before we can find out what they are.'

'Buried treasure!' said Theo.

'The central piece is a well, they believe.'

I walked back to the entrance alone. Behind the pillars, eight lines of shade lay across a low rise. I took refuge in one of these narrow shadows. It seemed inevitable that one day this place would be overrun, first by archaeologists and geophysicists and physical anthropologists, and when they had neatly polished it off, the tourist hordes would come. The tribes would relent, security would cease to be an issue, and somebody like me would walk about, hearing Sabaean history called out in four different languages, but they would be unable to stand and absorb the silence of the place, as I could.

Mounds of sand hugged the base of these spines, and it made me think of God. It was as if He had swept out the desert, leaving the sand-dunes clean and uncluttered, but littering Marib with its surplus rocks and detritus.

Christian's enthusiasm bubbled up in the necropolis where his team was working. We climbed down into the open-air passages, where he showed us engraved masks – images of the deceased – set into bricks outside tombs. 'Every echelon of Sabaean society is represented here – mass graves for commoners, tombs for the upper classes, mausoleums for the ruling families.'

'What's this got to do with *abasiyya*?' I asked.

'*Asabiyya*. Well, for one thing, the practice of multiple burials suggests that the individual was less important than the collective.' He crouched and wiped a low wall to show us inscriptions. Gemma leaned over him, apparently fascinated, though she had as much interest in anthropology now as in dead sheep. 'The script is amazing,' he said. 'At one time, it was written both left to right *and* right to left, alternately, but then they settled on right to left, like Arabic. And there are often two characters for one of ours. This fork represents an H.'

As we went back up the steps, a mini-tornado of sand came whirling towards us. I pulled my scarf over my face, closed my eyes and held my breath. It hurried along, throwing dust at us like a lorry spewing water on pedestrians, then dropped to the ground and disappeared. We unfurled like snails coming out of shells, gasping and rubbing our eyes.

'I hate those things,' said Theo, pulling off his glasses.

'We call them "jinn",' Fadhl said to Gemma.

'The Queen of Sheba was born of a jinn,' said Nooria.

'Like a genie coming out of a bottle and going back in again,' I said.

Christian wiped his hands. 'Like a genie,' he repeated.

Debilitated by the stinging sun, we dispersed, the way people do in heat, as if proximity to others exacerbates it. Christian was on his hunkers showing Fadhl another inscription. Theo was with Nooria, Gemma alone. This is a tough way to address your demons, I thought, watching her, standing here in this hard place.

Theo, who was enjoying the role of the over-enthusiastic tour leader who has to keep his charges moving swiftly along, called us back to the cars and we headed out to the old Marib dam. The remains stretched across a dry watercourse, Wadi Dhana.

'For centuries, this dam irrigated lands that fed up to fifty thousand people,' said Fadhl. 'In the Qur'an this area is referred to as the Two Paradises, because the lands on either side of the dam were so rich.'

'It was twice the size of the Hoover Dam in Colorado,' said Christian.

'What happened to it?' Gemma asked.

'The final collapse happened just before Islam emerged,' he said. 'The area dried up, returned to desert, and the people scattered.'

'Mice brought it down,' said Theo.

'Rats!' said Fadhl, smiling at me.

'Really?'

'You see,' he said, 'there was a prophecy that the dam would be destroyed by a giant rat so the Sabaeans put cats on every gate. But a huge red rat with iron teeth and claws killed the cats and started eating away at the foundations until the whole thing fell down.'

Christian smiled for the first time since we had arrived.

'So was it rats or mice or history?' I asked.

'An amalgam of factors, most likely,' said Christian. 'A build-up of silt, political unrest, economics – and another suspect is global warming.'

'Global warming?'

'Yeah. A volcano in Java erupted in the sixth century AD and ejected all sorts of crap into the atmosphere, which changed the climate. Here there would have been a long drought followed by intense flooding, under pressure of which the dam would have been blown out. Whatever it was, it changed this area for ever.'

Gemma ran her palm along the smooth brick wall. 'Just think,' she said to me, 'thousands of years ago someone touched these same bricks. I wonder who they were and who they loved and what they had for dinner that night.'

'Is your anthropological self trying to get out?' I asked quietly.

'Not really. University's a fog to me now. Thanks to him.' She put her hands on her hips and looked towards Christian. 'This is so weird. The heat, the sites, Christian doing his thing . . . It's like Jordan all over again. And the worst of it is that I still want to get under his skin . . . and into those clothes.'

You and me both.

After swimming at the hotel, we gathered in the lobby. Gemma had regrouped and the woman I knew emerged, smart, witty, dangerous – and beautiful, of course, with shiny straight hair falling to her shoulders, bright eyes and pale skin. It was all very familiar to me: the poise and posture; the way she cleared her throat while choosing her words; the way she used her lips – slightly open, lightly closed, pursed, licked, or locked in a confident semi-smile. In this subtle manner, I had regularly seen her destroy the opposition and get the man she wanted, but now my perspective had changed. *I* had become the opposition. The only obstacle Gemma was aware of, however, was Christian himself, and she had the means to make him unravel.

He took us to the house where he was staying. What it lacked in facilities the family made up for in their welcome. The landlady, Fatima, a sturdy woman swathed in garments, fussed over Christian as though he were her only son. She hurried us into the *mafraj*, where her daughters brought us tea. The rug was threadbare, the cushions dusty. 'Like good old-fashioned lodgings,' Christian said, sitting cross-legged with Gemma tight beside him.

A number of young men stood around the doorway. They spoke some German, some English, even a smidgen of French, so our conversation was haphazard but extraordinary. These boys had scarcely ever left Marib and yet here, in their country, they spoke to us in bits and pieces of other languages.

Gemma twittered a little too much. Don't gush, I thought, paradoxically wanting her to come across as alluring and bright, not bloody-minded and silly, but she was hanging on to Christian's every utterance like an awestruck child. For my part, every time the conversation took a dangerous turn, I swerved it away from the precipice, leaping from topic to topic like a sparrow landing on thorns, terrified someone would let slip about Christian and me – not least Christian himself.

'Are you tempted to come to work in Yemen?' Nooria asked Gemma.

'I'm sorry?'

'You are an anthropologist, no?'

'Oh, no. I didn't complete my degree.'

'It must have been the teaching,' Theo said.

'The teaching was great,' said Gemma. 'I wasn't.'

'You should have taken your degree,' Christian said flatly.

'I've done all right without it. I'm in the entertain-

ment industry. I'm much better suited to it than . . .
this. I meet all sorts of fascinating people.'

'More fascinating than multi-lingual kids like these?'
he asked. The rebuke made her blush. There was something odd in his demeanour still. He was unreasonably
ill at ease. I wondered about 'unfinished business'. Had
more taken place between them than I knew of – in
Jordan, perhaps? Was there more to this than that
bloody pavement?

'We should get back,' said Theo. 'We have an early
start.'

Fatima kissed our hands many times as we left.
Nooria tactfully hooked Gemma's arm and walked her
out to the street, but Christian said goodnight and more
or less closed the door in my face.

He was already in the empty hotel dining room, his
shoulders rounded as he swirled tea in his glass, when
I emerged at four the next morning.

We tried to eat, the two of us, but it was too early,
too fraught. When the others joined us, Gemma was
full of the delights of dawn. Here was my true rival,
awake now to the possibilities before her. She had
two days, maybe three, in which to make a fresh, and
profound, impression on Christian, and she went about
it with alacrity. In all the years of her infatuation, I had
never given serious thought to the possibility that he
might have returned her interest, but now I had to
wonder, especially in view of his extraordinary unease.
Perhaps Gemma had drawn him into an extra-marital
affair, which he had learned to regret and which, even

now, could be damaging to him. Either way, I had to step back. It pained me to do so. The gust of love that had whistled past me at Bab al-Yemen had to bury itself like a crab in the sand and nestle in where it could not be seen.

Something pressed into my lower back. Theo's hand, unobtrusively, absentmindedly almost. Solidarity. This would have been such a trip. With my new friends I could have sailed across Rub al-Khali, the Empty Quarter, like a wind, leaving a light but temporary imprint on the sands. Instead I was bogged down in someone else's past and would drag across them with heavy stride, too many footsteps alongside mine.

'Well?' Nooria beamed. 'Ready for your great adventure?'

I smiled. Damn it all, I *was* ready. To hell with these two thorns in my foot. I was going across the desert. I would see Shabwah, as Freya Stark had failed to do, and unlike her I would reach my destination.

An aspiration once foiled would not be foiled again.

12

Rachmaninov's second piano concerto was my choice of soundtrack for our departure, when we left Marib in the dark and headed in the general direction of Shabwah. Once the ancient capital of the Hadramawt kingdom, the still undiscovered Shabwah had been Stark's objective when she went to Yemen in 1934, but she never made it. An epidemic of measles, to which she succumbed, and further illness in Shibam prevented her. Instead a German, Hans Helfritz, was the first European to get there, although he was chased away by Bedouin on the outskirts. Now it was my turn.

Our Bedouin guides, in their own Toyota, stopped outside the town to let air out of the tyres, which would allow for greater grip in the sands. Gemma travelled with Christian, Ahmad and Farouk, one of the drivers from the excavation who had agreed to come along to share the driving with Christian. I went with the others. Leaving behind the lights and telephone poles of Marib, and eventually the checkpoints too, we settled in for the long drive. As dawn teased the landscape with light, low mounds of sand tinted by swathes of deep pink appeared around us. The horizon was a grubby mix of yellow and blue. Ahead, the tail-lights of our guide led the way. Excitement lapped about inside me. In that fresh, early air I could smell the day ahead. We were driving into it, into its heat and quiet. Nooria sat beside me in the gloom, her slim wrists crossed on her lap, her head turned towards the window. Theo was trying to read a map in the front seat, although there were no roads where we were headed, and fiddling with his GPS.

'Can't you stop being a cartographer for one day?' Fadhl asked.

'I like to know where I'm going.'

'But I don't know where I'm going and I'm driving!'

The morning stretched and got up. We passed an oil installation: glaring lights reflected off the sunlight and monster shapes jutted out of the ground, like dangerous toys left on the floor. 'Ugly,' I said.

'Necessary,' said Fadhl.

'I'd like to have breakfast again,' I said.

The sun was well risen. We drove across a flat expanse, lined with tyre-tracks, but the desert was becoming humpier and bumpier until even the flats were warped and there were dunes in every direction, an untidy multitude of heaps. Some were rounded, some peaked, others curved. They were like a whole busy population, a crowd at a rock festival, and those in the distance were like the people at the back, standing on tiptoe, looking over the shoulders of others. The moon struggled to make a blot on the sky, so faint it seemed no more than a thumbprint on the lens of my camera, and the sky was clean now – an even blue from one end of the dome to the other – featureless but for that lunar effort to smudge it.

I made them stop the cars so that I could run up and

down low, rippled mounds. The silence was as thick as the heat. I wanted to stir it. Away from the others, I said loudly, 'Yes.'

Christian came over to me. 'So?'

'I love it,' I said. 'I *love* it.'

'I didn't mean –'

'You should live out here. Look – no plants!'

'There's one.' He pointed at a mini-volcano of sand spewing green twigs. 'I suppose you'd like to pick it and shake it at me.'

I smiled. 'I wouldn't do that.' I wanted to run the back of my fingers along his chin, but Gemma was in my peripheral vision, back at the cars.

A whistle pierced the quiet. Theo.

Greater treats lay in store: serious dunes in the Ramlat al-Sab'atayn. We approached them at speed in the 4 × 4s to avoid getting bogged down, then climbed to the top and it was like coming to the crest of a wave, then surfing down the other side. Nooria and I squealed like children on a rollercoaster, laughing and holding on to our seats as we slid down into the trough.

'Is this safe?' I screeched.

'Do you care?' Theo called back.

'No!'

We flew along the intervening shallow, then took on another dune. On the crest, we had to get out. The line of sand along the top was sharper even than the rim of a wave on the point of breaking. I put my fingers into it, to untidy its perfect line, but that wasn't enough so, like a naughty child seeking revenge on a houseproud mother, I ran along the ridge kicking my feet left and right, flinging sand in both directions and leaving a pattern of inverted commas behind me. The wind would soon vacuum the dune and return it to its neat, orderly appearance – the haphazard creating perfection – but for now it endured my punctuation. Granules slid down the slope, covering the ripples like an incoming tide. I felt suddenly, magnificently, well. Christian and Gemma had dogged my every thought since I had been in transit in Cairo, and now they were with me in this, *my*, place, a curious duet – the lover and the loved – and a lumbering weight on my back. On the peak of that dune I threw them off and sat down to think of better things.

The first time Thesiger crossed the Empty Quarter, he had had to tackle mountainous sands known as the Uruq al-Shaiba: 'The sun was scorching hot and I felt empty, sick and dizzy. As I struggled up the slope, knee-deep in shifting sand, my heart thumped wildly and my thirst grew worse. I found it difficult to swallow; even my ears felt blocked, and yet I knew that it would be many intolerable hours before I could drink . . .'

With these words he had made me envious. *Envious.* I had read the book brimming with jealousy. Hundreds of miles south of Uruq al-Shaiba, I reconsidered. Wistful envy no longer stirred. As I sat within reach of cold drinks, snacks, cool air and effortless transportation, my strongest emotion was apprehension that our own 'ships of the desert' – those soulless machines that didn't grunt or have long lashes – would break down. Crawling up and sliding down dunes was a ride, not a challenge, but the sun was fierce and the stillness eerie, and the infinite humps of desert deeply intimidating. I wanted to get out of there as much as I wanted to stay.

'We have to run down it,' I announced, but only Theo followed when I leaped off the rim and buried my feet in the lee of the dune, then lumbered down the side. Grains of sand rushed ahead, creating glorious sliding patterns that gained momentum until a great swathe of sand was rolling along like silk on a counter. Our feet were almost left behind as we tumbled down and ended up in a dusty heap at the bottom, laughing. The guides smiled with forbearance.

'They must think we're mad.'

Theo stood up, brushing himself down. 'Why did I do that? I'll have sand everywhere.'

'Jesus, the heat.'

'Get up. Quickly. It's fifty per cent hotter down where you are than up here.'

'Well, we can't *all* be three metres high.'

'I'm serious, get up. The heat is very intense at ground level.'

I stood up. 'Who are you telling? God, you'd die here. You'd die in a flash.'

The jeeps came bolting down the slope and we stopped to snack on bread and bananas and even chocolate biscuits, brought along by Theo, whose predilection for them was such that he would eat them even as they melted in his hand. The guides brewed tea, and I would have taken ten glasses were it not likely to give me need of non-existent natural screens. Then we set off again, across a stretch of gravel. 'More dunes?' I asked Fadhl.

'Plenty more.'

Sure enough, we were soon throwing ourselves against the incline of another dune and skimming down the other side. Nooria looked seasick, especially on the downward slope when we toppled forward and it seemed as if Fadhl had lost control. Even I was wondering how much longer the novelty would last, although my eyes couldn't leave the rollercoaster horizons.

Occasionally, the guides' jeep disappeared beyond a dune, which filled me with anxiety until I caught the glitter of their vehicle as it climbed the next. At one point, they fell behind, and we stopped in a dip to wait for them. When they failed to show, Fadhl went back up and called that they were bogged down on the other side, so Theo got in with Christian and Farouk and they drove back to help pull them out, leaving Ahmad with us. Gemma wandered along the contour of the dune behind us. Nooria and I sat together by the jeep, drinking and thinking.

'You should travel with him a little,' said Nooria.

'He doesn't want me to.'

'*Ya Allah!* Why cannot you see what I see?'

'He has an interest in Gemma. I've put myself in the middle of something.'

Nooria wiped her glasses with the end of her veil. 'It is Gemma, I think, who has put herself in the middle.'

The voice distracted us. Sitting some way up the dune, Gemma was singing one of her favourite songs – a hymn-like ballad by Enya. Ahmad turned. In that sparse place at the height of the day, with the acoustics provided by sand-dunes, it sounded like the lament of a wandering soul.

Nooria said, 'What is this?'

'This is the unexpected. You can always rely on Gemma to provide it.'

'Yes, but . . . I don't understand it.'

'She's singing in Irish.'

'Oh, but it's lovely! What does it mean?'

'"*Deora ar mo Chroí*" – Tears on My Heart, or something like that.'

Plaintive and sad, it was well chosen, even if no one else understood it.

The jeeps appeared over the crest behind us and bounced forward, but Gemma was oblivious to them. The men switched off their engines and got out. Christian stood listening, with one hand on the car door, his expression softer than it had been. Her voice was hers to do with as she pleased, she had once said. She was certainly using it to good effect here, applying it like a balm.

I climbed some way up the dune, away from the cars and the performance. The ripples in the sand entranced me – parallel lines streaking the ground, the ageing skin of the earth. I saluted Thesiger, and Lawrence, and Charles Montagu Doughty. I saluted my other self – the one who would have come this way twelve years before, without a barrel-load of complications in her pack.

Some time later, Shabwah appeared, a shadow on the landscape. Not even a ruin, more like a ragged moonscape. It, too, had been on the frankincense trail, and caravans several miles long, carrying myrrh and incense from the coast, had had to pay huge levies to pass through. In fact, taxes were charged so often along the route that by the time the spices reached the Levant they were luxuries. Shabwah, like Marib, had been an oasis, but there was little left of it, and it stood forlornly in the wilderness, inhabited by a few families living off the local salt mines.

We had our picnic in the shade of some bushes. The newly monosyllabic Christian chose to eat with the guides. He looked good, hunkered on the ground like them, all sandy in his desert-coloured clothes, joining in their banter. There was laughter and raucous teasing. I would have liked to understand. Theo was consulting his GPS; Fadhl and Nooria were dozing in the shade of separate bushes. Gemma sagged like an old teddy bear on a rug, wearing my clothes. Nothing she had brought with her had been suitable. It was all too revealing, or too warm, so I had lent her some baggy shirts and long skirts.

She fanned herself with Theo's hat. 'I've cleared the air,' she told me.

'Hmm?'

'I apologized for what happened.'

'You shouldn't have,' I said. 'It wasn't your fault.'

'That's what he said — that I couldn't have been re-sponsible in any degree for such an unprovoked attack.'

How gracious, I thought, and yet he seemed no more reconciled to her presence than he had been. Gemma appeared unmoved by his simmering antagonism towards her, which surely made any rapprochement unlikely, but this was of little comfort because he was equally chilly towards me.

She closed her eyes and rested.

I walked among the ruins Freya Stark had never seen. 'I lay helpless,' she had written in Shibam, 'my journey crumbling like card-houses around me; and I felt ashamed that I should mind if others reached my city before me – for this matter of being first is not really a very creditable passion.'

Tumbled masonry littered the one-time capital. I scrambled through it to the base of the palace near one of the gates, which stood on a mound, but the ruins scorched the air, reflecting the sun and redoubling the heat. My feet ached as I wandered in what had been the palace, and the veins in my legs were throbbing. Unable to bear it, I sat down in the shade of my own broad-brimmed hat, my mind drab, and stared at my feet. Poor Freya, I thought, to have reached the gate, only to be turned away on the doorstep. I heard the scrunch of grit as he came towards me. Two desert boots stepped into my line of vision.

'I didn't expect her to haunt me this much,' I said, without looking up.

'Who?'

'Freya. It's unsettling, the way she's here but isn't here.'

'She made this spot her own, I suppose, by never reaching it.'

'She had a lover in Aden, you know. A Frenchman. And then she married a homosexual.'

'Vivien,' Christian crouched in front of me, 'I take it Gemma is the reason you didn't want to see me in Dublin?'

'She had strong feelings for you. I didn't want to hurt her.'

'I wish you'd told me you knew her.'

'Would you have pursued me if I had?'

'No.' Short and sharp.

'Then you're right. I should have told you.' I took off my sunglasses and wiped the sweat from the bridge of my nose. 'What on earth happened that night, Christian?'

'That night, that night!' He stood up. 'How the hell did that night end up *here*? In Shabwah!'

'It ended up here because Gemma did. And that, incidentally, has absolutely nothing to do with me. She's here because you're here.'

He took off his hat and pushed his hand through his hair.

'I only know what she's told me,' I went on, 'and what she's told me does you no favours.'

Christian snorted derisively. 'I'm sure it doesn't.'

'So tell me your side of it.'

He fanned himself with his hat, shaking his head. 'I . . . They . . . Look, it's all pretty foggy and it isn't something I dwell on if I can help it, but . . . well, I remember the party pretty clearly, the crowded rooms, and the smell of dope and body spray, and Gemma pressing against me at every opportunity . . . I made an early exit to avoid a showdown and went to my car —'

'You offered her a lift.'

'Of course I didn't offer her a lift – no teacher in his right mind would offer a student a lift in those circumstances – but there she was at the car, nonetheless, and she just . . . threw herself at me.' He stopped to see if I would contradict this, but I nodded. He went on, 'All I could think at first was, Shit, it's happened: a student. And then . . .' Christian swallowed, a dry gulp emphasizing the leap in his Adam's apple, and took several deep breaths of burning air. It occurred to me that I was not equipped to deal with what he had to say, especially there. It was no place to prise open cuts full of maggots, and he had become so agitated that I was about to reach out and say, 'It doesn't matter,' when he continued, '. . . there was a bit of a struggle and, well, I lost it.' His voice seemed loud in the hushed ruins. 'The next thing I knew I was being savaged.'

My arms hugged my waist.

'So if that's what you meant by saying I compromised myself, you're damn right I did, because it didn't leave me a leg to stand on, but in the bigger picture –'

The masonry was too hot to sit on any longer. I stood up and rubbed my fingertips together, trying to roll thoughts into words. 'How far did it go, exactly?'

He stared at me. All these conversations, taking place in glaring light, mingled with sweat and disorientation, were too sharp. Spoken in dead heat, the words stood grimly in the still air. Christian wiped his palms on his shirt. 'How far did it go?' he repeated. 'What do you want, Vivien? The biology? You want to know if we had sex, is that it? How it felt, maybe? Because if that's what you want, I'll also tell you what it feels like to have your lip ripped and your groin kicked several times. That's the biology that matters to me and it pisses me off that you're looking for details when the only detail that damn well matters is that I got away with my life.'

He walked off, back to Ahmad. I had learned nothing, nothing at all.

On a vast flat expanse, Fadhl put his foot down. 'You can do one hundred and twenty kilometres per hour here, no problem.'

'No speed cams, then?'

'In Holland,' said Theo, 'there is a group that destroys speed cameras. They burn them.'

'Can I have a go?'

Fadhl stopped and we swapped places. It took a while to accustom myself to the 4 × 4 – it had a mind of its own – but when I got the better of it, I stomped on the gas and moved across the plain like a motor-boat through water. The music blared, the air-conditioning hummed, and Nooria and Theo sat in the back discussing mosquito repellent. Christian appeared on my right; he also had taken the wheel. We raced. We pulled out and pulled back. We were courting, flirting, and nobody knew.

Having had too much *shai* after lunch, we soon had to stop, but when we got out the heat colonized us like flies on meat and the plain offered little in the way of concealment. A tiny pile of rubble, several hundred metres away, shimmered in the haze.

'That must be the ladies',' I said to Nooria.

As we trudged towards it, I thought of Doreen

Ingrams, who always travelled with male companions and had had to contend with a lot more than just peeing in the vast uncluttered spaces: 'The disposal of sanitary towels was always a problem on the stony plateaux, and the best I could ever do was to scratch a hole and bury them under a heap of stones. These memorial cairns were to be found all over the deserts of the Hadhramaut.'

Crouching behind the inadequate rocky screen, it was clear to me that I could never have been an Ingrams or a Stark, or even a Dervla Murphy, our own Irish traveller, who had seen the world on bikes and asses. Gemma had been right, way back, when she had said it was a conceit to fancy myself an adventurer. I was too well married to privacy.

We still had a long way to go. I dozed off, but woke with a start. I could not miss a moment, and it was a good thing I opened my eyes because we passed Bedouin families whose tents, goats and camels encapsulated my most romantic visions of the desert. The going got rough. A line of white tyres showed the way, but there were dangerous patches of soft, sliding sand to be avoided and great ruts left by larger vehicles to be negotiated. To the south, mountains shimmered in the distance and seemed to be moving towards us.

In the late afternoon, we stopped at an encampment where there was a kind of shack-café for a meal. We sat under an awning, limp with exhaustion.

'What is this?' I asked, looking at the meat.

'Camel,' said Christian.

'You're kidding.'

He and Theo grimaced at one another. The old joke: the one about me wanting to be a traveller.

'It's goat,' I said. 'I believe it's goat.'

'You'd eat goat, but not camel?'

'I'd rather not eat either.' I nibbled a piece of meat. Definitely camel. Its genealogy was in its flesh – the distances and deserts, the long hungry stretches, the packs, the grazing, the journeys without end. 'I've never eaten anything so big.'

After the meal, our guides made their farewells with considerable fanfare and took off in their Toyota. The mountains came steadily closer – it was as if they were taking great silent steps when we weren't looking, as in a children's game – until we hit Tarmac and filtered into the Wadi Hadramawt, an extraordinary gorge squeezed between two plateaux, the most beautiful valley, Fadhl said, in the Arabian peninsula. The Hadramawt is another country altogether, but then Yemen is full of other countries. 'Hadhramaut,' Doreen Ingrams wrote, 'means "death is present".' And yet our surroundings were coming back to life as we meandered, dazzled, through the greenery, where there were people and houses and trees.

'There are one million palm trees in this valley,' said Fadhl.

In the fields, women moved about, wearing the upright straw hat, the *mathalla*, native to these parts. But it was getting dark, and the glories of the Hadramawt were soon dimmed from view.

'Nearly there,' said Theo.

I had nothing to say. I was apprehensive. It was like

meeting someone with whom I had enjoyed a long correspondence for the first time. It was bound to be awkward. Perhaps, I thought, Shibam and I should never be introduced. Perhaps it would have been better always to think of it in its perfection, rather than be exposed to its flaws. Would the reality be able to match my expectations?

It was dark by the time Shibam appeared to our right. We stopped beyond the checkpoint to take it in. Rows of lights were all I could see, were all I needed to see, even as we swooped around the town and drove past it.

We reached al-Hawta Palace, which had been converted into a hotel, so tired that we could hardly stand at Reception. Christian was the first to be attended to and was given the main suite. I passed his open door and stopped to look in. He was standing beside a grand four-poster bed, placed right in the middle of the room; he looked up at me, eyebrows raised, hands outstretched. Here, in this sumptuous suite, among draped fabrics and carved timbers, we would have been together had things gone as planned. I went to the room I was sharing with Gemma, fuming.

After a light supper, during which we were mostly too exhausted to speak, Christian dropped his bombshell. 'I've decided to head back tomorrow.'

'What?' said Gemma.

'What about Shibam?' said Theo.

'I can see it another time. It isn't fair to keep Ahmad and Farouk hanging around while I go sightseeing, and I really should get back to work.'

'But you'll have to turn round and do another fifteen hours straight,' said Gemma.

'There's a tarmacadam road that's much quicker than the desert route.'

'Much quicker,' said Theo, drily. 'Nine hours. Why did you bother?'

'To make sure Vivien got here this time,' he said, without so much as a glance in my direction.

There were attempts to talk him out of it, but I didn't intervene. Shibam, like Sana'a, actually had more to do with Theo, who had made it his business to get me there. Christian and Gemma were distractions. For all my best efforts to ignore it, Durham had trudged behind us, like a mange-ridden dog, all day. Whatever had happened between them, it had not been, as Gemma implied, the culmination of mutual attraction. That much I had gleaned from Christian's irascibility, and while I didn't know why he was turning back, it had possibly as much to do with me as with her, which gave me an odd kind of comfort.

Since he would be leaving at dawn, Fadhl and Theo shook his hand before going to bed and advised him to drive carefully and be vigilant.

Gemma was stricken. She didn't know what to say but clearly had not yet said enough, for all that she had shadowed him. And so we both found ourselves tossing in our beds. He had pulled the rug from beneath us. We could not sleep. I, in fact, did not intend to. Gemma would now not see Christian again. Nothing had happened, beyond the rekindling of her feelings to absolutely no end. It must have been hard, in that single bed beside me, to ruminate over her actions of the last few days. Perhaps she was seeing her own folly at last.

The long rough day proved stronger than her distress but weaker than my frustration. She fell asleep. I got up. My turn for a little folly. I stepped into the corridor in my T-shirt and made my way to Christian's room. I pushed down the great handle ... The door was not locked. He was expecting me, or someone. I found him in the dark like a cat finding warmth. When I pulled back the sheet, he grabbed my wrist and held it, hard. Neither of us moved until he released his grip and slipped his fingers between mine. I pulled off my T-shirt and lowered myself on to him.

He fell asleep with his head resting in the crook of my neck. Eventually I went back to my room and slept until, in the dull light of dawn, Gemma's shuffling around the room woke me. I glanced over my shoulder. She was packing. 'What the —?'

'I'm going with him.'

'You are joking,' I hissed.

'No.'

'Gemma!'

'There's no point me trundling off with your little party. This is your adventure, your ...' she waved her hand around '... place. It means nothing to me, and I can certainly give Shibam a miss.' A twist of the knife. 'I didn't come here to be a tourist. I came to see him.'

'You don't seriously intend to take another shot at him? Not after what happened last time?'

She zipped her toilet bag.

'Gemma, don't be mad. I –'

'You really can't stand him, can you? You made up your mind about him long ago, before you'd even met. He hadn't a chance. You've been so rude to him, I've been embarrassed for you.'

'For God's sake, what's he going to think? You told him you came to see me and now you're asking to go back to Marib –'

'I'm not asking. He offered.'

She left the room. My tongue seemed to be lodged a long way down my throat. *He what?* I pulled on a skirt and hurried after her, down the dark cool corridors to the lobby. She went outside. Christian and Ahmad were tying supplies of water and diesel on to the roof of the 4 × 4. Christian glanced at me, his expression more relaxed than it had been for days. *Jesus,* I thought, *what the hell are you playing at?* Her. Me. Her. Me.

As Gemma loaded her gear, he came over. 'Say goodbye to the others for me.' He kissed my cheek and went round to the other side of the jeep, and in that cursory manner, our holiday affair ended, while Gemma looked on, none the wiser.

She gave me a hug. 'I'm sorry for invading your holiday,' she said. 'But beware, Viv. If you think seeing Shibam now is going to do for you what was never done in the first place, you'll be very disappointed.'

I've had an affair with him.

She got into her seat.

I hadn't said it. I'd meant to – that was why I ran after her – but it wouldn't come.

*

At eight, I went to Theo and Fadhl's room. Fadhl had gone for breakfast. Theo was shaving. I leaned against the bathroom door. 'She's gone. Can you believe it? She went with them.'

He glanced at me in the mirror. He had such a long back. The bumps on his spine went on for ever. 'Good,' he said.

Nooria made no comment about Gemma's abrupt departure, but there was an unspoken acknowledgement that we were better off this way. We had lost the Land Cruiser, which had followed us the day before like an unwanted suitor, and we none of us cared. Christian had been foul; Gemma racy. Now we could be four eager-beaver campers all together, gasping at our surroundings.

I felt light, bright. My conscience was easier than it had been in weeks. The boil had been lanced. The cost had been Christian, but he had never really been mine anyway.

Meanwhile we were weaving through the Hadramawt. It was forbidding and mesmerizing, and as we went back towards Shibam, I grew nervous again. Would it disappoint? Was I about to destroy something I should have kept sacred?

Theo's voice, somewhat muffled as if he were under a blanket, reached back to me. 'There it is,' he said. 'In daylight.'

And there it was, beyond my grubby windowpane.

Nooria squeezed my hand. Fadhl stopped beside a low white wall.

I wound down my window. The mud city stood before me, its skyscrapers facing out to the world. It was as expected. I had projected myself at last into *Paris Match* or *Life*, and although it seemed as if I had waited an age to get there, it had not taken so very long, after all, to arrive at this place, where too few come.

Shibam did not disappoint. It could not.

13

In a flux of warmth and lingering satisfaction, I enjoyed my last day in Yemen, invigorated by my achievements. I had seen Shibam. I had stepped beyond its gates and walked its shaded streets, skirting children playing hula-hoop. The town had surrounded me, concealed me among its towers, and while I had sat in the teashop just inside the gates, I had projected myself through time and seen the travellers, coming and going through those gates, as they all did. Thesiger bought his guns there; Stark lay ill on the outskirts; Ingrams collected her mail; Mackintosh-Smith hand-delivered a letter . . . They all came, *I came*, and the satisfaction was unquenchable.

And yet, two days later, when I had found myself wandering in the old town of Sana'a with Nooria, Shibam already felt like a well-consummated fling. Sana'a, on the other hand, was a love-affair that showed no signs of abating. It was a mystical, gripping place. In spite of the poverty and the rough, I was permanently, deeply, impressed. This country did not compromise, would not conform. It was a country so fierce in its sense of itself that I suspected it would never let me go, and when we stood on a street corner munching watermelon, I knew it was a moment I would revisit in the course of my life, over and over again.

It wasn't only Sana'a. That last evening, when Theo and Nooria took me to the roof of a hotel to get a panoramic photo of the city at sunset, I could see my own shadow in the frame and noticed, on either side of it, two other shadows standing by.

Gemma was still in Marib. Christian kept telling Theo he was bringing her back, but somehow he never got round to it. I was angry and perplexed, and deeply regretted going to his room in al-Hawta. I could no longer grasp my motivation. Or his. After snarling at each other for two days, we had come together like lions. I had been unable to resist licking the crumb, the morsel, Christian had left on the plate: that gesture – his arms and eyebrows raised, as he stood by his bed in that room. Had it been rebuke or invitation? It was hard to tell, but I had addressed both, and was sorry for it. But regardless of what had happened in al-Hawta, and was happening in Marib, nothing would be allowed to engulf my last hours in Sana'a.

That night, we took a final walk through the *suq*, meandering slowly among the evening shoppers. Scarves and materials aplenty were pulled out for me, and I bought incense and saffron, and miniature Sana'a houses for my kitchen. Bored, Theo wandered off. I was in active purchase mode when he came rushing back.

'Vivien! He's here!'

'Who?'

'The writer person. He's up there having tea with a bundle of *qat* on his lap.'

I threw money at the shopkeeper and we hurried after Theo. 'Are you sure it's him?'

'No, but you can ask him.'

'Ask him if he's him?' We ducked between the crowds. 'This is typical! My last night!'

'Have you got the book?'

'I always have the book.'

We reached the shop. There was no Englishman, with or without *qat*.

'*Bollocks.*'

Nooria asked the owner did he know where the foreigner had gone? Yes, he'd gone home. Did he know if he was a writer? Yes, he was a writer. He was Mackintosh-Smith.

Later, Nooria took me to a woman to have my hands and feet decorated with *naqsh*, a lasting black ink adornment. It was late when we got there, but Aisha and her children were up. Her *mafraj* was a long stretch from number eight: dirty orange walls, a bare cement floor, a few mats and a television. It was dim, with only a weak overhead bulb lighting the gloom. Before getting down to work, she served us cake, cucumbers and *qishr*.

Nooria fed me, and Aisha chatted about her fourteen births and eight surviving children while she painted intricate lines, loops and curves from my wrists to my fingertips, my ankles to my toes. When she had finished, she patted my hands and feet with Vaseline, then wrapped them in strips of cotton to stop the night air provoking irritation. Her teenage daughter crouched in front of me and, because I could not use my hands, offered to fix my scarf. Her unquestioning assumption that I would not wish to step into the street unveiled was deeply affecting. Her face inches from my own, she tied my headscarf tight beneath my chin and tucked away every suggestion of hair. Her concentration and my stillness welded us together like women in a still-life painting.

Bound in rags, I walked through the streets like the Straw Man in *The Wizard of Oz*. Nooria giggled as I hobbled along. At the house, we put plastic bags on my hands and feet, as recommended, to make them sweat. This would secure the *naqsh*, but it also meant I couldn't do my packing, so Nooria did it for me. Watching her and laughing with her had already become harder.

Later, in the kitchen, she scented my hair. She burnt charcoal in a burner, broke sticky blocks of incense over it and, when the charcoal began to glow, held the burner close to my neck and ran her fingers through my scrappy hair. 'I must smell like the Queen of Sheba,' I said.

'A pity Solomon is in Marib.'

'I'm sure Solomon has his hands full.'

We didn't sleep, but I agreed to rest while Nooria prepared breakfast and I lay down, hands bagged and hair whiffing of incense, in turmoil. Thoughts of Christian and Gemma had been superseded, knocked out, by the prospect of leaving Nooria and Sana'a. And Theo, of course.

We had breakfast in Nooria's flat before dawn. She tried to keep up the mood, ribbing me and making jokes, but we had little time left and couldn't rise to it. We went back to the other house. Theo was ready to go. I climbed to the roof and stepped out to spend a quiet moment looking at the mountains. Purple light meandered towards the city. Birds, sounding like the return action on an old typewriter, chirped at the morning light. I could hear myself breathing, could feel the sadness rising. I had overcome the obstacles, defied the cynicism, confronted my own apprehension, but I had still lost.

Nooria came out and put her arms round my waist, her chin resting on my shoulder. My eyes filled.

'Any time,' she said. 'You come back to me here any time and I'll show you what you can do.'

I put my hand on her wrist. She squeezed me, and we stood facing the light, looking across the rooftops.

I turned. Nooria shrugged. Nothing to be done.

Theo was waiting by the jeep. Nooria could not come to the airport. She might get stuck there all day, so it was better to part outside the house where we had spent so much time together. The only gesture available to us was an inadequate hug. As we drove down the street, I turned to see her standing in the warm sunlight, watching me go.

The airport was frenetic. There were no delays, but I had to fight my way through the security check where an irritating man with a very white beard almost caused a stampede by holding everybody back with his several trunks. Theo managed to battle his way through to the ticket desks.

'At least you won't be stuck here all day waiting for me to leave, the way you were when I arrived.'

'It was worth it.'

'Theo —'

'Don't say anything else, Vivien.'

He was right. There was no need for thanks and gratitude. We had chanced upon a friendship that, in its time and place, was pure and unfettered. It worked, simply. I would probably never see him again. His work would take him all over the world, so those three weeks were all that we, as friends, amounted to, and yet nothing would ever take them away. Theo would always be firmly stored in my memories of Yemen — but it was a wrench, a horrible wrench, to leave him there.

PART II

14

My apartment had been spoiled. Yemen had wrecked it. Stepping across my threshold gave me no pleasure. The plant in the hall, which usually greeted me with a faint rustle of its fronds, now seemed in the wrong place. I turned on the light and glanced around the clean, spacious kitchen. Sterile. I had a sterile, empty home. By sending that email, by allowing Christian's advances, I had created this cold hearth.

There was no milk in the fridge for a mug of cocoa, no Gemma curled up in her armchair reading the paper. Instead I was there alone and she was in Arabia Felix, with Christian.

The following morning my usual homecoming ritual – the *Irish Times* over an indulgent breakfast of bacon, toast and Barry's tea – offered no relief. No amount of fresh milk could lift the feeling that I was in the wrong place. Everything seemed incongruous. Theo's house was not small, nor was it spacious. The kitchen, the bedrooms and even the *mafraj* were neat little rooms. My flat, in contrast, was full of empty spaces and horrendously tidy too, with every item in its given place, not stacked willy-nilly on overladen shelves. It had the bland whiff of good hygiene. Being there was like playing Blind Man's Buff – every time I reached out, there was nothing but air, nothing to grasp, so I was relieved to get back to work, albeit to another starched environment.

My office was a poky room at the back of the gallery, which was always in a shambles because everything that had nowhere else to go ended up in there, including Shoukria. Far preferable to me was the clear space of the gallery itself, where a small desk half-way along the room was the only protruding item. All the other furniture was on the walls. This place I loved. I loved it even when the featured work repelled me. When there were photographs of hell or violent depictions of famine and savagery on the walls, I still rejoiced in being surrounded by the minds of others. All day I basked in the reflection of other people's ideas. It could be said that the gallery was as untidy as my office, cluttered as it was with the mess of clashing imaginations, but even though it was often empty, it was never lonely. The public came and went in small numbers, whispering as they moved from work to work, barely disturbing the library silence, as if speaking aloud would alarm the figures depicted on the walls and prompt them to jump into life.

If Shoukria happened to be sitting at the desk when people came in, their visit might be quite different, depending on her mood. She was an imposing presence, quite tall, with wavy black hair and a voluptuous figure, and she was likely to descend upon them like a snobby saleswoman in a smart boutique and show them round with intrusive enthusiasm; another day she was as likely to sigh loudly and scribble with her pencil, as though impatient for them to leave.

Over the years I had developed the gallery. A former storeroom had been converted into an audio room where the public could sit on a black carpet, surrounded by black walls, and listen to recordings. The current installation was the sound of water gurgling through the overflow in a bath. It was amusing, and soothing, this bath that never emptied. I had also let rooms upstairs for art classes and drama groups, which kept me particularly busy in the summer months. I had plenty to do when I got back, but none of it helped to shake off the draining homesickness for a place that wasn't home and never would be.

We always ate in my office – Shoukria didn't have one – and she would sit on my desk, munching her way through some exotic roll, while I sat with my feet resting on the open bottom drawer. We sat like this on my first day back, and I told her about Nooria and Theo, and everything we had done.

'Thank you,' she said, 'for the travelogue, but what really happened to you out there?'

'I've just told you.'

'You want to go back, is that it?'

'Have I said anything about going back?'

'Something isn't right with you.'

I put down my sandwich, and my feet, and opened my mouth to speak.

'I don't care how much you loved it, I won't have you resigning.'

'I'm not going to resign. If you must know, I'm getting over an ill-conceived affair.'

Shoukria's eyebrows wrinkled above her nose when

I told her about Christian. I hate the way beautiful women do that; while the rest of us get permanent lines from every passing frown, natural beauties can work their faces overtime and remain unscathed.

After I had covered everything from Dublin to Sana'a and back again, she simply chewed, ruminating, the food like a ball of *qat* on one side of her mouth. 'This isn't what I expected,' she said. 'I thought it might be the Theo person.'

'Theo is lovely, but this is about Linklater. *Gemma*'s Linklater.'

Shoukria knew the story. She pushed a protruding piece of lettuce back into her roll. 'Was it a very passionate affair?'

'Utterly. I couldn't move sometimes when he came into the room.'

'Love?'

'I'm holding it down like a festering cold.'

'So why did you end it?'

'Because it couldn't carry on right under Gemma's nose. Can you imagine Christian standing around our kitchen in his boxer shorts eating cereal? It would have been horrible for her.'

'Bof! It's not like he was her *huzz-band*!'

'No, but it feels like it. There's an unwritten rule that you don't get involved with friends' lovers, exes or missed opportunities.'

'Missed opportunity. Exactly. She missed it, you took it.'

'But that's what I'm not sure about any more. *Did* she miss it?'

Shoukria stood up. 'The *Sunday Tribune* is sending a photographer this afternoon. Make sure she takes the tree.'

Later that afternoon I paced the gallery. It was a particularly good group exhibition, with everything I liked in art: large canvases, multiple interpretations, pouring colours. One piece in particular pulled me in: a dripping palm tree on a blood orange background. For years paintings had been my life. I had been good to them and they to me, but as I stood in the aura of that particular work, it seemed as if we were parting company. The Ramlat al-Sab'atayn pulsed in my veins. It had been hot and hard in those sands, but entrancing. And yet I had only skimmed the surface. I had rushed across as if there were a train to catch and had toured the Hadramawt like a hornet. Tarim: yes, yes, with its wonderful minaret sprouting out of the oasis. Seyun: the imam's palace, all wedding-cake layers and peppermint trim. Villages clamped on to peaks, looking as if they were about to slide down the slopes and bury us in the gorge. Honey in Wadi Daw'an . . . The satisfaction of getting there had seemed, then, to be enough. In Shibam, I had studied the great wooden doors and their intricate carvings, but none of those doors had opened. I had taken the inevitable photo of the city at sunset and had been moved to stillness by the longed-for panorama. It was mysterious and fulfilling, but as I stood staring at that painting in Dublin, I knew it wasn't enough.

Gemma was due to arrive four days after my return, on the Saturday night. It was a torturous day. I mooched about the flat, tidying where there was no disorder, and cooked a special meal as though we would sit down, all chummy, and enjoy dinner together. It was April. The evenings were long. I waited in silence. Music would have been too much. There was enough noise in my head. I rang Theo, waking him in the small hours. He told me that he had taken Gemma to the airport and that the flight had left on time. Then he told me about his day, but I hushed him and listened instead to the silence of the Yemeni night behind him.

I feared Gemma's return. If Christian had told her about our affair, she would come home justifiably furious, and intolerably betrayed, but a worse prospect was that she would arrive smug and ebullient, having taken him back for herself.

As it transpired, she was neither angry nor gloating, but evasive. The key slipped into the lock just before eleven. I listened to the sound of her chinos rubbing against each other as she walked the length of the corridor to the living room. 'Hi,' I said.

'Hi.' She threw down her bag and sank into her armchair. 'Home!' My cat, Didds, jumped on to her lap.

'Good flight?'

'Long.'

'Do you want something to eat?'

'Toast maybe, but I'll get it.'

'So, how'd it go? How is everyone?'

'Yeah, yeah, he sends you lots and lots of love.'

'What?'

'Theo. Isn't that who you were asking about?'

'Oh. No, I meant everyone.'

'I didn't see much of Nooria.'

'Christian?' The word, dry in my mouth.

She smiled. 'He's good. Really good.'

'Great. So . . . you got whatever it was you went looking for?'

'God, yes.'

There came a lull. The *naqsh* faded from my skin, making my hands look grubby. Yemen was no longer yesterday or even last week. It was behind me, and still ahead. I returned there often, unconsciously and consciously, finding myself in Nooria's kitchen or Christian's bed. My dreams of Christian were usually erotic and never resolved, and everything else filled me with nagging incertitude. An opportunity had been missed, I was sure, but had it been Yemen or Christian? I kept flicking through my photo album, looking at the green terraces and the brown houses and the women scurrying away from the lens. Ingrams and Stark tugged at my sleeve. Every evening after the gallery closed, I emailed Theo and Nooria, then went home to Mackintosh-Smith and read about saints and scholars and tombs and civil wars: 'During the war I often recalled the old border post, out in the finger of desert beyond Marib . . . Ever since the days of the incense caravans, traders and travellers, nomads, pilgrims and smugglers have passed through that barren short-cut . . .'

In the hiatus we drifted on, Gemma and me, like two people living alone in the same space. Her dash to Yemen remained unfathomable, even shocking, to me.

It was beyond everything I had expected, even though I knew her to be a little crazy. (Spontaneous, she called it.) There could be no doubt now that, in spite of our confidences at that time, there had been more between her and Christian than I had known about. *Ergo*, there was more to Gemma than I understood. She had become like a shifting bullseye that would not come into focus, and I had to wonder what exactly had constituted resolution with Christian. I dreaded his coming to claim her; I dreaded finding him standing around my kitchen in his boxer shorts, tousled from *her* bed.

But what of al-Hawta? That remained the great conundrum.

One weekend I went home to get away from the flat, and from Gemma. I had come to reassess my parents over the years. When I was younger, they had sometimes seemed dull, especially in contrast to the Colberts, who were vivacious and even a little dangerous, while the steadiness of my own home was like an unsinkable barge. Now I fully appreciated our barge and the unassuming warmth of my parents' devotion.

My mother had shown her true colours when I had fallen in love with Bill. Instead of wrinkling her nose and disapproving of every untenable part of his being, of which there were many, she sympathized. We should each have at least one rogue in our lives, she told me, because it is the only way to learn. I didn't argue. Even then I suspected Bill was the one I would have to get over, the railings I would have to scale without becoming impaled, and when things went badly and I walked the streets at night distracted with confusion, Mum waited up. She nursed the illness, but didn't treat it. Her own rogue, she admitted, had been married. They had never consummated it, which she seemed to regret when she told the story of a cold November night spent in Tramore, in a bleak bed-and-breakfast at the far end of a spit, where they had intended to begin their affair. She had backed out, haunted by the knowledge that one day she might herself be a wife with a husband away from home. Years later, she became friendly with his wife at bridge and thanked her stars she had never cheated on her.

She looked well now, her grey hair swept up in a roll, her shirt buttoned at the neck, her cardigan manifestly expensive. In her bright front room, she listened to my tales of Arabia and looked at the photographs.

'No women?'

'They don't like to be photographed generally.'

She turned a page. 'Such nice faces. You can tell a good man from his face.'

'They're all good men.'

'So which one of them, is it, has you looking so worn out?'

I tapped a photo of Christian.

'Ah.' She looked more closely. 'Single?'

'Yes, you can relax on that score. He's divorced. Father of triplets.'

'Oh dear, I don't know about that. Is this tall one single?'

'This tall one isn't the issue.'

'But he looks so nice.'

'I'm sure his girlfriend would agree with you.'

'Girlfriends can be got rid of,' said Mum. 'Triplets can't.'

'There's no need to get rid of them. It was just a holiday thing and I have no intention of ever meeting his triplicated offspring.'

'Why not?'

'Because he lives in England . . . Oh, and then there's the thing about him being the guy Gemma was in love with who was eviscerated on the side of the road . . .'

Mum straightened. It was a severe gesture, which made her seem taller than me, which she wasn't. 'Oh, Vivien.'

'That's why she turned up out there.'

'Only to discover you'd taken him for yourself?'

'She doesn't know about that yet. I *will* tell her, but things aren't right with us and, besides, she's not telling me anything either. Honestly, Mum, it's horrible at home. It's like a marriage breaking up – the silence in the rooms, the separate bags of shopping, the "Would you mind not using my toothpaste?" cracks. She thinks I disapprove of her going to Yemen, and I bloody well do, but I'm mostly peeved that I had to give him up because of something that wasn't even real in the first place.'

After a significant pause, Mum said, 'So far as you know.'

'Mum!'

'Well, what do we know about what these people get up to?'

'What people?'

'The Colberts, for a start, and how can you be sure

he didn't encourage her in whatever it was she wanted to believe?'

I scowled. That was the problem – I couldn't be sure about anything.

'You should have stayed well clear of this,' Mum went on. 'I mean, Gemma's obviously still besotted with him if she went all that way to see him. The question is – where does *he* stand?'

'I wish I knew. There was something odd between them, Mum. I couldn't put my finger on it, but it was like the awkwardness between lovers when they meet up after an acrimonious split, except stronger, you know? I caught him looking at her sometimes, in a perplexed sort of way, as if he couldn't understand why it hadn't worked out.'

'So you think something *did* happen at Durham? I must say, I always had that suspicion myself. No innocent crush goes on for three years.'

'I don't know what to think, and Gemma isn't giving anything away. Since I blew a fuse when she turned up in Sana'a, she hasn't given me anything to go on, except all this . . .' I wobbled my shoulders '. . . suggestive stuff.'

'No wonder his marriage didn't last,' said my mother, in that sniffy way of hers, 'if that's the way he behaved. A *student*.'

I opened my mouth to defend him, but closed it again. The infatuation he had told me about with his colleague in London – could it have been, in fact, an infatuation, and even more than that, with a student in Durham? More than he could admit to, if he were to maintain any integrity? Had he deliberately blurred the lines? How much of what he'd told me could I actually believe?

Mum turned back to the photographs. 'Honestly, Vivien, I think it was tasteless of you to get involved with this man in view of all that murky business with Gemma, but you mustn't tell her. You know what they say about infidelity. Never own up.'

I lived in abeyance. At work, I stared out at people walking along the pavement and tried to summon up enough interest to do the publicity for an upcoming show. At home, I jumped every time the phone rang because I lived in dread of Christian coming looking for Gemma, or even for me: either eventuality would be fraught with difficulty. When, allowing a month either side of the date he had anticipated returning to London, I concluded that he would not come looking for either of us, relief and disappointment threw me back and forth. I tried to regain enthusiasm for my settled, single life and went back to my book club.

Then, one day in June when I was standing in a queue in Marks & Spencer waiting to pay for a bra, a thought, too well-defined, fell on me like a great cloak: I wanted to go back to Yemen.

Not only that. I handed the bra to the cashier. I *would* go back.

15

Shoukria was like a firecracker. America had tired quite suddenly of its war on terrorism and decided instead to attack Iraq. The transition from a war on terrorism to one on Iraq was almost seamless, but hard to fathom. The hunt for Osama bin Laden was thrown out; Saddam Hussein, who had had nothing to do with the assault on the World Trade Center, as far as anyone knew, returned to his cherished role as hate figure number one.

Shoukria's immediate family, her parents and siblings, were no longer in Iraq, but they feared for their extended family. The peace in the gallery was regularly disturbed by outbursts when she spoke to friends and relatives around the world. She walked about in short, angry steps, all her movements displaying restrained fury. Some Iraqi émigrés favoured an attack, if it would rid them of the regime, but most feared for civilians and the consequences of such a war. The consensus seemed to be that if America attacked Iraq, the Middle East would conflagrate.

'The American Institute of Suicide Bombers!' Shoukria railed.

Meanwhile, current suicide bombers continued to explode among Israeli civilians, and innocent Palestinians were locked into their own lands, their sense of injustice fermenting. Doddery old extremists on all sides sent the young to their unwritten fates, while the moderates just grew angrier.

One night, Shoukria and I sat despondently in her living room, watching the news – never an uplifting occupation, but particularly sobering that spring. UN inspectors were scouring Iraq for weapons of mass destruction, the discovery of which was the declared linchpin for war.

'There's even talk of a unilateral strike against Yemen,' said Shoukria. 'Did you hear?'

'Yeah, I heard. To "take out" fugitive al-Qaeda operatives.'

We were distracted by an item about a mysterious stomach bug that had hit British troops in Afghanistan. It lifted Shoukria out of her seat, like a pilot ejecting from a fighter jet. 'A tummy bug?' she yelled at the television. 'This is *news*?'

'Well, it's obviously serious,' I ventured. 'Potentially fatal.'

'And the people?' She turned on me. 'The Afghanis, who have paid the price for September eleventh and are still suffering and dying, where are they on the news? Nowhere!'

'Sit down. I'm not the enemy.'

'They have been forgotten. Completely forgotten! And now they're going to do it all over again to another country! *My* country!'

Her eyes filled, and I couldn't think of a word to say to her.

*

None of the war-mongering was conducive to my own plans, which I was contemplating one Saturday morning while jiving around the living room in a T-shirt and embroidered Chinese dressing-gown. I thought I heard the doorbell, but ignored it. I was too busy singing along to Dido about seeing the world again, which was exactly what I intended to do. My potential had been resurrected by Theo and Nooria, by the magnificent cliffs of Yemen, and by seventeen hours in Cairo airport. My dreams had been dug out of the hole in which they had buried themselves, allowing me to dance on the graves of my failures. It was exhilarating, and I whirled round the room bellowing Dido's song.

But that was definitely the doorbell. I went into the hall.

'That'll be ruddy Brendan,' Gemma called from the bathroom. 'Complaining about the noise.'

Flushed and breathless, I opened the door and said, 'Get a life,' to Christian. 'Jesus.'

He was leaning against the wall, his hands in the pockets of his jacket, his chin dipped into his collar. He was very tanned.

Instinctively, I pulled the door against my shoulder.

'Ah,' he said slowly, 'so my visit is indeed in-opportune.'

Before I could reply Gemma, also in a dressing-gown, pulled the door fully open from behind me. 'Christian!' She, clearly, had not been expecting him either.

'Gemma.'

'God,' she said. 'Come in, come in.'

He glanced at me. I waved him past. 'Mind the plant,'

I said, as he stepped in and the fronds were bent against his back. He jumped away, as if it were a bull terrier.

'I'll just get dressed,' said Gemma, visibly flushed. 'Put on the kettle, Viv.'

We stepped into the kitchen. Christian opened his mouth, suddenly close to me.

'I'll turn down the music,' I said, making my own escape.

When I came back, he was standing nervously inside the door, like a schoolboy sent to the principal's office. I busied myself with that vital prop, the kettle, filling it the slow way, through the spout.

Christian sat on a stool beside the wall. 'How are you?' he asked.

'Great. Fine. Yeah, excellent. You?'

He nodded.

'So what brings you to Dublin? Or is that a stupid question?'

'Very.'

'How's Theo? Everyone?'

'All well when I left, but that was weeks ago.'

Gemma came back, beaming, and reached for mugs. 'What a lovely surprise.' Her wet hair hugged the back of her neck. There were damp patches on her top. 'How are things?'

'Good, thanks.'

'And all my friends in Marib? Fatima, and those little angels of hers?'

He hesitated. 'Would those be the same angels you cursed for four days?'

She giggled and glanced at him coyly.

'I'll get dressed,' I said.

In my room, I sat on the end of my bed, my nails cutting into my palms. I considered going out, leaving them to it, but the night in al-Hawta prevented me. Instead I pulled on jeans. Bits of my hair were standing on end – the curse of the short haircut; after a night's sleep it presents like twisting beams of still-life sculpture. I failed to comb it down and returned to the kitchen.

'Where are you staying?' Gemma was asking Christian.

'At the Royal Marine.'

She handed me a coffee and we sat there on our high stools, the three of us, each in our own torment. We weren't even half-way into the maze, I thought, and nowhere near finding our way out again.

Gemma did most of the talking. It was the most I'd heard from her in weeks. She told me with relish about Marib – Ahmad's family, characters at the site, Christian's love-hate relationship with sand. So coy, and so bloody irritating. Christian dipped his chin when she spoke, and looked at her from beneath his brows. It must have been uncomfortable for him, listening to her telling me about their time together. Or perhaps I flattered myself that he would care. After all, he had no apology to make. I had dumped him.

When Gemma got up to make more coffee, Christian said, 'I was wondering if I could take you to dinner tonight.'

Gemma swung around, coffee jar in hand. 'That'd be lovely,' she gushed. 'Thank you.'

'Vivien?' he asked.

'Sorry. I'm going out. But you guys go ahead.'

'Where are you going?' said Gemma.

'To a film. With Shoukria.'

'Never mind,' said Christian. 'Some other time.'

He seemed to be backing out altogether, which prompted Gemma to say quickly, 'I've a better idea. Why don't we all eat here? I'll cook. I'd love to.' She waved a finger towards Christian. 'I certainly owe *you* dinner after all our outings in Yemen, and, Viv, you could go to an early viewing with Shoukria, then come back here to eat. I'm sure Shoukria would love to meet Christian.'

I'm sure she would, I thought, but before I could formulate another excuse, Gemma had turned to him. 'Let's say eight?'

'Lovely,' he said, and he glanced at me just as he had that night in Sana'a when Theo had invited him to Wadi Dahr and he knew I didn't want him there. He stood up. 'Thanks for the coffee.'

'God, no, don't rush off. Have another.'

His eye twitched when he looked at her, and for a moment I thought he was going to swipe all our mugs from the counter to shatter on the floor. Instead, he breathed in slowly. I heard it. Restraint. It was restraint that had etched the grooves of tension on his face. I longed to release him from it, to unhook him and see what would happen . . . Or perhaps I misread it. He said, courteously, 'Thanks, but I'm meeting some friends from Maynooth for lunch.'

After he had left, I turned on Gemma. 'What was

that about? I was giving you space. I thought you'd want to be alone.'

'You thought wrong,' she called, flouncing down the corridor.

'What happened in Marib, Gemma?'

'Enough.'

'Nothing happened in Marib,' Shoukria declared, when we met later that afternoon. She had had other plans for the evening, but I forced her to cancel them and meet me in a café in town. 'He has come for you.'

'God, I hope not.'

'But I thought you wanted this man?'

'I do, but not like this. Gemma's tearing around the flat right now, cleaning up, poring over recipes, like a seven-year-old before her birthday party. She may not have had her way with him in Marib, but she's behaving like someone who believes she soon will. And she's probably right. There were little looks going on between them. Vibes.' I shuddered. 'It was horrible. He obviously felt really awkward around me. At one point he looked like he was going to explode.'

'But of course! How frustrating for him to come all this way only to find that the woman he has come to see is cold and unwelcoming.'

'She wasn't unwelcoming, she was like golden syrup on a piece of French toast.'

'I meant *you*.'

'Don't, Shoukria. Don't get me started again. It was hard enough putting him away in that box back there,' I gestured behind me, 'and he has to bloody stay in it.'

'*Why?*'

'Because even if he is here for me, the timing is wrong, and the history is wrong, and I have other plans.'

'But you still want him?'

I pressed the heel of my hand into my forehead and groaned.

'Then be fair to yourself, and to him,' she said. 'This is difficult for him – he's navigating rocky waters, trying to read you, to see if he still has a chance. You *must* let him know that he does. Otherwise everyone loses out. Three people hurt for the price of one.'

'You're assuming an awful lot.'

'That's because I don't believe this has anything to do with Gemma. Even if there was something between them when she was in college, that was years ago. He has recently had an intense affair with you. That is what he is chasing, I am sure of it.' She leaned forward. 'The damage is already done with Gemma. Between the two of you. Whatever happens, you and she will never get over this. I'm sorry, but that's the way I see it. So don't lose both of them. At least he's still around, this Linkearly.'

'Later.'

She frowned and smiled at the same time – affectionate frustration. 'Don't be so . . . *tight*. It's exciting he has come. Now you can resume your passionate affair!'

'If you think it's so exciting, why don't *you* have an affair?'

Shoukria sighed. 'I can't. I'm happily married. It's so dull. I have to live vicariously through you.'

'Well, I hope my life is more fun vicariously than it is in reality . . .'

When we got back to the flat, half an hour late, Christian was sitting in the living room, nursing a glass of whisky. He stood up to greet Shoukria. She took his hand, stood an inch from his chest and told him what an honour it was to meet a television personality.

'Oh dear, you've seen my programmes.'

'No, but I'm sure they're very good.'

'I thought you weren't coming,' said Gemma.

'The film was longer than I expected.'

'What did you see?' asked Christian, clearly miffed by our lateness.

Shoukria and I had forgotten to synchronize our stories, so each sat down, allowing the other to speak, which resulted in neither of us saying anything.

'A silent movie, then,' said Christian.

'Sorry, no,' I said. 'It was a documentary about an arranged marriage in Palestine.' The most recent film I had seen.

'Yes!' said Shoukria.

'A documentary?' said Christian. 'On general release?'

'No,' I drawled, 'it was a one-off screening in a film club. A fly-on-the-wall thing made by an Australian woman. Exactly the kind of film you wanted to make in Yemen – just her and the camera and the family.'

'You want to make a film in Yemen?' Shoukria asked.

'I'd love to,' said Christian, 'but right now . . .'

'Right now is just the time for it!'

'Don't encourage him, Shoukria.'

'I am sorely aware of that,' he said to her.

Gemma had prepared an amazing spread and was flustered from the effort, but I felt like Thai chicken as much as I felt like cold porridge. The only appetite I had was for Christian. Shoukria directed the conversation like a traffic policeman, giving us cues with her eyebrows. Gemma made no attempt to compete and there was something endearing in her acquiescence. I felt a tug of love for her. There was no telling if she was glowing or groaning inside, but there was no discernible tenderness between her and Christian, although that might have been out of consideration for me.

'Vivien tells me you are studying clannishness,' Shoukria said to him.

'Well, that makes it sound a bit churlish. I'm interested in groupishness, if you like, solidarity and its implications.'

'It's called *abassiya*,' I said to Shoukria.

He sighed. ''*Asabiyya*. Group feeling.'

'But this *can* be very churlish, and inward-looking.'

'Yes, but there is a point of view that suggests it exists only when there's an opposite force working against it. In the Yemeni case, the northern tribes feel they're up against the government, and neither Islam nor nationalism is that hooked on tribalism, so there is a natural tension there.'

'So have you finished your research?'

'For the most part. All I have to do now is write it up.'

'It must be such an interesting place to work, Yemen, what with things blowing up here and blowing up there . . .' She was referring to a couple of ineffectual explosions set off in Sana'a by a group calling itself the Al-Qaeda Sympathizers.

'Shoukria, don't you start. You know it isn't like that.'

'Don't idealize it, Vivien,' Christian said.

'The whole world is so tense right now,' said Shoukria, with a world-weary sigh. 'It's such a worry. My husband is in Dubai, you know. Selling horses, or buying them, I'm never quite sure.'

'He sells them,' I said to Christian.

'Yes.' Shoukria sniffed. 'A horse trader, that's my Liam.'

When Gemma went to get dessert, Shoukria cleared the plates and followed her. Too hot to stay alone in the room with Christian, I opened the french windows and went out on to the terrace. He followed, stepping carefully round the lavender petunias and pink geraniums that were bursting out of their well-appointed tubs.

'Can we meet tomorrow?' he asked quietly. 'We haven't had a decent conversation since three days before I left Sana'a and we –'

'Probably don't need to either.'

'We do. I want to explain.'

'Explain what? About you and Gemma?'

'Yes.'

'It's really none of my business.'

'Perhaps not, but –'

'Pudding's up,' Gemma called.

'Come to my hotel in the morning. Please.'

Shoukria summoned us with a clap, and we returned dutifully to the table, where she entertained Christian with such flamboyance that he might have been a corporate buyer she wished to impress. Of course, he *was* impressed and, as the wine flowed, they became flirtatious. It filled me with lust, irritation and my now permanent companion, disappointment.

Wrap her in a *burqa*, I thought. But no, that would make her all the more alluring: better that her shiny black hair should go drab, her seductive accent become clumsy . . . But these were idle thoughts, provoked by idle lust.

Christian's determination to leave as soon as he had gulped down his coffee alerted me. There was no lingering, no waiting for an opportunity to be with Gemma. At the door, he turned to me and said, 'Give Theo my best if you're speaking to him.'

'Yes.' I held his eye and said again, '*Yes.*'

He nodded. 'Good.'

Propelled by idle lust, I went to his hotel first thing the next morning and rang his room from the desk.

'Come up,' he said.

'You must be joking.'

I paced the lobby. Up and down the steps, around the lounge. When Christian appeared, we stood awkwardly before one another. He wanted to hold me. I wanted to be held. We stood awkwardly.

He had not had breakfast, so we went to the restaurant. I could still feel the Thai chicken kicking about in my gut, but Christian ate, as always, with intent. He launched into the prevailing issue in a similar manner. No beating around here, no fiddling with knives and forks, and no consolation either.

'Those reservations you had in Yemen,' he began, 'did they all concern Gemma or was there something – someone – else?'

'It would have been difficult for her.'

'It would have been difficult all round, but you can't allow your life to be determined by others. You made that mistake before.'

I turned a dessertspoon around in my hand. 'Bill is her brother, you know.'

He bit into his brown bread and marmalade. 'Well,' he said, chewing, 'that follows.'

'What?'

'You don't see a certain pattern of erratic behaviour?'

'No.'

He sighed. 'I wish you wouldn't allow yourself to be a pawn to people who are weaker than you are.'

'And I wish you wouldn't presume to know me better than you do.'

'Oh, I do beg your pardon.' He turned his attention back to his breakfast.

I had inadvertently halted his flow. The click of cutlery on plates tinkled around the room, infused with the low murmur of other guests. My fingers drummed on the table.

'Bored already?' Christian snapped.

'Just restless.'

'You really are impossible.' He motioned for the bill. 'I'd better go and pack.'

Something shrank inside me. 'You're going back already?'

'Tonight. My flight's at seven forty-five, but I have to check out by twelve.'

'We could walk the pier, if you like. It's what people do in Dublin when there's nothing left to say.'

'Vivien,' he said, 'I haven't even started yet.'

After he had checked out, we strolled down the West Pier among Sunday-morning walkers. Children ran about, dogs crapped.

Christian took out his phone. 'Do you mind if I send some texts?'

'Go ahead.'

'I forgot to tell the girls I was going away so I ought to let them know where I am.' He tapped away on his phone as we walked – one message, and another, then another.

'Don't you send them all the same message?' I asked.

He put away his phone. 'Why would I do that? They're triplets, not clones.'

At the end of the pier we sat behind the wall and watched the sea gush against the smooth boulders that made up its heel. 'This is where I come to think,' I said. 'I've come here a lot recently.'

'To think about what?'

'You. Me. Yemen.'

It was a dull day, but there were sailboards flying across the bay and schools of yachts sliding through the waves – handy props to hold our gaze.

'I need to know about Marib,' I said.

'No,' said Christian. 'You need to know about Durham.'

'That too.'

He picked up a pebble and began scraping the rocks between his knees. 'When you turned up in Marib,' he began, 'I thought you'd changed your mind and had come to make a proper start with me. But then Gemma stepped forward – swirling up from nowhere like an evil jinn come to wreck everything. I couldn't believe you knew her. I mean, I'd finally met a woman who filled that great black hole,' he scraped the ground in earnest, 'but bugger it all if she wasn't the best friend of the girl who almost blew me out of the water.' He looked at me. 'When you told me you knew what happened, I thought you had the whole picture. As her friend, it made sense you would, but since then I've worked out that you don't know everything. You just think you do.'

'I know enough.'

'I really hope that isn't so because . . .'

There was a long pause while he struggled, doodling on the rock again and allowing every possible scenario to scuttle round my head. The grey sea shuffled on to the rocks a few metres from our feet, then slid back again. 'For such a big talker, Dr Linklater, you're not saying much.'

'Maybe Gemma should be in on this. It might be better coming from her.'

'I didn't come down here for fresh air, Christian. Get on with it.'

He chucked the pebble into the sea. 'It seems to me,

and I hope I'm right, that you don't know Gemma very well at all.'

'Of course I do.'

He sighed, impatient with my assertions. 'All right. If you say so. You know, then, that she was on the point of being thrown out of college when she took off?'

'Thrown out? Why?'

'Because she'd had her last warning.'

'About what?'

'Harassment.' He looked at me, as if to see whether that one word made everything fall into place. It did, and yet it didn't. 'She was guilty of harassment, Vivien, of harassing *me*.'

I shook my head, but not to contradict him.

'That woman was the bane of my life for three years,' he went on, his voice lower than ever. 'She was everywhere I went: round every corner I turned, in every class I gave, at every blessed lecture. And always waiting at the end of lectures too, with convoluted questions that took an age to answer. She was bright, and she worked hard initially, but then she completely lost focus. There was no passion for the subject that I could see, no sense that she was trying to get somewhere, and yet she became a fixture in the department. She'd hang around the corridor, waiting for me to come back to my office, and when I did, there was no getting rid of her. It was manageable at first. I mean, it happens. Students get fixated on teachers, teachers get fixated on students, but it quickly went from irritating to invasive. I'd come out of a lecture and she'd attach herself to me, no matter where I was going. Once she ended up in the car park, and another time she even came into the common room with me, chattering away, and sat down with my colleagues.'

'She wouldn't have the neck.'

'No?'

I bit my lip. Gemma had a lot of neck.

'It was so bloody time-consuming – hours and hours spent trying to get rid of her – until eventually she had the whole department on alert. The secretaries were fed up with her, but the more tricks we came up with to offload her, the more controlling she became.' He turned to me again. 'There was nothing naïve about this, let me tell you. Your friend has a confidence that is spine-chilling. She was cool – you might even say charming – and she had this smirk, which seemed to say, "You won't escape me." Nor could I – she was always there, walking across the same quadrangle, into the same shop, up the same staircase. She must have walked hundreds of miles in my pursuit. Sometimes I turned off the lights in my office so she wouldn't know I was in there, which sounds pathetic – but being stalked is a very weird experience.'

'*Stalked?*'

'What else would you call it? I mean, I never came home to find her sitting in the kitchen chatting to Diane. It wasn't *Fatal Attraction* – there were no pet bunnies left boiling in the pot – but it was fairly sinister just the same. It got to the point where I thought she was there when she wasn't.'

There was a terrible whiff of truth to all this. It was

the extension, the piece I hadn't been able to see. 'You encouraged her,' I said limply.

His eyes narrowed. 'Not once.'

'The time she walked into the door. You fussed over her.'

'Walked into . . . Oh, that. I didn't fuss, I walked away. I heard this clang, saw who it was and got the hell out of there.'

It was my turn to scrape the rocks with a pebble, overwhelmed not by anger but pity. 'Why was she given that job if she was such a pest?'

'What job?'

'The summer job in the department.'

Christian grimaced, his eyes firmly on the Sea Cat that had just appeared on the horizon on its way from Holyhead. 'Is that what she told you? There was no job, but one summer she hung around the university under pretext of doing research.'

'Why didn't you speak to her? Warn her off?'

'I handled it according to procedure. We had a system for dealing with these problems. In her second year, when it came to a head, she was approached by a counsellor and agreed to talk to her. And she did so, dutifully, for six weeks. During that time she left me alone. We thought we'd cracked it. But then she managed to get herself on to a trip to Jordan. We couldn't stop her – it was relevant to one of the courses she was taking – but every time I looked up in that village, she'd be watching me from the other side of the road or the bus or the room, with that unworldly smile on her face. As if we were lovers and it was our little secret.'

I couldn't speak. All those letters from Jordan . . . The conversations she could not have had with him; the private jokes they had never shared; the collaboration they had not enjoyed . . . The letters had been invention, fantasy, which she had brought to life, perhaps, by writing it down.

'This is not the person I know,' I said at last.

'I appreciate that, but there is a duality about her. I saw it in Yemen. She has remarkable control over whatever it is that drives her to pester me.'

I swallowed, trying to assimilate all this. 'What about Diane? Did she know?'

He nodded. 'And she was totally spooked. Stalkers usually extend their territory eventually, but Gemma, to give her credit, never came near the house to our knowledge. If she had done, she would have found herself in deep trouble.'

'Why didn't you do that anyway? Get a barring order or something?'

'A barring order would have interfered with her studies, which she managed to keep on track – obviously, because the course was her link to me – and I didn't want to see her thrown out of college. Nobody did. She was a young woman with a career ahead of her, who had some kind of personality disorder, and even when she'd had her last warning, I was reluctant to act on it.'

'For God's sake, I'd have noticed if she had a personality disorder!'

'Not necessarily. You aren't the object of her fascination. It is a recognized syndrome, you know, when someone starts focusing on one person, or group of people, and you have to be very careful because they read secret messages into everything. If I smiled at a roomful of students, Gemma was likely to think it was meant only for her. She probably went to Yemen because she'd somehow persuaded herself I'd be pleased to see her.'

I shivered.

'And then there were the phone calls,' he went on. 'They came sporadically all the way through, in spurts. I'd pick up and there'd be no one there, so I'd hang up, and the phone would immediately ring again. And it would ring and ring and go on ringing, but never when I had a tutorial – she knew my timetable better than I did – always when I was alone. It became a battle of wits. I knew it was her and she knew I wasn't picking up, but she somehow had the upper hand. Sometimes she'd ring seven times in a couple of hours, and that would happen three or four times in as many days, and then it would stop again, for weeks or months. I was frequently driven out of my office in frustration, but in the end I refused to give in and I'd sit there counting. Counting how many times she'd let it ring and how many hours' work I lost. We changed my number, of course we did, and I moved offices, but that was a kind of capitulation.'

'But surely –'

'Yes, yes, surely this, surely that, surely the other, but it's never as easy to deal with as it seems. These people don't take a hint. They can't tolerate rejection – probably because they didn't get enough love from their parents, I don't know,' he said, with an unsympathetic moan, 'but they protect themselves against it by refusing to see it. And the really difficult ones are those who don't break any rules, who hover around the median where what they're doing is wrong, but just not *wrong enough*. The ones who aren't patently deranged, who otherwise seem normal, are the hardest ones to handle.'

'Were you her supervisor?'

''Fraid not.'

The lies were stacking up. Any more and it would be hard to see past them. 'She described it all so vividly,' I said. 'Sitting with you in your office, eating chocolate from your top drawer . . . tutorials that went on longer than anyone else's . . .'

'Well, I did keep chocolate in my top drawer, but someone else took on her thesis for me, poor sod. She was none too pleased.'

'You shouldn't have let her away with it.'

He grimaced. 'Hindsight, of course, is a great thing. Besides, who's to say sending her down would have solved anything? Would she have gone meekly back to Dublin? Or would she have gone to my house?'

I didn't want to imagine.

Christian went on, 'Which brings us, I suppose, to the night of the party . . . When I came out and saw her waiting on the pavement – my own personal praying mantis – I was, well, nervous. Actually, to be perfectly honest, I was scared. I'd had so much of it by then, and she'd been drinking, and with the trip-trip-trip of her heels coming after me, I couldn't get to the car fast enough. When I reached it, the clickety-click just kept coming, so I turned and told her to back off. That was when she lunged.'

We both stared hard at the busy horizon. His voice was low, and slightly hoarse. 'She got me into some kind of clinch, with one arm round my neck like a vice, her other hand at my belt, and her teeth sunk into my lip. She just went for it. She had the element of surprise on her side, and she's tall, so you could say she had the upper hand.'

The cold of the rocks was working its way up my spine.

'Even when I pulled her off, she went at it again, kissing me in this manic way and I . . .' His hands were clasped tight together.

'You lost it.'

After a moment, he nodded. 'It was . . . unforgivable.'

'And stupid.'

'I sent her reeling, clear across the bonnet.'

'Wait a minute –'

'I swear I'd never hit a woman before, Vivien, and I never will again. There was no excuse, but –'

'You *hit* her?' Nothing was as I thought.

Christian bit his lip. 'Something like that. And those honourable gentlemen who happened to be coming along the street didn't think it was nice to hit a lady, so I got my comeuppance. They grabbed me by both arms and threw me against a wall.'

I felt sick. I put my hand over my mouth. It was as if I was there, could see it happening, from both sides, both ways. 'She said you tripped.'

'She's fed you a bucket of horseshit. To protect me, probably.'

'No, she told me most of this.'

'But not all of it. Not the bits that matter. And it didn't end there, you know. When I came round after the operation, I was very bloody relieved to be alive and shocked to have lost a kidney, but I wasn't given much time to deal with either before the police were pressing me for a statement. I had no idea what Gemma had told them. She could have had me up on assault charges. Attempted rape, even.'

'But she assaulted you before those bloody mongrels did!'

'I'm a teacher, Vivien,' he said, 'and teachers walk a thin line. A *very* thin line. It would have been my word against hers. I wasn't even sure how to explain what the hell I was doing with one of my students in the street at one a.m. just before her finals . . . The story was already all over the press – "Local don gets kidney shredded. Traumatized student can't sit exams . . ." If the rest had got out – the kissing and the slap – there's no knowing where it would have led. Whenever people in my position wander into a grey area, it's very, very difficult to get out again. Shit sticks, as you know. And I was right to be worried, because Gemma had unhelpfully told the police that I'd offered her a lift. I insisted I hadn't, but the cop who was taking my statement hassled me. He probably figured I was massaging the facts to protect my reputation, but I was pretty ill so he let it go and, anyway, our statements converged in every other respect. I didn't mention our tussle and, as it turned out, Gemma hadn't either. She told the cops she got the bruise on her cheekbone from one of the thugs.'

'That was what she said when she came home.'

'Well, it was me who did it. They didn't touch her. That much I do remember, because I was terrified they'd go after her next and I kept willing her to run, to get away, which she did. And that's the huge irony about this: I find myself curiously indebted to your friend. She could have destroyed my career. She chose not to.'

'But everyone knew she was harassing you.'

'Did that give me the right to hit her?'

'*Yes*,' I said. 'Maybe.'

'No. I abused my position. I lost control.'

'You were provoked.'

'It just isn't that simple,' he said impatiently. 'No matter which way you look at it, I'm the one who assaulted her.'

'Oh, for God's sake! She was all over you. What were you supposed to do?'

'Restrain her, somehow. Not fling her out of my way.'

I stood up. 'Jesus, I could throttle Gemma right now.'

'I've had that inclination myself. Especially when she behaves as if we're best buddies and everything's hunky-dory and she goes on about her wonderful career, whereas *mine* . . .'

'There's nothing wrong with your career.'

'I got it back on track, eventually, but it wasn't easy. I had to get out of teaching a year later.'

266

'Why?'

'Couldn't trust myself. Students made me nervous, and I kept looking for another Gemma. So I took a long sabbatical and had a lot of counselling before I went back into the system. In the interim I made documentaries.'

'I thought you were doing both at the same time.'

'Not during my "gap" years. The first series was a Godsend. It got me out of the country, away from academia, and it gave me options. When those programmes were well received, they offered me a second series. I had to do it. I needed the money and I needed an alternative career in case I couldn't teach again, so we decided to move to London and get away from Durham altogether. Eventually I got part-time lecturing, but there was no guarantee I'd ever have a permanent post so I kept up the television work. But every time one of those series came out, with all the attendant publicity, we were terrified Gemma would wriggle out of the woodwork and go to the press or the police, making God knows what allegations. It has happened before, you know – students have accused lecturers of sexual harassment long after they've left college. And I had a public profile. It might have been irresistible. She might even have made money out of it.'

'She wouldn't have done that. She was in love with you.'

'Give me a break. At least let's get the terminology right.'

'You're not going to say she suffers from erotomania or something?'

'God, I hope not. OCD, probably. She's a love-obsessive – perhaps only mildly so but they can be very destructive, if that's where they get their kicks.'

'But Gemma isn't vengeful,' I said. 'When those programmes came out, she just lay back and sighed over you.'

He closed his mouth, shook his head. 'She did more than that. Yemen wasn't the first time I'd seen her since Durham, you know. She showed up at the university a few years ago. Twice.'

'Jesus.'

'I thought then I was really done for – that she'd go after my family. Instead she was there one day, gone the next. I wondered if I'd imagined it, until it happened again a few months later – Gemma smiling at me from across a coffee shop, then gone. Nothing for the police to go on. There never was.' He stood up, pressed his hands into the pockets of his jacket and went to the water's edge. 'She's smart. She only ever goes so far, but she gets what she wants, and the little game she's playing right now makes me . . . ill.'

We stood by the water's edge. Out on the bay a dinghy capsized, slowly, slowly, as if the sails wanted to lie down and rest.

I said, 'You could have told me all this in Shabwah.'

'You led me to believe you already knew. And you were so quick to defend her. You still are.'

'Of course I am. I've known her for twenty years.'

'It's all documented, you know. In Durham. If you have any doubts, we can call Diane.' He took out his phone. 'She'll tell you what it was like trying to get me back to work.'

'Put that away.' In spite of the dull skies and cool breeze, the heat and stillness of Marib enveloped me and I was standing again by the jeep, with Gemma behind my shoulder and Christian hurrying over . . . 'When she turned up in Yemen,' I said, 'you must have been –'

'Stupefied. And then *you*. That you could be close to her . . . All the old paranoia returned. I thought I'd been set up – that you were some kind of bait sent ahead to snare me or something. It was hard to be rational.'

'But why did you come to the Hadramawt? You could have stayed behind.'

'No,' he said, looking at me, 'I couldn't. But I'm afraid one day spent trapped between you and her was more than I could handle. You wouldn't even get into my jeep. I had the pleasure of *her* company for fifteen hours . . .'

'God, what a bloody awful day that was.'

He nodded. 'Until you came to me that night.'

I sat down on the rocks again. 'I suppose she invited herself to Marib?'

'No, I asked her.'

'Oh? That's a little inconsistent, isn't it?'

'Maybe, but I wanted to get her away from you. She was up to her old tricks, manoeuvring us all round the chessboard, and I didn't want her messing you about, so when I saw her there in the lobby that morning, as she would be, whining about dreary Shibam, I just thought, Fuck her. She'd wrecked your trip to get to me. You were tense and tetchy, and so pissed off that I decided I'd salvage it all by taking her, and me, out of the picture. It seemed like a good plan, in the fog of dawn. Unfortunately I'm not at my brightest first thing in the morning, and we weren't far along the road when I realized what a jackass I'd been. I made sure it was a long, hard day for her, but she was too wily for me. In Marib, every time I went to fetch her to take her back to Sana'a she'd disappeared, which was bloody dangerous apart from anything else. I barely slept all the time she was there. I was surrounded by bodyguards and God knows what, but the only thing that really scared me was that woman. I've never been so glad of the rattle of a few AK47s.'

'You did that for me?'

'Did it help?'

'Oh, yes.'

'Good, because that day I left you in al-Hawta was the longest of my life and every day since has been only marginally shorter.'

There it was. The declaration I had sought in the ruins of Shabwah was made on the end of Dun Laoghaire pier.

'I've given this a lot of thought, Vivien.' He crouched in front of me. 'If I'd known in Yemen that you had anything to do with her, I'd have been out the door faster than you could have blinked. Coming anywhere near that woman is like walking into a viper's den for me, and getting involved with a friend of hers was sheer bloody madness.'

'So why are you here?'

'Because I couldn't stay away. And not for want of trying, believe me.'

My mobile phone rang. Gemma. We looked at her name on the screen. I took the call. 'Hello?'

'Where are you?'

'Walking the pier.'

'Oh. Look, I'm off home and I won't be back till late, but I've just finished the milk so you might want to get some. And cat biscuits. Didds is driving me mad. He won't touch the tinned stuff.'

'Okay. See ya.'

'Em . . . how do you think last night went?'

'The meal was lovely.'

'Do you think he enjoyed it?'

'Why don't you ask him?' I said.

'Oh, I will, I will. Later. Get milk,' she said, and rang off.

I put the phone away. 'How am I going to face her when she comes home tonight?'

'Tonight?'

'She spends Sundays with her parents.'

'Oh. Right.' Christian frowned, then nodded. 'And in the meantime?'

In the meantime, back in neutral, back at the flat, I poured him a beer and made myself peppermint tea. When I came along the corridor, he was standing by the living-room door. He took the glass from my hand and put it on the hall table, took the mug and did likewise. As was his way, he didn't leap: he simply stood very close and watched me, then leaned forward to kiss me, still watching. I gripped his shirt and pulled him closer. He pressed me against the wall. I held him as

I had wanted to in Arsh Bilqis, and Mahram Bilqis, and in the Ramlat al-Sab'atayn. It was the hug of a dozen different places. As we stumbled towards my bedroom, it seemed impossible that I had thought I could ever let this go.

We lay afterwards, released and relieved.

'I've imagined this,' said Christian, 'every inch between Marib and Sana'a, every mile between Sana'a and here.'

'And I've dreamed about it at every stop on the DART line.'

'So it *is* what you want?'

'Wanting is the easy part.'

'You're not going to say, "This is only a Sunday-afternoon fling", are you?'

'No, but what am I to do about Gemma? More to the point, what is Gemma going to do about us?'

Christian leaned on an elbow. 'Listen, Vivien, I'd love to say that if being with you means being with her, then I'll do it. But . . .' he ran a finger along my chin '. . . I can't say it because I won't do it. I won't be putting myself in her way again. No more chummy dinner parties or trips to Dublin. Not to stay here, anyway. I know that sounds like an ultimatum and I don't much want to come between friends but –'

'You came between us long ago. In Durham. We haven't been particularly close since she was at college, since I so singularly failed her . . . and you.'

He smiled. 'Don't.'

'She never quite forgave me for trying to talk her out of it. She desperately wanted an ally, someone to egg her on in her pursuit of you, but I wouldn't do it and sometimes I think that's why she went to Yemen. It was as if she wanted to taunt me with her determination to get to you, whatever I thought about it.'

'Exactly. That's exactly how she behaved with me.'

'But why? Why would someone keep going where they're not wanted?'

'To escape indifference. To force you into their lives, make you a part of their experience, even though you patently don't want to be there.'

'What am I going to do?'

'Tell her about us,' he said. 'That'll shake her up good and proper.'

'Don't be mean.'

'Can't help it.'

'Nor can she, I'm sure.'

He lay down again.

'I'm not telling her,' I said. 'Not yet. I need to think it through.'

'But —'

'No. You can't expect me to flip Gemma out of my life, like a piece of litter, just because you've turned up and declared yourself.'

'How long do you need?'

'I don't know. A few weeks, maybe.'

'What am I supposed to do in the meantime?'

'Wait. Don't phone. Don't contact me. Just wait.'

'Bloody hell, Vivien, I've been waiting for you since the day we met!'

'Not my fault.'

He sighed, and stroked my shoulder with the back

of his finger. 'All right, but don't muck about. The sooner we get Gemma out of the way –'

'There's something else getting in our way, Christian.'

'Good God, is nothing ever straightforward with you?'

'I'd been thinking about going back to Yemen,' I said. 'To live.'

'Christ.' He sat up. 'Just my luck! My first rival was a dead man, poor Eric, and now I'm competing with a bloody country!'

'It isn't just the country. It's the opportunities, the things undone, as Freya would say.' I put my hand on his back. 'I keep thinking about those women – what they're trying to achieve, the work they do, the sacrifices – and yet all these years that I've been a free agent, with no kids, no constraints, I've done nothing for the greater good.'

'You've nurtured artists, which is always for the greater good.'

'Shoukria nurtured them. I just straightened the paintings. I want, have always wanted, another perspective.'

'That other perspective could be *us*. Besides, it isn't all it's cut out to be, you know, this alternative lifestyle you hanker after.'

'That's a bit disingenuous coming from you.'

'And this isn't a good time to move to the Middle East. Al-Qaeda isn't done yet.'

'If al-Qaeda strikes again, the danger is here, not there,' I said.

'They could strike *anywhere*. And don't forget the

274

Americans. They have their beady eyes on Yemen, so leave it, please. If you want excitement, you can come on field trips with me.'

'You mean be an appendix to *your* adventures? Not quite what I had in mind.'

'What exactly *do* you have in mind?'

'I want to work at Nooria's centre, but she can't pay me so money is a problem. Leasing the apartment won't cover my expenses. It'll barely cover the mortgage.'

'So you can't afford to go back? Excellent,' he said smugly, sliding down to my side. 'Stay with me instead. Give this the chance it deserves.'

'But I'd be repeating history. Can't you see that?'

'No. There's no comparison. You were culture-shocked the first time and you had a crazy boyfriend who threw down his toys when he didn't get what he wanted.'

'Culture-shocked? I never said I was culture-shocked.'

'Erm . . . no, you didn't, but Theo did, after you left. It sort of slipped out.'

'Sod him,' I said. 'That was between him and me . . . and Nooria . . . and all the women at the *tafrita*.'

'Why not me?'

'Because of everything you've done. You probably think I'm a total wimp.'

'Culture shock has nothing to do with separating the wimps from the not-so-wimpish.'

We lay for a while without speaking, my head rising and falling on his chest. 'Do you know why bad memories remain painful,' I said, 'even years after the event?'

'Tell me.'

'Because the human survival instinct –'

'Now you're sounding like an anthropologist.'

'Shut up. Our survival instinct etches our failures into our brains so that we won't make the same mistake again.'

'But this isn't a mistake.'

We lay at either end of the bath, frankincense wafting from my Yemeni burner. Christian squeezed a soapy sponge between my toes. 'I have a horrible confession to make.'

'What?'

'It wasn't my fault, honest. I was just sitting there in Sana'a, minding my own business, when along he came with Edda and before I could do anything about it – we'd been introduced.'

'What are you talking about?'

'Mackintosh-Smith.'

I sat upright, heaving a wave of water on to the floor. 'You met him?'

He nodded. 'Good bloke.'

'You *rat*.'

'I was an innocent bystander!'

'What happened?'

'Not much. We had a chat. It was a bit embarrassing, actually, because I still haven't read his Ibn Battutah book.'

'That's terrible.'

'Excuse me, but I've been very busy. I'll get to it in my own good time.'

'I mean, it's terrible you met him. And so unfair.'

'I know. I said to him, I said, "Fancy meeting you now, when only a few weeks ago a friend of mine was chasing around Sana'a looking for you under every dustbin lid."'

'If you told him that, this relationship is over.'

'I *did* think about it, but I didn't want to spoil it for him. I mean, one day he'll be walking down a street in Sana'a, thinking about Ibn Battutah and all his many friends, and you'll abseil off one of those tower houses and land right on top of him with his book in one hand and a pen in the other.'

'And if he has any sense, he'll be delighted.'

That evening, as I made my way home from the airport, there was no battle raging within me. I was not torn between Gemma and Christian, and the very absence of such conflict was a source of distraction. I walked past our flat and went round the block. It all made sense, that was the horrible thing. Gemma had often manipulated me and I had allowed it, sometimes because I loved her, sometimes because I loved her brother. Our friendship, like many, worked on the basis of imbalance. She was strong, I less so. She held the rudder, usually, and I went where she took me, but in this instance she had led me way off course without my even being aware of it. I should have seen that she was compromising Christian, that even by her own account she was pushing the limits, but my mistake had been in not doubting that account. It had never occurred to me that she was drip-feeding me, using truth to disguise lies, and I was baffled by what she had pulled off. Why had she brought me so far, instead of leaving me behind? Why not simply lie about the whole thing? It was as if I had been led around a windowless house in Sana'a, along hidden staircases and blind alleys. In letters and late-night phone calls, she had made of me an unwilling voyeur, a bystander, to her frustrated delusions. 'Oh, it was rather more than a drunken kiss,' she had said, and I had seen it played out the way she drew it, filling in the gaps myself. I stopped on the pavement and covered my eyes. It was mortifying to be exposed to the desperation of someone else's longings. Fantasies are too hungry to be shared, and yet I had been roped in to Gemma's, probably because if *I* believed them it made them all the more real to her.

How could I possibly be fair to her when I was involved with him?

I came to our front door. The lights were on. She was home. I had been very careful, before leaving for the airport, to wash down the bath and open the windows, clear all vestiges of our torrid afternoon, and yet I stood on the doorstep, terrified of being found out. It was a horrible, choking feeling. It could not happen again. There would be no more secret trysts, no hiding or dissembling.

Yet when I stepped inside and Gemma asked me cheerfully where I'd been, I lied. Of course.

16

A student sat cross-legged on the floor in front of a painting, sketching. I sat at the desk, staring at his back. Outside, people hurried about. Lunch hour. I was aware of them, aware of the waves of movement beyond the window. Particular voices drifted in and out of my hearing, like fireflies sailing in and out of sight. In theory I was waiting for these people to come in, or some of them anyway – that tiny slice of the population whom we hoped to attract; the ones who would step in, nod at me, and move quietly around the room, viewing the work. What a curious job, I thought. Working with the public, depending on the public, yet barely engaging with them beyond a smile and a hand stretched out with a catalogue or to receive a cheque. What a very odd, silent relationship. Sometimes when a customer approached me with a query, I had to struggle to find my voice. I would search for it in my throat and hope to find with it the administrator's tone, the professional's delivery, and when the purchase was finalized and the buyer gone, my voice could retreat to below my ribcage, which was where I usually found it.

It had been a week since Christian had been over. Nothing had changed. Nothing had been done. I had retreated, like my voice, into the pit of myself, and I had no means, or inclination, to come back out again.

I stood up and walked the length of the gallery. I loved our floor. Canadian maple. My steps were sharp, my heels meeting the timber with resolution. Pacing is so much more satisfying than walking. It has attitude. But my pacing, and my thinking, were getting me nowhere.

I turned, did another length of the room. The student tore a page from his pad and threw it aside, just as I, repeatedly, threw aside opportunities and considered approaches. I spent hours, like this, formulating ways to broach the subject, to break the news with the least possible impact. The dread was two-fold: causing hurt would be bad enough; handling the explosive reaction would be no less difficult.

The current exhibition, called *Black and White*, was by an artist Shoukria had found in Donegal, and it had brought in the press in good numbers. At first glance each piece looked the same – a white canvas with two thin black cylinders more or less in the centre, standing side by side, one slightly smaller than the other. The differences between each painting were minimal – the cylinders were a little taller or slimmer, or placed further to the left or the right – but it was the titles that made the point: *Love*, *Hate*, *Envy*, *Fear*, and on through eight other emotions (none of which was *Gutless*). From the middle of the room, it looked as if we were exhibiting twelve copies of the same painting. I had told Shoukria they would never sell because they couldn't stand alone, but she was right and I was wrong, as usual. A bank had bought the whole collection for its headquarters.

'Enough with the pacing,' I said aloud. The student

turned. Enough with the pacing, because there was only one step I needed to take and I would not see Christian until I did so.

'I'll tell her outright,' I said to Shoukria, later that day, when I was looking at slides on a hand-held viewer. 'I'll just throw it out, clear-cut and bare. She's Syrian, this woman?'

'Yes, based in Frankfurt. She has exhibited a lot already, with others.'

'And you want to give her a one-woman show?'

'What do you think?'

'It'll be next year before I can find a slot.'

Shoukria nodded. 'Don't be brutal with Gemma. Feed her. Lead her. It will be easier if she comes to it herself.'

'But that could take weeks.'

We both looked up. There was a pounding on the ceiling. Shoukria was standing by the window, sucking a pen. I pointed upwards. 'This is what happens when I leave you in charge. I go away for three weeks, and I come back to discover that the ceiling's coming down because *you* let the room to an aerobics class. Aerobics for the over-size-sixteens!'

The ceiling shook again. 'Is that a crack?' Shoukria asked.

'The vibration could damage the work. You'll have to kick them out.'

She pouted. 'That's your job.'

'No way. You booked them, you can unbook them. Just go up there after the class and say, "I'm sorry, ladies and gents, but your combined weight is bringing down the building."'

Christian was breaking all the rules. He sent me text messages every morning. The first time he did so, my phone was lying on the kitchen counter when it beeped. I had to dive for it in case Gemma saw the English number on the screen. Subsequently I never switched it on until I was safely on the DART. Every morning he sent me a few words, and every morning I enjoyed it, but sent no reply. So he started phoning me at work. There was no stopping him. 'How can I think straight if you keep phoning me like this?' I asked, exasperated.

'That's exactly why I do it. I don't want you to think straight. I just want you to act.'

'Like you did? In Durham?'

I had become edgy. At home, if a door banged or Didds sprang on to a chair, I jumped. Christian's story had made me nervous. It was as if I had absorbed his experience. I was living with a stranger, an unknown quantity, and my head was filling daily with revived memories of once-forgotten events: scenes from a childhood, from a friendship, from a love-affair. Gemma, years back, locking herself in a cupboard because we disagreed about what film to watch and refusing to come out for three hours. Bill, disappearing from my life for ten days because I had become exasperated with his loafing. But above all I thought about their parents: the distracted mother, who sometimes appeared to have trouble remembering which of her boys was which; and the father, throwing tantrums on his rare appearances at home because his children were not excelling at school. Dissatisfaction and disregard – neglect, in fact – had been their lot, yet I had envied them their freedom . . . The result had been petulance in one, and an obsessive determination to have her way in the other, but it was Christian Linklater who had paid the steepest price.

Gemma frightened me now. It scared me that she had so little grasp on other people's rights, and privacies, and wishes. I felt her watching me when she wasn't even there, sensed a presence behind me when I was alone, and one day at work I looked up and saw her face pressed against the window. I gasped.

She burst into the gallery.

'Jesus, it *is* you!' I said.

'Who'd you think it was?' she asked.

'No one. I didn't think it was anyone.'

'Fancy lunch? I want to talk to you.'

'Okay.' That sweat again. The creeping sweat that broke out every time I thought I'd been found out. She had not set foot in the gallery for years. It spooked her, she said – all that space with nobody in it. It spooked *me* that she chose to turn up now. Had she heard something? Seen something? Found the photos of me and Christian that I had tucked away in a drawer?

Nothing so helpful. Instead, when we had settled at a low table in a nearby pub with tuna salads, Gemma said, 'Fancy a weekend in London?'

'What?'

'You know, a girls' weekend away.'

'We haven't done that for ages.'

'Exactly. We could both use a break, especially with the way things have been recently, and a weekend away might give you the kick-start you need.'

'To do what?'

She sighed in exasperation. 'Okay, look, no one else is saying it so I'm going to: if you don't want to be here any more, *don't* be. If you want to be with Theo and Nooria and all your many friends – fine. Do it. Go. I mean, this long face you've been going around with since April is doing my head in, and I don't understand what's stopping you. You've been working in that place for *seven years*. You're stagnating. So take the bull by the horns and go abroad, if that's what you want, and see if you can hack it.'

Oh, the little nick, the reminder that I had not been up to the challenge the last time. 'Well, thanks for your . . . concern, but that isn't the only thing that's been on my mind.'

'I *know*,' she said irritably. 'I know very well that you're pissed off with me for going after Christian again, but I wish you'd get off that high moral ground you're standing on because what I do with Christian is nobody's business but my own.'

'I'm not on high moral ground.'

'Fine. Great. I'm glad to hear it.' She tucked into her salad. 'So let's put all that behind us and go away for a bit of *craic*. Come on, Viv. Everything seems so sour these days. We need to re-bond!'

At that moment, I would have forsaken Christian for ever, just to have that wicked smile, that zest, in my life again. 'All right,' I said, smiling. 'But let's go to Paris instead.'

'God, no.'

'Why not?'

'It's just, well, I fancy London.'

Silly me. Silly, naïve, dependent little me. 'I see. And I suppose, while we're there, you thought we might just call in on Linklater?'

The shrug. 'It crossed my mind. After all, he dropped in on us.'

'What a bonding session *that* would be,' I said. 'You and me and him. Just like old times.'

'But it isn't like old times,' she said earnestly. 'That's the point. Everything's changed. He'd be dead pleased to see us.'

'He wouldn't. He'd hate it, and you bloody well know he would.'

Her brows went up and down in slight, swift movements as she pressed food on to her fork.

'Nothing happened in Marib, did it?' I said.

'Not exactly, but –'

'Nothing is ever going to happen.'

Suddenly her eyes were on mine, anguished and honest. 'But why did he come over two weeks ago? Why did he turn up like that?'

'He has friends in Maynooth.'

'You don't really believe that's why he came, do you?'

I pushed away my plate. 'No, I don't.'

'Right, so –'

'He came to see me.' I picked up my bag and slid along the bench. 'Sorry, Gem.'

I hurried back to work. *Stupid, stupid, stupid.* I could have been gentle, could have explained, but confronted once again with her relentless sculpting of events to suit her own peculiar mould, I dropped the load and ran away. I pulled out my phone and began a message to Christian, my fingers shaking. 'Help,' I wrote.

'Vivien!' Gemma was coming after me.

I pushed the door into the gallery. She came hurtling in behind me, but before either of us could speak, Shoukria came out of the office. 'Oh!'

'What?'

'A call, Vivien. For you. Quickly.'

I reached for the phone.

'Not here,' said Shoukria. 'Take it inside.'

Hell, I thought. *Christian. What timing.* I made for the office.

'Gemma,' Shoukria said loudly, 'thank you so much for dinner the other week! Such a lovely evening . . .'

It was Christian, all right: leaning against my desk, with his hands in his pockets and his ankles crossed.

I raised my hands and shook them in the air.

He smiled.

'Gemma's outside!' I hissed.

'Oh, shit.'

'Is *right*.' I put my ear to the door. Shoukria's voice was a little too high. I could just imagine her steering Gemma towards the entrance. Christian touched my arm. I pushed him off, my ear pasted to the door. He kissed my neck. I elbowed him again, but he persisted, his mouth sliding inside my collar.

'She's gone.' Shoukria put her head round the door. 'May I come in?'

'How did you get rid of her so quickly?'

She wrinkled her nose. 'She was determined to speak to you, but I said, no, no, we should give you some privacy because it was that nice anthropologist calling from London.'

'That might work,' said Christian, nodding.

I straightened, instilling the gesture with all of my mother's severity. ' "Might work"? Is this some pest-eradication problem? Nothing needs *to work*. I have already dealt with this, and bugger the both of you for interfering. You had no right, either of you, to mess around with Gemma's feelings.'

'What have I done?' Christian asked.

'You turned up!'

Shoukria raised her chin. 'I had to keep her out of here, didn't I? I saved your ass!' She flounced out.

Christian chuckled. ' "*I saved your ass!*" ' he mimicked. 'No wonder you can't get away from that woman. She's gorgeous.'

As he spoke, Shoukria came scurrying back into the room, her eyes wide, with Gemma right on her heels.

She stopped dead when she saw Christian. Her elbows drew back, and she turned to me, astonished.

'I didn't know he was here either,' I said.

It took only a fraction of a second. With that increasingly familiar twist, Gemma absorbed the situation and made it her own. 'I've just heard!' she said, stepping over to Christian and taking his arm with both hands.

'It's lovely. *Lovely.* And you two have so much in common – me!' She giggled. She kissed his cheek and, in a mock-whisper, said into his ear, 'Just don't tell her what we got up to, darling!' And then she was gone.

The door was open. Shoukria, Christian and I stood staring at it.

I said, 'Did I imagine that?'

'No.' Shoukria looked out into the gallery.

'Where is she?'

'Gone,' said Shoukria. 'Here and gone. Your problems are over.'

'Someone get me a drink,' said Christian, sitting into the nearest seat. He looked shaken.

We spent the night in a city-centre hotel. It was a muted evening. Christian was subdued, reflective. He stood looking out of the window, muttering occasionally. 'Mistakes,' he said, at one point. 'Too many mistakes.'

'What could you have done differently?'

'I should have thrown the law at her, but I was too busy being the Compassionate Tutor, flattering myself that I had it in hand. Diane was right. I should have thrown the book at her.'

'You and Diane disagreed about it?'

'Frequently. But don't worry – I ate humble pie and gave her credit, from my hospital bed, when she was proved right. If I had dealt with it at the outset I wouldn't still be dealing with it now.' He looked out again. 'I just don't understand how Gemma keeps the upper hand.'

'She doesn't have the upper hand. She just performs . . . And it must be pretty bleak backstage.'

'No matter what I do she wheedles her way back into view. And now I have you, but somehow she's . . .' He turned to me. 'She'll wreck this.'

'Christian, come here.' He came reluctantly to the bed and sat down. 'When you got up this morning, you were presumably looking forward to getting here. Now you look like you wish you hadn't bothered.'

'Yeah, I do.'

'Thanks.'

'The one day I turn up at your work so does she. I mean, what are the odds?'

I touched his face. 'Stop. Don't perpetuate it. As far as you're concerned, it's over.'

'Is it?'

'Yes, especially now that she knows about us.'

'It's a habit, Vivien, and habits are hard to break.'

'But I'm going to break it for her. Just you watch.' I pulled him over and made him forget all about Gemma Colbert.

He was more cheerful when we woke early the next morning and had coffee before he left. 'Come to London for a weekend,' he said. 'See what I have to offer.'

'Like, for instance, three children? I'm afraid I'm not ready for the Linklater triplets.'

'I'll lock them in a cupboard.'

I smiled. 'Actually . . . I *am* longing to see the Queen of Sheba exhibition at the British Museum, so if you promise you won't foist a family gathering on me I'll consider it.'

'Done.'

*

289

Dublin was out of sorts that evening. It didn't look well as I made my way home from work, and an odd, indistinct feeling pursued me when I got off the DART. I kept turning round to see if someone was following me.

I came to our front door. The apartment was suffering the same apprehension as the streets. There was bad air about, as if someone had left the gas on unlit. Gemma was in the living room, sitting at the dining-table, flicking through a magazine. If I had expected to find her meek and broken by my revelation, I would have been disappointed. She was in marketing mode, wearing high heels and a tight green dress – the outfit she wore to make a presentation to a new client.

I didn't care what she said, or how she raged: I just wanted to be spared the trouble of speaking.

'You're sleeping with him,' she said, without looking up and flicking another page.

It was a statement not a question, but I said, 'Yes.'

She stood up, crossed her arms, and walked up and down in front of the french windows. Then she laughed. 'No wonder you were so pissed off when I turned up in Yemen.'

I put down my keys.

Gemma turned. 'I can't believe you could do that to me. After everything I'd been through . . . the years I'd spent . . .'

'You didn't own him.'

'I held the copyright.'

It was hard to argue with that.

She looked at me as though I were some vile creature crawling about in the underlay of the carpet. 'Why didn't you tell me? All you had to do was send me an email saying, "Linklater's here and he's hitting on me." It would have been so easy.'

'Not for you. Give me some credit for trying to get it right.'

'Get it right? You let me think he was available.'

'He *was*. He was fair game by the time you turned up. I'd already ended it.'

'Not on my account, surely?'

'Yes, on your account. Why not?'

'Well, thanks for the consideration, but it was a bit late, don't you think?'

I sat down at the table.

'Don't get me wrong,' she said. 'I know Linklater. I know his charm, his way under hot suns, so I know what you were dealing with. I can't say I'd have been happy about it but, God, I would have been fair to you.'

'Like you were fair to him?'

'You allowed me to make a complete fool of myself in front of Christian and Theo and all those people . . . You hung me out to dry. You couldn't even spare me the humiliation of rushing out to Marib – and back again. Why didn't you stop me?'

'There *was* no stopping you. There never has been any way to stop you, has there, Gemma?'

Her eyes dropped to the floor, but she continued to stride back and forth. 'He's filled you in.'

'I wish he hadn't.'

Her stilettos were ineffectually silent on the carpet. This exchange would have been far more intimidating on parquet.

'I mean, Jesus, Gemma, what were you thinking? He could have brought charges against you. Serious charges. He still could, after Yemen.'

'Don't be ridiculous.'

''There are witnesses, official records.'

'Oh, really? Well, if it comes to that, I have stuff on him too, you know.'

'Listen to yourself,' I said quietly. 'Would you please just listen to yourself?'

For the first time, she looked slightly meek, and maybe even beaten.

'I just don't get it,' I said. 'In spite of everything that happened in Durham, you just kept on going – from London to Sana'a to Marib. Why? I mean, explain it to me, would you, because I really don't understand?'

She stopped pacing. After a long, still silence, she said, 'I had to be near him. That's all.'

'At any price?'

'You should have told me,' she said, 'when I got to Yemen. You owed me that much.'

'I know, and I'm sorry, but I'm telling you now.'

Gemma sighed loudly, shook her head and resumed pacing, as if I were a tedious irritation in her busy day. I had expected worse – either a vicious personal attack or convulsions of remorse as the whole thing fell out of her at last – but all she could come up with was the body language of corporate displeasure.

'I intend to stay with him,' I said, 'and if Christian

ever again looks over his shoulder and sees you there, he won't let it go because I won't let him.'

'Is that a threat?'

'A warning. Enough is enough, Gem.'

The cat came in. We both looked at it. In response, it purred loudly, and the soothing ripples of sound reproached me.

'This wretched business has been eating you up for years,' I said gently. 'You should get help, counselling of some sort.' The cat brushed against the leg of my chair and mewed, but its purr had had no mollifying effect on Gemma.

'Don't be so patronizing,' she snapped. 'You fell for him same as I did. What's the difference?'

'The difference is that you as good as attacked him!'

'Oh, for God's sake, we had a shag.'

Revulsion rose in my stomach. So, too, did a Trojan horse full of doubts, as intended. She said it with such easy conviction.

'Do you really think I would have gone out to that place without good reason?' she asked. 'And do you seriously expect him to own up to it? It would hardly make for very salubrious pillow talk, would it? And it certainly doesn't make him look good.'

As I stared back at her, feeling as stretched as the rope in a tug-of-war, a simple thought came to me. The parties at either end of the rope collapsed simultaneously. 'You know what, Gemma? The only thing that matters to me about that night is that you both survived it.' I stood up. 'So if you really did have a shag, I hope it was a good one and I hope you enjoyed it because it isn't going to happen again.' I made for the door.

'I'm moving out. And I'm not giving a month's notice.'

I turned. 'That's probably for the best. I don't suppose you'd find it very comfortable with Christian around, and I won't find it particularly comfortable living with someone to whom deceit comes so easily.'

'I don't know why not,' she said. 'It came pretty easily to you.'

I slept better that night than I had since I'd got home. Denying myself had wearied me to the core.

Gemma left early the next morning. She closed the door quietly, but I had heard that click before. The first time Christian had moved towards me in the dark alcove, I had heard the click of the door that would close behind Gemma.

17

An empty flat, an empty life. Christian in London, Gemma gone. Sometimes I fancied I heard her showering in the mornings or muffled music coming from her room . . . Often I came home to find items gone. Her armchair, her bookshelf, and then smaller things were taken – the vegetable scraper she had bought and the funny beaded lamp she'd got in Cork. Like a magpie, she swooped when I wasn't there, and I'd reach out for something, once shared, now repossessed. Then one day I came in from work and found her keys on the mat.

It was the end of a lot of things – my link to Bill, still unmarried and restless, and to their family and the mad teenage years I had spent among them, and to an uneven but long friendship. It should have been poignant, but it was like stepping into a quiet corridor after closing the door on the fractious Colberts. The sadness was slight, the relief almost palpable.

The way was clear. The path had opened up ahead. I could be with Christian without a bad conscience, yet I continued to feel oddly constrained.

In my faded *Shorter Oxford English Dictionary*, printed in 1950 and given to me by my father, the word 'commute' had yet to absorb its current association with trains and planes. I looked it up in an idle moment in my quiet home, curious to find out when exactly the word's workload had increased. Its primary meanings in 1950 were to change, or exchange, and so I became a commuter in the original sense of the word: I exchanged one person for another, and was about to exchange one town for another.

Christian and I also commuted according to modern usage. For a month after Gemma left, he came over every weekend and we headed into the country, where there was no chance of running into her or mutual friends. I made my first visit to London in July, drawn not by the daunting prospect of meeting his daughters but by the Queen of Sheba, and a special exhibition in her honour.

Stepping across Christian's threshold was like entering a warren. Someone else's warren. He led me down to a broad kitchen, which looked on to a plain, untended garden. The flower thing, obviously.

'Why don't you put down some shrubs?' I asked.

'I do enough digging in my professional life.'

'But you could mow the lawn . . . an odd time.'

It was a homely room, with dining and kitchen on one side, and a sitting area and fireplace on the other. There was clutter around the shelves, girls' stuff, and piles of books and periodicals. Christian poured me a glass of wine and set about cooking dinner. A long oak dining-table ran alongside the french windows. Outside, weeds sprouted between the tiles on the patio.

'Are you sure one of your daughters isn't about to

burst in and turn this romantic weekend into a family affair?'

'I specifically suggested this weekend because they're away. Diane's taken them hiking in the Lake District so no one's going to come looking for a cup of sugar.'

'Thank goodness for that. I don't know how you cope with this arrangement.'

He smiled. 'It *can* get confusing. I never know on a given morning who's in the house. I've even been known to bring mugs of tea upstairs, certain I'd heard life, only to find empty beds. And once or twice I've brought women home convinced we were alone, only to have them run into a daughter on the landing in the middle of the night.'

'What a prospect.'

'Never fear. I wouldn't land you on them like that.'

Land *me* on *them*?

We had sex and croissants for breakfast the next morning, then set out for the British Museum, where the Queen of Sheba greeted us in all her glory. Handel's 'The Arrival of the Queen of Sheba' played quietly in the background as we walked around.

'Yemen in a glass case,' I said.

'Ancient Yemen. Long-gone Yemen.'

We wandered in the muted atmosphere of the arc-shaped room, in which desert colours on the walls – deep reds and yellows – gave the impression of an underground cave where treasures had been stashed. In spite of my role as gallery administrator, I usually hurry through museums. Nothing is worse than being stuck with a guide who lingers before each piece and warbles on, scarcely audible over the noisy hush of feet and the screeching voices of other guides. But this exhibition slowed me down. I felt like a personal guest of the Sabaeans, who pervaded that room more even than they had their own former lands. I had walked through their fallen temples and seen their inscriptions on slabs left where they had been for three thousand years, but everything had shimmered in the desert, pulsating with heat and forbidding concentration. There, inscriptions had been like scribbles in the sand, the detritus of a collapsed civilization, but in the hushed and regulated atmosphere of the museum, under the glare of spot-lights, Sabaean culture coalesced and carried me back. Their script, one of the first alphabets, was tidy, geo-metric, its lines and curves reminiscent of the decor-ations on Sana'a houses. In front of the glass case displaying coins, I heard the sounds of the market-place, the rattling exchange of these little knobs of black metal, and smelt the spices wafting about me.

'Look at these statues found at the Awwam temple,' said Christian, 'men wearing skirts much like the *futah* they wear at *qat* chews today, and carrying daggers in their waistbands. Some fashions never change.'

One of these bronze statues, virtually undamaged, depicted a man wearing a lion skin with an inscription running from his chest, across his skirt, to his knees. 'Who's he?'

'Ma'dikarib,' Christian said. 'They had wonderful names: Lahayathat, Hammi'athat, and over here, look at this alabaster stela.' He showed me an engraving of a woman sitting on a stool in a striped dress. 'Abibahath, wife of Tubba'. And the greatest Sabaean *mukarrib*, or king, was called Karib'il Watar!' He was brimming over again. 'Not quite Jack and Jill.'

A huge photograph of green terraced slopes covered an entire wall. 'I shouldn't have brought you here,' said Christian. 'It'll make you pine.'

I stared at the photo. 'It hasn't done with me yet.'

'Yes, it has.' He covered my eyes. 'It doesn't even know you're gone.'

I took away his hand and held it against my collar-bone. 'But I do.' I turned to face him. 'There's still so much I haven't seen – the Tihama, Mukalla, Socotra. And I've been thinking about doing a book. A travel book, driven by Yemeni art. I'd take a handful of artists and go looking for the particular features that inspired them.' Christian was ready to counter-attack, as though we were arguing. 'Take Antelak's depiction of women in their tall hats – I'd go to Wadi Hadramawt and find all those shapes she reflects in her work. And those exploding wombs I told you about – that's about disen-franchised women, so I'd find them. And the bog-standard still-lifes of the *suq* and the desert . . . It'd be like following a trail, finding a country through its art.'

Christian pursed his lips. 'Vivien, there's something I should have told you in Yemen.'

'Oh, God – you've got a wife and three children?'

'Yes, but no.'

'Some ghastly infectious disease?'

'Not so I've noticed.'

'What then?'

'I'm in love with you.'

Another panoramic photograph covered the wall behind him: a Toyota flying across a flat expanse of sand, leaving a trail of dust behind it. The route we had taken. 'Since when?'

'I'd say that day we stood in Bab al-Yemen, when you were expecting your past to fly at you from every alleyway, was a pivotal moment.'

'Why didn't you say anything?'

'I was going to. I thought we were on the same track, but then you took the wheel and started driving us about like a learner on an obstacle course. Since then, since we've been home ... you've been so reluctant to commit to anything that I wasn't convinced it was what you wanted to hear. And you probably don't want to hear this either: come to London. Live with me here.'

Three elderly women, each apparently alone, stood staring into glass cases, waiting for my answer.

The blue paint in the bedroom would have to go; the carpet too. There were bound to be good floorboards underneath, which would relish a varnish. The house had potential – it needed only a personal stamp on its décor, a determined assault on its mood – and the unadorned jungle behind it begged to be cleared.

London had potential too. There were jobs in the *Guardian* for which I was qualified, and being with Christian had its own attractions, of course. When we curled up in front of the television that Sunday night with pasta and salad and a bottle of wine, an ugly foreboding settled in my stomach. I didn't want to go home. Dublin had come to feel like someone else's town. There were pubs, restaurants, even cinemas I avoided for fear of running into Gemma, and there was a gaping hole in my flat where she used to be. Even the gallery, every time I stepped into it, seemed to say, 'You? *Still?*'

A light kiss brushed my face before Christian left for an early flight to Paris at dawn. My own flight to Dublin was later, so I didn't get up until eight when I went downstairs and sat at the kitchen table imagining myself coming home to it every day. I breathed in the house to see if it made an easy passage. It did. The garden needed tending. Christian needed tending. So did I.

When the taxi came, I grabbed my bag, ran to the front door and pulled. It wouldn't yield. I yanked it. Nothing happened. The taxi beeped again. Turning the knob, I pulled hard, but the door was locked farther down – Chubb-locked. Christian had locked me into his house.

A frenzied search for keys – to the front door, back door, or windows – while the taxi driver waited on the doorstep, revealed nothing. Nor did an irate phone call to Christian, who had just arrived in Orly and had no clue where I might find spare keys. Like the taxi driver, he found my predicament amusing.

'Let's see . . . Try the kitchen,' he said. 'Look in a few jugs or whatever.'

'*Or whatever?* This is your contribution to getting me back to work?'

'Look in my study. Under the stairs. Outside in the shed.'

'That'd be difficult! And why are all your windows locked? It's a fire hazard!'

'I didn't know they were locked, but here's a thought – why don't you ask the fire brigade to get you out?'

'You're doing yourself no favours, Linklater.'

'It was five a.m! Pure habit.'

'It's your habit to lock women up?'

'No, but it will be nice to come home tomorrow to my very own Rapunzel.'

'Oh, fuck off.'

There was nothing to be done. I had to let the taxi go. I paced, turned, swore. Then I rang Shoukria and explained I would be late for work – by several days.

My perspective was immediately altered. Christian's house could never be *our* house: it belonged to, smelt of, smacked of him and his multiple daughters. It reeked of family life. I would become a step here. A step-person, step-mother, step-wife.

There was no milk, and only Yemeni tea is good without it. The fact that the other Linklaters were away had become a gross inconvenience. They could have released me. I was cold and bored. I thought about doing housework, but only mothers do other people's housework for nothing. Instead I went into Christian's study and spent hours on-line, then rang Theo for a long chat. Christian's phone bill would register this little misadventure. 'He wants me to move here,' I told Theo. 'It's the last place on earth I ever planned to live, but London looks quite attractive at the moment.'

'And Christian?'

'Christian looks quite attractive too.' I laughed.

'But Nooria says she's waiting for you. What about Yemen?'

'Oh, God, I don't know. I honestly don't know what to do. It seems I'll have to choose – again – but I don't want to miss out on either. Tell me what to do, Theo.'

'Never.'

'Gee, thanks. So how's Roos?'

'She's here right now, but she doesn't like it. She says she couldn't live in a country that treats its women as they are treated here.'

'Have you not introduced her to Nooria?'

'*Ja*, but, you know – fireworks.'

'Really?' I was gloating.

'Roos thought, here is an intelligent Muslim woman, someone she could discuss these issues with, so she asked Nooria why she wore the veil when it was so constricting and sexist. Nooria asked her why she wore a bra.'

I snorted. 'Well, you tell Roos that it isn't so long since women in the West wore headscarves, and that we've only had the vote for less than a hundred years, and in the sixties women in Ireland who worked for the public service had to give up their jobs when they got married, so you ask her why the Arab world should keep pace with *our* sexual politics.'

'Why don't I just send her over to you?'

'She wouldn't be able to get in.'

*

303

The chicken tikka for one that I found in the freezer wasn't half bad. I watched a film and had an intimate conversation with Christian, he in his hotel bed in Paris, I in his bed in London. The next day, I watched soap operas. Christian was due home at seven, so I sank into a bath at half six and heard him coming in as I was getting out. I pulled a towel round me and hurried to greet him. As I came round the bend in the stairs, three identical pairs of eyes looked up at me.

I yelped. They stepped back, as one, like a well-calibrated machine. Bad enough to find them there at all, but it was additionally disconcerting that they looked the same. *Huey, Dewey and Louey*, I thought – or maybe I said it aloud, because one said, 'Goldilocks.'

18

In September, before the bright evenings stepped back into winter, I took Christian to one of my favourite places – the home of friends who lived the organic life on a two-bit plot in a harsh Atlantic landscape in County Mayo.

'So Tess is another best friend?' Christian asked, on the long drive west.

'Do you have a best daughter?'

'Of course not.'

'Well, friends are the same. Different relationships, equally important. Tess is special, though. She never sees the outer casing. If you asked her what colour my hair is, she'd hesitate, but she'd be able to give you a perfect map of my soul.'

'Then I really must meet her.'

Tess and Declan had lit a fire, which we huddled round while a storm raged outside, and they served a wonderful dinner of stuffed pork and lemon soufflé, during which, as had become inevitable at any recent gathering, there was talk of Iraq and war.

'How does Shoukria feel about it?' Tess asked.

'Totally against. She wants rid of Saddam, but not this way.'

'It can't happen,' said Declan. 'There's too much opposition worldwide.'

'Bit odd, isn't it,' said Tess, 'to live in a democracy and be totally powerless to stop something we feel so strongly about?'

'Aw, that's not true,' I said. 'We'll get to march. And sing. We'll get to march and sing John Lennon songs. There's democracy for you.'

'If there is a drawn-out war,' Christian said to me, 'neither Bush nor Blair will survive the next elections. *That*'s democracy.'

'Well,' I snapped, 'I'm sure that will give *enormous* comfort to the Iraqi civilians and American soldiers who have to die in the meantime . . .'

'Come on,' said Tess. 'Let's change the subject.'

So I regaled them with a flamboyant account of my unravelling in London. '"Goldilocks", they called me!'

'Sounds about right to me,' said Tess.

'When I arrived,' said Christian, 'the four of them were sitting there, with the strategic teapot in the middle of the table, and I knew it was Worst Case Scenario.'

'Poor kids,' said Tess.

'Poor me!' I protested. 'I had to keep reminding myself they were children, not wives.'

'And now I can't get Vivien back there,' said Christian.

'I'll meet them again when I'm good and ready and have my clothes on.'

While Tess and Declan toiled the next morning, feeding goats and mucking out sheds, Christian and I walked the shoreline. It was sunny, but still quite windy; there were white caps on the untidy waves. Sandpipers ran like children into the sea in busy flocks, then ran away again. Their matchstick legs took them back and forth in tiny, speedy steps until, all in a swoop, they took off and darted above the surf like a waltzing cloud, then landed again and resumed the curious ritual of running in and out of the water. I watched them, saying, 'We will go. We won't go. We will go. We won't go.'

'A bit like you,' said Christian.

Yellow foam slid back towards the sea, as if trying to become froth again, but the waves just pushed it on to the beach and left it, like unwanted waste in someone else's backyard.

'Like walking through the top of a pint of Guinness,' said Christian, linking my arm as we stepped through it. 'Vivien, do you ever think about having kids?'

'Golly. Where did that come from?'

'It's just – I wouldn't want you to think I'd be averse to having another family.'

I stopped, foam sloshing about my ankles. 'Now, why wouldn't you want me to think that?'

'Can we get out of this stuff?'

We stepped over to dry sand. 'Rest easy,' I said. 'My body clock ticks unobtrusively, even now. But if you don't mind my saying so, you're a deeply questionable prospect in the fathering department.'

'I am?'

'How could I overlook the multiple-birth syndrome you carry, which, incidentally, you and Diane did not survive?'

'But it's an excellent service, and so economical!

Three for the price of one pregnancy, one labour, one spell of broken nights.'

'You'd really do all that again?'

'Oh, yes.'

At the end of the beach, I sat on a rock shaped like an armchair. Christian inhaled, his eyes sweeping across the bay. 'You know I'd move here tomorrow if it weren't for the girls?'

'I know.'

'So when are you going to get off your arse and come to London? Commuting is expensive and I'm sick of the long empty weeks in between. I loathe being without you.'

'I'm just . . . you know, waiting for the ripples to disperse.'

'The Yemeni ripples?'

'Mmm. And I have a lot to sort out.'

'But you haven't even started. I don't believe you responded to any of the job adverts I emailed you.'

'So maybe I haven't, but you make it sound so easy. I know it *is* straightforward for you – you want to be with me, and that's all there is to it. Well, I want to be with you too –'

'I'm very glad to hear it,' he said.

'But what am I to do about this *draw*, this *pull*, towards something else? If I ignore it, won't we pay for it further down the line?'

'No. You're just fretting because of what happened last time. But I'm not Bill, and you're not twenty-one any more.'

'I know that.'

He pulled me to my feet. 'What will it take, Vivien?'

'I don't know. A kick up the ass might do it.'

Christian smiled. He had great lines. They spread out from the side of his eye like fingers. He carried a whole range of punctuation on his face. Semi-colons and parentheses when he smiled; oblique dashes when he didn't. 'A kick up the ass?' he said. 'I'll organize it.'

We had a clear view of Downpatrick Head and its enormous stack, and could even see the waves breaking soundlessly against the foot of the cliffs. 'I'm going to take you over there tomorrow,' I said. 'There's a blowhole I want you to meet.'

Significant days begin like insignificant ones. The next morning I woke in an empty bed and went downstairs. Christian was out in the goat pen with Declan; Tess was cooking me a big fried breakfast. I put my feet into some very large, cold wellington boots and went outside. Christian waved as I pushed open the gate and waded through mud and dung to reach him. A cow mooed.

'Let's chuck it all in and move here,' he said, smiling broadly. 'We could live like this. You could get a job in an office, and I'll study Irish and unearth ancient burial sites.' He took a vigorous breath of fresh morning air. 'God, I'd love it.'

'I love you.'

His eyes widened, comically. 'Good grief. Those aren't words that trip easily off your tongue.'

'Oi,' Tess called from the door. 'Breakfast!'

'Get thee inside, wench,' said Christian, 'before the

farmhand sees you in that transparent gown.' But he couldn't disguise his delight.

I trudged back through the mud, holding my nightdress above my knees. On the kitchen table, a place was set for one and a huge fry laid out. 'What's all this?'

'You look like you need a little spoiling,' said Tess.

'Do I?'

'You still have Gemma on your conscience.'

'I don't, you know. Not really,' I sat down, 'although I probably should have. After all, I was as dishonest with her as she was with me, giving her snippets but holding back on the rough stuff.'

'You were trying to protect her.'

'Don't glorify it. I simply took what I wanted. Nothing admirable in it.'

'Either way,' said Tess, glancing out the window, 'he's worth it.'

'You like him?'

'Very much.' She sat down opposite me with a mug of tea. 'So is this it? Is it *lurve*?'

'It had better be because I've just told him so.'

'You're not sure?'

I was buttering soda bread. 'I *think* I'm sure. I mean, how are we supposed to recognize love? Does it come up and introduce itself?'

'In a manner of speaking.'

'So what was it about Declan that made you settle on him, throw your lot in with his?'

'Instinct.'

'What?'

'It was *instinct*, not love.'

'You didn't love him when you got married?'

'I did, but I'd loved lots of men,' said Tess. 'The decision to marry was instinctive.'

'The only time *my* instincts spoke to me was when they warned me not to get involved in this particular relationship.'

'But that was about Gemma.'

'Was it?'

'Well . . . are there any vibes coming through about him now?'

I stopped chewing my bacon and scanned the ceiling. 'Nope. Not a thing.'

Tess threw her long dark plait over her shoulder. 'How could you possibly have doubts?'

'Because doubting is easy. Certainty has the trajectory of snipe.'

'Meaning?'

'Snipe fly in a zigzag. They're very erratic and hard to shoot. Hitting on certainty is just as difficult, if you ask me.'

'So why don't we take your doubts and my certainty out for a drive?'

She took me to a circle of modern standing stones erected on a bog. An old leather suitcase lay discarded just outside the circle, the lid open. 'What a superb piece of installation art that would make,' I said. I stepped inside the circle and did as one does – leaned against one of the stones and looked up at the cloudy, temperate sky, so different from the clear blue expanse above the columns at Arsh Bilqis. 'It was terrible,'

I told Tess. 'There we were in this extraordinary place, but I had one eye on Christian, the other on Gemma . . . Even the Queen of Sheba couldn't compete with the ghosts of Durham.'

'Do you think she'll get help?'

'The Queen?'

'Gemma.'

'I don't know. I just want to put the whole thing right out of my mind, but it won't go. It's all so embarrassing. I know way too much.'

We drove on, out to the beaches of Belmullet where we threw coins into a Marian shrine hidden among sand-dunes that was supposed to restore sight to the blind. 'I'm boxed in,' I said. 'What Christian has to offer is enticing – a relationship that actually works, companionship, compatibility. Everything you and Declan have. It's right there for me, waiting. All I have to do is endorse it, which is such a small thing, and yet I can't seem to get there. It's like being in a traffic jam. I can't see what's blocking the way and I really want to get where I'm going, but I can't move, in any direction, and Christian just doesn't get it.'

Tess took my arm as we walked away. 'It will clear,' she said. 'And probably very suddenly.'

Unwilling to turn back, we drove on to the tip of the peninsula, listening to David Gray singing 'Forgive Me' on the radio. We bopped about, seatbelts straining, until we came over the brow of a hill and a magnificent sweep of beach stretched out below. Tess screeched to a halt. Across the bay, the mountains of Achill Island lay slumbering in hazy sunshine. We couldn't stop jigging about, so we turned the radio up very loud and got out. We were hemmed in by graveyards – a modern one on our left and an old one on the hill to our right. Surrounded by the dead, we jived.

We wriggled our hips and reached for the sky. We called out to one another and sang at the swallows, who dipped and dived. We were dancing in the streets, dancing at Lughnasa, dancing at the crossroads. We threw off our jackets. Then the song slowed, spiralling down to just the voice. I stretched my palms across the warm bonnet, gasping. Tess doubled over her knees. 'Better than sex,' she panted.

I glanced across at Achill Island, magnificent and glowing, and at the beach below us. Then, with a tic-tic-a-tic, the rhythm built up and we danced again, clapping our hands and wiggling our bums.

There was a beep. We swung round. Behind us stood a hearse, and behind the hearse a long string of cars full of mourners, going up and over the crest of the hill – all blocked from the cemetery. Tess dived into the car and pulled on to the verge. The cortège drove slowly by. In the back seat of the first limousine, a young woman looked out and gave me a little smile.

On Downpatrick Head that evening the wind buffeted Christian and me. It had been another windy night and the heave on the sea meant the blowhole was performing like a geyser. The spray was jumping so high that we had to keep our distance so as not to get spat on as we passed it on our way up to the cliff edge. On the magnificent stack opposite, seagulls nested and squawked. Its flat top was covered with lawn. That's what it looked like: a carefully maintained carpet spread over the wild piece of jagged rock. If it had been Yemen, they would have built a palace on it.

We lay on our bellies and crawled across little mounds of spongy grass to reach the very edge of the cliff and peek at the waves below as they clashed fiercely against the rocks and shattered into a million white shards of water. They growled at Ireland for getting in their way, forcing them to retreat, but kept renewing the attack. It might take millennia, but they would eventually beat Ireland down.

'It's like the Empty Quarter,' I said, looking out at the Atlantic. 'Extreme and mostly empty. Bigger, though.'

'And a bit wetter.'

'And yet more people cross this ocean than ever cross the Empty Quarter, so what I want to know, Mr Anthropologist, is why more people are drawn to the sea than to the desert.'

'The extremes of the desert are worse than those of the sea.'

'But the sea moves and swells.'

'So does the desert.'

'Not violently.'

Christian rested his chin on his wrist. 'Maybe it's because we've found the means to cross the sea in comfort.'

'Air-conditioned 4 × 4s don't make you seasick or throw you overboard.'

'Er . . . We can protect ourselves against the cold, but not the heat?'

'What about the wet?'

Christian groaned. 'Thank God I never had to teach you. Look, maybe the difference is that the sea is often benign, the desert never.'

'That must be it.'

'Phew.' Christian rolled on to his back, perched on his elbows, and looked at the white foam spewing high out of the blowhole.

'What are you thinking about?' I asked. 'What do you English think about in places like this?'

'What do the Irish think about?'

'I think, *Mine*. All mine!'

'Greedy you.'

'But we know I'm greedy.'

'The Aborigines wouldn't agree with you. Their understanding of our relationship *vis-à-vis* the earth is –'

'No anthropology lecture, please. Just tell me what you were thinking about.'

'Diane.'

'You think about her a lot.'

'Habit.'

'You still love her.'

'I love *you*, extravagantly, but I wish she could have had something like this with Eric. The romantic weekend. The abandon.' He turned to me. 'The years ahead.'

I got to my feet. 'Let's go have a shower at the blowhole.' We made our way down the slope. 'Tess told me a terrible story about this place. Well, there are lots of stories, but the worst has to be the one about the woman who threw herself and her three children into it. In the days before it was fenced off, obviously.'

Christian stopped behind me. 'How? How did she do that?'

'I don't know.'

'I mean, with two you'd put one under each arm and jump, but three . . . Did she throw one first or —'

'Christian!'

'But the logistics. How's it done? That's horrible. *Horrible.*'

'Don't let it take away from the raw power of this beautiful thing. Just listen.'

We had come to the high wire fence round the hole. A dreadful moaning came from the sea below, like a planet lowing.

'It sounds like Hades,' said Christian. 'Full of tormented souls.'

A huge spout of water leaped out and rained down on us. I screeched, but Christian wandered round to the other side, preoccupied by that poor woman and her children. I stood, happy and wet, waiting for the next spray — it was like waiting for a cat to pounce — knowing it was coming but not when, exactly, the geyser of sea would spew out. It rumbled down there, like underground trains.

'Vivien?' Christian called from the other side. He was quite far away, greyed out by the mist-filled air, his fingers in the netting. The rocky chasm between us took a great raspy breath.

'Yeah?'

'Let's get married.'

'What?'

He smiled. I smiled. He knew I'd say yes.

The white foam shot up, reaching for heaven, and stopped there, millions of watery droplets hanging in the air.

PART III

19

Knocking. Knocking. Knocking.

I came round slowly. It was Saturday. I rolled over and thought about breakfast. Breakfast was still my friend. The hammering went on. My bell was broken. So was the loo-seat. Someone was banging on the door. My mother probably. I opened my eyes. It was Friday, not Saturday. Nine a.m. on a Friday. I'd overslept again.

I pulled on my dressing-gown and stumbled along the corridor. In the waking world the knocking was hesitant, not insistent. Not my mother, then. I opened the door. Gemma.

'Sorry,' she said. 'I thought I should come.'

'Gemma! Come in.' It had been months since I'd seen her.

She followed me into the kitchen. My limbs were shaking. I reached for the kettle.

'Are you all right?' she asked. 'You look like you haven't slept.'

'No, I did. I took something.'

'It must be hard.'

My hackles rose. 'It is, but you surely haven't come to commiserate? Because if you want to gloat –'

She was very pale. 'Gloat? No, I just ... I don't know. I heard it on the radio and found myself flying out the door. Old habits die hard, I suppose.'

'Heard what on the radio?'

Her expression changed, horribly.

'Gem?'

She took a step back and her eyes seemed to be reading an autocue behind my head. 'Christian.'

'What about him?'

'You haven't heard?'

'What?'

'Oh, God, Viv. He's gone missing. In Yemen.'

20

Pity the tea drinker. Airport caterers worldwide must work to some unspoken international agreement according to which they strive conscientiously to provide the most unpalatable brew imaginable. Variations of café latte, mocha, espresso and hot chocolate are available everywhere, but 'tea' always means a teaspoon of dust in a square bag made of sanitary-towel tissue. At Dublin airport, when I needed something sustaining, I had to make do with tinted water and UHT milk. I railed silently against teabags, caterers and airports. A Norwegian study once revealed that sixteen per cent of all couples meet in airports. Western couples, one assumes. I am part of a percentage. Or was. Sitting on the edge of a chair in the bar, rocking, I cursed myself for leaving that percentage.

Gemma had brought me the bare outline of the story. Earlier that morning, on Radio 4, she had heard that the TV anthropologist had gone missing in the Yemeni hinterland and was presumed kidnapped. I had tried, but failed, to reach Theo or Nooria, but had been more intent on getting flights. Gemma insisted on driving me to the airport; I was too needy to refuse. She even packed for me while I spoke to airlines and embassies and engaged tones. When I told Aer Lingus I was the fiancée of a man who had been kidnapped, they promised to put me on a flight to London as soon as a seat became available. And so we sat there in the bar, the two of us, with cups and slopped-upon saucers on a low round table before us.

'What the hell was he doing out there?' I muttered.

'You didn't know he'd gone back?'

I shook my head.

'How come?'

'Probably because we broke up five weeks ago.'

'But you told the airline you were his fiancée.'

'I'm his ex.' She had not heard. The grapevine had failed, which was a measure of how well we had disentangled our lives. I resumed my rocking. 'What kind of stupid bloody thing was he up to? And the timing. Such awful bloody timing!'

'Why?' said Gemma.

'Because there's a war brewing, or hadn't you noticed?'

'I meant why did you break up?'

I stared at the slop in my saucer. 'Search me.'

These were busy times in the world. Busy, bad times. In the new millennium, there was no safe place to go. Two hundred people had recently been blown up in a nightclub in Bali. Holidaymakers; kids. A young Australian bride had lost her entire bouquet of bridesmaids – four young women killed in the blast. Then a Moscow theatre had been invaded by rebels and the people inside were subsequently gassed by the authorities. Over a hundred dead. Germans were killed in Tunisia, Americans in Kuwait. America's allies were being picked off one by one by terrorist groups, leaving Britain, as yet untouched, in a state of high alert. In fulminating about Iraq, the US had taken its eyes off the ball, some said.

The rest of us waited. The Iraqis waited. Women who had been at school with Shoukria looked at their children and waited.

Yemen, inevitably, had risen to the surface. The Americans had been true to their word about taking out suspected terrorists. Only days before, a jeep and all but one of its occupants were blown up in the desert near Marib by a Predator missile – the very type of drone, indeed, about the use of which the US had frequently rapped Israeli knuckles.

In the midst of all this, Christian Linklater, a Briton with a television profile, had disappeared.

Gemma poured more 'tea'. 'So who's living in my room?'

'Hmm? Oh, I haven't filled it yet. I haven't really tried.'

'Why not?'

'I'm leaving.'

'Leaving? How come?'

'I'm going to live in Yemen, when I've saved a bit more and found someone to take the flat ... or that was the plan before this happened.'

'Something always gets in the way, doesn't it?'

I eyeballed her. She turned away, eyebrows raised, her point made.

'I miss your flat,' she chirped, turning back. 'It's so hard to get a nice place.'

'Gee, thanks.'

'Look, Vivien, the bottom line is I wouldn't have done what you did. I would never have got involved with a guy you liked.'

'Well, that's very laudable, especially coming from someone who threw herself at a married man and father of three.'

We looked in opposite directions. Shoukria was right. There was no way back.

Just then, Shoukria herself appeared in the doorway of the bar and came over, pulling off her leather gloves. Her fake-fur coat slipped off her shoulders and on to the seat beside me. 'That wretched man keeps taking you out of the office.'

'Sorry.'

She sat down and twisted round to catch a passing waiter. 'Sparkling water, please.' Then back to me. 'This is about the Predator ambush. This is revenge.'

'Shoukria, *please*. I need reassurance, not –'

'What ambush?' Gemma asked, alarmed.

Alarmed for Christian, I supposed. 'The other day,' I snapped. 'The al-Qaeda suspects blown up by the Hellfire missile.'

'Oh, that.'

'Yes, that.'

'But those guys were involved in September eleventh, weren't they?'

'Even if they were, does that make it okay?' asked Shoukria.

'About as okay as it was for all those people in the Twin Towers to go to work that day and never come home.'

'Do you two mind?' I said.

'I'm sorry,' said Shoukria. 'Let me get you more tea.' She went to the bar and returned with another pot. 'By the way, you're fired.'

'What? You can't fire me. I'll have you for unfair dismissal.'

'Yes. Good. Then I'll have to pay you an *awful* amount of money in compensation. I'll be forced to give you a severance payment.'

'Thanks, but the way things are going, I'll be home in a week.'

'Even so, you can't have your job back. Enough is enough. Move on. To that man or that country or wherever it is you're going. But while you're fired I want you to do some work for me. You must round up these women and their paintings, and send them over. I'll cover the costs and put on an exhibition.'

'This is the weirdest dismissal I've ever heard,' Gemma said.

'I'll have no mind to work when I get there – *if* I get there.'

'It can wait until he's . . . come back from wherever it is he's gone to.'

An old woman came towards us, and I realized with horror that it was my mother, dwarfed in her big grey coat, her face creased like a bunched-up tissue. 'You're not to go,' she said to me. 'This is no time to go out there.'

'It's also no time to stay at home.'

'I forbid you.'

'Have some tea, Mum.'

'Please, Vivien.'

'You know very well I was going to go back to Sana'a anyway.'

'You never really left,' Shoukria muttered.

'But you promised you wouldn't move until after the war!'

'Yes, but things have changed somewhat, wouldn't you say? The only thing that matters now is finding Christian.'

Gemma put one hand over the side of her face.

'What matters is that there's a war looming!' My mother's grey eyebrows had turned white. Her hands, gathered in her lap, were thin and knobbly, veins showing through translucent skin.

I put my hand over hers. She was cold. 'I'll be fine. I'll probably be home in a few days anyway.'

'*Insh'Allah*,' said Shoukria. 'This will be resolved soon and the war is unlikely to begin for months.'

'And it probably won't even happen,' I said to my mother. 'The UN inspectors haven't found any evidence of those damn weapons so –'

'Pfff!' Shoukria threw her eyes up. 'The only weapon of mass destruction we have is Saddam himself.'

'*I* think it'll happen,' said Gemma, unhelpfully. 'I heard a guy on the radio the other day, some American commentator, saying, "At this point, the Security Council should just get out of the way."'

'Exactly,' said Mum. 'There's going to be a war whether we like it or not and you could get stuck out there, in the middle of it all.'

'I won't be anywhere near Iraq!'

'And what about bin Laden?' My mother was all earnestness. 'The papers say he could be in Yemen.'

'I know,' I said wearily. 'He escaped the bombing of the Tora Bora mountains, crossed into Pakistan, took a dhow to Oman, followed all the old trade routes through the desert, and he's hiding out on the fringes of the Empty Quarter – and nobody saw him do it.' I glanced at Shoukria. 'A new take on the Incense Trail: incensing America.'

'If he's there –'

'If he's there, Mum, it's highly unlikely I'll run into him.'

'Don't be smart.'

'I'm sorry, but you haven't expressed one word of concern for Christian, and you really ought to care about him because he's about the only person who can stop me moving permanently to Sana'a!'

She recoiled. They all recoiled.

'My only concern is for you,' my mother said quietly.

Shoukria frowned. 'What will you do about a visa?'

'The Yemeni Embassy has promised me one, except they won't fast-track it so it could take days going through the normal channels, but there's a Yemenia flight tomorrow night and I'm determined to be on it. I'm going to ask his family if they can get me an emergency visa. They'll have the ear of the embassy. I won't.'

My mother was horrified. 'You're going to his *wife*?'

'Ex-wife. What else can I do? I'll shrivel up if I have to wait five days. I'm going to throw myself on her mercy.'

*

It was another three hours before I was offered a flight. My mother wouldn't come to the gate, but walked away across the concourse in her overlarge coat. She had shrunk recently. She had not taken to Christian, but it was the dip I slid into after he left that had drained her. Now I had taken another few inches off her.

Shoukria wept, elegantly. 'I have no fears for you,' she said, hugging me, 'but I don't expect to see you soon.'

Gemma squeezed my wrist. 'Bring him back safe.'

'Oh, for Christ's sake, Gemma. Get over it!'

Four hours later, I was standing on Diane Linklater's doorstep, ready to beg.

One of the triplets answered the door, I couldn't tell which. She stared for a moment before letting me in. My hand reached out to her – an inadequate gesture that reduced us both.

A woman looked out of the kitchen. 'Who is it, Tan?'

'Vivien.' She turned to her mother. 'Dad's . . .' No word to describe me.

Diane came forward. We considered one another. Her dark hair had blonde streaks and was pulled into a ponytail. She was wearing jeans with a pyjama top and dressing-gown. The bags under her eyes weren't recent. 'What are *you* doing here?'

'I need to speak to you.'

'Yes, but . . .' She frowned, then led me into their sitting room. It was a mirror image of Christian's house down the road. I sat rigidly on the edge of the couch.

Diane stood by the mantelpiece looking down on me with sunken grey eyes.

'Are you going to Yemen?' I asked.

'Of course. The girls are adamant.'

I squeezed my hands together. This was one major hurdle overcome – we shared the same instinct, however irrational, however useless. They, like me, just wanted to be in motion, to step on to a plane and move in his direction. It would have been far more sensible to sit by the phone and hold hands, but that would have been impossible. We had to get to him, or make ourselves believe that was what we were doing. I said, 'I need to go with you.'

'I thought you were already there.'

'No, I . . . Well, I'm not, and . . . Look, I haven't been able to hear much news. What happened exactly?'

Diane shook her head. 'Nothing has happened. He just hasn't been seen for two weeks. Everyone thought he was out doing fieldwork, but there's no trace of him anywhere, and with the way things are at the moment, the diplomats are nervous. That's as much as we know. And now the media are on to it . . .'

Over her shoulder, on the mantelpiece, there was a framed photograph of her standing by a Christmas tree, smiling and cheerful, with another man's arms round her. How had Christian endured it?

'I was wondering,' I said, 'if you could help me get a visa?'

Her mouth fell open. 'A visa? I thought you'd come because you were concerned for the girls, but you're looking for favours!'

'I'm looking for help.'

'There's nothing I can do. The FCO –'

'The what?'

'The Foreign and Commonwealth Office – are trying to stop us going, as is the family liaison officer from Scotland Yard, so we're up against it every way, and you're neither family nor British so –'

'But if you could include me in your party . . .'

She crossed her arms, still looking down at me. 'If Christian is so important to you, you had ample opportunity to demonstrate it without waiting until he'd been kidnapped.'

'*Presumed* kidnapped. Please, Mrs Linklater. You won't see me once we get there, but if you could just help get me *in*.'

'I can't. The embassy has issued only five visas.'

'Five?'

'My brother is coming.'

I swallowed hard, and let it out. 'Let me go in his place. Please.'

Her demented eyes shot on to me. 'You have some nerve!'

'I'm sorry, but what can I say to persuade you? Who is more important to Christian? Me or your brother?'

That threw her, but she said, 'Christian would want us to have someone with us. Someone to be there if things don't work out. I have to think about the girls. If this turns out badly, I'll need all the support I can get.'

'It won't turn out badly. If he has been kidnapped,

he'll be released within days. Most kidnappings in Yemen end quickly.'

She sat down. 'This is different. The officials haven't ruled out al-Qaeda.'

Although I cannot have been unaware of this possibility, hearing it like that gave me a severe jolt. Diane nodded. We sat for a moment, staring at the floor.

'Could I use your phone? I haven't been able to speak to anyone in Sana'a since I heard and –'

'You know people there?'

'Yes, friends of Christian's. They're bound to have heard something.'

She hurried me out to the hall and thrust a phone at me. Theo's number rang only once.

'Vivien? At last! I've been trying you all day.'

'Jesus, Theo, what the hell is going on?'

'You've heard.'

Diane backed into the kitchen.

'Who's taken him? Have there been demands?'

Theo said, 'There have been no demands.'

'But doesn't that mean it isn't a traditional kidnapping?' I said quietly. 'It could be some terrorist group that'll just kill him and dump him somewhere.'

'Those people are afraid to put their noses outside the door after the Predator attack. They're not going to take chances with missiles flying around the desert.'

'So where is he?'

He sighed. 'I don't know.'

'Tell me what you do know.'

'He went off with Ahmad to do more fieldwork a few weeks ago, just before I left for Amsterdam. When

I got back, nobody had heard anything from him, but I didn't think about it until a guy at the Dutch Embassy told me the British were concerned. They made inquiries in Marib, but there's been no sign of either of them.'

'Jesus.'

'*Ja*, but don't worry. They'll be fine. I'll ring as soon as I hear anything.'

'No need. I'm on my way. I'm in London with the Linklaters. If I can get a visa today, I'm going to do everything possible to get on that flight tomorrow night, but if I can't, I'll come on the next one.'

'You'll be here soon?'

'I hope so.'

'*Great*.'

'Theo, why didn't you tell me he'd gone back?'

'He asked me not to.'

Diane came out of the kitchen as I hung up. I told her what Theo had said. She sat on the stairs, dazed.

'Mrs Linklater, if I were his wife now, as I could have been, I would have *your* rights. I would be certain to go, along with your daughters, but if you turned up on my doorstep, wanting to travel with the girls, what justification would I have in turning you away?'

'You forfeited those rights.'

'So did you.' I sat beside her. 'Look, we're not adversaries. We just love the same man.'

'If you love him so much, where have you been this last month?'

I ran my hands through my hair and suppressed an urge to scream. 'When Christian and I . . . disagreed, he was still in love with me, and I don't believe that can have changed in the space of a few weeks.'

'I am all too well aware of that.'

'But then surely I should go to him, or try to? In view of our disagreement, it's all the more important that I see him. I need to get there every bit as much as you do.'

'You aren't the mother of his children. Whatever you fear, I feel *fourfold*.'

A tired, thin man, a professorial type in tweeds, came up from the kitchen. 'Gordon . . .' said Diane.

Christian's father. We'd never met.

'. . . this is Vivien.' She turned to me. 'My father-in-law, Gordon,' she said, slipping up on the 'ex'. It seemed fair. They had been family for nearly twenty years.

'Oh, my word,' said Gordon, shaking my hand warmly. 'I've heard a good deal about you.'

'Vivien wants Ben's visa,' said Diane.

'Ah,' he said.

I couldn't look at the man, although I was inclined to fall to my knees and beg his support. But I already had it. 'It's probably what Christian would want,' he said gently.

'That's what I was thinking,' said Diane, wearily. I almost burst into tears.

Their kitchen was full of people who looked alike. Christian's daughters were like younger versions of Bess and Emily, his identical twin sisters – a confusing scenario. Diane's brother Ben was also there with others: an attractive woman in a grey suit; a man with a red beard and bushy hair; and Gordon, who was smoking long black cigarettes but speaking to no one. There was a ripple of interest when Diane led me in, indicated the teapot and offered a mug.

It was like every funeral I had ever attended – the unspoken mutual support structure that builds itself between the closely bereaved: tea permanently on the brew; the phone ringing as soon as a call ended; mobile phones beeping and ringing in different tones, interrupting the quiet murmur of the gathered assembly. Ben brought me a chair.

'Ben, there's been a change of plan,' said Diane. 'I need to speak to the embassy.'

'Oh?' Several faces looked up.

'It seems only fair to Christian that Vivien should come with us, if that's what she wants to do.'

Her daughters looked at one another, then all looked at me.

'Diane –' said one of the twin sisters.

'It's fine. We'll manage. And she knows the country.'

'What's there to know?' Ben asked. 'Except that there are fifty million guns being bandied about like toys and that this is the homeland of Osama bin Laden!'

'And of sixteen million desperately poor people,' I countered. 'There is a lot to know about Yemen you won't ever hear on the news.'

He was about to retort, but Diane stopped him. 'The girls, please. The thing is, Ben, I could use someone who's been there before.'

Christian's sisters were equally unimpressed. 'Diane,'

said one, 'I really think one of the family ought to go. If not Ben, then perhaps Gordon.'

'Good God, no,' said Gordon. 'Not me. I'd be an encumbrance.'

'Well, one of us, then,' said the other sister. 'I'll go.'

'Thanks, Bess, but . . . I'd like Vivien to come. She knows people, and Christian simply wouldn't forgive me if I stood in her way.'

So I sat in a corner and waited out the nightmare among strangers. Someone proffered a plate of chocolate biscuits. With the inclination of a child at a party, I almost pocketed the whole lot to stash them away for Theo. Images of the day kept rushing at me – Gemma at my door, my mother's busy hands, Shoukria 'firing' me.

The evening wore on, and I was reminded of a recurring dream I had had as a child in which I was swimming through thick air. I kept pushing my arms behind me, trying to make progress, but for all the effort, and in spite of a desperate determination to get somewhere, I never moved. Christian's father continued to smoke, with a slight shake in his hands, and the television was never switched off, not even when Diane complained of a pounding headache. News channels returned regularly to the disappearance of the British documentary-maker, showing grainy old footage of Yemeni terraces. There were no foreign news teams in Yemen, so no on-the-spot coverage. Instead, they replayed bits of Christian's programmes, along with a commentary suggesting that he was well equipped to survive the conditions to which he might be subjected.

Because he was recognizable, this was easy fodder for newscasts, although any story in which 'al-Qaeda' could be bandied about made news.

It wasn't the conditions that worried me – it was the outcome; but I learned quickly to keep such thoughts in a box. Torment had lodged itself firmly in my gut and was better kept down there, in order to avoid the psychological meltdown that would occur if I coherently addressed what was happening. Better to move from one hour to the next in a kind of self-induced torpor than press towards the next stage and whatever horrors that might uncover. It was better not to think too much, in limbo.

An official from the Foreign and Commonwealth Office arrived and was brought into the kitchen. When he was informed about my addition to the party, he was exasperated, and reminded me that my own government had advised against non-essential trips to Yemen.

'How could any trip be more essential?' I asked.

'As you wish,' he said curtly. He was far more concerned for the teenagers. The situation was unsettled, he warned, and following the drone attack, any foreigner might be a target for revenge. Christian's daughters were not unperturbed – one bit her nails, another kept stroking her hair behind her ear – but they weren't cowed either. The Yemeni Embassy, they said, had promised protection from the moment they arrived. Nothing would stop them getting as close to their father as they could.

'You'll make our job very much harder,' the official said.

'Harder than it is for us to sit here doing nothing?' Diane asked.

'But what exactly,' he said, 'do you propose to do when you get to Yemen?'

Diane was stumped, and so was I, but one of the daughters said, 'We'll be there, that's all.'

The Yemeni diplomats were more amenable. They gave me a break, and a visa, and our passports were couriered back to us that night with our tickets. We had all been booked on to the Yemenia flight the following evening. Just as I'd hoped. A business-like meeting was held at the kitchen table, to which I contributed nothing. It was not for the baggage to dictate the route.

It was a pleasant room we sat in, but an awful place to be. Newspapers phoned, colleagues called round, and a neighbour dropped in an enormous chicken and broccoli casserole. *God*, I thought. *He isn't.* But I had to shut out a voice that whispered, *'You hope.'*

The meal was a dreary affair. Christian's daughters were admirable, if naïve, in their determination. I was impressed by these seventeen-year-olds, who might have been my step-daughters, but they had no feelings for me. It was hardly surprising that they had not been overly friendly some months earlier, when they had come upon their father's lover in a towel on his landing, but they were too preoccupied, now, to be judgemental. I was a tolerated appendage, whom they accepted because they believed Christian would want to see me. I wished I could be as certain.

When there was a lull in the phone calls, after eleven, I phoned Theo again. 'Sorry to wake you.'

'You didn't.'

'I've got a visa – and a seat on tomorrow's flight.'

'Fantastic.'

'Tell me more about Christian. When you saw him, how he was . . .'

There was shuffling at the other end as Theo turned on his light. 'I didn't know he was here,' he said. 'Not many people did, which is why nobody really noticed he . . . wasn't around. I ran into him at the Taj just before I left and he looked, you know, a bit . . . nervous because he thought you might be in Sana'a and he'd been avoiding me to avoid you. But we had dinner the night before he and Ahmad left. He said he had people to meet in Marib.'

'Did you try to talk him out of going?'

'No. *I*'m still travelling around. Why would I stop him? And things weren't so tense a few weeks ago.'

'You don't think . . .'

'What?'

'Well, you don't suppose he's . . . I've been wondering about that mad little plot he had to make a documentary. If he were to get footage now of what's going on, it'd be strong stuff. He and Ahmad could do it too. Ahmad would take Christian anywhere.'

'*Ja*,' said Theo. 'The same thing occurred to me but . . .'

'What?'

'He didn't expect to be away long. He told me he'd

be gone from Yemen by the time I got back from the Netherlands.'

'You should get some sleep,' Emily said to Diane. At least, I guessed it was Emily. The twins did little to assert their individuality, at least in sartorial terms, which seemed odd for women in their forties, and made it difficult to tell them apart. Happily their nieces did not take after them in this regard. They were alike in looks only and, determined not to fall into the trap of mistaking one for another, I spent the evening memorizing which was which. They all kept their hair long and parted on the left, which didn't help, but Tania was wearing a cerise pink sweater and had somewhat larger breasts than her sisters, Melanie had five earrings in one ear, and Rebecca had a ponytail, which made her look like one of those horsy types. There had to be tics, mannerisms, which would help me differentiate them in time, but for now I used these props – earrings, ponytail and breasts – to avoid calling one by another's name.

They packed, despondently, coming down occasionally to ask me what they should bring, how hot it would be, what they might be expected to wear. I was becoming more useful by the hour, and more tolerated. As the night wore on, I blended into the disaster. When sleeping arrangements were being organized, Christian's sisters agreed to sleep in his house and assumed that I would too.

'No, no. I'll go to a guesthouse.'

Diane shrugged. 'That's stupid. Christian's house is empty.'

Empty of people, perhaps, but not of recriminations. Dark and cold, and like a dog wondering when its master would return, it was a very different house from the one in which I had spent that happy weekend. Bess put on the heating. We climbed the stairs to the landing outside Christian's room.

'You'd better sleep in here,' Emily said.

'I don't know if I can.'

She shrugged. 'Up to you.'

They made their way up to the girls' rooms. 'I wonder what he's going through right now,' I heard one say.

'Best not to think about that.'

I stepped into his room and switched on the light. He had left a mess behind him: a shirt hanging out of the laundry basket, socks on the floor, drawers open. I fell on to the bed, my stomach rolling around like a pebble in the surf. It would be four a.m. in Yemen. He would be on some mud floor, waking to another day away from us all, wondering, perhaps, when this would end. I wondered too. How, I asked myself over and over, had he let it happen?

It was a foul night. When I slept, I dreamed, and when I dreamed, it was terrifying. I was wandering in the mountains calling, calling my name, looking for myself, and from the tower houses balancing on the rock faces above me a voice called back. My own.

The next morning one of the twins came with tea at half past eight. It was too milky, but it brought me round to a continuation of the day before. I sat up against the pillows, trying to find a way to still the lurching sickness in my belly.

Placing my hand on the sheet beside me, I wondered if we would return together and lie there again. I sent my love across the continents, calling out to him that I was coming, and that I was sorry.

In such circumstances there is no such thing as time. We move through it, mindless of the hour or the day. To engage with time means engaging with the end of the ordeal, so it is better not to dwell on what lies in between. Perhaps that was why my fingers lay on the sheet without moving. Perhaps that was why I was calm, and patient.

That evening our grim party hurried down the steps of Diane's house and into taxis. Neighbours watched us go. Christian's daughters were nervous. They imagined Yemen to be a wild place with gunmen on every corner and populated by angry people who believed in holy wars. I hoped they would return much wiser.

At Heathrow we were shepherded into a lounge and offered refreshments. I kept myself apart, sustained by the thought that when morning came I would be with Theo. The others whispered as if we were standing in a mortuary with an open coffin, fearing the dead were eavesdropping. *Christ,* I thought again, they have him buried already.

I went to buy chocolate for Theo and nice pens for Nooria. Then I dawdled, among sunglasses, cameras, perfumes and things, things, things, so distracted that

343

I bumped into Rebecca and she into me. We ambled together. I wondered what they had been told about our split.

Our flight was called. A Yemenia official led us, with our carrier-bags and mangled hearts, along corridors as endless as the day. Emily or Bess should have been going in my place, but nothing would make me part with my fraudulent claim to Christian, whom I had twice rejected. I had, in fact, no right to be boarding that flight, but I was driven by instinct. The very instinct, perhaps, that Tess had spoken about, when we suddenly know what to do and how to do it.

Diane and Tania sat across the aisle, Rebecca and Melanie in front of them. I took a window seat and furiously texted friends before take-off, as if I, too, believed I was heading into some wilderness from which I might never return. The buzz of my phone was a lifeline. A beep in the dark. Dublin calling.

During the flight, Tania took an empty window seat in across from her sisters. It seemed odd to leave Diane by herself, so I offered to join her. We fiddled with our dinner.

'Will they feed him, do you think?'

'They'll share their food. Hostages are treated like guests. If he *is* a hostage.'

'Stupid, stupid man! Going off like that.'

'But why did he go? He'd finished his research.'

'I thought he'd gone after you. That at least made sense.'

'He *did* think I was there, but he was actively avoiding

me, according to Theo, so it had nothing to do with me. It must have been some kind of work.'

'What abominable timing. Bloody typical male conceit!'

I touched her wrist.

'You know the country,' she said. 'What do you think will happen?'

'I don't know the country well, but I don't understand why there have been no demands. It could be a good sign, or a bad one.'

'Why did you leave him?'

It came out of nowhere, just like that. I turned to her. 'Why did *you*?'

Her eyes were glassy with exhaustion. The fork shook in her hand. 'I was in love with someone else. There seemed to be no good reason for what you did.'

She had thrown me back and I was standing there again – the water stopped, mid-air, its drops hanging, the growl silenced, and Christian almost obscured behind the veil . . .

I cannot explain it. I was going to say yes, *yes*, but I couldn't speak. Nothing came.

His eyes crinkled. He leaned into the wire. 'Vivien?'

Still nothing came.

Christian nodded slowly, then walked round to me. 'And you're not going to move to London either, are you?'

'I don't know.'

'I do,' he said, and he walked away from the blow-hole, away from me.

Neither of us spoke in the car. When we got back to the house, he went upstairs and started packing. I stood at the other side of the bed.

'What are you doing?'

'Going home.'

'But you can't just –'

'I can't hang around any longer, Vivien. I've been going back and forth like a bus for months, and it's pretty bloody clear nothing is going to change. You're perfectly comfortable here in this nowhere zone where you don't have to make any decisions.'

'I've made plenty of decisions. Hard ones. You're the one who's had it easy.'

'You call this easy? Sitting around airports?' He flung a shirt into his case. 'Hanging about like a dog for a bone that may or may not come its way? Well, it isn't easy.'

'You're asking me to leave my home, my job, my parents and friends. Not to mention giving up something that I've wanted to do all my life!'

'I'm asking you to be with me. It isn't complicated.'

'Not for you. All you'll have to do is change the sheets and make space for my clothes.'

He snapped his case shut. 'Look, I'm just trying to have a relationship here – it's supposed to be fun, uplifting, but it's more like standing on a precipice. I've no idea which way I'm going to fall or where I'll be next week. It's one step up and two steps back with you.' His fingers spread across the corners of the suitcase; he looked vulnerable, suddenly, and hurt. 'Even when we're together, Vivien, there's only part of you here.

346

It's as if you're looking over my shoulder at something else. And the truth of it is, you *are*.'

My legs gave out. I sat on the end of the bed.

'Maybe you *do* want to be with me,' he said, 'and maybe you do love me in fits and starts, but when it comes to it you're just not prepared to drop anchor. Not for me, anyway, so I might as well take the hint.' He took his suitcase off the bed and stood by the door. 'If it's all the same to you, it's time I cut down on my air miles.'

'Just like that? Out of the blue?'

'It's been six months. I think I've been fairly patient, don't you?'

'No, I don't. It is possible, you know, to want and need two irreconcilable things at the same time.'

'Yes, and that's why we have to grow up and make choices. You've just made yours.'

He went downstairs. I stayed in the room and, from the small white window, watched the car disappear down the lane. There was no point in tearing after him, and nothing fair in begging for more time. He was right. Put to the wire, I had made a choice, and he had not been part of it.

I had to travel back by train the next day, late for work again. We had had no contact since.

Diane was still waiting for my reply, but there was no easy explanation, except that something had held me back that day by the blowhole and I had had to take heed. *We must not travel the road that is not ours to take.*

'It was having no good reason that made it hard,' said Diane. 'He believed you loved him.'

347

'I did. I do. But he's the one who walked away.'

'You made no attempt to stop him.'

'Excuse me, but you threw him out of his own house for a dead person. Explain that.'

'All right, I will.' She held out her cup to the flight attendant for tea. 'Living with Christian after Eric died was an unspeakable strain. It was like living with infidelity day in, day out. I didn't want to be with him, I wanted to be with someone else. I *longed* for someone else, do you understand? I couldn't tell Christian, I couldn't spell it out like that, especially with him being such a saint, nursing me patiently through my bereavement. Only it wasn't just bereavement, it was a love-affair. Eric was dead, but I was in love, and I didn't want to be around another man, let alone my own husband. I could see the hope in his eyes, the belief that once I'd "got over" it, we'd go back to being Diane and Chris. But you cannot go back to loving one man when you've started loving another, even if that man happens to have died. You can't. And it wasn't fair to keep Christian hanging, so – yes, I threw him out. He would have settled for anything just to be with his daughters and maintain the status quo. He begged me not to do it. Really begged.'

That must be why, I thought, he never so much as queried me. He had probably resolved never to plead again.

'When you came along, I was pleased,' Diane went on. 'I wanted Christian to have what I'd missed, but then he came back from Ireland like a piece of cloth that had got caught in machinery, and I wished he'd never met you. I had to put him back together again, you know.'

'We're quits, then. I tidied up the mess you'd left behind.'

She allowed a reluctant smile, which momentarily shaded the anguished expression. She may not have wanted him as a husband, and I wasn't even sure about that, but she was not travelling for her children's sake alone. Christian might have been amused. The two women who had rejected him were sitting side by side in an aeroplane, desperate to be with him.

'What did he ever do to deserve us?' I asked aloud.

Diane almost laughed.

I walked the length of the plane, wondering why I had hesitated at Downpatrick Head. Not for want of love, clearly. This sudden pilgrimage, this nightmare of air-craft air, was a testimony to love. My mistake had been in trying to hold it back because, inevitably, it had come crashing down like a slow-building wave, landing on me with all its pent-up force and throwing me around in its wake. I should never have resisted. A wave will always break.

The overhead screens informed us that we were more than half-way to Sana'a. Local time flashed up, along with the mileage done and the mileage yet to go. My heart began to thunder, my bowels rumbled, and the ordeal took real shape. I went back to my seat, feeling sick.

The worst part of that long flight was having no phone. Not being able, even, to *wait* for it to ring. We were in Information No Man's Land. The flight attendants handed out blankets. We tried to sleep. I closed my eyes. '*May I?*' he had asked, coming to sit with me somewhere over Egypt. That voice. The boyish eagerness. The flirtatiousness I had laboured to misinterpret.

The plane veered and my heart slid sideways with it, drawn back, drawn to Yemen, again.

None of us slept, but we spent two hours trying to, then began to move about, checking up on one another with eyes and brows so as not to disturb other passengers. As we drew closer to our destination, the girls gathered around my seat. Should they cover up? Would they be searched? How should they behave?

'Cover your arms and legs, and be yourselves. And there's something else – it's Ramadan now, the holy month. People fast between sunrise and sunset so you should respect that. Eat and drink discreetly. Don't go swinging water-bottles around.'

There was a faint blue light on the horizon. Dawn. A shiver went through me, as if I was meeting an old lover at a graveside. I'll get my hands painted again, I thought, only to be immediately horrified. This was no holiday! We took a great aerial step downwards, and another, and I felt cushioned. Closer to him. With every aeronautical mile put behind us, we came closer to him, wherever he was. Did he hear our jet? Was he listening somewhere below us? Had he thought of me?

We had come in over Yemen. Slumbering in the early light, it welcomed me with that same conceit. It had been expecting me. The engines pulled back. We dropped again, and the arid plains came a little closer. A weird landscape stretched out beneath us. It was like a vast, sea-less beach. Not desert, but an empty beach with no coastline. Black and brown. Cratered mounds, like gigantic dog turds, rose from the ground. There were mountains in the distance, and more and more mud-brick villages on the plain.

As we came in to land, I was so caught up, so full, that tears gathered behind my eyelids, and when we bumped down, they escaped. The aircraft turned at the end of the runway. I had never meant to return like this.

Our little party jumped to its feet. We grabbed our bags, an agitated posse, and hurried towards the doors, desperate for news. Things might have changed during our seven-hour suspension. An English diplomat came aboard to greet us. There were pleasantries, formalities, documents handed over, but no news. I couldn't wait. 'Excuse me.' I pushed past everyone and hurried down the steps and into the terminal.

The official party came in behind me. The diplomat introduced himself as Geoff and took my passport. 'I'll get you all through Immigration. Shouldn't take long.'

My stomach churned. The Linklaters stood, eyes wide, shifting about on their feet, fiddling with their headscarves. The business of immigration might well have been rushed through, but it seemed an eternity before we were finally released. I took off like the electronic hare at a greyhound race and barged through the doors. This time there was no confusion. My Dutchman was there, towering above the crowd, and he looked to me like the only man I had ever known.

21

I stood in the street, looking up at our house. 'For months I've imagined myself standing here, but it never felt like this.'

We headed straight for the kitchen, but the kettle had not yet boiled when a high-pitched squeal called out in the stairwell.

'Nooria!' I ran down the steps. We slapped into one another on the landing outside my room.

'Aieee, Vivien!'

'It's so great to see you!'

'I don't think so. Not this way.' We walked hand in hand up to the kitchen. 'What's happening?' she asked Theo.

'No news. You?'

'Na. No one knows where he is. *Ya Allah!* His daughters have come?'

'Yes, they're at the Taj. And his wife. Ex-wife.'

The phone rang in Theo's room. He ran to it.

'You are stupid woman,' said Nooria.

'I beg your pardon?'

'Why did you not marry him?'

'I swear if I'm asked that question again I'll kidnap myself and make no conditions for release.'

'Well?'

'I didn't want to get married.'

'Why not? You are not a young woman.'

'Oh, thank you.'

'You want children, no?'

'Yes, but don't worry – there's still a little bit of time left for that. And *you* can talk.'

Theo came back. 'Work,' he said.

'I take it you saw him?' I said to Nooria.

'Just once, here. He blamed Yemen. I told him is not Yemen's fault you stubborn person.'

Theo sat beside her, one leg resting on her chair, his bony knee protruding above the table, and I thought, not for the first time, what a pair they would make.

'How come *you* haven't asked me why I wrecked everything?' I said to him.

'Sometimes there are things we can't do,' he said.

Nooria nodded at him with a gentle smile. 'God's way.'

'If it's God's way, why were you yelling at me about it?' I asked.

'Because I can't yell at God.' She got up and hugged me. 'I must go to work.'

''Bye, see you later.' I stretched. 'I feel better now I'm here. Have I really been away?'

'Too long.'

The waiting began in earnest. I thought it would be easier in Sana'a, but the day was sluggish and my heart jerked whenever the phone rang, then palpitated un-comfortably until it regained its rhythm. When Theo went out to some site on the Hodeida road where he was working, I lay on my bed and tried to rest. The room seemed to hold Christian's scent, his presence. I waited for him. I expected his gentle rap on the door, the rattle of plates as he brought breakfast, but he didn't come and I didn't sleep. In the *mafraj*, I sat against cushions and waited for him. When he came, we would replay the scene in which we made love on the rugs with sunlight filtering through the multi-coloured panes. But he didn't come. The empty house roared at me. I wished Nooria wasn't working. So often, she and I had sat around the *mafraj* giggling and lazing. *Why cannot you see what I see?* The only place that held no memories was Theo's room. I went to his bed and slept.

He was there when I woke, taking off his shirt. 'What time is it?' I asked.

'Four thirty.'

'Any news?'

'The British Embassy has advised all the British to leave, actually.'

'Shit. Because of Christian?'

'Due to a "heightened threat of terrorism to America's allies". It's . . . I don't know, intelligence. "Increased chatter on the lines", they call it. More even than before September eleventh, apparently. Shall we go to the hotel after I shower?'

The Linklaters were at the coffee-shop in the lobby. As we approached, Theo, who had already met them at the airport, muttered, 'Which one is which?'

'The one with the earrings is . . . is . . . Oh, God, I can't remember.'

The diplomat, Geoff, was briefing Diane on developments, such as they were. The government was adamant that this was not a traditional kidnapping – there had been no demands and no car had been found – but that left the prospect of involvement by more sinister, and ruthless, groups. As far as anyone could work out, Christian had left Sana'a the day before the missile attack. He had been issued with an exit permit, but had apparently travelled without security, except in the form of Yemeni friends. There was clear irritation that he had not made his plans known to the embassy, but things had not been so fraught then.

'Officials are making inquiries up-country,' said Geoff, 'and the army is scouring the area east of Marib. And there is, of course, the other possibility – that if his work took him off the beaten track, so to speak, he might have got lost.'

Diane gasped. 'But surely to get lost out there is to be dead?'

'Mum,' one of the girls said, 'why do you always have to look on the black side?'

'We mustn't have false hope, darling.'

'But you must have hope,' I said. 'Does he have a GPS?' I asked Theo.

'Even if he did, batteries run out.'

Geoff gathered his papers. 'I'll call in again later.'

I asked them how their day had been. Rebecca shrugged. 'Some woman called Jane came round. She wanted to bundle us up and take us home for lunch, but we don't much feel like going out, especially with those guys around.'

Three policemen stood by the door, smart and clean in their blue uniforms.

'Our official bodyguard,' said Diane. 'The Blue Meanies.'

'Are they mean?' asked Theo.

'No, no. Sorry, I stole that expression from a film.'

'Ah,' he grinned, '*those* Blue Meanies. *Yellow Submarine.*'

She smiled. 'Yes.'

I had no idea what they were talking about.

'We're not to go anywhere without them.'

'But you must still go out,' I said. 'Hanging around the hotel won't do any good. Go and look around. Christian would want you to see this place.'

'I hate this place,' said Melanie. I was learning. It was their personalities that differentiated them, not physical pointers.

'*He* doesn't,' I said.

'He will now.'

'No. He won't.'

The girls went to their rooms to watch satellite television. 'I never thought I'd hear myself say thank God for television,' said Diane, 'but it takes their minds off it. I wish it could do the same for me. Now that we're here, I'm not at all sure why we came. I expected something to happen. I thought things would move once we got here, as if that journey would be enough to bring this to a close or that they'd see his daughters and take pity ... Instead – inertia. Doldrums. It's unspeakable.'

On the steps of the hotel, after we'd left Diane, Theo stood with his fingers in his hip pockets, looking up and around. 'It's dark.'

'Yes, Theo, that's right. It's what happens when the sun goes down.'

'Good. Fadhl and I have been asked to a *qat* chew. Let's do that instead of sitting by the phone.'

'A *qat* chew at night?'

'Yes, because of Ramadan. It has to be after dark. Will you come?'

'I'm a bit knackered to tell the truth.'

'The *qat* will help.'

'It won't help me sleep.'

'It will help you relax. We both need a bit of that.'

'True.' But it was the prospect of sitting in number eight, staring at the walls, waiting for a phone call, that really persuaded me to go with him.

The house where the *qat* chew was taking place was particularly tall, which was unfortunate in view of my exhausted state, and there was also a black-out when we arrived so we had to climb to the top in darkness. We went in single file, with Fadhl, holding hands. Theo pulled me up the steps; it was like walking upwards into a deep, unlit basement, until he came to a sudden halt. 'Shit. I've walked into a wall.' He dropped my hand to feel his way.

'Don't let go! I'll never find you again.'

'Oh, I get it.' The stairway, which had been turning up to the right, was now going to the left.

We continued on until we reached a landing and stepped into a large, L-shaped, candlelit room. Huge windows overlooked the blacked-out city. The men were all in *futahs*, the Yemeni skirt traditionally worn at *qat* chews, and talking quietly among themselves. They

357

greeted Theo and Fadhl and made space for us in a corner.

'We must change, Theo,' said Fadhl.

'Into what?' I asked.

He held up *futahs*. 'Skirts.'

I was the only woman there, but no one paid any heed. When Theo and Fadhl returned, Theo spread his *qat* across the rug.

'Where's your phone?' I said. 'Is it on?'

He tapped his shirt pocket. 'It'll vibrate.' He held out some *qat*. 'Have some. You need it.'

I took it and lay back. 'The best thing about this stuff,' I said, 'is that there's no such thing as passive *qat* chewing.'

Theo threw in snippets of information about *qat* and old houses. 'They store the *qat* in the left cheek and they lean to the left as well.' As with other chewers, the sparkle in his eyes grew brighter as his cheek swelled. In the middle of the floor three water-pipes were bubbling away, which the men occasionally puffed at.

The *qat* dissolved in my mouth. I had not learned how to chew it and store it, but my fitful anxiety was slightly quelled, either by the juices of the plant or by my surroundings – the gentle murmur and the haloed flames, the reclining bodies and mellow minds. No better place to rest.

The city called me out to the terrace, as had become its habit. In spite of the circumstances, I could not be unmoved by my return. Candlelight flickered at windows all over town. Families yelled at one another.

Children wailed. It could have been any century, any century at all.

Theo came out behind me.

'There's nowhere like it,' I said. 'I haven't travelled much, but I know that there is nowhere in the world like this.'

'I know.' After a moment he added, 'What will you do when Christian comes back? Go to live in England?'

'God, I wish I had your certainty. "*When* he comes back?"'

'He will.'

'I bloody well hope so, because this is like . . . like slow suffocation.'

Theo put his arm round my shoulders.

'Whoever he's with,' I said, 'wherever he is, he'd better get himself out of there fast because . . . because . . .'

'It's okay.'

'He could be injured, ill, trapped. The jeep could have gone over a ravine or – or they could have got caught up in some tribal trouble or wandered into those no-go areas . . .'

'I don't think so. Come on, we'll go home.'

Back at the house, we took our seats opposite each other in the kitchen where, over tea, I ran out of tears and sat with a stinging face and sore nose. 'I drove him to this. He got careless because he didn't actually care what happened to him any more.'

Theo sipped his tea.

'Oh, for God's sake, Theo, can't you at least contradict me?'

He ran his hand round the back of his neck. 'I can, if you want me to lie, but it's partly true what you say. He wasn't . . . focused. Sana'a was hard for him.'

'Did he talk about me?'

'There wasn't much to say. You'd turned him down.'

'I didn't turn him down. I just didn't *accept*.'

'It comes to the same thing. You think it's easy, asking someone to marry you?'

'No, but I don't understand how marriage came into it. We'd never discussed it. It came out of the blue. And then he took off!'

'Of course. There was nothing to make him stay.'

'I needed more time.'

'He didn't think time would make any difference,' said Theo.

'Clearly.'

'It's hard to stay with someone who is unsure.'

'It's hard to *be* unsure.'

I went to my room, exhausted and depressed. The same yellow sheets, the little vase of dried flowers. The fleas, too, no doubt. Wakefulness took hold as soon as my head met the pillow. An hour later, I went back upstairs. Light shone beneath the bedroom door. I knocked.

He called me in. 'Can't sleep?'

'Not a chance. I don't suppose the Linklaters can either. Any of them.'

Theo was in bed, propped up against the wall, reading. I plumped up a pillow and sat beside him. We speculated again.

'If terrorists wanted revenge, they'd just kill him and dump him where he could be found, wouldn't they? They wouldn't delay like this.'

He shook his head. 'Who knows how they think?'

'Are you on the road tomorrow?' He was looking at my feet. 'Theo?'

'God, but you've got nice legs.'

'Hello?'

'I've never seen them before.'

I whacked him. 'You shouldn't be seeing them now either – at least, not until we're married.'

'Yes, I am on the road tomorrow, not far from town, actually.'

'You'd better get some sleep, then.'

As I leaned over to turn out the light, he said, 'Roos left me.'

'Seriously?'

'*Ja*. She wasn't cut out for the life.'

'But you could give up the life.'

His eyes were smaller without glasses. 'Why?'

'You shouldn't be alone. It's a waste of good material.'

'Look what happened to *your* waste material.'

'Oh!' I grabbed a pillow and hit him with it.

He hit me back with his own. 'You treat your lovers like rubbish.'

'You!' I whacked him again, knocking books off the table, but he swiped back, and we went on swinging and laughing until we exhausted ourselves and fell asleep at either side of his big bed.

*

The call to prayer woke me, and as consciousness crept over me, the fear came back with it. The room was sunny, but not stifling. I opened my eyes – I was still in Theo's room. He was breathing deeply. A cool breeze filtered through the window. I slithered off again, into sleep.

Theo was gone when I woke at ten, full of thoughts of Christian and the high times we had spent there. After showering, I walked to the hotel. Having told Diane I wouldn't be glued to them in Sana'a, I now couldn't wait to be with them. I needed to be with those who had been suspended, like me, from the normal course of events; to be where nothing was happening because it was the only place where something might.

On account of Ramadan, the streets were quiet, almost dead. People had stayed up until dawn and were sleeping it off. Dusty cats prowled around al-Qa Square. The view ahead had been splintered once again. I had been saving hard and looking for suitable tenants for my flat (who were prepared to pay the slightly elevated rent) and, contrary to what I had told my parents, no war was going to stop me coming back as soon as I could afford to. After all, I'd paid a high price to make it possible. And here I was, sure enough, but with every certainty swept away. My determination to live there had been thrown into the broth of Christian's disappearance and was now heavily diluted, almost gone. This was the kick up the ass I had needed – not a proposal of marriage, but the prospect of losing him. And yet there was a spring in my step as I negotiated the broken pavements of Sana'a. Streets that had once intimidated me were now like my own personal suburb.

The triplets were swimming. It wasn't hot, but it was warm and sunny and the heated pool was a world away from grim November evenings in London.

'Takes their minds off it,' said Diane, sitting in the shade of a parasol. She was such a tired woman, had been tired, I believed, long before this happened.

'News?' I asked.

'They're closing the embassy.'

'Oh, God.'

'Until further notice. Closed to the public, at any rate, while they review security. It doesn't affect us. Geoff is still keeping us informed, but they clearly want us out of here and I can't say I blame them. We're not helping matters, and yet the girls have this idea that it's what they must do. It's quite affecting, really, the way they think they're being so loyal and mature, while Christian would be apoplectic if he knew they were here. He'd be furious with me for not stopping them.'

'So why didn't you?'

'I couldn't stop *myself*, let alone anyone else.'

We sat for some time, not speaking. Language had become thwarted. Gestures, the flicker of an eyelid, were more useful tools when mouths were dry and when all thoughts, anyway, covered the same ground. Little wonder I had always loathed the waiting state, but I, who had never got the hang of it, now had to endure the worst possible interlude, one that had no foreseeable end and was spiked with fear and horrible imaginings. Those fears held us to ransom – the dread of what punishment might be inflicted and the terror that he might not survive it, or the flip side: the imagery of a merciless desert and its killing thirst. We were numbed, paralysed, by such thoughts and by the relentless effort of trying, not quite successfully, to shut them out. There was nothing to be done, save sit through hour upon hour of ignorance, unable to prevent our minds dwelling where they would. We had no purpose other than fretting. No event altered our situation. No movement at the side of the eye helped. It was never what we hoped.

'Diane?'

'Mmm?'

'Last night Theo and I had a pillow fight. I fell asleep laughing.'

She smiled. 'Well, laughter *is* a form of hysteria . . . And maybe, wherever he is, Christian heard some echo of it.'

When the girls got out of the pool, I suggested we go to the *suq* that evening. 'Nooria says it's wonderful during Ramadan. Everything comes to life after dark, when the fasting is over.'

'What's the *suq*?' asked Tania.

'The market, in the old town.'

'I'm not going *shopping*,' said Melanie.

'No, you're going for a walk.'

'It's dangerous,' Rebecca said.

'It isn't. Look, don't miss out. This country isn't responsible for what's happened to Christian, so don't hold the whole population to ransom.'

'An unfortunate choice of words,' Diane muttered.

'Sorry. The thing is, most of them are in sympathy with you. They'd like you to see the better side of their country.'

'I'm up for it. I could use the distraction,' said Diane. 'I'm going mad inside these walls.'

A more apprehensive party had never left that hotel, but after four days stuck indoors, in London and in Sana'a, cabin fever had set in and the Linklaters were at least willing when Theo, Fadhl and I shepherded them through Bab al-Yemen. The Blue Meanies fanned out like geese. The girls were nervous, as if this very protection unit was going to take us, but the policemen were friendly, jovial, and kept a reasonable distance as we walked, the least enthralled of tourists. The *suq* was livelier than I had seen it, buzzing with the excitement of Ramadan, as people hurried about the shops, looking forward to the night ahead when they could eat and drink. The Linklaters were distracted, even a little mesmerized. In the fabric *suq*, Diane seemed on the point of buying the materials spread out before her. 'Emily would love some of these,' she said vaguely. A shawl held her interest even longer. She fingered it, unaware that the woman who ran the stall was bargaining hopefully with Fadhl, while all Diane wanted to say was 'Christian brought me back one of these the last time.'

Our feet were heavy. I glanced up at the towering blocks, the overhanging balconies, and found myself turning on the spot, thinking, Where are you, Christian? Where in the labyrinth have you gone to?

I came to an abrupt halt. Theo had grabbed my arms. 'Stop. Stop turning.'

'We should get back,' said Diane. 'There might be news.'

News. That ghastly little word. We were slaves to it.

'Let's eat first,' said Theo. 'Geoff has my number.'

We took them to the restaurant we had been to that first night in March, but it was much busier on account of Ramadan. There were foreigners, mixed parties, Yemenis; even an Italian family with four children.

'I don't get it,' said Melanie. 'I thought Westerners weren't supposed to be in Yemen.'

'There are thousands working here,' said Theo. 'Like me. Most won't leave.'

'But aren't you worried?'

'I would rather be in a country like this, with people like this, than take a train to the office every day. The risks are never as much as they seem.'

'But everything's going on as if nothing is happening,' said Melanie. 'Everyone's partying.'

'You would party too if you had not eaten since before dawn,' said Fadhl.

I kept hearing Christian's voice among the crowd. It was disconcerting.

'It's odd,' said Diane, 'but I feel safer here than in that hotel.'

The girls devoured the crisp *rashoosh*, but picked warily at the fish, even though they had seen it subjected to intense heat in the ovens, and Diane and I, also, made little impact on the grand Ramadan spread. It was easy to fast with the Yemenis by day: we had no appetite. Breaking the fast in the evenings was the difficult part.

When we were leaving, we stood by the entrance while Theo paid the bill, and I sensed again that Christian was there somewhere, in the restaurant behind me, sitting with another party, perhaps, and leaning across the table to make his point, in Arabic. The impression of his voice came in Arabic, so it was probably a Yemeni who sounded like him, although I kept imagining it to be Christian. I glanced around the crowded room and found myself looking straight at him. He *was* leaning across a table towards his companion, making a point in Arabic. I stared open-mouthed until, aware that eyes were boring into him, he looked up.

I closed my mouth and held his gaze: 'I find myself looking towards the place where the sun must have just disappeared. This high above sea-level we are spared the more vulgar sort of sunset. The afterglow is dusty, the sky above the city like the inside of a shell. But I'm looking towards it, not at it — there's a distortion in the windowpane, interesting and annoying at the same time.'

Mackintosh-Smith looked away. I followed the others on to the street.

The next morning I woke with a headache. I had come to hate my room, riddled as it was with memories of Christian balancing on the edge of the mattresses and of Nooria laughing on that last night when my hands were in plastic bags. It was a stuffy, lonely room.

News later that day threw Diane into a panic. A terrorist arrested in Kuwait had talked. He divulged a plot to car-bomb a hotel in Yemen used by American military personnel. Whether it was the Linklaters' hotel or not was beyond the current scope of Diane's rationality. She wanted them to get out of it immediately. The embassy offered them sanctuary in diplomatic homes, but she refused. 'Anyone who works for the embassy is a target. Where are we to go?'

'You could come to us,' I suggested. 'It'd be a bit crowded but . . .'

'What about the bodyguard?'

'I don't know. You'd have to speak to the embassy – and Theo and his boss.'

Even before an agreement had been brokered, her daughters had been despatched, with me and without bodyguard, to the house. A forlorn trio, with their hastily packed bags, they sat slumped in the *mafraj*, deprived now of their television. I had no idea what to do with them. Theo, meanwhile, refused point-blank to allow the police near his house, but said the Linklaters were welcome if they would forgo the bodyguard. The embassy and security services urged Diane not to do so, although even Geoff admitted that there was something to be gained from blending into the background. After much anguished deliberation, she decided to move in with us. I gave up my room, intending to sleep in the *mafraj*, but neither small bedroom could accommodate two people, so Tania and Rebecca took the *mafraj*; Melanie and Diane took the single rooms and Theo ended up on the floor in his own room.

In his lackadaisical way, he did not embrace the overcrowding, but I was pleased to have the Linklaters there. I wanted to nurse Christian's women, to mind them for him, while Theo and Nooria minded me.

We took them on to the roof for drinks before dinner. They were, all four, mesmerized by the mountains.

'Is that where he is?' Tania asked. 'Up there somewhere?'

'Beyond, I'd say.'

In neighbouring houses families were gathering to break the fast. Laughter, shouting and the smell of cooking wafted towards us, a soothing aromatherapy.

'This is better,' said Diane. 'That hotel had become so small and tight.'

Nooria had issued us with one of her threat-like invitations to Ramadan breakfast: 'If you're not there by the time he calls, "*Allahu Akbar*", I start without you!'

We got there just after the muezzin's evening prayer had announced the end of the day's fast; the dawn prayer would herald its beginning. We were treated to salted porridge and onions, followed by bread, yoghurt and salad, then *qishr*, with custard and fruit for dessert. Diane and I did our best, glancing at each other in encouragement whenever another mouthful went in and then down; an achievement every time. The girls were overawed by Nooria, but without her they would never have known Yemen. They would have seen only a five-star hotel with an Arabic column in the menus.

I liked sleeping in Theo's room, up by the roof. It was nice to cancel out the empty spaces of the long house that had echoed between us until then, accentuating the darkness of night and the length of it, with its hours of silence when no phone rang. I didn't abandon him to the floor. It was a wide bed, and we had already shared it. We slept well together. Even if one rolled into the other, there was no sense of trespass: we simply shuffled away, as if we had accidentally smothered the cat. Once, after a spell of sleep, we began a conversation, and in the early hours we went out on to the roof to let the spotty sky mess with our vision. There was comfort in seeing the same stars that Christian could see. I shivered in the night air, absorbing the void out ahead, and promised myself that when Christian turned up, I would take him back to the blowhole and we would stand on Downpatrick Head and watch the waters fall again from where we had left them hanging, until every drop had returned to the sea.

Family chatter in surrounding houses grew louder. Theo looked over the parapet towards Nooria's house. 'Hungry?' he asked.

'It's four a.m.'

'Nooria's up. Let's go and eat with her.'

She might have been expecting us. She hadn't bothered to sleep and had been cooking for some time before we arrived. We sat around the kitchen table. For the first time in days I felt hungry.

'I don't suppose Christian will be able to drink all day, wherever he is,' I said.

'He won't eat when he's with Ahmad anyway, so it makes no difference,' said Theo.

I yawned, and rested my elbow on his shoulder. 'You're so sympathetic, Theo.'

The muezzins began their prayer. At the call of *'Allahu Akbar'*, Nooria put down her fork.

Later on I brought Diane a glass of tea and found her sitting on my mattresses, bloated with crying. 'He could be dead already. He could be . . . God knows, lying somewhere on a hot plateau. We might never find him. I thought . . . I don't know, that we'd get here and he'd turn up and we'd all be together. Instead this interminable *waiting*.'

Unable to reassure her, I rubbed her back and let her cry and rant, and when there was nothing left, she whispered, 'This is worse, you know.'

'Worse than what?'

Still whispering, lest a ghost might hear, she said, 'Worse than Eric dying.'

With those four words, I lost Christian.

22

Melanie, Tania and Rebecca swam quietly around the heated pool. They wouldn't forgo the pleasure and assured Diane that if a car bomb went off outside, they'd be safe at the back, in the water. They were acquiring the right mindset. The hotel seemed to be empty, but for a few idle waiters and two other guests reading in the sun. If American secret agents were staying there, they were well disguised.

The fact that nothing had happened yet was, we were told, cause for a little optimism. Kidnappers would have come out of the woodwork by then, it was generally believed, but that was small comfort in a screaming vacuum of hard facts, and it left the arguably worse possibility of an accident on some distant dirt track, miles from help of any kind. Diane had aged. The girls, in contrast, were more relaxed, and Rebecca had even taken a fancy to Youssuf, the gorgeous manager of the leisure centre, whom I had noticed myself eight months before.

'I envy you,' Diane said to me. 'You have only yourself to worry about. You're so *free*. Once you have children, you become bogged down in love and you labour through life trying to get things right, suffering all their hurts. It's unbearable to see them go through this, trying to be so brave and mature, when deep down they're terrified . . . Tania simply won't be able to cope without him. He's the only person who really understands her. I don't know what she'll do if –'

'Tania will be fine. You'll all be fine.'

'The authorities were right. We should never have come. It isn't doing them any good. Or Christian. What on earth was I thinking, dragging the children over here?'

'*They* dragged *you*, remember?'

'I should take them home and get them back to school. These people aren't making progress. They don't know where he is.'

'Diane –'

'I must take them home. It's what Christian would want, don't you think?' She waited for my reply.

'I suppose so.'

'But you'll stay, won't you? I don't want him abandoned.'

'Of course I'll stay, but you can't just bundle the girls into a taxi and take them away. I don't believe one of them plans to leave here without their father.'

'Then you must help me persuade them.'

We sat watching the girls. There was something endearing about the way they mirrored one another. It made them seem younger than they were, or perhaps it was the gentle way they swam about, as if reluctant to disturb the water, that made them seem vulnerable and sweet to me.

Diane said, almost to herself, 'It really isn't fair. We've been through so much already . . .'

'I know. You've had a horrible run.'

'It doesn't seem right, does it, that the same man could be assaulted twice? And with only one kidney, he's so much more susceptible to disease and infection ... If he doesn't get enough to drink ...' Tania spiralled round in the water and did a languid backstroke. 'He's done so well,' Diane went on. 'He did so well to pull it all together – only for that woman to come back at him again, and now *this*.'

I had wondered if Gemma would come up, and here she was. 'I'm sorry about Gemma,' I said. 'It was my fault – this time round, anyway.'

Her eyes swung towards me. 'She's your friend, I know, but I can't be kind about her.'

'I don't blame you. It must have been terrifying.'

She rubbed her shin, her hand going up and down as if she was trying to soothe a freshly inflicted bruise. 'Whenever I think about that person – and I try not to – I see Christian in hospital, hooked up to things, and the girls, little mites that they were at the time, edging towards this unrecognizable mess like a low moving wall. He was so pleased to see them, but he couldn't smile or enunciate so his attempts to reassure them were terrifying. Their visit did him a power of good, but I had to handle the nightmares back home for a week afterwards, and that was only the beginning. I'm afraid I hold your friend entirely responsible.'

'Me too.'

'She left a mess behind her,' Diane went on. 'The physical damage was one thing, but Christian was shattered. He lost his nerve. He went out every day shaking. That's why I insisted we leave Durham. I couldn't stay there any longer, worrying all the time that she might be round the next corner. Even *I* kept expecting her to spring out at me, so God only knows what it was like for him. Luckily I had a bit of cash put by from my mother's estate so we could afford to move south, but even in London it took him a long time to really come home again.'

'Christian said you met her once.'

'Yes. In his office. She came bursting in.'

'It must have given her a jolt, seeing you there.'

'Not one bit,' said Diane. 'She looked at me as if I was completely irrelevant. She had everything just the way she wanted it and she looked at Christian – well, as if they were lovers. If I hadn't known him so well, I'd almost have believed they were.'

'She can be very persuasive.' I stood up, and pressed my fingers into the small of my back. 'At one point, she had me believing it.'

'*Did* she? But she's delusional.'

'I know, but when you're up as close as I was, it can be hard to tell which bits are delusional and which aren't.'

Diane looked at me. 'Heavens, Vivien. How long did she have such a hold over you?'

'Since she gave me the nod at school, I suppose, and made me visible. She was like an extra skin on me. It was hard to wriggle out of it.'

'Well, I hope you have now, because I'd hate to see her do to you and Christian what she did to us. She stole years from us, you know. First there was the stalking, then the attack, then the recovery . . . Christian had to fight to get his health back, then struggled to maintain his integrity – in his own head, as well as with some of his colleagues, who had questions about how he'd got into that situation – and then he had to find some other way to make a living. And the worst of it is . . .'

'What?'

'That I didn't stick it out.'

'You did. You carried him through.'

'No. I turned back. I ran out of sympathy way too soon.' She turned her head away. 'I wanted things to get back to normal long before it was reasonable, and I resented Christian going off on those long trips, leaving me with the kids, when we were all trying to find our feet in London . . . I'd managed to get some physio hours in a rehab unit – back-breaking work, lifting grown men and heavy women, then going home to housework and schoolgirls – while Christian, as far as I could see, was enjoying his exotic travels. I never wondered what it was actually like for him, having to scrape around trying to do something he'd never done before and make it work – ad-libbing to a camera when his confidence was at an all-time low . . . No, I didn't give him credit for anything, and by the time he had pulled himself together, really found his ground, I had moved on.' She shook her head in self-disgust. I handed her a tissue and sat down. 'That's why I'm here now. I won't let that man down again.'

Youssuf came over to greet her. He had a low, soothing voice, and as they chatted I noticed how beautiful she was, how very pleasant and gracious. She always wore eye-liner, and her streaked hair was usually off-side in a bundle, but now it was loose and, when she threw it over her shoulders, I saw the lover she would have been. Christian's lover. Lithe and taut, confident and intense. When Youssuf moved along, her thoughts swerved right in front of my own.

'I suppose,' she said, glancing towards the hotel, 'you and Christian became lovers here?'

My breath caught in my throat.

Diane touched my arm quickly. 'I'm sorry. Don't answer that.'

'I'd done it before,' I said. 'That's why I couldn't . . .' Words and tears began tumbling out. 'I abandoned all this once before and spent a dozen years regretting it. Like a kid who finally reaches the top of the queue and gets her ice-cream and she's so bloody pleased with herself that she goes and drops it on the road and has to watch it melt away! I was afraid to give up on myself again. To let myself down. I mean, how many times can you get away with that? Theo has my life now – with his little house and his days spent exploring everything from abandoned wells to villages on moun taintops. I wanted all that. I tried to pretend I didn't any more, but I *did*, I wanted it so badly, and then Christian . . .'

'Got in the way.'

I nodded.

'His timing has always been off.' Diane handed me a tissue. 'Our own private language – handing each other tissues.'

Geoff burst through the restaurant doors, mobile

phone to his ear, and looked around. Diane raised her arm. He made for us, talking into his phone, and there was a swoosh as Tania heaved herself out of the pool. News? Here was news at last, coming towards us like a Predator with a Hellfire missile on board.

Theo had been on the road since dawn. Curled up on his bed with a towel round his waist, he had fallen asleep after a shower. I needed to wake him, tell him. But I sat beside him and listened to him breathe. I put my hand on his side and left it there, rising and falling with his breathing. He sighed deeply, raised his eyebrows, but didn't wake, so I curled up beside him.

He opened his eyes. 'What?'

'Christian.'

Theo leaned on his elbow. 'What? What have they done?'

'It's been confirmed.'

'What has?'

The words came out, slow and flat. 'Some tribesmen reported back. They saw them a few days ago. There's no al-Qaeda or kidnap or anything. We were right: he's out there, doing his Wilfred Thesiger thing. Travelling around with some Bedu doing God knows what.'

'*Verdomme.*'

'They've sent someone to find him.'

'*De klootzak!*'

Tears slipped across my face. 'Why are you speaking Dutch all of a sudden?'

Theo touched my shoulder.

'I'll kill him,' I whispered. 'I tell you, I'll kill him for this.'

How long those twenty-four hours, and how still. The quiet days of Ramadan were rendered quieter by unspoken thoughts and a large degree of embarrassment. With all Christian's experience, how had he so drastically mistimed his adventure? Did he care?

The next day the Linklaters had lunch at the embassy, but later we congregated at the hotel where there was more space for our shifting restlessness. The girls wanted to swim and lounge. I had lost all inclination to make tourists of them. Nobody knew when Ahmad and Christian would be tracked down, but we were less nervous than we had been. It was a painfully slow day. Diane and I were playing cards when Theo got back from his work on the Hodeida road.

'We're nearly ready,' I said. 'Just let the girls dry off.'

'Actually,' he said, 'I don't think we should leave the hotel tonight.'

Everyone looked up.

'They've located them,' he said. 'They're on their way to get them.'

Diane cried out, then put her hands over her eyes and wept. Her dripping daughters gathered around, screeching.

Theo sat down and squeezed my hand. 'It's over, really.' But I was shaking uncontrollably.

'How long?' said Tania. 'How long?'

'It will be some time yet. They're a long way off.'

'Jesus.'

Geoff spun in, as had become his habit, grasping papers. 'We must remember to buy him a briefcase,' I whispered to Diane.

'Yes, yes,' he confirmed, 'we know where they are – somewhere in al-Jawf, one of the trickiest parts of the country. Apparently he's been moving around with some tribesmen. As soon as the army make contact, we'll be informed.'

'Poor Dad,' said Rebecca. 'He'll be so embarrassed.'

Hours more, then, but we didn't care. This wasn't like waiting, or if it was I had become good at it.

Managers and waiters who had tiptoed about us for days now shook our hands and wished us well. The mood in the hotel seemed to lift. People from the embassy came and went; well-meaning ex-pats turned up, and journalists. Nooria and Fadhl joined the vigil. After dark, we sat in the lobby, drinking tea and coffee, nibbling pastries and allowing the sway of relief to take us back and forth between jokes and tears. Every time the phone rang at Reception, at least five people stood up. The manager never left his shift.

'It's really happening,' said Tania.

'Let's not get carried away,' said Diane. 'They haven't reached him yet.'

'Mum, stop being so bloody negative.'

'I'm being realistic. Anything could still go wrong.'

'Sometimes I think you want it to!' Tania snapped, so suddenly that Nooria and I jumped.

A family row, whipped up like a jinn, vanished almost as quickly, and we returned to our fidgeting. I walked round the pool thirty-eight times. Nooria did a few turns with me.

'What a way to get my attention,' I said.

'And he has it now, your attention?'

'Oh, yes. I only wish it hadn't cost so much, especially for his family. And there is another price to pay.'

'Your plans to stay here?'

'Scuppered. I'm sorry, Nooria. After all you've done to make it possible.'

'I want you to be happy, that's all.'

'Those women who picked me up that day in March to take me to the *tafrita* taught me a Yemeni expression: "*Kama 'sh-shams ba'd al-matar.*"'

'Very good pronunciation!'

'Thank you. They worked hard on it. Anyway, that's what you are to me: like the sun after the rain. I'll miss you.'

'Your friends in Yemen will always be here.'

'But I won't be. If he'll have me back, that is.'

'Of course he will. The man I met a few weeks ago would have you back even if you had goat's feet like Bilqis.'

We went inside, where I coincided with Diane in the ladies' room. With one hand on the tap, she looked at me in the mirror. 'What if they've moved on by the time our people get there?'

'You know what I love about you?' I said. 'You're as much of a pessimist as I am. I haven't had to pretend this week. I haven't had to summon up fake optimism.'

She sprinkled water over her face. 'Ditto.' She turned off the tap. 'It'll be nice to have you down the road.'

'Diane . . . why did you let me come instead of one of Christian's sisters?'

'Because,' she said, standing very close to me, 'Bess and Emily are two of the most irritating women you will *ever* meet!' She smiled. 'And you're very welcome to them.'

The phone call came that night at thirteen minutes past eleven. None of us noticed. Geoff was at Reception. The rest of us were draped around the coffee-shop in varying states of discomfort. I was slouched in an armchair. Theo was reading. Nooria was sitting at another table, talking animatedly with some Yemenis, eating their way through the hours of darkness. The lobby was much livelier during the night, when everyone was up feasting. Diane was sitting upright, arms crossed, staring blankly at the floor. The girls were curled up on one couch, lying around each other as they might have done in the womb.

When Geoff called out, 'They've got them!' we leaped simultaneously to our feet and hurried over. He was still on the phone, nodding and listening.

'Are they all right?'

'Yes, yes, everyone's okay.'

'Let me speak to him,' said Diane.

'He's in a different car, but they're on their way.'

There were cheers and yelps and clapping all around us. The triplets brimmed not only with relief, I fancied, but with the satisfaction of being in the right place at the right time – something they had achieved against great odds. They had come of age.

'They'll be here by morning,' said Geoff.

'*Al-hamdu lillah!*'

We returned to our seats, where I sat with my head in my hands, filled to my chin with relief that the last time I ever saw him would not be that day in the bedroom in Mayo, when he was unhappy and frustrated and his fingers were spreading across his suitcase. Here was my chance to undo all that.

After the initial euphoria came a jittery interim. We were offered rooms, but nobody took them. The girls managed to doze, but Diane and I remained rigidly awake even though we were physically limp: relief had siphoned off our energies. We sat slumped, struggling even to speak.

At some point during the night I shook off the torpor and went out to the pool. The lights had been turned off. I took a deep breath of light Sana'a air. Time to leave again. My stomach twisted.

Theo came looking for me. 'You okay?'

'I don't know.' We sat by the edge of the pool, our feet in the water. 'I don't know where I am any more.'

'You're with us all in Sana'a, just like you wanted to be,' he said, almost cheerfully, then added, 'But you'll be leaving now.'

'Not immediately.'

'Today or tomorrow.'

'You think? So soon?'

'They'll debrief him and get you all out of here as quickly as possible.'

'Oh.' We kicked our feet about in the water. 'Leaving has become something of a habit with me. A very bad habit. Maybe I'll stay on for a few days.'

'Christian won't like that.'

'He needs time with his family and I need time to say goodbye to this place, properly.'

'It seems a pity,' said Theo, 'that you have to leave after getting back – twice.'

I sighed. 'It is. It is a pity, but real life calls. It was never meant to be, Yemen and me.'

'Are you very sure about that?'

'I am now. It seems I never *was* fated to live in this country after all, and the worst of it is, after leaving this time, I'll never come back.'

'How do you know?'

'Because everything else will get in the way – career, finances, Friday-night shopping . . . Who knows? Babies, even. That's why I'm in absolutely no hurry to leave.' I put my toes on the bridge of his foot.

He lifted our feet slightly out of the water. 'I'll be finished here soon.'

'What?'

'My work is done, for now. I'll have to come back next year to do more, but, *ja*, I'll be leaving soon as well.'

'God. I can't imagine this place without you.'

'You don't have to. You won't be here either,' he turned to me, 'will you?'

'No, I'll be in London, with Christian . . . Come and see me, won't you?'

'*Ja*, you and Christian, in London.'

Nooria and Fadhl had to eat before sunrise, so some of us migrated to the dining room to keep them company. Diane and I had more tea.

'So,' I said to Geoff, 'is the ambassador going to rap Christian's knuckles?'

'I dare say she will.'

'But he didn't know what was going on. They're better informed on the international space station than out in the Yemeni wastelands.'

'He must have known about the Predator attack. For my own part, I cannot understand why he didn't come in when that happened.'

'He wasn't to know everyone would get so nervous. He's just doing his job.'

'No academic paper is worth the manpower that's been put into finding him.'

'But he wasn't lost!'

'Look, I'm not the enemy here, Vivien. If it weren't for the co-operation of the British and Yemeni governments, he would still be unaccounted-for and very possibly at risk, and you'd be none the wiser. Dr Linklater concealed his intentions in very tricky territory during incredibly difficult times. He has some explaining to do. I'll go and check on their progress.'

Nooria pushed away her plate. 'This is stupid. Waiting, waiting!'

'Now there's a girl after my own heart,' I said.

'They won't be long,' said Theo.

Diane sighed. 'Might as well be the next millennium.'

'Let's go out,' said Nooria.

'Out where?'

'Go to meet them.'

Our eyes flashed from one to the other to the other.

'They'd never allow it,' said Theo.

'We could sneak out the back,' said Diane. 'There must be a back entrance.'

'What? All of us?'

'No,' said Theo. 'Much better to stay here.'

'But what harm can it do?' I said. 'They'll be coming in on the Marib road. Let's get out there. Give him a reception party.'

He scratched his chin. 'We'd never fit into the jeep.'

Nooria slapped his arm. 'What is wrong with you? Your friend is coming!' She raised her hand again, playfully, an empty threat, and when he grabbed her wrist to protect himself, their hands fell momentarily on to his knee.

'I won't go,' said Fadhl. 'I must get home.'

The triplets came into the restaurant in single file. 'What's going on?' asked Melanie. In low voices, we shared the plan with them.

'Excellent!' said Tania.

'No,' said Rebecca. 'I want to stay here.'

'We could ask Geoff. He might be fine about it.'

'But he might say no,' said Tania. 'Let's not chance it.'

'What about checkpoints?' I asked.

'If we don't get through, we'll wait there,' said Nooria.

Theo looked at his watch. It was coming on for five o'clock. 'We'd probably run into them not far from town.'

'Oh, let's do it!' said Melanie.

'Let's not,' said Rebecca.

'It'd be so great for Dad,' said Tania.

It was decided, plotted and put into action. Theo, Nooria and I went through to the lobby, waved casually to Geoff and told him we'd see him in a few hours. He looked at us oddly. 'You don't want to be here when they arrive?'

'Of course, but,' I glanced over my shoulder, 'we feel we should make space for the family. We'll be back for breakfast.'

We went outside, nodded greetings to the Blue Meanies and hotel security, then made our way to the car. My heart was racing. 'They're bound to come after us,' said Theo. He started the engine.

'Here are the others.'

Tania, feigning a fainting fit, was being helped out of the hotel by Diane and her sisters. 'Take deep breaths,' Diane was saying, as she propelled her down the steps. We pulled up in front of them, they jumped in and Theo hit the pedal. The policemen ran after us, but we were on to the main road before they reached their own cars. We drove along the *sailah* and out of the city.

A thin blue band of light skimmed the horizon. After an initial burst of hysterics, like boarders sneaking out of school for a smoke, we became subdued. I sat beside Theo, too excited to speak. Christian was in for a shock. The women he loved were about to appear on the horizon.

'They're coming!' said Tania, but she was looking behind her, not ahead. Two Toyotas were hurtling after us. The Blue Meanies. Theo accelerated with some glee. The schoolgirls urged him on. His phone rang. 'You could have asked!' Geoff roared.

'Get us through the checkpoint, will you, Geoff?'

He did, with help from government minders when they caught up with us, but it took some negotiating and a degree of arguing with the soldiers on duty, who were facing a long shift without food or drink. Sitting by the window, Nooria made spirited contributions to the debate going on outside, while the rest of us sat still.

'We're through,' said Theo, getting back in.

The soldiers smiled and waved us on.

This needed a soundtrack. I turned on the radio. Arab music belted out at the morning. Cymbals. A voice yodelling. Nooria held my hand.

Tania leaned out of the window, waving at the jeep behind us, and called out to the road ahead, 'We're coming, Dad!'

There was a shimmer in the distance. 'There!'

A glitter in the early-morning light. Vehicles. On a straight stretch of road, the convoys headed towards each other, like two arrows on a collision course. The triplets laughed. Diane squeezed my shoulder. I smiled at Theo, barely thinking about Christian, about the logistics, the reunion, what I'd say, what he'd do. I was too giddy to see ahead.

The convoy had come well within sight. Tania and Rebecca hung out of the windows waving scarves and calling, 'Dad, it's us. It's us!' Someone in the lead vehicle waved back. About a quarter of a mile away, the trucks slowed perceptibly and, as Theo hurtled towards them, stopped altogether. We swerved to a halt on the side of the road a couple of hundred yards away. Geoff's driver had to veer right off the road to avoid hitting us.

Diane, Tania, Rebecca and Melanie jumped out and

ran along the road like Olympians. I couldn't get my seatbelt open. Theo pulled at it. As I tumbled out of the jeep, I saw Christian emerge from the vehicles. I ran. He ran. Screams of 'Dad' filled the air, and my legs slowed to a halt.

His family were upon him, and his arms, as if elongated, embraced them all at once. Some way back, Theo and I stood on the road. Like honeycombs, the Linklaters blended. I could not tell one from the other: they were all of a huddle. They rocked, this five-in-one, as they cried out and hugged. I heard Christian's voice – consternation, disbelief – carried on the air.

'Vivien,' said Nooria. 'Go. He has not seen you.'

I shook my head.

'But this is where they part like the Dead Sea,' said Theo, 'and he sees you standing there.'

As he said it, Christian did indeed look up, his family glued to him like an ill-fitting extension, and saw me. He was unshaven and a headcloth was thrown round his neck. He turned back to his family.

'Theo? Get me away from here.'

We had breakfast in silence. It was unlike us to have nothing to say. I nibbled at bread, then lay on Theo's bed and stared at the ceiling. I felt light. A coat of armour had slipped from my shoulders. The worry was gone; expectation, terror, apprehension – all gone. The waiting ended, and nothing left. Since March I had been swaying like a skyscraper, minimally but significantly, so it was peculiar to find myself stilled; still and light, and with nowhere to go.

Theo didn't go to work. For part of the day, he lay with me, staring at the same crack on the ceiling. The Linklaters were probably at the embassy. I slept for an hour, Theo for longer. When I got up and went to my favourite perch on the parapets to look out across the roofs, my other suitor was waiting for me, like a dusty man sitting in a corner, twiddling his thumbs and glancing at me furtively, as if to say, *I'm still here.*

It was coming on for five o'clock, although I had no idea how that had happened. I had been an absentee from the day. My fellow absentee joined me.

'It's silly,' I said, watching goats rummage around, 'but I thought there'd be this big jubilant reunion where we'd hurl ourselves into one another's arms and I'd say I was sorry, that it had all been a terrible mistake, and his family would look on approvingly . . . Instead the sod's gone back to his wife.'

'What you saw on the road was a family reunited, not two people getting back together.'

'He looked away from me.'

'That doesn't mean anything.'

'It means I've burnt my bridges. He won't come back, and I don't blame him. I haven't been good to him or for him. He saw me there and for the second time decided against.'

'You think.'

'You saw what I saw.'

After a moment, Theo nodded.

The sun began to dip, throwing a yellow haze into the air. 'So here I am again – no flatmate, no job, no lover, nothing to show for any of it. Now, who does that remind you of? Vivien Quish – *circa* 1990, maybe?'

Theo smiled. 'Don't say that.'

'Every time I come to this country everything goes haywire. It toys with me, this place does.'

'But this time,' he said, taking his phone out of his pocket and handing it to me, 'you can fix it.'

I looked at the phone. 'You're dead right,' I said, taking it. 'I can and I will.' I dialled Nooria.

She sounded tired. 'Has he come yet?'

'Who?'

'Christian.'

'No, and you know as well as I do that he isn't going to.'

She didn't contradict me, which was as depressing as Theo's acquiescence on the point, but there was no misreading the manner in which Christian had turned away from us with his ex-wife cradled under his arm.

'Nooria, go to your window.'

A moment later, she opened the shutter and called over to me. 'What is it?'

I leaned over the parapet. 'Did I wake you?'

'You're always waking me.'

'Does that job offer still stand?'

'It isn't a job,' she said. 'There is no pay.'

'Even so. I'll take it – if you'll still have me.'

'Of course I will. My need never changes.'

'Excellent! Thanks.'

'You know, someone asked me yesterday about English classes for three sisters. I thought about you, but then I thought, *Ya Allah*, she will be going back to England!'

'Well, I'm not going anywhere so I'll start tomorrow.'

'Okay.'

She was about to close the window when I called, '"Okay?" Is that all you have to say?'

Nooria shrugged. 'Didn't I tell you that God knows what is right for us?'

'If you ask me, God's been a little undecided in my case.' She waved and closed the window. I put Theo's phone back into his pocket. 'Happy now?'

'Very,' he said seriously. 'This is a good decision. If I had champagne I would open it.'

'During Ramadan?'

'Even during Ramadan!'

We laughed. Theo touched me lightly, his fingers on my forearm. 'You know, it was stupid of you to fall in love when you came here. I like Christian,' he said, 'very much, but he asked a lot. You've had a successful career, a proposal of marriage –'

'Two!'

'– and twelve years to find other things to inspire you, but it was never enough. And Christian, actually, wasn't enough either. You shouldn't forget that.'

As he spoke, the numbness I had pulled about me that morning to shut out the panic of losing Christian began to slide away. I looked around at my new home. 'What will I do without you, Theo, when you leave?'

He was leaning over the parapet, his hands clasped. 'What will *I* do?' Then he added quickly, 'I don't mean to be unsympathetic. I *am* sorry about Christian.'

'And I'm sorry about Nooria.'

His fingers tightened round his knuckles.

'It must be hard.'

'It gets worse every day,' he said.

'It can't work?'

'No.'

'Why not?'

'Her work. Her ambition. My work. My ambition.'
He shrugged. 'Anyway, this country needs her. She'll
go into politics. She's already on all the committees and
focus groups. She's helped get other women elected
It's only a matter of time.'

'So stay and support her.'

'And do what? There is no long-term work for me
here.'

'You could do something else.'

He shook his head. 'Don't start pushing for romantic
endings. It isn't going to happen for me any more than
for you. Nooria has made that clear.'

'God, what a mess,' I said. 'We got this all wrong,
you know. We could have saved ourselves a lot of
trouble by seducing one another instead.'

'*Ja*. It might have worked too.'

I nudged him. 'Maybe it isn't too late?'

He looked at me, horrified. 'But I promised the
soldier! I cannot break my oath to Allah! . . . Not during
Ramadan, anyway.'

'Pity,' I sighed, 'I could have lived all over the world
and had *very* tall children.'

Like a lightning bolt coming up from Hades,
Christian's voice echoed in the stairwell. 'Theo?' he
called. 'Vivien?'

We swung round as he came through the door. Theo

embraced him, but Christian pushed past him and threw himself round me.

I pressed him to me like a lost child.

'I couldn't believe it when I saw you on the road,' he said, into my neck. 'I thought I was dreaming.'

We drew apart. No longer the wreck I'd seen that morning, he had showered, shaved and changed. He was thinner, but there was light in his eyes. I squeezed his arms. They were solid.

'You're all right?' Theo asked.

'I'm fine. Fine.' And then to me, 'I can't believe you're here.'

Anger slid between us. 'And I can't believe you did this. What were you thinking?'

'I know. I'm sorry. I didn't mean to cause such incredible consternation.'

'Consternation?' I pulled away and scraped my fingers through my hair. 'Jesus, Christian.'

'I am so sorry.'

'Not good enough. Not nearly good enough.' Still holding my elbows round my head, I said, 'Got good footage, did you?'

He looked sheepish, and he was still smiling. 'Don't say that word again until we're out of the country.'

'Oh. They'll take it off you, I suppose. Dynamite, is it?'

He glanced at Theo. 'It's unbelievable. I've got this whole sequence of when the news of the missile attack came through and deliberations about Osama ... It's going to be —'

I thumped him. 'You bastard!'

'Vivien.'

'No. Fuck you. You put us through all that for what? A TV programme? Some little piece that might win the ethnographic film award? When can we view it?'

Theo put his arm between us. 'Come on.'

'Diane has already done the guilt trip on me,' said Christian. 'I have the bruises to show –'

'Well, good on Diane!' I said. 'And what *about* her, Christian? And what about your kids standing up to the authorities to come here? Where the hell have you *been*?'

'I'll go and put the kettle on,' said Theo, his accent always more pronounced when he was stressed.

'I was with Ahmad and his uncles. We moved around. North-east of Marib and around the outskirts of al-Jawf, going to camps and hearing what they had to say.'

'Which was no doubt absolutely bloody fascinating!'

He put his hands on his hips, resigned to this attack. 'Yes, actually, it was.'

'How could you do that to us?'

'I had no reason to believe anyone would notice. I had my pass to get out of Sana'a and I left – give me a break here, Vivien. How was I to know all this would happen?'

'You can't just take off when you want to, where you want to. Not at times like these!'

'But there was no other time to do it, don't you see that?'

'So why didn't you tell anyone?' My voice was carrying across the rooftops and probably waking neighbours from their Ramadan slumbers.

'People at home would have worried. People here would have stopped me.'

'Yeah, and dead right, too. Have you any idea what we've been through?'

'No, I don't suppose I do.'

'And if you're lucky you never will,' I snapped. 'I hope you're embarrassed. I hope you're absolutely bloody *mortified*.'

'I am! And you can be quite sure my humiliation will be total when the media gets hold of this.'

'You asked for it. You're supposed to be a professional.'

'That's exactly what I am. This job can't be done in the safe zone of college corridors, you know.'

'That doesn't mean you can piss off into a danger zone either!'

He raised his hands. 'Maybe you'll understand when you've seen the work.'

'Tell that to your children. I'm sure they'll really value "*the work*"! You're obsessive, do you realize that? Obsessive. You and Gemma deserve each other.'

His expression hardened. 'That's unwarranted.'

'So is disappearing at a time like this!' I turned away, my chest heaving. It didn't matter what I said, the fury continued to boil.

'Vivien, cut me some slack. It's bad enough knowing what I put the girls through, but I thought you at least would understand.' He came round me to face me and tried to take my hands, but I pulled away. 'No one can reproach me more than I reproach myself. It was selfish and thoughtless, and I deserve to be whipped, but the thing is . . .' He glanced towards the door. 'Look, I don't have much time. I have to get back to the others. I just came to say –'

'Don't.' I waved my hands in front of my face. 'Don't say it because I really, honestly, don't need to hear it. Seeing was enough.'

'Sorry?'

'I'm glad for you. Really. Diane is wonderful.'

'What?'

'I'm delighted for all of you,' I said, and then I kissed him suddenly, because I very much wanted to and never would again.

'Hold on,' he said, but we had to kiss more before he continued. 'I'm not following. Is that why you took off this morning? Because you think I'm going back to Diane?'

'Aren't you?'

'No.'

'Well, you should be. It's so obvious – to me, and Theo, and anyone who has been with them these last days. You have a great family. They love you.'

'And you don't? Why are you here?'

'Where else would I be?'

'Vivien, they're my family, but I love *you*.'

'But Diane wants you back.'

'She doesn't.'

'She does! Don't blow it again, Christian. She said this was worse than losing Eric.'

'And if anything happened to her it would tear my

heart out, but that doesn't mean I'm in love with her, any more than she is with me. Do you know what she said when I left her just now?'

'What?'

'"Don't blow it again, Christian." I wish you two would stop speaking the same language. It's unbelievably confusing.' He took my elbows. 'Listen to me. Forget Mayo. I won't do that again. There'll be no more talk about kids or marriage. No pressure, I promise, but can we please just *get on* with this?'

He kissed me again, but there was an odd taste in my mouth, as if I was eating an orange after brushing my teeth, and something akin to an earthquake rumbled ominously in the Yemeni ground.

'No pressure,' I said. 'Do you mean that?'

'Of course I do. I nearly blew it last time.'

'Good,' I said, 'because I've made arrangements to stay here.'

He drew back, his eyes hard on mine. Then he shook me gently. 'No.'

'Sorry.' I looked past him.

'Oh, Vivien, don't. Please. Come home with me. Give us some time together.'

The sea was still up there, in the air. I wanted to bring it down, but it wouldn't come. Still it wouldn't come.

'Vivien?'

A weight round my ankles. Intense gravity pulling at me.

Theo came out, holding three glasses of tea.

'Don't let Yemen stand in the way again,' Christian said. 'Please.'

I thought I saw Theo shake his head, so slightly that I might have imagined it.

'Yemen isn't standing in the way,' I said. 'You are.'

Sana'a, shimmering in the evening haze, seemed, from the corner of my eye, to be dancing in the background. I heard music that wasn't playing, voices that weren't singing.

'It's your turn to choose, Christian. You can leave me, or you can leave me here.'

His shoulders dropped beneath my palms, his hands fell to his side.

A glass of tea slipped between Theo's fingers and shattered on the ground.

'*Klote!*'

23

I have my own belvedere. It seems unlikely, but there it is: I have my own belvedere. It is not perched atop the seventh storey of a glorious old tower, but is on the third floor of a fairly squat building in a cul-de-sac. Nonetheless, it is on the roof and has great windows, and it is in the old town.

I have let my flat at last – to Gemma and her brother – and can live for a while on my severance pay. When the world has settled, I will organize an exhibition of Yemeni artists in Dublin for Shoukria.

Theo is in Ougadougou on a job. He has left me a GPS so that in future I will always know where I am. We miss him. Nooria is distracted by his absence, but she has me to boss around now, which is some compensation.

Christian waits. Neither patiently nor graciously, nor even with any certainty that it will be worth his while, but he waits and I am thankful for it. His documentary was hastily aired (I have the video, but no VCR on which to view it) and was apparently riveting, but not, Diane insists, worth our days of torment.

Iraq has not yet been invaded. The global nausea continues, but no one has yet thrown up. Everybody waits.

Whatever happens, I will be here in my *mafraj*, pretending to be the great travel writer that I will never be, and would never have been. It doesn't matter any more. It is enough, now, that I have travelled, and I do write, as I sit here in Sana'a, which must be seen.

Acknowledgements

A number of people helped, at various stages, to bring this book into being, and for their time and assistance I would like to thank: Eamon O Tuathail, Jean Morgan-Bryant, Ger and Steven Lee, Mechteld Schuller, Angela Coffey and Carol Hodder; Dr Iris Gerlach of the German Institute of Archaeology, Sana'a, Fadhl Maghafi, of the Yemeni Embassy, London, and his wonderful family in Sana'a, and Dinny Hawes, of the Catholic Institute of International Relations, who, twenty years ago, over a cup of coffee in a café in London, made it possible for me to go to Yemen for the first time.

I must also extend special thanks to Kathleen Hindle and Anita Culazzo who shared their instincts and experiences; to Guido Ferrari and Michel Lambotte, for their professional input on all matters cartographical; and to Professor Abd al-Aziz al-Maqalih, for special permission to use an extract from *The Book of Sana'a*.

I would never get anything done without the indulgence and patience of Tamzin, Finola and William; my excellent editor, Patricia Deevy; and my agent and pal, Jonathan Williams.

I would most particularly like to thank the many women of Sana'a who welcomed me into their homes, their work-places and their gatherings with hospitality and friendship, including Jamila Awadh, Amnah al-Nassiri and Antelak al-Mutawakel.

This novel also has four outstanding godparents to whom I am indebted: Dr Fatima Kahtan, of the University of Science and Technology, Sana'a, for opening so many doors and for much else besides; Janet Starkey, of the University of Durham, for her generous input on many fronts not least anthropological; Yousuf Mohageb of Arabian Ecotours, for just about everything; and Tim Mackintosh-Smith, for sourcing and translating from *The Book of Sana'a*, and for his unstinting encouragement, guidance and good-humoured forbearance (especially when asked to appear).

Although he is gone, I'd like to acknowledge a debt of gratitude to Sir Wilfred Thesiger, for igniting the passion many years ago.

Finally, Gavin and Koukab, wherever you are – thanks.

Woodstock, Cork, December 2004

Permissions